"No!" She pushed aga

He hesitated briefly
wrenched herself away
half-crumbled wall of th

"No, Jake. This is not why we came here."

His chest rose and fell with the labored force of his breathing. Emerald eyes burned as he stared at the wet spot his mouth had left on her bodice. Gillian's breath caught. Her breasts ached to be touched.

He dragged his palm along his granite jawline, then slowly licked his lips. "Ah, princess." His hands moved to the buttons on his shirt and he yanked the top one free, saying, "Yes, princess, I think it is."

He stepped forward. She retreated and felt cool stone at her back.

Determination rumbled through his voice. "I think this is precisely why we are here. I think this is why I'm still in Scotland and not on a ship headed south."

"But—"

"I want you, Gillian Ross. It's a clawing in my gut and an aching in my bones and a hunger in my blood. I'll have you, here and now."

Tremendous Acclaim for Geralyn Dawson's Hilarious, Heartwarming Romances

Simmer All Night

"Delightfully spicy. . . . Perfect to warm up a cold winter's night."

—Christina Dodd, author of *Someday My Prince*

"A romance buoyed by lively characters and Southern lore. . . . Dawson sustains readers' attention with her humorous dialogue and colorful narration."

—*Publishers Weekly*

"Once again Geralyn Dawson has come up with a winner. . . . Great verbal sparring, delightfully funny at times and also extremely touching at points."

—*Romantic Times*

"*Simmer All Night* is an entertaining blending of a western romance with a Victorian romance. The mix works as the characters imbue a special jocular charm into the story line. Geralyn Dawson shows she is a gourmet chef who serves simmering hot Texas chili with a cup of tea."

—*Painted Rock Reviews*

"*Simmer All Night* is a wonderful, delightful, and gratifying book that is not to be missed."

—*Denver Rocky Mountain News*

The Kissing Stars

"Dawson, who is known for her comedic style, has a knack for creating hilarious secondary characters."

—Publishers Weekly

"I loved it! Gabe and Tess are wonderful. Geralyn is a favorite at our store!"

—Kathy Baker, Waldenbooks

"Geralyn writes a fun story. Rosie and the camels were a delight. I enjoyed all of the Aurorians."

—Thea Mileo, Cover to Cover

"The Kissing Stars is a delight. A zany cast of characters and unique plot leave the reader with a smile on her face and a warm feeling in her heart."

—Betty Schulte, Paperback Outlet

"Once again Geralyn has taken a unique snippet of Texas history and turned it into the backdrop of a wonderfully warm and witty story. The characters are well-drawn and as eccentric as their setting. The colorful phrasing Geralyn is known for always brings a chuckle at just the right moment."

—Norma McDonald, Echo Paperbacks

"The Kissing Stars is one of Geralyn Dawson's finest books yet. It's chock-full of charming, whimsical characters, with the Dawson trademark combination of love and humor done to perfection. This is what romance is all about!"

—Sharon Walters, Paperback Place

Books by Geralyn Dawson

The Wedding Raffle
The Wedding Ransom
The Bad Luck Wedding Cake
The Kissing Stars
Simmer All Night
Sizzle All Day

Published by POCKET BOOKS

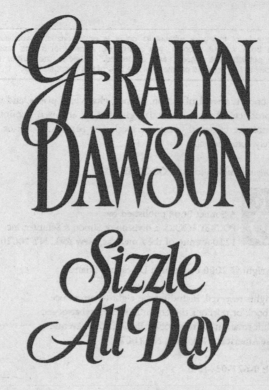

GERALYN DAWSON

Sizzle All Day

SONNET BOOKS

New York London Toronto Sydney Singapore

This book is a work of fiction. Names, characters, places, and incidents
are products of the author's imagination or are used fictitiously. Any
resemblance to actual events or locales or persons, living or dead, is
entirely coincidental.

An Original Publication of POCKET BOOKS

A Sonnet Book published by
POCKET BOOKS, a division of Simon & Schuster, Inc.
1230 Avenue of the Americas, New York, NY 10020

ISBN: 0-671-03448-0

First Sonnet Books printing September 2000

10 9 8 7 6 5 4 3 2 1

SONNET BOOKS and colophon are trademarks of
Simon & Schuster, Inc.

Cover art by Ben Perini

Printed in the U.S.A.

Fightin' Texas Aggie Band:
Gig 'em

A-Battery Zips '03

Acknowledgments

I want to offer my sincere thanks to my editor, Caroline Tolley, her assistant, Lauren McKenna, and my agent, Denise Marcil, for their insight and expertise. To my dear friends and Monday Night Buds, Pat Cody and Sharon Rowe, I'd be lost without you. Thanks to Lana Ridl, for doing all the yucky stuff at home, and to Jody Allen, for so kindly answering my e-mails and recommending my favorite Scots reference book. Y'all are the best.

one

Scottish Highlands, 1884

JAKE DELANEY WAS a man on the run.

From his mother.

"It's damned embarrassing," he told the small dog sharing the saddle with him. "I'm thirty-four years old. I'm my own man. I've driven cattle from Austin to Wichita. I've fought a gun battle with bandits in the West Texas badlands and won a knife fight with card cheats in a San Antonio whorehouse. I took my first drink when I was ten, loved my first woman when I was fourteen, and bought my first property when I was eighteen. I truly believed I had my share of sand."

The dog snorted.

So did Jake. Sand, hell. He'd taken one look at that matchmaking light in his mother's eyes and had run for the hills. The hills of Scotland, that is.

The dog gazed up at him with liquid brown eyes, her long ears flopping in cadence to the horse's gait. She'd been a good, if unexpected, companion on this trip north. Jake liked females who listened well and didn't wear out a man's ears with talk of hair styles and fabrics and fashion.

That's all he'd been hearing of late. He'd spent the past few months escorting his mother around London. Elizabeth Delaney had returned to England after more than twenty years in Texas, thrown herself into the welcoming arms of a blue-blood society, and decided her son needed to follow suit. Literally.

"A bit of wenching is fine, don't get me wrong," he told the dachshund he'd christened Scooter. "But I'll be damned if I'll marry one of those simpering English misses. If I did want a wife—which I don't—I'd want a female with some pepper in her. I like heat in my women."

And in the weather, too, he silently added as the dog whined and burrowed her way inside his coat. Here it was the middle of summer, but the day was cold as a dead snake in an ice house. Think of how miserable he'd feel had he made the trip during the winter months. That's when he'd first learned that the missing copy of the Republic of Texas's Declaration of Independence was likely hidden in a castle in the Scottish Highlands, and he'd been elected to go get it.

It was, Jake believed, a worthy quest. When the state capitol burned four years ago, Texas's lone copy of the historically significant document was lost to the fire. Recently, research by the Historical Preservation Society in San Antonio confirmed that in 1836, five copies of the Declaration had been penned and sent by courier across Texas in order to inform citizens of the official creation of a new republic. What, then, had happened to the four unaccounted-for copies? The Society had made it their objective to find out. They would locate the lost Declarations and bring them home to the people of Texas.

Jake became involved because at that time, his mother had been an officer in the club.

Originally, Cole Morgan—Jake's brother-in-every-way-but-blood—had been charged with the task of retrieving the copy rumor had placed in England. Cole's search proved to be quite an adventure, netting him in the end one wife—Jake's sister Chrissy—but no Declaration, only a lead about where to look for it next. Supposedly, a lost copy of the Republic of Texas's Declaration of Independence could be found in the Scottish Highlands, in a place called Rowanclere Castle.

"So here I am," he murmured. "Cold enough to spit ice."

Jake might have been born in Britain, but he was South Texas bred. He thrived in the sizzling heat of a Texas summer, and he wasn't cut out for cold. He was more than ready to reach his destination, recover the Declaration of Independence for the people of Texas, and start living his own life for a change.

Jake had plans. For years now he had spent his time fulfilling responsibilities to family, friends, and country. But now his sister was blissfully married to his best friend, his mother happily reconciled with her British family, his land sold, and his law partnership in San Antonio cheerfully disbanded. As soon as this last duty was accomplished, Jake would be free to shake off the clay that had long weighted down the wings on his feet.

He craved adventure. The wilds of Africa, the islands of the South Pacific, and the mysteries of the Far East were lures he need no longer resist. He couldn't wait to see it all, experience it all. To live it all.

Thinking about it spurred him into picking up his pace. A short time later, his horse rounded a bend and Jake spied the end of the current trail. "Rowanclere Castle," he murmured, reining his mount to a halt so he could study the place.

He scratched Scooter behind the ears as he blew a soundless whistle of appreciation at the sight of a fairy tale come to life. Turrets and towers and thick, weathered walls of stone rose high above the deep blue waters of a narrow lake—or loch, to use the vernacular. A colorful flag fluttered from the long pole reaching up into the sky from a tall, square keep. The rest of the castle was a hodgepodge of gabled roofs and towers and crenelated lines that softened the keep's imposing facade.

Jake had visited larger castles since arriving in Britain, but this was certainly the most beautiful. Rowanclere possessed an air of welcome lacked by the others he'd seen along the way. This castle was no forbidding hunk of stone and mortar, appropriate as a setting for one of Shakespeare's tragedies. Rowanclere was more a light-hearted, fanciful romance, a place for a princess to dance with her prince.

"Princess?" Jake muttered aloud. Hell. The cold must have frozen his brain. Next thing you know, he'd be composing poetry.

He'd damned well better get his head on straight. Castles were historically places of intrigue, and the search for this lost document had already come close to costing his sister Chrissy her life. Besides, he didn't want to die before getting a good look at those bare-breasted Tahitian women.

Tucking that warm image pleasantly in mind to combat this wretched cold, Jake snuggled Scooter close to his chest, signaled his horse forward, and headed for the castle by the loch.

Gillian Ross stood at a tower window and watched the broad-shouldered man guide his horse across the small stone bridge spanning the burn. The wings of a thousand butterflies fluttered in her stomach as she sent up a silent prayer for the success of the plan she prepared to put into action.

Mr. J. A. K. Delaney of Texas had sent word to expect his arrival today. How would he react to what he found at Rowanclere Castle?

"Oh, I am having second thoughts," her twin sister, Flora, insisted as she nervously twisted the wedding band on her finger. "We should not do this."

"We have little choice at this point."

Flora grimaced and her arms fell to her sides. Dejection filled her voice as she said, "Aye, you are right."

Gillian couldn't help but smile at Flora's woebegone state. Adopting a cheer she didn't feel, she said, "Though I could happily skelp Uncle Angus for forcing this upon us. And our brother for abandoning us to our grand-uncle's whims."

"Now, Gilly. Nicholas left Scotland two years before Mama and Papa were killed. He did not abandon us."

"What would you call it? We have not heard a word from him in the longest time."

Flora shook her head. "Let us not argue over Nicholas. He has nothing to do with this. David is the one—"

"I will not speak of David," Gillian snapped. Then,

mindful of her sister's delicate condition, she reached
for Flora's hand and gave it an apologetic, reassuring
squeeze. "We've more important matters to occupy our
minds. Lord Harrington arrives in little more than a fortnight."

"Aye," Flora said with a sigh. She trailed a finger along
the wide window casement painted in Gillian's favorite
color, a deep forest green. "Whether we wish it or not."

Gillian shared her twin's lament, though she refused
to voice it. Not now. Not when doing so could serve no
positive purpose. "That is beside the matter, sister. After a
year of search, you and Uncle Angus have found a potential buyer for Rowanclere."

She returned her gaze to the window and the stranger
approaching the castle. "All we need do is successfully
navigate these next few weeks and come first snow,
Uncle Angus will be safe from the danger this castle
poses upon his health."

Flora resumed her hand-wringing. "But you will lose
your home."

Gillian took her sister by the hands and stared into
bluebell-colored eyes identical to her own. "Never. My
home is my family, wherever we are, and I do not intend
to lose a one of you. You and your Alasdair and babe to
come. Uncle Angus and Robyn. And Nick, if he ever
returns to us."

Flora's eyes closed and her shoulders slumped forward as she relaxed. "You are right."

"Of course I am right," Gillian said, her lips twisting
to smother a smile. "I am always right. Rowanclere is just
a place. As long as we are together—or within a day's
ride, in your case—in a place that provides safe shelter, it

matters not where we live." Turning back to the window, she watched as the man reined in his horse. He removed a wide-brimmed hat and raked his fingers through dark auburn hair as he sat staring toward the castle. "Besides, Flora, you know how much I believe in fate. Fate put you and Uncle Angus in that hotel dining room at the same time as the Earl of Harrington. Fate caused your tongue to slip when he asked The Question."

Flora moved to stand beside her sister. Together, they saw the visitor signal his horse forward. "I opened my mouth to say no, Gillian. I promise I did. I dinna ken what came over me."

"Fate, Flora." The grin broke free as she gave her sister a sidelong look. "Or, perhaps a brownie. They are mischievous ghaists, after all."

"Aye, that I do know. I learned the wee detail from all the reading you forced upon me." She hooked a thumb toward a stack of books and pamphlets atop Gillian's bedside table. "*Spiritual Magazine* has an interesting article about brownies in its winter issue."

"I read that piece," Gillian said. She'd read them all, in fact. She'd started collecting the material four months ago after Flora ran weeping into her bedchamber upon her return from Edinburgh. With tears flowing down her face, her twin had stuttered out her story.

During luncheon with Flora and her husband Alasdair Dunbar at an Edinburgh hotel, Uncle Angus had suffered an attack of severe chest pain. A gentleman seated nearby was quick to offer his assistance, and Alasdair requested he keep Angus and Flora company as he left to summon a physician. While they waited, the man who introduced himself as the Earl of Harrington from Devon, England, went out of his way to distract Flora from her worries by asking innocuous questions about her home. Flora had told him that while she now lived at Laichmoray, she had spent her youth at Rowanclere Castle. The earl then expressed interest in buying a Scottish castle of his own, and Uncle Angus caught his breath enough to inform Harrington that he wished to sell his Highland home. In reply, the earl had asked his fateful question: *Is Rowanclere haunted?*

Flora, who seldom spoke a falsehood, had opened her mouth, looked him in the eye, and lied. *Aye, we have a very active ghaist, in fact.*

Her claim captured Harrington's imagination. A Spiritualist and a fellow in the College of Psychic Studies, the earl had a keen interest in everything relating to the supernatural. Though he did wish to buy a Scottish castle, not just any castle would do. He wanted to study supernatural beings. He must own a *haunted* castle.

Wasn't it convenient, Flora had told him, that they had a haunted Scottish castle for sale.

The Englishman immediately made arrangements to call at Rowanclere.

"I do so hope we have not missed something important, Gilly," Flora said, her teeth nibbling at her bottom lip.

"I don't know what it would be. I think I must have read everything that has been written about these ghost hunters in the past five years."

Upon learning of the earl's impending visit, Gillian set about studying both Harrington and those whose interests mirrored his own. She'd found a wealth of material available. At least a dozen magazines had been born in the wake of the Spiritualist movement as it swept from America to Europe. Newspapers wrote of the séances that were the rage in London society these days. Clairvoyants provided entertainment at parties, and spirit photographers held showings in galleries. From her research, Gillian compiled a list of what talents and abilities Lord Harrington might expect of Rowanclere's wraith.

Now she prepared to evaluate her research using Mr. J. A. K. Delaney. If all went well, the Texan would get first glimpse of their apparition.

Gillian leaned forward, staring harder out the window when their visitor paused to rearrange something he carried on the saddle in front of him. Idly, she wondered what it was.

Her sister said, "I had difficulty sleeping last night so I picked the most recent issue of *Spiritual Magazine*. Did you read Lord Spaulding's article theorizing that ninety-eight percent of all castles in Scotland are haunted by at least one ghaist?"

Gillian blinked. "Ninety-eight percent?"

"Aye. Considering our luck, I am surprised it is not higher."

Outside on the drive, the rider nudged his horse into a trot. Gillian clicked her tongue. Delaney sat his horse quite well. "Well I think our luck is about to change, Flora. I think fate is working on our side this time."

Flora smoothed a hand down the front of her dress across her belly, swollen with child. "Possibly. Though I hesitate to place my faith in it. Gilly, are you certain we must take this path? Could we—" She broke off abruptly and grimaced as she rubbed her back.

"What's wrong?" Gillian demanded.

"Nothing. I am fine."

"Indeed now." Her muscles tight with sudden tension, Gillian took her sister by the arm and led her to a chair beside the fireplace. "I insist you rest."

When Flora lowered herself into the seat, Gillian folded her arms and pinned her twin with a scowl. "I forbid you to worry one second longer. It is bad for the bairn."

Both hands resting protectively on her stomach, Flora lifted her chin and sniffed. "Do not start that lecture again, Gillian Ross. You do me insult with it. I am not so daupit as to put my child at risk."

Gillian blew a frustrated sigh, then attempted to explain. "You are careful, but you are also a worrier. That, in turn, worries me." She paused a moment before confessing, "I fear I should have refused your help and sent you back to Laichmoray."

"Would have been a waste of breath, that."

Gillian couldn't help but smile at Flora's expression of disdain. "Aye. Like Uncle Angus always says, you are a stubborn lass."

Flora lifted her chin and wrinkled her nose. "I am your twin."

Laughing outright, Gillian dropped to her knees and sought her sister's comfort by joining their hands in a clasp. "Oh, Flora. The selfish part of me is very, very glad to have your help. Alasdair Dunbar is a fine man to allow you so much freedom. Most men in his position would insist you remain home the final two months prior to your confinement."

Her sister hummed her agreement. "I married a prince. He understands how important my family is to me and how I need to be with you through this upcoming . . . challenge. He is aware of how difficult it was for me to leave Rowanclere when we married."

Gillian's answering smile was shaky. She, too, would find it hard to leave her home when the time came. But the leaving must occur. Uncle Angus had made up his mind and he was laird of the castle. Besides, knowing he had provided for his grandnieces' futures would bring him a measure of peace. Heaven knew he'd earned that.

And, in all honesty, she'd rather leave her home than be forced into a loveless marriage in order to save it.

She closed her eyes, sent a quick prayer heavenward for her loved ones' continued good health, then stood and said, "Are you feeling well enough to go downstairs? Our guest will be knocking at the door shortly. Maybe I should—"

"I'm fine, Gilly. I'll rest another minute or two just to be careful. I've asked Mrs. Ferguson to act the butler and show him to the red drawing room if I'm not downstairs when he arrives."

"Good." Rowanclere had few servants, and the cook was the only one informed of their plans concerning Delaney and the earl. "Mrs. Ferguson is a fine judge of character and I should be glad to have her observations about the man." Then, anxious to soothe away the lingering lines of worry on her sister's face, Gillian addressed a concern her twin had mentioned earlier. "Flora, before this all begins, I have something I want to say. Dinna fash yersel' about the lie. Uncle Angus said he would have told Lord Harrington that Rowanclere was haunted. I know I would have."

"'Truly?" Her sister's brows arched. "You would have invented a wraith for Rowanclere?"

"I may well have created two of them."

Flora's brow wrinkled in thought, then she nodded. "Aye, I don't doubt it. You always did tend to exaggerate. Still, I find this entire scheme troublesome. If only I—"

"Stop. I'll not listen to any more wheeking about what happened in Edinburgh. You did the right thing. Remember what we are about here. Remember what's important."

"Uncle Angus."

"Aye."

A slow, grateful smile blossomed across her twin's face and Gillian was heartened. Flora didn't need to deal with guilt on top of everything else.

"Now," Gillian continued. "How do I look?"

Flora frowned and studied her twin's face for a long minute before she stood, licked her thumb, then reached out and smudged the black theatrical paint that covered Gillian from the line of her golden hair to the base of her neck. "Quite frightening."

"Good. And quit spitting on me, please. I do not feel frightening with spit on my face."

"You look absolutely awful. So awful, in fact, it worries me. What if we truly frighten Mr. Delaney or Lord Harrington? I hate the thought of being cruel."

Gillian lifted her gaze to the ceiling in frustration. Who was this insecure, vulnerable woman? Acting in such a manner was so out of character for Flora. Normally, she was every bit as strong as Gillian.

The pregnancy. It must be the pregnancy.

Of course. Gillian's heart went soft, and she gave her

sister a quick, fierce hug. "Our guest is from Texas. Think of all the things Uncle Angus has told us about Texans. Remember what Nicholas said about them in those early letters of his? I doubt a moving picture or unexplained sound will cause him much anxiety. And as far as Lord Harrington is concerned, he is coming to Rowanclere in order to look for ghaists. He won't be frightened to find one. He will be thrilled."

Flora nodded and brushed a streak of dirt off the filmy white gown Gillian wore. "Aye, you are right."

Flashing a smile, Gillian repeated her earlier observation. "Of course I am right. I am always right."

Her twin shot her a droll look. "What you are is annoying."

"In that case, you will want to leave now. Hie yourself downstairs, sister, and see to our guest."

"I haven't 'hied' myself anywhere for months now," Flora told her glumly. "I shall waddle my way to care for our guest. What is his name again? This man who is writing a book about castles in Britain?"

"Delaney. Mr. J. A. K. Delaney."

Gillian rubbed her itchy nose, careful not to disturb the paint. Delaney was to be the test. If she could fool him, she would be more confident in her ability to deceive Lord Harrington.

Glancing out the window once more, she watched their guest cross the drawbridge. The butterflies in her stomach once again gave a flutter, and her mouth went stone dry. "He is a brawny one."

Her sister stood beside her. "He looks chilled to me. What is that in his arms?"

"A dog, I believe. A wee one." Gillian saw the man

swing gracefully from the saddle, confirmed that he was, indeed, an extraordinarily tall, imposing figure.

Flora said, "He's here. I'd best be going. I expect to be at least ten minutes taking him up to his room. That should give you plenty of time, should it not?"

Gillian nodded and her sister turned to leave, stopping at the doorway to add, "Good luck, Gilly. Now that the moment has arrived, I do believe you will do fine."

"So do I," Gillian said, reassuring them both. Then, lifting the black kerchief from the table beside a large doll's head, she tied it around her hair, concealing its long golden strands.

As her sister disappeared from the tower room, Gillian gathered up the rest of her supplies, then felt along the wall for the catch that opened a concealed door granting access to Rowanclere's hidden passages. A musty smell surrounded her as she stepped into the dim, narrow space and made her way along the twisting and turning tunnel toward her destination.

Upon her arrival in the guest wing, and with voice trumpet in one hand and doll head in the other, she turned her ear to the wall and prepared to listen. Softly, she muttered, "Mr. J. A. K. Delaney. Prepare to meet the Headless Lady of Rowanclere."

Jake carried Scooter in one arm, his saddlebags over his shoulder, and a small satchel in the other as his beautiful landlady led him along a warren of hallways and staircases. At one point as he followed Mrs. Dunbar up a narrow, spiral set of steps, he warily eyed the bulge beneath her gown and said, "I'm sure I can find my way myself, ma'am. No need for you to make this climb in your condition."

She flashed him an amused smile. "Worried, sir?"

"Terrified, ma'am."

She laughed. "Ach, Mr. Delaney, you remind me of my Uncle Angus. No need for concern. I'm fit as can be, and the bairn will not be arriving for months yet. Now, tell me what is wrong with the puir wee beastie."

"She hurt her back and can't move her hindquarters," Jake replied as Mrs. Dunbar paused outside an arched wooden door. "Her owner was a . . . friend I made in London, and she couldn't bear to put her pet down so she asked me to see to it. When the moment arrived, those big brown eyes got to me and I couldn't do it, either. But Scooter here has adjusted to her problem so I decided to keep her."

"Are not you the kind one."

"No, I wouldn't say that. I'm a . . ." Jake's voice trailed off as the door swung open. The room was dominated by a bed hung in deep green and gold silk. The tables sitting on either side were a heavy oak and old, and while the marble mantel was fancy enough, the room lacked the delicate froufrou he'd come to expect from British guest rooms. It was homey. A man's room. "Well, isn't this nice. I've always liked this shade of green."

"Thank you. This particular guest chamber is my favorite."

"It's nice of y'all to put me up, Mrs. Dunbar. I want you to know how much I appreciate the opportunity to include Rowanclere in my study of castles. I'm told you don't often entertain visitors here."

Judging from the color creeping up her cheeks, he had embarrassed her. "Rowanclere is a simple household and but for my elderly uncle, primarily one of women.

We have learned to be careful. Your letters of reference, however, assured us you are safe."

Safe? Jake debated whether or not to be insulted. He also noted the lady made no mention of a husband. Was the ring on her finger an excuse? Was her pregnancy part of their being careful? Ordinarily he'd consider such questions none of his business, but in light of the purpose behind his visit, he knew not what piece of information might prove of value.

Mrs. Dunbar pointed out a few features of the room, then said, "Your letter indicated your home is in Texas. From what part of the state do you hail? My brother once visited a town called Dallas."

"I'm from San Antonio, ma'am," he said, striding over to the window. "That's a good ways south of Dallas. Did your brother have business there?"

"Nae. He wished to see Dallas, Texas, the town named after our own." She wrinkled her nose and added, "He's gone exploring, Mr. Delaney, for no better reason than he wanted to do it."

"A man after my own heart, then. I hope to do a bit of that myself soon. Once I'm finished with my book, that is. I . . . well, twirl my spurs!" he exclaimed, distracted by the view of the loch and hills beyond outside his window. "If this isn't one of the prettiest sights I've seen since leaving home."

It was, he concluded, spectacular enough to rival his hostess' face.

They spoke of the countryside around Rowanclere for a few minutes, then she said, "I have kept you from your comfort long enough. Dinner is served at eight in the dining room, but if you prefer a tray in your room we shall be happy to provide it. Also, you are welcome to make use of the library, billiard room, and drawing room downstairs should you so desire. We've an excellent selection of whisky any time you've a mind for a wee dram." She gestured toward a cabinet against the far wall and added, "You'll find a bottle of the local barley bree there."

"I could use something to warm my insides," Jake said with a smile.

"The Rowanclere malt will certainly do that."

"Do you mind if I build a fire?"

Mrs. Dunbar's brows arched as if to say *This time of day?* Audibly, she said only, "I'll send a maid immediately."

"No need. I'll do it. I prefer it, in fact. A man who builds his own fire warms himself twice." Also, doing it himself meant he built the blaze to suit him. In England, they'd always made puny little fires that hardly warmed a man's hand, much less his bones.

"Very well. I'll leave you to your ease then, Mr. Delaney."

Jake was already reaching for the whisky before his hostess cleared the door. He poured a healthy amount into a glass, then took a generous sip. The liquor left behind a smooth, smoky taste as it burned down his throat and hit his stomach. Rays of welcome warmth spread through him.

Scooter dragged herself to his feet and whimpered. "No," Jake told her, his smile apologetic. "This is not for you. Let me get a fire going, though, and you can have the prime spot in front of it."

Jake set about the task, and soon felt a welcome heat steal over him. Scooter plopped down to the left side of the hearth, so he took the right. "Feels good, doesn't it?" he said to the dog as he warmed his hands.

He'd have loved to take a hot bath, but after downing a second drink, he decided to settle for a change of clothes. To that end, he removed pants, a shirt, and clean underwear from his satchel and hung them near the hearth to warm. Then, pulling a rocking chair close to the fireplace, he sat, tugged off his boots and socks, and stuck his feet toward the fire. Heat soaked into his skin and he groaned aloud. It felt so damned good.

A few minutes later, greedy for more of that delicious warmth, he stood and shucked out of the rest of his clothes, toasting his front side first.

From behind him, he heard Scooter start to whine. "What's the matter, girl? Why did you leave the fire? You need to stay over here if you're cold."

Ordinarily, the dachshund would tug her way toward the sound of his voice, but this time Scooter ignored him. Curious and with his front side finally warm, Jake turned his back toward the heat and—

What the hell?

A filmy white figure floated where a portion of the room's plastered wall appeared to have dissolved. Jake's heart leapt to his throat. He stared at the apparition holding a glowing lantern at its side in one hand, and its . . . oh, God . . .

It held its head in the other.

"Sonofabitch!" Jake whispered, taking an inadvertent step backward.

At the same instant, the ghost let out a squeal. "Dear Lord in heaven! Where are your breeks?"

Jake froze in shock at the very human voice, and a

number of things happened at once. The fire hissed, then popped. It spat out an ember that landed on his rear. He jumped as pain shot into his skin, then grabbed the nearby water pitcher, intending to cool the burn.

While Jake tended his posterior, Scooter darted forward and began nipping at the ghost. In addition to the dog's barks, Jake heard a tearing sound from the direction of the wall as he doused his left buttock.

Then the figure literally lost her head.

It rolled toward him, its long tresses twisting like a golden rope. The pitcher slipped from Jake's grip and shattered against the stone floor. Revulsion swept over him, even as he recognized the object as nothing more than a painted wooden model. When it rumbled to a halt at his feet, he stared at it in frozen surprise until a distinctly feminine gasp grabbed his attention.

His gaze trailed the length of white cloth that now stretched between Scooter's teeth up to the prettiest set of plump, rosy-tipped breasts he'd seen this side of the Atlantic.

"Sonofabitch," he repeated, breathing hard. He took a step forward even as the lamp flickered off, the opening in the wall closed, and the figure disappeared.

Damn. That was no ghost. That was a flesh-and-blood woman. *And fine flesh it was.*

Bending down, he lifted the head by the hair and held it out in front of him, studying the grotesquely painted face in the firelight. What sort of trick was this? What had she been trying to accomplish?

He stood there, naked, pulse finally beginning to slow as he stared at the wooden head dangling from his hand.

Then a voice seemed to come from the mouth mere inches from his manhood.

"My, my, my," said the snickering ghost. "I have long been told they grow things bigger in Texas. Now I see it is the truth."

Jake yelped and the head hit the floor with a thud.

two

◆

IT WAS A debacle, a disaster, but Gillian couldn't stop giggling. She lay sprawled across her bed, her face wiped clean and the voice trumpet with which she'd pitched her words lying beside her as she chortled her way through the story.

"You said *what?*" Flora asked, scandal in her tone as she grabbed hold of the embroidered blue silk bed hangings.

"That they grow things bigger in Texas."

"You didn't."

"I did. And you know what? It is true. I had no idea some men wore such a great sword."

Flora choked, her eyes rounding with scandalized mirth as she clutched her hands to her chest. "Oh, Gilly, you are wicked."

Then, after a moment's pause, she asked, "Just how big is he?"

Gillian sat up cross-legged and rolled her tongue around her mouth in thought before shrugging. "My experience is limited. I've only David and that wicked Jamie Ross to compare him with."

"Jamie Ross!"

"Be calm. I was not personally involved. I stumbled upon one of his staged seduction scenes years ago."

"You never told me that."

"That is because he threatened to hurt you if I mentioned it to anyone. Later on, I forgot about it." After a moment's pause, she added, "He wasn't that impressive."

Her sister giggled. "Unlike Mr. Delaney?"

"Aye. Unlike Mr. Delaney."

Flora plucked at a loose thread on her gown. "And David?"

For the first time in months, Gillian found herself able to smile at the mention of her former betrothed's name. "David? He's half the man at best. I tell you true, sister, Mr. Delaney is a muckle great man."

The women's eyes met, then they both burst out in laughter that lasted until tears ran down their faces. At some point—Gillian couldn't tell exactly when—those tears of laughter transformed to tears of worry, and she gazed up at her sister and said, "Oh, Flora, what if this fails to work? The sale of Rowanclere must go through. I fear Uncle Angus winna last another winter here."

Her twin sat beside her on the bed and gave her a quick, hard hug. "Dinna give up yet, Gilly. All will be well. That was your first attempt, and it is understandable you lost your concentration under the circumstances. I truly doubt you'll be faced with a nakit man next time you pretend to be a spirit." After a moment's pause, she teased, "Although, if you suspect it might happen again,

I may decide to play along. You've whetted my curiosity concerning Mr. Delaney."

Now it was Gillian's turn to act scandalized. With a groan, she flopped back down on the bed. "Alasdair would kill us both. We could haunt Rowanclere in truth."

"Aye, he would nae be happy. In that case, I should content myself with playing hostess rather than a haunt." Laughing softly, Flora stood and crossed toward the door, pausing long enough to frown down at the torn swath of white lying against the tartan carpet. "What happened to the gown?"

"His dog," Gillian said with a grimace. "Vicious little thing tore it."

"Vicious? Why, Gilly, the wee dog is crippled."

"The wee dog's jaw works just fine, believe me."

Shaking her head, Flora bent awkwardly and scooped the gown off the floor. "Oh, I see what you mean. This is ripped right in two." She shot her sister a questioning look and said, "You are lucky Mr. Delaney did not see more of our ghaist than you intended."

Gillian smiled crookedly and kept the baring-of-the-breast detail of the incident to herself. As busy as he'd been dousing his burning buttock, she doubted he saw anything he shouldn't.

Maybe.

However, even if he did note her in-the-flesh state, it wouldn't ruin the plan. According to the magazines she'd read, some types of bogles took an earthly form. The Headless Lady could be one of those types of ghaists. "Leave the gown with me, Flora, so I can repair it for my next haunting."

"You will give it another go, then?"

Shrugging, Gillian said, "I need the practice. It appears that Mr. Delaney is in for a few more supernatural exposures."

Flora shot her a look of surprise. "Delaney? You cannot haunt Mr. Delaney again. You literally lost your head to the man."

"Who else do you suggest I haunt?"

"But he is bound to realize you are a guiser."

"That is a risk I must take."

"No, it is not," Flora said, flinging up her arms. The diaphanous white gown she held floated like a bedraggled flag as she added, "Haunt the servants or Uncle Angus. Haunt me. It is practice you need. What does it matter if we ken the Headless Lady of Rowanclere is really you and not a death bogle?"

Wishing to soothe her sister, Gillian scooted off the bed, took Flora's hand, and spoke in a soft, solemn tone. "Please do not get so upset. It worries me. Flora, I realize the Texan will be a difficult man to dupe at this point, but consider this. If after this day's fiasco I can convince him that Rowanclere is haunted, I shall surely be successful with Lord Harrington. If I can dupe Delaney now, I can cozen anyone. It will be the perfect test."

"I don't like it," Flora snapped, absently rubbing the bulge of her belly. "But I can plainly see your mind is made up. What exactly do you intend to do?"

Gillian walked to the window and gazed out over the castle's great lawn and the road leading to Rowanclere's front door. The roses need tending, she absently thought as she dwelled upon her sister's question.

Aloud, she said, "Since I've already spoken to him and thrown something at him, I think I should probably be a mischievous specter."

Flora sniffed. "As if you could be any other kind."

Gillian ignored that. "I shall need to do something which will make it appear as though the Headless Lady threw the head on purpose. As a joke, perhaps. Maybe I could throw some other things at him. I could be a poltergeist."

"What things?"

"I don't know. I'll need to go through my books and determine which tricks or illusions would best suit a mischievous, talking boodie."

"I have an uncomfortable feeling about all of this."

Gillian glanced over her shoulder. "It is the bairn making you uncomfortable."

"It is my twin." Flora folded her arms and rested them on her belly. "What about the séance? Do you still intend to host one of those?"

Gillian pursed her lips and blew a gentle breath that made a circle of fog on the windowpane. "Perhaps. That should be a perfect opportunity for some mischief, don't you think? I do believe I shall save the magic slate and tapping hand for another time, although I would feel better if I rehearsed everything I might need once Lord Harrington is in residence."

Silence descended as the two women considered the situation. Gillian pictured herself tossing various items from the castle's hidden doorways, crawl spaces, and blind spots.

She swallowed a groan. *This will never work.*

I must make it work.

Each day Uncle Angus found it more difficult to get up and down Rowanclere's numerous staircases. Each day he appeared to suffer greater pain. Each day he asked after her progress, and worry did him no more good than it did Flora.

Gillian refused to accept defeat. Her granduncle had surely saved her and her sisters' lives when he rescued them from their abusive Ross relatives following their parents' death. 'Twas her turn to save his.

"The sale of Rowanclere must go through," she said grimly. "Lord Harrington will be convinced this castle is haunted." She plopped back down on her bed, sat cross-legged, and declared, "I shall haunt this castle so very well that Mr. Delaney will shake in his cowboy boots."

"Guid fegs." Flora shot Gillian a sharp stare, then took a seat in a floral upholstered chair. "You have that look about you again, Gilly. Tell me. What did he do? Taunt you? Bait you? Challenge you?"

"No. Nothing like that."

"Then what? You only get that particular sparkle in your eye when you are planning something wicked."

"Wicked?" Gillian protested, giving her head a toss that sent her long hair flying over her shoulder and bringing a theatrical hand to her chest. "Me?"

"The innocent look doesn't fool me. You love to do wicked, dangerous things. That attack of nerves you had in your room before Mr. Delaney arrived was highly unusual. Now you are back to your normal self."

Gillian studied her fingernails. "Do not be silly, Flora. What could be dangerous about darting along Rowanclere's secret passageways pretending to be a ghaist?"

Flora leveled a stern look upon her sister. "I'd say you might fall and hurt your head upon the steps, but we both know it's more likely that hard head of yours would crack the stone."

Their gazes met and battled silently for a long moment before Flora asked, "What are you hiding?"

It was at times like this that Gillian wished she didn't have a twin. They could not keep any secrets from one another. "All right. It is Delaney. The man bothered me."

"Bothered you how?" Flora's expression grew stormy as she added, "Did he touch you, Gilly?"

"Nae. He did not come near me."

"What, then?"

Gillian swallowed a sudden lump in her throat. "He's from America."

Her sister blinked. "So?"

"I dinna like Americans."

"You dinna know any Americans!"

"Aye, I do."

"Uncle Angus? You love him."

"Not Uncle Angus. Besides, he considers himself a Scot despite all those years in Texas."

For a moment, Flora looked at her twin with a blank stare. Then slowly, the light dawned. "Oh, Gilly. You canna be that unfair. Mr. Delaney should not be blamed for the fact that David Maclean acted the cad and married that American heiress. Mr. Delaney had nothing to do with David's betrayal."

"I know that. David hurt my heart, not my mind. But they say in the village that the woman used wicked wiles to ensnare him, and I would not be surprised if such behavior were an American trait. Think of the risks we face. If Delaney suspects we are staging the hauntings, he could use the information against us. He could tell Lord Harrington."

Flora nibbled at her lower lip as she considered her

sister's argument. Then she shook her head. "Nae. I dinna believe that. I quite liked Mr. Delaney. He was charming."

"Exactly." Gillian nodded forcefully. "Which is what has me concerned. Did we not have a similar first impression of Mrs. David Maclean?"

"Actually, my first thought was that David stole a bairn from a cradle. But you canna compare our guest to—"

Gillian shook her head. "Mr. Delaney was much too charming and far too flirtatious when addressing a woman well advanced with child."

"Don't be ridiculous. If he flirted with me—and I am not saying he did, mind you—it would be because I am obviously . . ." she glanced down at her stomach ". . . safe."

"Safe? I seriously doubt Alasdair would agree. No matter, Delaney was still too forward in his actions, just like Mrs. Maclean was when she stole my betrothed."

"She bought your betrothed, sweetie, and Mr. Delaney wasn't forward. He was courteous."

"He was cocky."

"Aye, I believe you mentioned that already," Flora said dryly.

Gillian's mouth twitched with a grin at that, though the seriousness of her point quickly quashed the urge. "Cocky as in bold and brash, sister dear. He claims to be a writer, but for all we know, he could have come to Rowanclere for nefarious purposes."

"He had references from a full dozen English peers."

"So? Sleekit men can fool anyone. Perhaps he is a thief who is here to steal our valuables."

"Now you are being silly."

"True," she said flippantly. "We have no valuables. Uncle Angus's brother sold them all."

"Gillian."

Hugging one of her pillows to her chest, she sulked a few moments before saying, "Ah, all right. Perhaps I should not be so distrustful. Still, I sense Mr. Delaney is more than he presents himself to be."

A wicked light sparked in her sister's eyes. "Considering your description of how much the man presented, that is saying quite a lot."

Jake tucked Scooter beneath his arm as he made his way downstairs the following morning. He'd slept surprisingly well for a man so recently "haunted" in his bedchamber. Probably because he would have enthusiastically welcomed the seductive spirit into his bed.

He'd heard tales of headless ladies and green ladies and gray ladies, various ghouls, bogles, and brownies, and while he didn't necessarily believe in them, he wasn't prepared to discount the stories entirely. However, such phenomena had nothing at all to do with the shapely flesh-and-blood woman who had invaded his privacy yesterday. Even before he'd pulled on his pants this morning, he had decided to track down the elusive illusion while he was here at Rowanclere. There was no reason he couldn't keep an eye out for her at the same time he searched the confines of the castle for the piece of Texas history suspected to be harbored within its walls.

After all, he ought to get some fun out of this trip.

Last night and again this morning he had examined the portion of the wall where the apparition had appeared, and while he was certain a hidden passage existed, he'd failed to locate the mechanism that opened it. He'd decided to look for it again at different times throughout the day. Changing light altered how a room appeared, exposing different details.

Right now, however, he wanted to survey the lay of the land, get his bearings, and develop a plan on how to best conduct his search. In light of yesterday's events, his decision to conceal the true purpose of his visit appeared to have been the right one. Rowanclere definitely had its share of intrigue.

Reaching ground level, Jake eventually found himself back in the centrally located room that presently served as Rowanclere's entry hall. He eyed his choice of doors. The most appealing led past the dining room he'd noticed yesterday. The least appealing led outside. Out of doors where he should take Scooter. Where a light mist fell. An undoubtedly cold, light mist.

Jake gave the dog in his arms a scowl and muttered, "Pest."

Outside, he surveyed the surroundings for an appropriate spot to set Scooter down, settling on a spot of green grass beside rosebushes in bloom. With her business taken care of, Scooter happily took to sniffing around. Jake flipped up the collar on his jacket, hunched his shoulders, stuck his hands into his pockets, and burrowed in to wait on her. Damn, but he was miserable cold. Here it was the middle of summer and he could all but see the fog of his breath on the air.

"It's a helluva way to live," he observed to Scooter, who had fastened a hunter's gaze upon a lark perched upon the spreading branches of a nearby birch tree. The brainless mutt had yet to accept she was no longer fast enough to catch birds. Although Jake had to admit, even on two legs and dragging a hind end, she was still faster than most men. The dog was actually quite amazing.

And hungry, judging by the way she'd caught a scent and was scooting off.

"Whoa there, pooch." He stepped after her, reaching into his jacket for the rope sling he'd fashioned from a long strip of sheeting to assist her mobility. Slipping it under her belly, he lifted her rear quarters from the ground and she took off, dragging Jake along with her.

They wound up at what he deduced from the aroma to be the door to the kitchen. Within minutes, a playful Scooter had secured for herself not only a bowl of choice table scraps, but also a nice warm spot in front of the fire. Still chilled from the early morning cold, Jake was tempted to plop down beside his dog. The scandalized cook wouldn't hear of it, however.

"Just like Miss Gilly," the matron said, clucking her tongue. "She always has preferred to eat here. When will you gentry learn to act like gentry?"

"Who is Miss Gilly?"

She ignored the question and continued. "Guests will eat in the dining room. You will find a cheery fire built in the hairth and our breakfast is superb, if I'm allowed to boast a bit. I suggest the Arbroath smokie this morning. It is a fine bite of fish."

Jake knew a losing argument when staring down the wooden spoon at one, so he offered a rueful grin and said, "The food and fire sound wonderful, but could you tell me how to get to it without going back outside? It's colder than a banker's heart out there."

A kitchen maid flashed him a flirtatious smile and said, "I can show him up the servant's stairs, Mrs. Ferguson. That is the quickest way."

"Excellent," Jake hastened to say when Mrs. Ferguson appeared to hesitate. Along with finding the fireplace more quickly, this might give him the opportunity to clandestinely study the young woman's shape for the purpose of eliminating her as a spirit suspect. Every woman at Rowanclere was a possibility. Except for Mrs. Dunbar, that is. Jake's headless lady had no baby growing beneath the most lovely breasts Scooter had managed to reveal.

The flirtatious young kitchen maid—whom he quickly deduced was not his ghost due to an overabundance of hip—chattered like a mockingbird as she led him up the narrow servants' staircase. In short order he learned that the elderly laird of the castle, Angus Ross, was slowly recovering from a lung inflammation, that Mrs. Dunbar's husband loved to salmon fish, and that Mrs. Ferguson's haggis had won a prize at this year's fair. Other delectables, the girl told him with a wink, could be found in the cottage with green doors and shutters at the north end of the village once dinner duties at Rowanclere were done.

Jake declined her offer in a well-practiced, roguish manner and she ushered him into Rowanclere's dining room with a regretful sigh.

He was disappointed to find the room empty. Addressing the maid, he asked, "Before you go, could you tell me where I might find the mistress? I've a question or two to ask her."

"She took a breakfast tray in the drawing room this morning, sir."

"Thank you. And please tell Mrs. Ferguson her breakfast does smell delicious."

As promised, a fire burned in a marble fireplace, and Jake crossed the room toward its welcoming heat. Warming his hands, he eyed the steaming dishes lining the carved mahogany sideboard and gave the air an appreciative sniff. Ham. Eggs. Fresh bread. Something with cinnamon . . . apples perhaps?

His hunger aroused, Jake headed for the buffet, but a sound coming from beyond the dining room had him veering out into the hallway. There he stopped and listened again.

A thud. A bump. And a woman's humming. Coming from the room next door.

Having strolled toward the sound, he paused at the doorway of a small drawing room. His gaze flicked past the embroidered mahogany chairs, marble-topped tables, and portrait-hung walls to settle upon the delightful vision of a woman. Her back was toward him as she bent forward at the waist while reaching through the opened window to pluck a mist-kissed yellow flower from a vine. Golden hair piled high upon her head and quality of silk in her skirt convinced him he'd found Mrs. Dunbar. Before proceeding any farther, Jake did what any red-blooded man would do. He gave a soundless, appreciative whistle at the appeal of round, shapely buttocks pointed in his direction. Then, shifting his gaze from the view to the window, he cleared his throat, and said, "Y'all sure do have some beautiful scenery here in Scotland. Good morning, Mrs. Dunbar."

She gasped, dropped the flower, started to turn toward him, then abruptly stopped and did something downright strange. Yanking the midnight blue drapery toward her, she wrapped it around her like a bulky, badly pleated kilt before turning to face him. "Mr. Delaney. I didn't hear you come downstairs."

"I took the long way around."

Silence fell between them as Jake was distracted from his purpose by the sheer beauty of his hostess' face. A splash of pink embarrassment on either cheek was bridged by a light dusting of freckles across a pert little nose. Her eyes were the exact shade of bluebonnets. A wildflower, Jake was reminded, that legend claimed originally came to Texas via shipments of wool from Scotland.

His gaze drifted downward and he puzzled over why she had wrapped herself in the drapery. Was she embarrassed about her size? Had his comments yesterday upset her, made her worry about her expanding waistline? He hoped not. He hadn't meant any criticism, only concern. Personally, Jake had always thought expectant mothers especially beautiful. This was a time when their femininity shone like no other . . . oh, damn.

Jake's downward glance stopped abruptly at the sight of her bare feet peeking out from below her lilac-colored hem. His eyes narrowed. Heat flowed into his loins.

He'd always had a passion for a woman's bare feet.

Right along with the surge of lust came a wave of shame. Dammit, Delaney. What kind of lecher was he? She was a married woman. An expectant mother. He shouldn't even be looking at her, much less hankering after her.

Desperate to change the direction of his thoughts, he cleared his throat and said, "I, uh, think you should know, ma'am, I had a disturbance of a sort in my bedroom last night."

She blinked once. "Did you?"

"Yep. I think somebody was trying to play a joke on me. I think I was supposed to believe this person was a ghost."

"I see."

Jake waited for more, but she wasn't forthcoming. Eventually, he gestured toward the settee. "Maybe you should sit down and listen to my story. I think this is something you should hear."

Her smile was fast and as fake as a tonic peddler's pitch. "I'm fine as I am. Please continue, Mr. Delaney."

Suspicious, Jake folded his arms. "Not until you sit down, ma'am. It's not good for a woman in your condition to be on your feet too much."

Now the fake smile got some emotion in it. Heat. The woman was piqued.

She opened her mouth to speak, then abruptly shut it. Keeping herself wrapped in the drapery, she took two steps forward, reached out and grabbed the back of a desk chair and tugged it toward her. Before Jake quite realized what had happened, she had taken the seat, folded her hands on her lap, and pasted on a smile that was downright challenging. All the while, she kept herself covered by the drapery.

"Are you cold, Mrs. Dunbar?"

"Just curious, Mr. Delaney. Please, tell me about your ghaist. Rowanclere has a number of them, you see, and from your description, I am uncertain which one made himself known to you."

"Herself. She was definitely a woman. A living woman. I saw her . . . breathe."

Mrs. Dunbar sat a little stiffer in her chair and her chin came up. "We have the spirits of at least three different women haunting the castle. One is a brownie, who keeps out of sight and is often quite a help around the castle. At times, however, she delights in mischief. She loves to play tricks by moving things around. Another is My Lady Greensleeves, who legend tells us threw herself from a tower window after her father murdered the man she loved, a stablehand here at Rowanclere. Last, of course, is the Headless Lady of Rowanclere. She, too, is full of mischief. She dresses all in white and likes to frighten people by popping up in unexpected places at unexpected times. She carries a head that is but a wood model, and often leaves it behind following a haunt. I have seen the Headless Lady myself. She left a head in my room the day I departed Rowanclere to marry Mr. Dunbar."

"Really," Jake drawled, making no attempt to hide his skepticism.

Her chin rose a little higher. "Did your spirit resemble either the Headless Lady or Lady Greensleeves?"

"No, more like Lady Godiva."

The woman blushed red as the tartan that hung in Rowanclere's entry hall. "Well, 'tis neither here nor there. None of our ghaists are dangerous. Well, except for the bogles. They have been known to cause injury, although only to obnoxious men. As long as you are kind to the women of Rowanclere, you should be safe."

"That's reassuring to know," he replied, his lips twisting in a half-smile. Damned if she wasn't chock full of spirit. Feisty thing. Funny, she hadn't struck him that way at all yesterday.

She hadn't loaded his pistol yesterday, either.

It was, of course, the heat he sensed in her today that did it. Jake did like his women with some sizzle to 'em.

Again, his conscience gave him a rap on the skull. *She's married, Delaney. What's wrong with you?*

Giving his head a quick shake, he pushed to his feet. "I reckon I'll see to breakfast now."

She didn't rise, but simply flashed him a brilliant—and relieved—smile. "Be certain to sample Mrs. Ferguson's haggis. It is a prize-winning recipe."

"So I've been told."

He was halfway back to the dining room when the drawing room door closed and he heard the snick of a lock. Hmm. Friendly one minute, ill-tempered the next. *Maybe that has something to do with the pregnancy.*

In the dining room, Jake headed for the buffet. He lifted a fancy, blue china plate from a stack and began to pile it high with Texas-size portions of scrambled eggs, ham, stewed pears—he'd been wrong about the apples—and haggis, which experience had shown him tasted like a dully spiced sausage. He skipped the porridge and black pudding, and added an Arbroath smokie as recommended by the cook. Jake liked this Scottish custom of having fish with breakfast.

His plate filled to near overflowing, he reached for one last item, a roll. But the basket moved.

Jake blinked, certain he had imagined the movement. Once again, he reached for the bread.

Once again, the basket moved.

What the hell?

Abruptly, he grabbed for the basket. This time, his fingers brushed the straw before the basket scooted beyond his reach. "Sonofabitch," he said, setting down his plate, torn between annoyance and anticipation. Obviously, his "ghost" was up to her tricks once more. Unless, of course, these hijinks were the effort of Mrs. Dunbar's brownie and Jake didn't much believe that.

Shoot, he would suspect Mrs. Dunbar of being the culprit had last's night's seductive shade not proven beyond a shadow of doubt that she was not far gone with child. However, someone was making this bread-basket dance.

Jake stood still as a fence post, visually examining the sideboard for sign of a line, which was the most obvious explanation for the shenanigans. He saw nothing, but then a dark thread against the dark wood would be diffi-cult to spot. "You know," he said aloud. "This effort is juvenile compared to last night's."

At that, the basket jerked and slid completely off the cabinet, sending rolls tumbling onto the floor. Jake tucked his tongue firmly in his cheek and said, "Yeah, flying bread is definitely amateurish. Now, the naked bosom showed promise. Among other things." As he spoke, he bent and picked up the basket, fully expecting to find a thread attached to it.

He didn't.

"Well, well, well. Maybe you're a better mischief-maker than I thought."

Five minutes later, breakfast forgotten in the wake of the intriguing mystery, he lay on his back halfway beneath the sideboard, studying the bottom of the furni-ture. Hearing footsteps, he twisted his head to see the swish of lavender skirts revealing a pair of trim, graceful ankles. And, to his masculine dismay, a pair of shoes.

"Mr. Delaney," came his hostess' censuring voice. "I realize that Texas has a reputation for being less civilized than other parts of the world, but you should know that here in Scotland we take our meals from a table rather than the floor."

Some things Jake simply wouldn't listen to, and criticism of his home was near the top of his list. "Oh, I'm not down here eating, ma'am," he drawled, looking to turn the tables, so to speak, as he scooted out from underneath the cabinet. "I was looking for a likely spot to stash my gum, except somebody beat me to it. There's a dozen wads or more down here already."

"Gum?"

"Chewing gum."

"Chewing gum?" Fire lit her eyes.

Jake bit back a grin. "Sticky stuff, that gum."

He wouldn't have been surprised to see steam rising from her ears. "I'm going to wring Robbie's neck."

Then, while Jake climbed to his feet, to his surprise, the very pregnant woman dropped down onto her hands and knees. "Uncle Angus's, too," she muttered.

Jake's mouth dropped open in shock and a fair measure of horror when she compounded her folly by lying on her stomach—on her stomach!—and sticking her head beneath the sideboard to confirm his claim. "I rue the day my granduncle introduced the child to that nasty habit. Chewing gum on a Sheraton sideboard. The girl is—"

"Mrs. Dunbar, please! I don't think it's a good idea for you to be down on the floor like that in your condition."

"—such a trial. Oh!" She broke off abruptly. "Aye. My condition." Then, with a grace that belied her advanced state of ripeness, she scrambled to her feet. Her cheeks were once again stained a bright red. Failing to meet Jake's horrified gaze, she started for the door, murmuring absently, "Excuse me, Mr. Delaney. I have a lass to locate. Enjoy your breakfast."

Then she was gone and Jake was left staring after her, his arms folded and his eyes narrowed to slits.

Damned if in the past couple of minutes, Mrs. Dunbar's baby hadn't dropped.

three

DARTING BACK INTO the drawing room, Gillian went straight to the hidden passageway she'd so recently "haunted," and disappeared inside. In the narrow, airless corridor, she paused long enough to tug the stuffed corset she'd fashioned to assist in her masquerade back into position before setting off in search of her younger sister.

She hurriedly made the long climb up to Uncle Angus's suite of rooms where, when her granduncle felt up to the task, the child was directed to spend time each morning in educational pursuit. She found the elderly Scotsman asleep and Robyn nowhere to be found.

Next Gillian checked Robyn's favorite hiding place in the passages—a former dungeon she'd transformed into a "treasure room." After that, she made the trek to the playroom off the girl's bedchamber and finally, headed for the muniment room in the older section of the castle. As she marched down the hallway, the clash of a sword against stone told her she'd finally run her quarry to ground.

The scolding tones of Flora's voice filtering to her ears indicated she had not been the only one looking for Robbie.

". . . at this rate you'll never learn your Latin."

"So?" Robbie shook her shoulders. "I dinna care to learn Latin. I wish to learn languages people still speak so when I grow up I can go exploring like Nicholas and Uncle Angus."

"That gum-chewing scoundrel," commented Gillian as she swept into the room to see her twin and younger sister squared off on opposite sides of a table. Robyn clasped a sword in her right hand while the left rearranged the metal body parts lying strewn across the tabletop. "And you, young lady, would be well served to repair that suit of armor you destroyed and don it. I don't doubt my tongue is as sharp as your sword at the moment."

Spearing a look toward Flora, Gillian finished, "Your little sister has stuck wads of chewing gum beneath the sideboard in the dining room."

"Oh, Robyn," said Flora with a long-suffering sigh. "How many times have we warned you? It will be sentences I'll have from you, lass. Twenty-five saying 'I shall not stick gum on furnishings.' "

"Make it thirty-five," Gillian added. "This made me so angry I put the plan at risk." She gestured toward her stomach. Flora's eyes widened, then knitted in a frown.

"What in the world have you done to yourself?"

Wincing, Gillian reached down and tugged her "baby" back into position yet again. "This is never going to work. I make a dampt puir wicht."

As Flora frowned, young Robyn piped up. "Let me be

the ghaist, Gilly. I should be wonderful. I have been thinking of a way to string a harness from the ceiling of the portrait room. Can you not see me flying around all our ancestors?"

"Vividly," Gillian grumbled. "Which is why I shall do all the haunting."

Continuing to frown, Flora grabbed her twin by the arm and pulled her in front of the tall wall mirror. According to plan, the women wore identical dresses. Gazing at their reflections, Flora compared the shape of their bellies, then reached over and tugged her sister's stuffing up where it needed to be. "Gilly is right, Robyn. We would never chase you back into the schoolroom if you could fly away from us."

The girl gave a dreamy sigh at the thought. Gillian winced and sank into a nearby chair. "The rate I am going, we will never get me off the ground."

"What happened?" Flora asked.

Gillian allowed her head to drop forward until her chin rested on her chest. "First he sneaked up on me in the drawing room before I'd strapped on the 'bairn.' I had to hide behind the drapery while I talked to him so he wouldn't see my lack of stomach."

A giggle burst from Robyn's mouth, and Gillian shot her a glower before continuing her story. "Then after he went in to breakfast, I cozened him with the breadbasket and thread trick, tugging it just right so that the knot slipped when I needed. He was not bothered at all. The man actually talked back to the empty room, told me the haunting didn't compare with last night's."

Robyn pursed her lips and blew a soundless stream of air. "The Headless Lady is an awfully good wile, Gilly."

"Not the way I did it. Besides, I cannot be a one-feat ghaist. I will not convince Lord Harrington with but one apparition."

"Do not discount playing the mischievous, invisible brownie," Flora said. "Just because Mr. Delaney is skeptical . . . well . . . we know little of the man. Perhaps he does not believe in spirits and such. If that is the case, I should think he might question your . . . appearances . . . more closely than one whose mind is open to such phenomena."

"Aye. If he is a nonbeliever, the Texan—" Gillian broke off abruptly at the sound of a barking dog. A fast approaching barking dog.

Mr. Delaney would not be far behind.

Her gaze flew to Flora's panicked blue eyes. One of them needed to disappear. Fast.

Gillian pointed toward the wall holding the muniment room's entrance to Rowanclere's hidden passage system and Robbie jumped to trip the catch as the Texan's voice drifted toward them. "Scooter, get back here."

The small brown beastie came scooting into the room, growling and barking, as Flora, being closest to the wall, ducked into the passage. Robyn shut the door, then positioned herself between the hidden entrance and the yapping dog. "Why, sister, look at the puir wee thing. Her legs dinna work."

"She certainly has no trouble with her mouth," Gillian muttered.

"How does she move so fast?" asked the girl, both voice and expression filled with wonder.

"Exuberance for life," Jake said as he sauntered into the

room. He grinned at Robyn, scowled at the dog, then arched a brow toward Gillian. "The chewing-gum enthusiast, I assume?"

"Aye. Mr. Delaney, allow me to introduce my sister, Miss Robyn Ross."

"You may call me Robbie," she piped up, smiling with delight at the antics of the dog, who thankfully had abandoned her inquisitive sniffing at the hidden door along the wall. "What happened to your dog?"

Delaney repeated the story he'd told Flora, then apologized for allowing Scooter to run loose through Rowanclere. "Ordinarily I walk her with a sling, but today when I wasn't looking, she took it into her head to go exploring."

"I'd prefer she limit her investigations to something other than my ankles," Gillian responded dryly as Scooter commenced to nipping at the hem of her dress.

Gillian sensed the Texan's gaze as she tugged her skirt from Scooter's mouth. Glancing up, she caught the puzzled look he directed toward the bulge around her midriff. Hidden behind a polite smile, Gillian ground her teeth in frustration. The man paid altogether too close attention.

Then his gaze drifted upward and lingered a second too long on the cleavage displayed by her neckline. Gillian held her breath. While ordinarily a comparison of hers and her sister's bosom revealed little difference, pregnancy had made Flora's bounty more bountiful than usual. Would he notice?

Men always notice.

Wonderful. Now she must worry about her belly and her breasts.

Thankfully, Robbie summoned Mr. Delaney's attention by kneeling beside Scooter and scratching her behind the ears. "She just drags her hindquarters everywhere she goes?"

The Texan explained about the sling he used to assist the dog, and Robyn's face lit up like a gaslight. "May I take her for a walk, please? I'll be careful with her, I promise."

"Certainly. If it's all right with your sister."

Gillian nodded, welcoming the ankle-nibbler's riddance. "You may have half an hour. After that you must return to your studies, Robyn. Today is no holiday."

The Texan's eyes twinkled with mischief as he gave her a wink. "It's not? And here I thought it was National Chewing Gum day."

Gillian couldn't reply. The wink had struck her dumb.

Mr. Delaney was a handsome man. With that roguish glimmer in his eyes, he curled a woman's toes.

She stammered some nonsensical reply as he helped Robyn slip the dog into the sling and the pair took off at a run, leaving Gillian and the Texan suspended in a silence she found both uncomfortable and . . . stimulating.

Probably because he was staring at her again, only this time he concentrated on her lips. A faint crease of worry marred his brow. Gillian found herself wanting to lift her thumb and smooth it away.

He cleared his throat at the same time she summoned up a cough. His lips twisted in a quick, self-deprecating grin, then he said, "So, I take it this is Rowanclere's weapons chamber?"

"The muniment room. We're in the oldest section of

the castle, part of the fourteenth-century keep. In an attempt to preserve our history, renovations here have been kept to a minimum."

"I see." Delaney lifted a piece of breastplate armor from the table and examined it casually. "Looks like this fella died in battle."

"I don't know about the man who wore it, but the suit itself lasted centuries until the Terror of the Tower did it in."

"Terror of the Tower?"

"Robyn attacked it with a broadsword last week."

"Ah." He flashed a grin and added, "Reckon she could use her gum to put him back together?"

Gillian forced her toes to uncurl. "Better beneath his breastplate than her dinner plate."

His laughter sent her toes curling up again. *At this rate I'll wear holes in my stockings.* "Tell me about your book, Mr. Delaney."

"My book? Oh, yes, my book." He wandered around the room inspecting the feel of a crossbow, then testing the sharpness of a claymore blade as he rattled off a convoluted tale of the differences between Old World castles and frontier forts. He ended by observing, "Imagine what might have happened if the Texans had a place like Rowanclere to defend instead of an insecure mission like the Alamo. So, Mrs. Dunbar, I'd like to begin my research of Rowanclere by mapping each room. I'll be as brief as possible in the private areas of the castle, of course."

"You can't," she automatically responded.

"Sure I can. While I prefer to take it slow, I can work fast when desired."

Slow. Fast. Oh, my. The memory of how he'd looked

standing in his bedroom naked flashed in her mind, and Gillian felt the warmth of a blush crawl up her neck and sting her cheeks. "I mean we do not allow visitors to some areas of the castle."

Delaney frowned. "Surely you'll make an exception in my case, considering this is scholarly research? I promise not to get in your way." He lifted the claymore and tested its balance with a pair of smooth swings, his shirt stretching tight with the movement.

Gillian tore her gaze from the breadth of his shoulders and forced herself to take a breath. Her mind was foggy as a London night. Instinct told her to put some distance between herself and this man. Fast. So she opened her mouth and spoke the most foolish words she'd uttered since accepting David Maclean's proposal of marriage. "All right. You may tour the entire castle. Meet me in the Great Hall this afternoon at one."

I can't believe I lusted after a married woman. A married woman whose apron is riding high.

Jake stared at the painted wooden ceiling high above him and pondered the state of his own mind. Maybe the water in this part of the world had something funny in it. Maybe he'd gone way too long without a woman. Maybe he'd left his sense of ethics and morality on the other side of the Atlantic and transformed into a disgusting lecher.

Because, no denying it, Mrs. Dunbar lit his wick.

As if his wicked thoughts had summoned her, her voice floated toward him from across the Great Hall. "Good afternoon, Mr. Delaney."

He braced himself for another sensual assault and turned around.

Damned if that baby hadn't gone and moved on her again. "Afternoon, Mrs. Dunbar. You sure you're feeling all right?"

She drew back as if surprised by his question. "I feel fine. Do I appear otherwise?"

"No, no. You're glowing. You look beautiful, ma'am." Only, she looked beautiful in a different sort of way than she had earlier this morning.

And it didn't get to him nearly as bad.

"Why thank you, Mr. Delaney. Now, shall we begin your tour of Rowanclere?"

Nodding, he clasped his hands behind his back and listened half-heartedly as she launched into her castle tale. "We know Brodie ancestors have lived in this spot since 1285, but the exact date of the present building is not known. The caphouse on the southwest tower reads 1560 and we assume it records the completion date."

As Mrs. Dunbar spoke of corbeled battlements and bartizans, Jake pondered the puzzle of his reaction—or more precisely, his lack of reaction—upon conversing with his landlady this afternoon.

What a difference a few hours make. It was the strangest thing. Last time he saw her, she tied him in knots. This time she stirred nothing more than concern for her continued good health.

Maybe it had something to do with the way she carried the kid. Jake wasn't overly familiar with expectant mothers. Maybe it was normal for babies to do all that up and down moving around. Maybe he was naturally attracted to pregnant women who carried their children high instead of low.

Maybe I've lost my mind entirely.

Hell, Mrs. Dunbar had nothing to do with it. Jake was experiencing these lust surges and wanes because his body's juices were all out of whack. This was what happened when a healthy, adult man spent six months escorting his mother around the London social circuit instead of devoting some time to his own social inter-course—in the most private sense of the word. He'd been too long without a woman—no ifs, ands, or buts. Why else would he have a hankering for a pregnant married lady one minute, then feel like her big brother the next?

Maybe he should look up that come-hither kitchen maid, after all.

Jake took a moment and considered the thought. Though it might solve his immediate problem, the idea held little appeal. He hadn't come to Rowanclere to diddle the help; he'd come to find the Declaration so he could get on with his life. Maybe though, he'd alter his adventure itinerary a bit. Once the Declaration was on its way to Texas, rather than setting out to explore Africa first, maybe he'd head straight for the South Sea islands. From what he'd heard, the native women would revel in curing him of this condition. If they didn't kill him in the process, that is. "But what a way to go."

"Pardon me?" Mrs. Dunbar asked.

"Oh, nothing. I'm sorry. Please, go on."

She shot him a puzzled smile before continuing her lecture. "He died at the Battle of Pinkie, fighting Henry the Eighth's army during the 'Rough Wooing,' when he attempted to enforce the betrothal of the infant Mary, Queen of Scots to his son Edward. Over the years, each laird left his stamp on Rowanclere, some better than others, which is why you see the mishmash of styles we have today. Now, if you like, I shall show you the guard chamber. The vault is the best example of the late sixteenth-century rubble masonry construction of the house."

Jake had to duck to enter the dreary, windowless room. As his eyes adjusted to the dimmed light, his gaze was drawn not to the cement work, but to the small skeleton hanging from a metal bracket on one wall. "What the he—heck is that?"

"Oh, we call him Young Fergus. I'm afraid we don't know his true name."

His jaw gaped. "You keep a boy's bones hanging on a parlor wall?"

The woman shrugged, a this-is-nothing-unusual lift and lower of her shoulders that left Jake speechless. " 'Tis the guard chamber, not the parlor, and Young Fergus likes it here. We dinna ken when someone strung him together and hung him in this room, but we've found references to him in Rowanclere papers dating back three hundred years. Just last autumn we tried to give him a decent burial, but he was quite . . . loud . . . in his protest of our efforts."

Jake's gaze narrowed. "Loud?"

"All but raised the roof with his shoogles and skrieches."

"Shoogles and skrieches?"

"Shakes and screeches. Sometimes terrible moans."

Jake paused a beat, then arched a brow. "We're talking about the skeleton."

"Aye."

He shifted his stare from his landlady to the skeleton.

On second glance, something about the bones struck him as off, but he couldn't put his finger on what. Still, bones were bones and they did not "shoogle and skriech."

"So you're claiming Young Fergus left more than his bones behind?"

She flashed him a brilliant smile. "We call him our guardian ghaist."

As if on cue, the damned bones rattled, the arms and legs swinging like a puppet's. Jake all but jumped out of his boots.

Embarrassment flooded him as he sucked in a deep breath and attempted to calm his racing heart. He was glad of the dimness of the light filtering through the small window slits because he feared at that very moment, his face might be tinted a bit red. Although, come to think of it, a blush was a damned sight better than pasty, scared-as-hell white.

"What kind of trick is this?" he groused, striding toward the skeleton.

"No, Mr. Delaney!" cried Mrs. Dunbar, darting clumsily in front of him, effectively blocking his path. "Ye canna touch Young Fergus."

"Sure I can," he replied, stepping around her.

She grabbed his arm and planted her feet, attempting to pull him to a stop. It worked. Jake wasn't one to push around a pregnant female.

He dragged a hand down his cheek. "What's going on here, ma'am?"

She hauled him toward the doorway. "It's for your own safety, sir. Young Fergus won't abide being touched by strangers. He can be quite the wicked deevilock when he so wishes, and I'll not have harm done to you. My conscience would not bear it." She paused and sighed dramatically. "This tour was a mistake. This is precisely why we tend not to encourage visitors. Please, promise me you'll allow the puir wee one his privacy. Otherwise, I fear I cannot in good conscience continue your tour."

Jake couldn't help but grin. She'd managed to talk him right between a rock and hard place. As much as he wanted to piece together the mystery of these pranks being perpetrated on him, he needed to find the missing Declaration more. "All right, Mrs. Dunbar. I'll leave Young Fergus in peace." *For now, anyway.* "What's next on the tour?"

"The library," she said, beaming a smile bright as sunlight reflected off the loch.

Again, Jake was struck by his hostess' beauty. Taught by experience, he braced himself against an anticipated, though unwelcome, surge of lust.

It never came. Not when she smiled at him. Not when he followed her out of the guardroom and into the huge, high-ceilinged library. Not even when she familiarly took his hand in hers and pulled him from bookshelf to bookshelf, pointing out old histories and tomes, pride ringing in her voice and the scent of rosewater teasing his nose.

It didn't make sense. What was this on-again, off-again reaction he had to Mrs. Dunbar? Why did just looking at her sometimes make him hard enough to drive nails, while other times he felt only the compulsion to make her sit down and put her feet up to rest?

It made no sense. Sure, he'd endured stretches of celibacy in the past, but it had never affected him like this. Maybe that wasn't the problem. Maybe it was something more.

A sense of trepidation crept up his spine as Jake shifted uneasily on his feet. Maybe something was physically wrong with him and this was an early symptom.

Maybe he was developing a Condition.

Hell.

While his hostess rattled on about the room, Jake took renewed interest in the books lining the shelves. He scanned the titles searching for a medical text, or maybe one of those marriage books he'd heard was popular, if furtive, reading in England.

Now that the horrible possibility had occurred to him, Jake Delaney needed to know the truth. For all his education, this was a subject he knew nothing about. Men didn't discuss it. The very idea gave them the shakes. Jake could feel the shudder in his limbs even now.

He interrupted Mrs. Dunbar. "Does your library have medical books?"

"Why, yes. We have a few. Folk remedies, mainly, but I think we might have a text recommended by the medical school in Edinburgh."

"Where? May I look through it?"

She nodded, then moved to a section of shelves on the north wall. "There. The fifth shelf. It's too high for me, but if you'll—"

Jake grabbed the leather-bound tome she indicated off the shelf. Immediately, he began to leaf through it.

He prayed he'd find the answer to his question between its pages. Now that the dreaded idea had occurred, Jake simply had to know.

Could an indecisive cock be the first sign of impotence?

*   *   *

Seated behind a spyhole into the library, Gillian listened to her sister rave on about books—her favorite subject outside of her husband and the child she nurtured in her belly. Gillian rolled her eyes. Only Flora would lose herself in books at a time like this. "Give me the signal, sister," Gillian whispered.

To her dismay, Flora kept on talking. Gilly peered through the wall, confident of her anonymity. Mr. Delaney would need to possess an extraordinary sense of detail to notice the eyes in the portrait of a sixteenth-century Brodie ancestor hung high above him had changed from a flat gray to a very lifelike blue.

Besides, he hadn't so much as glanced in her direction. For the past ten minutes his gaze had been glued to the pages of the book he was reading. Flora didn't seem to mind. Gillian wasn't certain she'd even noticed. Once her twin started talking books, she tended to get lost in her own enthusiasm.

"My mother-in-law disapproves of fictional literature," Flora was saying. "As a result, Laichmoray's library suffers a lack of novels. Thank goodness we don't have that problem here at Rowanclere. I, for one, fail to see the harm in spending a few pleasant hours lost in an imaginary world. What about you, Mr. Delaney? As a writer, do you consider reading a fictional story a shameful waste of time?"

"What was that?" Jake said, glancing up.

Flora repeated her question and the Texan drawled his reply. "No, ma'am. Can't say I have a problem with reading stories or writing stories, either. But the other kinds of tale-telling . . . well, I reckon I don't hold much truck with that."

"Hold much truck?" Flora repeated. "I'm afraid I am unfamiliar with the term."

"Approve of. I don't approve of lying, Mrs. Dunbar. Or of preying upon people's fears with tricks and pranks. That's just a different type of lying . . . or fiction, if you will."

Gillian's eyes narrowed at his words, and she grimaced as she watched her twin's smile turn sickly. *Oh, Flora, don't let him bother you. Remember the reasons why we are doing this.*

It was as if her sister had heard her. Flora's shoulders squared, her belly went out, and her chin lifted. But before she had a chance to voice her reply, Robyn burst into the library holding the mongrel in her arms and calling Flora's name.

"Finally," the young girl said, her breath coming in pants. "Scooter and I have been looking all over for you. Mrs. Ferguson wants you in the kitchen, Flora. She says Mr. Douglas has come for the supply order, and you need to review it so we have everything we need when Lord Harrington arrives next week."

Flora shook her head and clucked her tongue. "Oh my. You will have to excuse me, Mr. Delaney. I must see to Mr. Douglas. He can be as grumpy as Young Fergus when he is kept waiting. Feel free to use the library this afternoon, if you wish. I'll be happy to continue the tour later, after dinner, perhaps. Robbie, come with me please. You'll need to stop me if it appears I am over-ordering. I find it difficult to judge these days."

Flora dashed from the room, followed by Robyn, who paused just long enough to give Jake time to scratch the dog and say "Howdy, Scoot. You having fun with your new friend?"

Almost before Gillian realized what was happening, Jake stood alone in the library, the scheduled haunting never set into motion. Leaning away from her peephole, Gillian blew a frustrated breath. What was Flora thinking? Mr. Douglas would have waited.

Flora's appetite wouldn't. One of the results of her sister's pregnancy was a marked increase in the attention Flora paid to food. Anything could trigger it—a smell, a word, the shape of a cloud. Residents of both Rowanclere and Laichmoray had quickly learned that whenever the mood was upon her, they put themselves at physical risk by standing between Flora and the larder.

"I guess I'll have to finish this on my own," she murmured. If it even mattered.

The haunts planned for today were the easiest to physically perform. Therefore, this afternoon's practice had been intended to help Flora more than Gillian. Her "ghaist tales" were as much a part of the visitation as the rattling of Young Fergus's bones, or the moaning, groaning, and chain clanging Gillian presently sat poised to begin. Without Flora around to talk about the Headless Lady and Rowanclere's other deevilocks, ghaists, and bodachs, any noises Gillian might make would be no more than that—noises.

Besides, after that pithy comment about tale-telling a few moments ago, she might as well throw in her chains. She hadn't fooled Delaney one little bit.

What did she expect after that first debacle of a haunting?

Gillian scowled down at the Texan. He'd finally put aside his book, and when he tugged the library steps to the end of the southern wall of bookshelves, her gaze lingered on the seat of his trousers as he climbed and reached for a volume on the topmost shelf. Despite her annoyance with him, she couldn't deny that Mr. J. A. K. Delaney was a fine figure of a man.

After all, she had seen the nakit truth.

So distracted was she by the memory that it took her some time to notice what he was doing. When she did, she leaned away from the spyhole, blinked her eyes hard, rubbed them, then looked again.

Nothing had changed. The skellum was ransacking the shelves.

Gillian sat frozen, watching the scoundrel work. Not ransacking, perhaps. Searching. That was what he was doing. Proceeding methodically, he removed a book from the shelf, felt the empty space behind it, then eyed the volume closely before turning it upside down and flipping through the pages. If nothing fell out, he replaced the book and reached for the one beside it. A time or two, a slip of paper did flutter from the inner pages and he'd catch it, read it, then return it to its place.

Gillian's mouth gaped open in shock at the man's audacity. Why was he doing this? Was Delaney a thief? A swindler? A fraud?

He was most certainly a liar.

Gillian pushed to her feet and began to pace the passageway. That man. What was he looking for? Money? Jewels? Not information about the castle like he'd claimed, obviously. And to think he tried to make poor Flora feel guilty about stretching the truth with these specter schemes. What a bleen o' blethers that was.

It made Gillian furious.

She had to do something. She had to find out what

he was about. A hundred different possibilities flitted through her mind, each more troublesome than the last.

She had to find out the truth. But how? Confront him? Cajole him? Accost him in his sleep?

A dozen or more minutes ticked by as she walked the floor and considered the question. Eventually, her path took her toward a corner where a spider web snagged on her hair and floated in front of her face.

Gillian reached up to bat the web away, but froze when the sticky silk adhered to her finger. "Spiders."

She spent long seconds lost in thought before her mouth bowed in a slow, wicked smile. "Spiders. Of course!"

Gillian returned to the spyhole and watched the rascal continue about his task. A soft chuckle escaped her mouth. "Don't look now, Texas. But you are in for the fright of your life."

four

THE TIMELY ARRIVAL of Mr. Douglas allowed Jake three unsupervised hours, which he utilized to make a methodical search of the library. While he didn't find the missing Declaration of Independence tucked between two of the numerous volumes of love stories, he did find a section of books that caused his heart to skip a beat.

One entire set of bookshelves held issues of early Texas newspapers bound into books. He took his time, flipping through each page of every volume, expecting at any moment to come upon the handwritten document he sought.

He didn't find it. Not in the newspapers, nor between the pages of any of the other books he searched. Still, he'd come to the right place. He knew it in his bones. Besides, when he began to sense he'd spent all the time he dared in the endeavor, he still had another whole wall yet to explore.

Jake was forced to face a truth. Making a one-man physical search of a place as big as Rowanclere Castle would not get the job done. He either would need to reveal his true purpose or trick the information out of them. After a few moments' deliberation, he settled on trickery. It seemed to fit the folk of Rowanclere better than telling the truth.

Following an early supper, he had just sunk the eight ball in a practice game of billiards, then settled into a chair pulled close to the fireplace to read the newspaper when Mrs. Dunbar swept into the room and said, "Well, Mr. Delaney, are you ready to continue your tour?"

Jake frowned. His hostess had changed clothes since the last time he'd seen her, and she looked particularly fetching in a gown of rose pink silk. "I thought I was scheduled for a visit with the laird of the castle."

"I am sorry." Her dainty brows dipped into a worried frown. "Uncle Angus is not up to seeing visitors. He's poustit this eve. Suffering the pains, the rheums."

Jake thought for a moment, interpreting the unfamiliar words. "Your uncle suffers from rheumatism?"

"Aye. Some days, like today, it sinks its teeth into him fiercely."

"I'm sorry to hear that. Chronic pain can wear a man down. Let's hope he feels better tomorrow."

"Aye." She appeared distracted for a moment, then, to his shock and chagrin, she gave her head a shake, paired a devilish smile with a wicked twinkle in her bluebonnet eyes, and crooked her finger right at him. "Allow me to show you the delights of Rowanclere, Mr. Delaney."

Damned if every drop of blood in his body didn't feel like it headed south.

Jake brought the newspaper with him when he stood, using it to shield his body's reaction. In a way, he was reassured by the response this woman elicited from him. Were he developing a performance problem, surely his pistol wouldn't load so fast.

No, the trouble wasn't with him. It had to be her. The trouble was he had a beautiful hostess who couldn't decide which personality to present: gentle Madonna or flirtatious vamp. Either way, she twisted him into knots.

Jake's temper kindled. To hell with going slow. Folks here at Rowanclere were big on bluffs, what with this ghost business and all. Maybe he should run a bluff of his own. Maybe he should pick her up, carry her to his chamber and tie her to his bed, refusing to let her go until the missing Declaration of Independence was in his hands.

He could see her lying stretched out before him, her hair spread around her a golden waterfall, her eyes flashing blue fire, her breasts heaving with the force of her breaths, her belly. . . . Sonofabitch!

"She's pregnant, for God's sake."

"What was that, Mr. Delaney?"

He shut his eyes and shook his head. "Nothing. Never mind. By all means, ma'am, show me your castle."

The next half hour was a whirlwind education on furniture, architecture, and Clan Brodie history. If she dwelled a little heavily on the bloodthirsty parts, he didn't mind. Gory detail kept his mind off other unsavory things.

Like how the burr in her words seduced him like the stroke of a velvet ribbon against his skin.

The cook offered him a lemonade when they toured the kitchen, and he gulped it like a man dying of thirst, hoping the drink would cool him down. "Maybe now's a good time to give me a look at the outer wall, Mrs. Dunbar," he suggested.

"The outer wall? But I thought you wished to remain indoors out of the weather. It is much cooler outside now than it was this morning."

"No, ma'am. A good dose of cold sounds right good to me about now."

"Very well." She shrugged her shapely shoulders and added, "We'll take the dungeon route from here and exit to the spot where the old wall stood, all right?"

Dungeon. Lovely. Better hope she can't read my mind or she'll lock me in down there.

Never having been one to enjoy jail cells of any kind, Jake didn't look forward to the next portion of the tour. He needed to see them, however. Dungeons were great hiding places for all sorts of things—like a stolen copy of an historically significant document, for instance.

For the thousandth time since being sent to the freezing north to retrieve the document, Jake wondered how the Declaration ended up at Rowanclere to begin with. The Texas memorabilia collector who'd come so close to killing Chrissy claimed to have purchased the item from a member of the Rowanclere household for a ridiculous price. Someone from Rowanclere had then purportedly stolen it back. Now that he was here, he found himself even more curious about the whys, wheres, and hows of the story. He liked a good mystery, and between this and the "ghosts," Rowanclere was certainly providing that.

His hostess opened a doorway cleverly hidden in the back of a food pantry and while holding a torch, led him down a steep, dark, spiral stone staircase. She droned on about this clan and that clan and this ghost and that. So much so, that by the time they reached the bottom of the stairs, he was feeling more than a shade dizzy.

He felt real dizzy, in fact.

Jake swayed on his feet. He saw two Mrs. Dunbars. Then four. Then none, because the light winked out.

"Ma'am?"

A low, keening groan sailed out of the darkness and swirled around him. Then a cackle, a witch's call.

Jake shuddered at the sound.

"Well, sir," came the disembodied voice from out of the darkness. "Welcome to my lair."

"Who are you?" he gasped, his consciousness fading. *Drugged. I've been drugged.*

This time the voice sounded feminine and amused. "Oh, I don't know, Texas. Why don't you call me Death."

Gillian watched him sway at the bottom of the stairs and wished she knew more about sleeping potions. Obviously, she'd given this man too much. He appeared about to drop.

"Bide a wee, Delaney," she said, jumping forward to offer him her support. "You must make it down the corridor a bit, first." If he fell before reaching the bed she had readied for him earlier, she would have little prayer of moving him.

And she did so wish to torture him.

Gillian had questions that demanded answers. Why had the Texan searched Rowanclere's library? Was he truly a writer come to study Scottish castles? Or was he here for more nefarious purposes? Most important of all, was he in any way a threat to her family?

Gillian intended to find out.

With one arm wrapped around his waist, the other holding his arm which was draped around her shoulder, she guided him down the narrow passageway. With every step, she was forced to accept more and more of his weight. "You are a big lug," she muttered.

His arm slipped off her shoulder, but settled around her waist. His hand landed on her stomach, dislodging her stuffing.

"Wrong," he murmured, his voice slurred.

She made no effort to reply, but kept all her energy focused on getting him to the bed in the chamber she had prepared.

They made it. Just. He started his fall close enough to the bed that a good shove from her sent him sprawling across it. She wrestled with his legs, then yanked on his arms, and finally got him where she wanted him, more or less.

He was snoring peacefully a few minutes later when she approached with the rope, and Gillian felt a prick of unease as she fixed first his hands, then his feet to the bedposts. She'd never done anything like this before in her life. In fact, the past few weeks had been filled with firsts for her. Lying, scheming, and trickery were foreign to her nature, although once she got started, she admitted to having a flair for it.

Gillian stepped away from the bed and stared down at her captive in the flickering light of the torch. The man truly was magnificent. Relaxed in sleep, the masculine angles of his face softened just enough to give him a fallen angel's beauty. A lock of overly long, deep auburn hair spilled across his brow and tangled with the thick, curling lashes of his eyes. Gillian's fingers itched to reach out and brush it back, but she clenched them into a fist instead. What was it about this man she found so . . . haunting?

Now there is an irony for you.

But it was true. Since the moment he arrived at Rowanclere the Texan had seldom left her thoughts entirely. Was this guilt at work? Did thoughts of him plague her because she felt bad about using him to practice being a wraith?

She thought about it for a moment, then shook her head. No, that wasn't it. She did feel a twinge of shame, but it was easily dismissed. Causing a few moment's fright to this bonny, brawny man was nothing compared to seeing that Uncle Angus spent his declining years in peace.

"Besides," she grumbled, "I don't believe I have caused him so much as a twitch of fear up until now."

That, she told herself, was about to change. She wasn't a woman who indulged her temper often, but when she did, she made it count. His methodical search of Rowanclere's library proved he had more than castle architecture on his mind. In order to protect her family, she needed to know what. That was why the Wraith of Rowanclere intended to get mean.

Gillian discarded her belly, gathered up her string, scissors, a bag full of feathers, and went to work.

Jake awoke from the old nightmare about the time during the cattle drive to Wichita when rustlers had him trussed like a beeve waitin' on the iron. In his case not a branding iron, but a shootin' one. He'd have been one dead cowpoke had his best friend and recently wed brother-in-law Cole Morgan not ridden to the rescue.

His capture that day had been a nasty event, and as a result, those ugly feelings lingered as he drifted back to consciousness. The pounding head and aching muscles didn't help anything. Neither did realizing the sensation of being tied down was not a dream.

Sonofabitch. This wasn't good.

Warily, he opened his eyes. To blackness. Blindfolded. Hell.

He strained against the ropes, testing. No give at all. Damn.

Twisting his head, he felt something brush his cheek. Something soft and ticklish. He jerked away from the sensation, only to have it repeated against the other cheek. "What the——?"

"Spiders," came the disembodied voice from out of the darkness to his left. "My grave is filled with them . . . and other creeping, crawling things."

Jake wasn't impressed. Bugs didn't bother him one whit. Now, had he awakened sharing space with a real ghost, he might have experienced a fright or two. The woman who called herself Death was very much alive and back to her old tricks.

And this particular trick had gone too far. "Are you Mrs. Dunbar?"

Her laughter bubbled like a brook in a dense, dark forest. "Nae, that sweet lady has gone visiting in the village this afternoon. I am the one who led you here. I took her form. I am good, am I not? I fooled you completely."

Jake scowled and something crawled along his cheek. He blew a breath from the side of his mouth attempting to blow it away. Though spiders and insects didn't give him the willies, he'd just as soon keep them off the menu. Whatever hung beside him swung back and brushed him, and he blew it away again. "If this is the way you treat all your guests at Rowanclere, I wouldn't expect much company."

"I would not expect many of Rowanclere's guests to conduct a clandestine search of the library."

"Hmm." Jake pursed his lips in thought. "Caught, was I?"

"That you were. Now I wish to know why you insulted your hosts with such activity."

Rather than answer immediately, he listened carefully, probing his surroundings. He sniffed the air, detecting only the closed, musty scent of an underground chamber. She was alone. A woman alone. He thought about that for a moment, then said, "Suppose I don't want to tell you?"

"Then I shall torture you. The Rowanclere dungeons are well equipped for such activity."

"Oh?"

"I warn you, it will be very frightening."

She sounded so fierce. And . . . cute. Damned if he could decide whether he was angry or enjoying this. He waited a count of ten before asking, "Painful?"

He heard a sniff on his right, but when she spoke he definitely heard it on his left. "Who do you think I am, Young Fergus?"

She was pitching her voice somehow. Like she had last night. "If I remember correctly, I do believe that earlier you introduced yourself as Death."

"True, sir. However, ways exist to torture a person, to kill a person, without even touching them."

"Yeah, but those ways are not necessarily pain free. Take last night's torture, for instance."

Suspicion clouded her voice. "What do you mean?"

"That was you in my bedroom last night, wasn't it? Believe me, honey, you had me hurting all night."

"Hurting? From what?"

"Let's just say that after your unveiling, if I'd had to sleep on my stomach, I'd have broken something off."

The "ghost" softly gasped. Jake swallowed a chuckle. Yes, he definitely leaned toward enjoying himself at this moment, ropes and all.

"You are a wicked man, Delaney."

A smile was his only reply.

Frustration bristled in her voice as she said, "But I am an evil wicht. I can be more wicked than you. Answer my questions, or I shall prove it."

He shrugged as best he could manage tied spreadeagle to the bed. "One problem here, ma'am. You haven't asked any questions yet."

This time he heard a definite feminine growl before she snapped, "Why did you search our library?"

"Didn't your mother teach you it's not polite to spy on a person?"

"I could ask you the same question, but that is not an answer I seek. Who are you? What is your real name, Mr. J. A. K. Delaney, and why have you come to Rowanclere?"

Jake debated his response. He wasn't about to tell her he was here for the Declaration, but his story of writing a book about castles obviously wouldn't hold water anymore. What would? To buy time, he said, "My name is Delaney. James Allen Kenneth Delaney, but you can call me Jake. And you are right. I am not an author."

Smug satisfaction filled her tone. "Then what are you?"

A dozen different possibilities floated through his mind. He chose the one most outlandish, the one that made him smile. "I'm actually Father Delaney, a Benedictine monk, and I've come on the trail of a rare manuscript stolen from a church outside of Rome during the second Crusade."

"You a priest? Hah." Scorn lashed like a whip. "And I am the Queen of England."

"I thought you were a ghost."

Fabric rustled, then he sensed a presence. He tried to peer through the blindfold, to no avail.

"Actually, I am the Scourge of Rowanclere and I'm running out of patience. Answer my question. Why were you searching our library?"

Her voice sounded different now and came from his right. Damned if she didn't sound like Mrs. Dunbar. But the scent was different. Not roses, but something else. Something more complicated, more exotic. More erotic. "What's that perfume you're wearing? It's different. Jasmine and spice."

"You are a lunatic."

"It's wonderful, though. You smell wonderful."

"It's called Coffin Cologne. Now tell me why you are here."

Coffin Cologne. He grinned. Wasn't she something?

Damn, he wanted to touch her. Maybe if he made her angry enough . . . "Fine. I'm a robber. I was looking to steal your jewels."

"My jewels?" Now she laughed, low and husky, and the sound sent a seductive shiver up his spine. "If that is the case, you are out of luck. Any jewels owned by this family were lost by Brodie ancestors long ago."

"So you are a Brodie, then?"

"A Ro—" She broke off and went silent for a long minute. "You tried to trick me."

"Yes ma'am, I did. Almost worked, too."

He heard her mutter something beneath her breath and the sound of her footsteps as she paced in a circle around him. Then suddenly, the air seemed to bristle. He felt her presence as she leaned near. Menace loomed in her voice as she spoke into his ear. "I have been told that in Texas you have spiders as big as a man's hand. Tarantulas, I believe they are called? Is that correct?"

"Yeah."

She moved away again, chuckled softly. "I am certain they are most frightening, but can they possibly be as wicked as my wee little friends here? Let me show you, Texas. You decide."

He caught a whiff of her heady scent and felt the heat from her body as she leaned over him once more. *Closer, honey. Stay awhile. It's drafty down here and I purely hate the cold.*

Then he heard the twist of a jar lid.

He felt it first on the back of his left hand. Tiny brushes that seemed to barely touch his skin. They moved up his finger, then played across his knuckles.

Jake frowned. This didn't feel like little spiders or any type of bug, for that matter. In fact, it felt rather . . . intimate.

That wasn't too surprising. After all, he was alone with a woman in what amounted to the dark from his vantage point. While bondage games weren't ordinarily his cup of tea, Jake was willing to give just about anything a try. Especially when an intriguing woman was involved.

The featherlight strokes moved higher, toward where

the rope bound his wrist. Jake concentrated on the sensation. Not spiders, but what?

Her voice blew across him like a soothing, sensuous summer breeze. "Dinna fash yersel' if you feel a bite or two. My pets are but a wee bit poisonous. They will only make you ill. They'll not kill you."

He clicked his tongue. "Now you're being vicious, honey."

"Answer my questions and I'll save you from my spiders."

Jake lay silent for a few moments, distracted by her perfume as he considered what to say next. How should he follow up his claim of being a robber? What sort of lie might work?

How anxious was he to end this "torture"?

The last was answered when her "spiders" breeched the vee of his shirt below his neck. All thought of declarations of any sort evaporated as a bolt of pure lust speared from his chest to his loins.

Jake strained against the ropes. He wanted free. He wanted to stay just where he was forever. Now he knew why he found this incident so stimulating. Feather Nell. The woman was an artist when it came to making a man sweat.

Back during the less discriminating days of his youth, he sometimes visited a sporting house up near Bastrop run by a woman named Nellie Blair. One of Nellie's favorite tools of the trade was a plain-old-every-day turkey feather. For the men of central Texas, she gave a whole new meaning to the notion of Thanksgiving.

But after a few minutes in the dungeon at Rowanclere, Jake concluded this woman could give Feather Nell a run for her money.

Clearing his throat, he said, "Torture me some more, honey. Unbutton my shirt."

The stroking stilled. "What?"

"You gotta give those spiders more room to move around to get the full effect."

Again, a pause before she asked in an incredulous tone, "You *want* the spiders to crawl across your chest?"

"Oh, I do. I really do." Damned if he didn't pant the words. "I've done this before, and that's a great place to start."

"By my faith. You are . . . the spiders . . . well, dampt!"

Her dismay told him a couple of things. First, the ghost might have been around the ol' graveyard a time or two, but probably no more than that. She picked up on sexual innuendo, but didn't take it anywhere. Second, the woman didn't care for spiders one little bit. For her, the illusion of being at the mercy of a passel of roving arachnids truly was a form of torture.

Damn, wasn't she just the cutest thing?

"I really want to see you," he told her.

"No."

"Will you show yourself to me if I promise to tell the truth?"

"You must tell me the truth no matter what. I shall not release you until you do."

A shade past innocent with a backbone. A combination damned near irresistible to a man. His lips quirked into a smile. "Honey, there is something you should know about me. Back home, I'm a lawyer by profession. In order to serve my clients to the best of my ability, I've learned to tell a darn fine lie. I could tell you the sun rises in the west and make you believe it. I'm that good.

So, this little exercise you've arranged—though interesting, I'll admit—won't succeed without my cooperation. You might as well untie me now."

"Nae. That winna do."

Footsteps shuffled once again as she paced beside the bed. Jake could almost hear the wheels turning in her head.

Abruptly, she stopped. "So you admit to being a liar. Do you believe in God, sir?"

"Yes, I do."

"So if I make you swear on your eternal soul, I can place my faith in it?"

The woman was bright, too. Definitely a risk-taker. Definitely the most provocative ghost he'd ever run across.

"Yes, you can trust my word," he replied honestly. Of course, it was her responsibility to listen closely when he gave it. Jake could bend words with the best of them. He would tell her the truth, but he'd do it in the way he wanted it told. "What about you? Do you stand by your word?"

"Aye."

She said it immediately, without hesitation, and Jake believed her. "All right, then. I'll show you mine if you show me yours."

Her unladylike snort made him grin. Yeah, a shade past innocent. If he played his cards right, this trip to Scotland might qualify as the beginning of his life of adventure.

"You answer my questions first," she said. "Then I'll release you."

"And you'll show yourself to me."

"I will. Now you must give swear on your soul that everything you tell me will be the truth."

"I swear." The scent of jasmine drifted past his nose and he savored it with a smile.

"Very well. First, I want to know——"

"Wait. You forgot to seal our bargain. A kiss should take care of it."

Instead of a kiss, she pinched his arm. Hard. "Consider the bargain sealed," she said. "Now tell me who you really are, what has brought you to Rowanclere, and why you were searching our library."

"You are not a very friendly ghost, lady," he protested. "In Texas our ghosts——"

"Your true name?"

"I really am Jake Delaney of San Antonio, Texas." Then he sighed and gave her the truth that had little to do with the questions she wanted answered. "I've come to Rowanclere because I'm a man on the run."

"From the law?"

"In a manner of speaking. My mother is the daughter of the Earl of Thornbury. The woman is attempting to use her father's influence to meddle where she shouldn't be meddling. This trip was the best way I could find to escape the . . . consequences . . . of her influence."

"What consequences?"

Even though Jake intended to use this line of conversation as a distraction, he still found he had to work himself up to say the word. It sounded as sour as it tasted. "Marriage."

Damned if she didn't laugh. Grumbling, he asked, "Would you untie my right hand, please? My fingers are going to sleep."

She ignored that, instead asking, "You are betrothed?"

"No, and I'm not gonna be. It's actually all my sister's

fault because she got married last winter and that turned my mother's attention to me. Mother and Thornbury have only recently reconciled after being estranged for years. Therefore, anything she wants, he moves heaven and earth to make happen."

"She wants you married."

"And I'm happy as an armadillo digging grubworms being a bachelor."

"An armadillo digging grubworms?" she repeated dryly. "Lovely. But what does any of this have to do with Rowanclere? With our library?"

So much for distractions. Now came the time to talk the tightrope between truth and fiction without giving away the game entirely. "That has to do with an Englishman. A baron. Tell me, are you familiar with a fellow by the name of Bennet? Lord Bennet of Derbyshire?"

All sound ceased and the dungeon seemed to grow even colder. In a thin, thready voice, she asked, "Who?"

"Lord Bennet. He has an estate called Harpur Priory."

"Did he send you here?"

"In a manner of speaking, yes."

Without warning, she moved. He felt a fast tug at his left wrist, then his left ankle and the ropes fell away.

She spoke in a voice as flat and chilly as the grave. "Leave Rowanclere today, Delaney. Never return."

What the hell? Shocked by her response, he was slow to tug off the blindfold. Twisting his head around, he searched for her in the shadows and spied a movement right before the light died, accompanied by the hiss of fire in water. She had doused the torch.

For the first time since the haunting farce began, Jake

felt just a shiver of unease. "Wait a minute. What about our bargain?"

The burr of Scotland thickened a distant voice trembling with anger. "Take a lesson home with ye from Scotland, Texas. Bargains are like guid shortbread. Baith crumble easily."

Then she was gone.

"Sonofabitch," Jake said into the silence that lingered behind her. He blew out a long, slow whistle, then picked at the knots in the line binding his right wrist and ankle, pondering what had just taken place. What can of worms had he opened here? What had that bastard Bennet done to the people of Rowanclere Castle?

Judging by the woman's reaction, it had to have been bad.

Free now, he felt his way along the cold stone wall toward a door and the corridor beyond, where in the distance, a burning torch cast a faint light.

One thing was certain. He wasn't leaving Rowanclere. "Shortbread, hell," he muttered.

Crumbled or not, that gal owed him a cookie. He wasn't leaving till his sweet tooth was satisfied.

"What do you mean you sent him away!" the old man roared, his fist pounding the bed beside him. "You sent him away before I had the chance to meet him? He's a Texan, lass. A Texan! Do you know how long it has been since I visited with one of my own?"

Lamplight flickered against the painted plaster walls of the small bedroom built high on the castle wall. Gillian gazed at her granduncle with love and replied, "Aye, quite some time."

"Then how could you do this to me? How could you. . . ."

Hands clasped behind her back, she listened silently as her granduncle continued his scolding. It took all her discipline not to betray a silly grin, so pleased was she to witness the improvement in his spirit. It appeared that this latest attack of the rheums was done. Gillian prayed it stayed that way.

Then a breeze swirled around Gillian's ankles, reminding her of the drafty nature of this chamber. She shivered and wished for at least the thousandth time that her beloved Uncle Angus were not such a stubborn man.

The Crow's Nest bedroom was Angus Brodie's way of keeping the vow he'd made upon leaving Rowanclere shortly after his father's death fifty years ago. During the falling out with his elder brother who had inherited title, castle, and control over Angus's trust fund, Angus swore never to sleep another night beneath Rowanclere's roof. He held to his promise even when John Brodie died childless and the castle came to him. One thing about Uncle Angus, he always kept his word, despite the potentially harmful consequences.

When he paused for a breath, she seized her chance. "Uncle, I am sorry you did not have the opportunity to discuss Texas with that man, but if you will allow me to explain, you will see why I thought I had no other choice."

"No choice?" Angus frowned. Narrowing his eyes, he gave the collar of his nightshirt a sharp tug, then folded his arms and studied her. "Explain."

Gillian returned his look, noting the way the furrows on his brow had deepened with concern. She wanted to reach out and smooth them away with a gentle touch.

She also wanted to throw herself into his arms seeking comfort like a bairn.

She settled on exhaling a weary sigh. Such was the way of their relationship at this time of their lives. Sometimes Gillian was still the child; more and more often she played the role of parent. It was a difficult adjustment for them both.

She and Flora had been seventeen when their parents were killed in a carriage accident. Nicholas was gone from Scotland and his whereabouts were unknown, so the sisters, along with two-year-old Robyn, were sent to live with less-than-loving Clan Ross relatives. After six months of misery, their granduncle Angus swooped into their lives and rescued them from their mean existence.

From that moment on, the grandest of all uncles had served the girls in the role of adoring father. Now in his eighties, age had finally caught up with the brave, braw man. His body was failing him. Pain in his knees and hips made it impossible for him to walk more than a few steps at a time. His hearing had weakened, and his lungs proved susceptible to every ague that came along.

But for all his body let him down, Uncle Angus's mind was still sharp as gorse. "What happened, lass? Did he insult you? Did he hurt you? Do I need to kill the limmer?"

She couldn't help but smile. She needed only to nod and, crippled or not, the stubborn Scot would do his best to see Jake Delaney's life brought to an end.

"No, Uncle. He did not harm me. However, he did lie to me."

Angus waited expectantly, obviously not impressed by that bit of news.

"I spied on him after Flora left him alone in the library. He searched it, Uncle. Thoroughly."

"He was looking for hobgoblins."

"No. He went through the books. He pulled them one by one from the shelves, then flipped through them, searching for something."

Angus's entire demeanor changed, going from dismissive to suspicious in a heartbeat. "What?" he demanded.

"That's what I attempted to find out." She outlined how she'd drugged him and led him to the dungeon room a long-ago laird of Rowanclere had furnished for romantic assignations. When she repeated the part about the spiders, his bushy white brows arched and he snorted. "It was a good thought, lass, but I am not certain spiders were the best source of torture. You know one of the storerooms down there is filled with devices designed for such a purpose."

"I could not actually hurt him," she replied. "Besides, I did convince him to talk. He brought up a name, Uncle. It is why I sent him away, although I wonder now if I might have been a bit hasty in the doing of it. I reacted emotionally." She took a breath, then exhaled in a rush. "You see, he said he was sent here by Lord Bennet."

"Bennet!" Angus gasped and struggled to sit up. Forty years in Texas drowned the Scotsman in his voice as he spoke through gritted teeth. "This Delaney fellow is in cahoots with Bennet? Holy hell!"

"You see why I reacted as I did."

Angus scowled and nodded. "He's used that dog of his to befriend Robbie. That's how the Englishman got what he wanted, befriending the lass. Where's Robbie?

Has she sold him our china for a pork roast or two? Has she traded something of value for the price of a two-legged dog? Get me my canes and my gun, Gilly. I got me a varmint to kill."

Gillian took a seat in the chair beside her granduncle's bed. "I spoke with Robyn right away. Jake Delaney didn't ask her for anything and besides, she learned her lesson after the debacle with Lord Bennet. She'll not sell any property of yours ever again, no matter the price. No need to worry over that. Also, now that I've had the opportunity to reflect on matters, I do not believe Jake Delaney is Lord Bennet's minion. I cannot picture the man using that dog to take advantage of Robbie. You should see him with Scooter, Uncle. He is terribly sweet with her, even when he thinks no one is watching."

"I have seen the bick. Robbie brought her to me. She's a pitiful but brave wee beastie."

Gillian nodded in agreement. "It speaks to character, does it not? If Delaney were a wicked man like Lord Bennet, would he be so caring of a crippled dog? No, I don't believe he is working for the Englishman. He may, however, be working for himself."

"What do you mean?"

"He was looking for something he might expect to find hidden in the pages of a book in the library at Rowanclere castle. He's from Texas and he has had some sort of dealing with Lord Bennet. What is the obvious connection?"

Angus Brodie's gaze shifted to meet Gillian's, then together they looked toward the framed document hanging on the wall opposite the bed. "Of course," he said. "I should have realized it immediately. The pieces fit together too nicely to ignore."

Grim faced, he added, "I treasure it, you know. My best friend gave it to me as he lay dying on the San Jacinto battlefield. I was born a Scot and I'll die a Scot, but a part of me will always be Texan."

"I know, Uncle Angus."

"Of course you do. It's why you took it upon yourself to go to Bennet's estate and retrieve my treasure for me after he swindled it away from Robbie. You were right to send this Delaney away, love. As much as I'd like to swap stories with another Texan, it's not worth the price of giving up my copy of the Republic of Texas's Declaration of Independence."

five

THE CASTLE CLOCKS struck three A.M. as the figure stealthily made his way up the servants' staircase. The twisting, narrow passage was pitch black and drafty with cool night air, and the slightest scrape of foot against wood magnified a hundredfold to the intruder's ears. As a result, he took extra care to remain quiet. He hadn't hidden in the cold, damp forest half the night to get caught now. No, he was the one out to do the catching.

Jake Delaney had come to call on his ghost.

He hadn't anticipated anything quite so much in months.

Following the incident in the dungeon earlier that afternoon, Jake had been escorted from the premises by a burly stable hand and the barrel of a pistol. The fellow gave him money for the horse he'd ridden to Rowan-clere, then tossed Scooter and the rest of Jake's belongings into the bottom of a rowboat. After insisting Jake man the oars and row across the loch to a village on the post route, the man paid for Jake's ticket, then watched until he'd boarded the coach. He'd added to the insult by grinning and waving a salute as the stage rumbled out of town.

Of course, Jake had talked his way off the transport before the second curve in the winding road. He'd used the horse money to rent a boat, then rowed back across the loch. Hiding out in the ruins of a watchtower a short distance away, he'd settled in to wait, dozing off and on into the evening. He'd wanted it to be good and dark before he made his move, and being this far north, that meant the middle of the night.

The castle wall had been relatively easy to breach, despite the presence of a watchman. He had not noticed the guard previously, and he wondered if the watchman was present on account of him. *Did I spook you, princess?*

He grinned at the thought.

Finally, he reached the landing that led to the guest bedroom he had occupied. He cracked open the door and listened hard for a good half-minute before concluding the room was unoccupied. Then he slipped inside.

His first task was to find and light the lamp. He felt safe doing so because the room faced away from the main body of the castle; therefore the risk of discovery was slight. That accomplished, he reached into the front of his jacket and removed the extra weight he'd carried with him through the castle. He held Scooter up before him, then gazed into her eyes. "I'll take the muzzle off, but you have to promise to be quiet. Is that a deal?"

He then removed the strip of cloth he'd tied around her snout. The first thing she did was lick him. "Hmm . . ." he murmured. "First you tolerate a muzzle, then you give me a kiss. Scooter, you are the perfect female."

Setting the dog on the floor, he said, "Now, let's get to work."

Jake's plan was to find the hidden entrance to the room, then track down the spirited specter. This old fortress was bound to be riddled with hidden passageways, which explained how the woman had accomplished her tricks. She would have left signs of her passing—like maybe an extra head or pouch of feathers—and he would use them to trace her to her lair. After that . . . well . . . "You reap what you've sown, lady."

He searched for twenty minutes before he found the concealed latch, and even then he'd have missed it were it not for Scooter. While dragging herself toward the meat pie he'd set down for her in an effort to keep her quiet, the dachshund managed to hang herself up on the small lever cleverly disguised as an andiron.

"Remind me to swipe you a bone next time we wander through the kitchen," he told her as the hidden door yawned open.

Jake tucked Scooter back into his coat, lifted the lamp from the bedside table, then stepped into the passageway. A damp, musty odor hung on air that felt cold enough to hang meat. Jake grimaced and thought longingly of a warm bed, warm blankets, and warm fire in the fireplace. *One more thing you owe me for, sweetheart.*

He couldn't wait to collect his due.

Because of the darkness in the narrow corridor, the going was slow and the tracking difficult. A short hallway led to a staircase that took him down to the main floor. There the hallway widened slightly before splitting off in three directions. Jake scowled. He'd expected cobwebs and footprints in the dust to lead him to his quarry.

Instead he found dust rags and a broom. Actually, the broom found him when he stepped on the bristles and the handle conked him on the temple.

"Ouch," he muttered. Hell, what kind of woman cleaned a secret passage, anyway?

One who was afraid of spiders. Jake rubbed his sore head, his lips twisting in a rueful grin. Helluva way to confirm he was on the right track.

He eyed the three corridors. "Well, Scoot, what do we do? Which one do we choose?"

Because she'd brought him luck earlier, he decided to follow the dog. He set her down, withdrew her sling from his jacket, and passed it under her lame hindquarters. Scooter took off.

She chose the center hallway and followed a twisting and turning path for almost five minutes before careening to a halt at the foot of a staircase. Jake took the hint, carried her up, then set her down at the top. She was off again.

They passed a dozen doorways before she finally stopped. Jake would have bet his favorite hat that they stood outside young Robyn's sleeping chamber. He doused his lamp and cracked open the door. Peering into a moonlit room, he spied a small lump lying crossways across a wide bed, hands hanging over the side. Who else but Robbie would sleep with a fishing net clasped in her fist? He wondered what she dreamed of catching.

Using his foot to block Scooter's attempts to get inside her buddy's room, Jake silently closed the door, then bent down and muzzled poor Scooter once more. "Sorry, sweetheart," he whispered. "But if this is the family area of the castle, we have to be extra quiet. Don't want to wake the 'dead' before we're ready, now do we?"

His gut told him his prey had Brodie blood. No servant would be so bold.

Jake moved to the next door in the corridor. Cautiously, he cracked it open and peered inside. His heart jumped and lodged in his throat.

Mrs. Dunbar was awake and pacing the room, rubbing the small of her back with one hand, the bulge of her belly with the other. She looked tired and achy, but beautiful enough in her plain white nightgown that Jake wondered why her husband had let her out of his sight.

If he were Mr. Dunbar and he caught someone spying on his wife in her bedroom, he'd kill the sonofabitch.

Uneasy with playing the Peeping Tom, Jake stepped back and closed the door, then continued his search for the wrathful wraith. The room next to Mrs. Dunbar's proved to be uninhabited, as did the four he checked after that. Anticipating the confrontation and ready to find a fire to warm his bones, Jake's patience wore thin.

A canine whimper reminded him he wasn't alone. He looked around to find that while he'd been searching the empty bedchambers, Scooter had dragged herself on down to the end of the corridor where another, extremely narrow staircase spiraled up into the darkness. The dog whined again. "You think she's up there?"

Jake shivered as a draft of cold air swirled around him. "Or, are you cold and you just want me to carry you around? No offense, Scoot, but I prefer a different sort of female to cuddle up with when I'm trying to keep warm."

Tucking the dog back into his jacket, Jake started up the stairs, thinking how miserable the Scottish weather was and what he wouldn't give for a nice blast of Texas summer heat right about now. Too bad the situation required quiet or he'd run up these steps and work up a sweat.

He ascended what was obviously a tower, pausing to inspect what lay behind the three doorways he spied on the way up. He found a small library, a drawing room, and another bedchamber. Each of them was unoccupied. Finally, he reached the top of the staircase and the last door in this particular portion of the castle. Mentally picturing Rowanclere and the route he believed he'd taken in this maze of hidden tunnels, he concluded he stood catty-corner to the bedchamber where he'd begun this particular adventure.

He dimmed his light, flipped the latch, and cracked open the door. This was somebody's room, all right. And somebody was cuddled beneath the bedcovers in a fanciful bed hung with emerald green silk.

The scent of jasmine wafted deliciously heavy on the air. Success!

Grinning, Jake shifted back into the passage, took off his jacket and fashioned a bed for Scooter with it and the sheeting he'd used as a sling. "Take a nap, sweetheart. This might take a while."

Moments later, he stepped into the bedchamber and pulled the door shut behind him. Moonlight cast a silvery glow about the room, and as he moved closer he saw not a ghost in the bed, but an angel.

Golden, ethereal, and so beautiful she made his teeth ache. At first glance, the sleeping beauty puzzled him.

This wasn't Mrs. Dunbar, though she looked just like her. He'd seen Mrs. Dunbar only minutes ago, awake and walking in her room. The biggest clue was, of course, the baby. Mrs. Dunbar couldn't hide hers. This woman didn't have one.

This *was* her. His sneaky spirit. Had to be.

He recalled how she'd looked during the very first "haunting" and his fingers itched to tug down the covers and check those breasts to make a positive identification. But that would have to wait. He would not assault a sleeping woman. However, he did have something else in mind.

Jake reached into his pocket and tugged out the tiebacks of soft red silk he'd appropriated from the bed hangings in one of the unoccupied chambers. Then it hit him. *Sisters*, he thought, approaching the bed. She and Mrs. Dunbar were sisters. Twins. Relief swept through him as finally, he understood.

He hadn't lusted after an expectant married lady. He wasn't the twisted lecher he'd feared. He didn't suffer from some distressing sexual sickness. This female had played a role, pretending to be the expectant mother in public and the mischievous gremlin in private. Jake had sensed the difference every single time.

Damn, I'm good.

And she was beautiful. And sneaky. And ornery as a snappin' sow.

Then he heard a noise, and he stopped and listened and grinned. With each inhalation, she let out a tiny little feminine snore. Wasn't that so damned cute?

He realized he couldn't wait to see what sort of noise the Headless Lady of Rowanclere made when she realized she'd lost the use of her hands. So keeping his touch as light as possible, he set about securing her wrists to the bedposts, taking care not to awaken her.

That done, he studied the lump in the covers that marked her feet and debated what to do. Though she had tied him spread-eagle, Jake couldn't do that to a lady. Should he tie her ankles together or leave them be?

No, better tie them. This gal struck him as the kind of female who wouldn't think twice about kicking a man where it mattered.

That decided, he carefully drew back the covers and his mouth went a little dry. Her white linen nightgown had ridden up to mid-thigh as she slept, revealing long shapely legs that seemed to stretch on forever. Jake had a fierce, sudden vision of those naked limbs wrapped around his hips and fought for self-control.

Dammit, he wasn't here to drool over her. He was here to teach her a lesson.

After that, maybe he could slaver a bit.

He made quick work of binding her ankles together, expecting her to wake at any moment, but she continued to sleep. That task accomplished, he stepped away and debated his next move. He had a cloth for her mouth with him, but he'd prefer to leave it in his pocket. However, if his spirit was a screamer, that wouldn't be a choice.

His preparations made, Jake was ready to begin the show. He lit the bedside lamp and waited for her to awaken.

And he waited. And waited. And waited.

Hell. He had tied her and shined a lamp in her face, but she continued with that cute little snore. The woman slept like the dead. Jake's lips quirked in a grin. *Well, she is a ghost, after all.*

As he glanced around the bedchamber, his gaze snagged on an item hanging from the back of a chair. "Well, well," he murmured softly. "What do we have here?" Checking to see that his prisoner still slept, he strode over to the chair and lifted the article. He held the contraption out in front of him and studied it.

It was a homemade . . . well . . . truss, he guessed was the word. Straps likely went over the shoulders while others buckled in back. The pouch, which would have been her "baby," was stuffed with, of all things, feathers. Quite effective, he thought. Then, recalling the incident at breakfast and the way the hump had dropped, he whispered, "Unless one lies down on the job, so to speak."

Looking back toward the devilish angel in the bed, he deliberately dropped the prop onto the floor and the buckles clanked against the stone. At the noise, she rolled her head from one side to the other. Still, she did not awaken.

With a roll of his eyes, Jake ran out of patience. He bent down, reached into the pouch, and withdrew a handful of feathers. Turnabout was fair play, after all.

Approaching the bed once more, he studied her, and chose a place to begin. *Her nose. Tickle her nose,* the gentleman within him said.

The man in him wanted to begin with her breasts. Jake envisioned his hands reaching out and tugging down her neckline, baring her bounty to his appreciative gaze. Her round, pink nipples would be soft in her sleep, but he'd stroke her once, twice with the feather, and they'd pebble up, pert and pretty and ready. Then he'd kneel down, lean over, and replace the feather with his tongue and taste her, feed upon her. Drown in her.

Heat surged in Jake's loins. A part of him—the honorable part—felt a tweak of shame at his behavior, but he simply didn't have the heart to pull himself out of the fantasy.

In fact, he sank into it even deeper.

In his mind, they both were suddenly naked and rolling on the bed. He nuzzled her neck, ran his hands up and down that satiny skin. Learning her, even as her hands learned him. Her long, thick hair spilled over him like a golden waterfall. He imagined her rising above him, wet and ready, then easing down upon him, taking him to the hilt. Her passage around him a soft tight glove. Then she moved, slow and languid, killing him. He wanted more, deeper and faster. Faster. Faster.

His blood pounded, his loins ached. He reached for his shirt buttons, undoing two before a gust of wind rattled the window and woke him to reality.

Jake was shocked at himself. Shocked and physically aching. Painfully aching. It sent his temper soaring. What the hell was he doing? He hadn't come here to be a damned Peeping Tom, to lose himself in fantasy like a fuzz-faced boy. He'd come here to find the stolen Declaration of Independence. That and get a little innocent revenge. Letting his lusty imagination run rampant was something else entirely.

Guilt perched on his shoulders as he removed one feather from the bunch in his hand and tossed the others away. While they floated toward the floor, he strode to the side of the bed, then shoved out his hand and tickled the tip of her nose.

She wrinkled her nose, but didn't wake up.

He stroked the feather against the same spot a second time.

She turned her head away and continued to sleep.

Sonofabitch! Mouth set in a grim smile and brow furrowed, Jake leaned over her, glared down into her face, and rubbed the feather back and forth across her nose, over and over again until she responded with a loud, "Achoo!"

But still, she didn't wake up. What was it going to take to get this snoozing specter to rejoin the living?

He'd shake her, but he didn't trust himself to touch her. He could shout in her ear, but in truth, he hated to do that. That's the way his father used to wake him up, and he'd always sworn he'd never do that to another human being. "Of course, I forgot you're not supposed to be human are you, Miss Wraith of Rowanclere?" he muttered. "It shouldn't matter if I holler—"

Jake broke off abruptly as another thought occurred. A smile melted across his face like warm butter in a bowl of grits. Pivoting, he walked to the secret passageway door and opened it. A moment later, he returned carrying his own personal alarm clock.

He plopped Scooter down upon the woman's chest, then stepped back, folded his arms, and prepared to watch the show.

Sure enough, the dog acted just like she did with Jake almost every morning. The dachshund poked out her snoot, stuck out her tongue, and started licking the lady's face.

Jake almost always awoke at the first wet stroke of tongue. Scooter got the woman five times—twice right on the mouth—before her lashes fluttered and lifted.

"Hello, wee sweet pup," she murmured before her eyelids sank once more.

Jake snorted. He couldn't believe it. She even slept through this?

Then Scooter gave her a particularly enthusiastic lick and the woman's brow furrowed. "Finally," Jake muttered.

One arm flexed, pulling at the bindings. Then the second repeated the action of the first. Her frown deepened as her hands fisted and simultaneously pulled at the strips of silk.

She opened her eyes and focused on the dachshund. Then she blinked. Her eyes narrowed. Blinked again.

Then, the spirit spoke. "Thank God 'twas the dog that kissed me. For a moment there, Texas, I feared it was you."

The problem with bravado, it could backfire on a woman. Some men one simply didn't challenge. Jake Delaney was one of them.

And Jake Delaney was back.

A part of Gillian recognized she wasn't terribly surprised. Nor was she afraid of him. Well, not very afraid. She should never have mentioned kissing.

A variety of emotions glittered in the Texan's eyes as he loomed above her. She read threat and anger and indignation. Anticipation and . . . *megstie me* . . . lust.

"Afraid of my kisses, are you?" he drawled, as he plucked the dog from her chest and set her on the floor. He propped one knee on the bed and leaned over her, his hands supporting his weight on either side of her shoulders.

Gillian swallowed hard as her pulse accelerated. She

hadn't intended to dare him. She wasn't that foolish. She was tied to a bed and at the mercy of a man who was basically a stranger. She should be frightened to death.

But she wasn't.

It was because of Scooter. He was so kind to the dog. He wouldn't hurt her. She was certain of it.

Delaney's gaze dropped to her mouth. "Aren't you going to answer me, darlin'? Does the thought of my kiss scare you?"

No, not at all. Thrill was a better word for what she felt. But she dare not tell him that.

As the moment dragged out, the tension thrumming in the air thickened. Gillian's mouth went dry. He would do it. He wanted to do it. She could see it burning in his emerald eyes.

What should she say? What answer would distract him? Did she even want to distract him?

No, she wanted him to do it.

Gillian bit back a groan. Now that was being foolish.

He lightly brushed her cheek with the tip of one finger, though the look in his eyes was anything but gentle. Maybe he would kiss her, then not stop. She knew that sometimes men, and even women, lost control during the heat of passion. She might feel safe, but the reality was that as long as she was tied, she was vulnerable.

Now, suddenly, Gillian felt nervous.

She drew a deep breath, prepared to scream. He clapped a hand over her mouth before she managed so much as a peep. "Don't do it, darlin'. Don't make me have to gag you. Now, back to my question." The hand covering her mouth shifted to cup her cheek. "What's your answer? Are you scared of my kiss?"

One more tender touch and she'd be lost. Gillian cleared her throat and used truth as her defense. "Yes, the thought does frighten me, Mr. Delaney. My experience is limited and has left an unpleasant taste behind. The last man I kissed broke my heart."

He drew back and scowled down at her. "Limited and unpleasant. Are you trying to provoke me, or do you simply not know better?" After a slight pause, his eyes narrowed and he added, "Or maybe you mean to wave your words around like a red flag in a bullring. Are you asking for it? Is that it? Do you *want* me to kiss you?"

The man was an excellent observer.

"No," she lied. "Of course not." Then, hoping to diffuse the situation with something absurd, she added, "We have not been properly introduced."

Momentary shock registered on his face, then he laughed, a quiet chuckle that brought Scooter's head up from her reclined position in front of the fire. "I reckon you're right. You've seen me buck naked, and I had a most delicious glimpse of your bare breasts. Nothing proper about those introductions."

"Sir—"

"Now that we're face to face, in the light and sans disguise or blindfold, we should at least swap names before we get around to swappin' spit." He sat on the bed, took her right hand in his, his finger playing with the trailing edge of the silken binding. "Jake Delaney, at your service," he said, showing a snappy grin. "And you are Miss Ross, I presume? Miss Robyn's sister and Mrs. Dunbar's twin?"

She saw no reason to deny him at this point. "Miss Gillian Ross."

"Miss Gillian Ross," he repeated. "Now that's pretty. Suits you much better than Young Fergus or Headless Harriet. So tell me, Miss Gillian, how long have you been haunting Rowanclere Castle?"

Why was he bothering with this? Why didn't he simply do the deed and get it over with? *Is that what you want, Gillian? Are you yearning to "swap spit" with the Texan? And maybe more?*

Ignoring all the questions, she said, "Mr. Delaney, my Uncle Angus lived much of his life in Texas. He has always told my sisters and myself that gentlemen from your home state pride themselves on their gallantry. I realize you have a legitimate argument supporting the manner in which you . . . approached . . . me tonight. However, as a Texan, do you not agree that binding me to my bed is less than chivalrous?"

"Chivalrous!" He snorted with disgust as he tickled the inside of her wrist with the trailing edge of the red silk tie. "Pardon me, but was I alone down there in the dungeon yesterday? I don't believe so. I didn't think of this—how did you say it, manner of approach—all on my own. Damned right I have a legitimate reason for tying you to the bed."

"So this is revenge?"

"Well, like you said, it ain't chivalry." He twirled the tie like a watch chain. "Let me tell you something else about Texans, Gillian. We don't take kindly to being made to play the fool."

"I don't believe I ever fooled you, though, did I?"

"Not about the ghost business, no." His gaze drifted down her body, then back up again. Softly, he accused, "You did drug me, however. You tied me up and you threw me out of the castle. Because of you, I had to spend hours out in the bitter cold."

"Bitter cold?" She forced a laugh. " 'Tis the middle of summer. The weather is balmy."

"And you're batty if you believe that. I owe you, Miss Gillian Ross, and in Texas where life tends to be a poker game, revenge beats gallantry nine hands out of ten." Having said his piece, he dropped the silk tie, then stood. He braced his hands on his hips and glared down at her.

Gillian restrained herself from sticking out her tongue. "Very well. You've bound me to my bed and achieved your revenge. You can leave now."

"Not on your life. Now we're gonna talk. You had questions I answered. I want you to return the favor. First off, I want to know why you kicked me out of Rowanclere."

Gillian closed her eyes and sighed dramatically. Honestly, she was in a clatty situation. Why, then, did she feel so excited? So alive? "My arms have gone numb. I would think more clearly and provide you more thorough answers were I untied."

"You're not tied tight enough to go numb. The quicker you provide answers to my satisfaction, the faster you'll get loose. Now, talk to me about Lord Bennet. That's when you turned on me. What about his name set you off?"

Gillian's heart hardened and her eyes narrowed at the name. "He is an evil man. We at Rowanclere want nothing to do with him. Since he sent you here, we want nothing to do with you."

Delaney visibly bristled. "I said he sent me in a manner of speaking. You didn't give me the chance to explain.

Instead you threw me out into the cold where I all but wore my shoulders out with a pair of oars. That just really chaps my hide, gal."

"I am sorry. I reacted instinctively, without thought. You see, the threats he made were so . . ." She closed her eyes and shuddered.

"Threats? What threats? What did that Englishman say and why did he say it?"

Gillian's skin grew cold at the memory. She closed her eyes and replied, "He basically stole something from Rowanclere and I went to England and took it back. It did not set well with him. He came here once and tried to force his way inside the castle, but we managed to keep him out. Rowanclere is still a fine fortress. After that he wrote letters. Made threats."

"Tell me what he said, Gillian."

Her mouth went dry, her throat tight, and she worked to force the words. "Apparently, Lord Bennet is quite a taxidermy enthusiast. He threatened to kill me and have my body stuffed for his special trophy room."

Shock registered on the Texan's face, then his mouth set in a grim line. "Damn. He'd have done it, too. You're right, the man was evil. You have no idea how much I wish I'd been the one to shoot him. At least the scoundrel died hard."

Gillian waited for a moment and allowed the words to filter through her mind. Then she lifted her head off her pillow. "Excuse me? What did you say? Someone shot Lord Bennet?"

"Yes. My sister. He was trying to kill her."

Gillian simply stared, trying hard to take it all in. He had a sister who shot Lord Bennet. "He's dead?"

"Dead as a fly in molasses. Has been since winter."

Gillian froze. He was telling the truth. She could read it in his eyes. Relief washed over her, and as her head dropped back against the pillow, she murmured, "I wish I'd known. I've been plagued by terrible taxidermy nightmares."

Jake's mouth tilted in a wry grin as he approached with a wicked looking knife and sliced through the silken ties. While he took hold of her arms and pulled her into a seated position, she imagined the look on Flora's and Angus's faces when she told them the news. The threats had made them all uneasy.

Jake sat beside her on the bed and gently rubbed her wrists where the fabric strips had bound her. Though it reflected poorly upon her to feel pleasure at another person's demise, Gillian couldn't help herself. He had just freed her from a fearsome burden and it filled her with delight. Pulling free of Jake's tender hold, she beamed a smile at him. "Oh, Texas, this is the most welcome news."

She threw her arms around his neck and yanked him to her.

Then, Gillian kissed him.

For the first time since arriving in Scotland, Jake Delaney wasn't cold. He smoldered. He steamed. He sizzled.

He was hot.

Damn. He knew from experience that females had a talent for surprising a man. His sister Chrissy was a fine example of that. And hadn't Scooter knocked him for a loop earlier today at the watchtower when she somehow managed to catch a bird? He had been shocked senseless when the pooch approached with her trophy in her mouth.

This particular surprise didn't knock him senseless. No, this surprise kept his senses very much in working order.

At the first touch of Gillian's lips against his, he felt an instant, intense jolt of lust. Sensation bombarded him. She tasted delicious, an intriguing combination of sunshine and sweetness. She smelled heavenly, surrounding him in a cloud of jasmine and temptation. Then the sound she made when his hands clasped her waist—that little, dazzled hitch of breath—made him want to howl.

Instinctively, Jake took control of the kiss. He changed the angle, deepened it. Invaded her mouth with his tongue. She whimpered once, and then responded, seducing him completely. Every impulse in him yearned to lay her back, to strip her naked, to take her and make her his.

But the pesky voice of reason, of honor, could not be silenced for long. She was no lightskirt or lusty widow, but a young, unmarried woman of good family. Undoubtedly, a virgin.

Virgin. Virgin. Virgin. The word echoed like a death knell in his brain.

Well, hell. If he didn't watch himself, his mother might hear those wedding bells after all.

It required a Herculean effort, but Jake pulled away. He wrenched himself from the bed and stalked across the room to the fireplace where he hunkered down and scratched the dog behind her ears. He didn't look at Gillian. He couldn't. After two bouts of serious sexual frustration in one evening, he was dangling at the end of his rope.

So he forced himself to tie a knot and hold on. He got

busy thinking about something else. Though he cleared his voice, it still emerged sandpaper rough when he asked, "What were you and Bennet fighting over?"

She didn't immediately reply. As the silence dragged out, Jake finally had to glance over his shoulder. She sat as he had left her, a stunned expression on her face. Jake didn't know whether to be flattered or insulted.

He raised his voice. "What did Bennet steal from Rowanclere?"

Slowly, she turned her head toward him. The dazed look in her eyes faded. "It's not important." She reached for the robe lying at the foot of her bed and shrugged into it. "Mr. Delaney, I think I should apologize for being so forward. I didn't mean—"

"I know. Neither did I. Tell me what he took."

She straightened her shoulders and lifted her chin, visibly affronted. Jake knew better than to grin, although he found himself wanting to. When she wasn't busy being beautiful and alluring, the woman was just so damned cute.

She gave the belt on her robe a hard tug. "Something that belongs to my Uncle Angus."

"And this something is—?"

"Not your concern."

Rising to his feet, Jake grasped the fireplace poker and stirred the coals. He knew the answer, of course, but he wanted her to confirm it. Gillian was the woman who had taken the Declaration of Independence from that damned Texas Room at Bennet's country estate. The pieces all fit.

Now he had to find a way to convince her to give it up to him. Not an easy task, considering the effort she'd made to get it away from Bennet.

Jake replaced the poker in its stand, then turned to face her. Moonlight cast a luminous glow upon the highlights in her hair. Now, for the first time, Jake could believe she might in fact be supernatural. The reincarnation of Helen of Troy was who came to mind.

"Jake Delaney, you and your sister have done my family a great service. I made the mistake of sharing Lord Bennet's letters with Uncle Angus, and he has fashed himself over the threats ever since. Such strain is not good for him. I think the pain in his bones worsens with worry. Now, that burden is lifted. We owe you a debt of gratitude."

A debt? Jake checked Gillian's hands for signs of a silver platter. Yes, there it was, imaginary but about as shiny and pretty as they came. Never in his life had he been handed such a perfect opportunity.

It can't be this easy.

But the sincerity he saw shining in her face suggested it was. *What the hell. Why not?* He curled his fingers and stared down at his nails. "Debt is such an unpleasant commodity. I think it's always best to discharge an obligation as soon as possible, don't you agree?"

"Yes, I do."

"Good. Because you see, I do know a way your family can pay my family for the good turn we have done you."

She must have heard something in his voice, because her eyes narrowed. Warily, she asked, "What is it?"

Jake flashed her a smile and called her bluff. "You can hand over the copy you have of the Republic of Texas's Declaration of Independence."

six

GILLIAN DIDN'T KNOW whether to laugh or cry. That accursed document. She rued the day Uncle Angus stepped ashore on Scottish soil with it in his possession. First Lord Bennet brought trouble to the family because he coveted the thing, and now Jake Delaney wanted it. If it were up to her, she'd give him the bastartin piece of paper just to be rid of it.

But it wasn't up to her. The document was Uncle Angus's treasure, his to keep or give away. She tried her best to make her smile sincere. "I am sorry, I have no clue as to what you are talking about."

"C'mon, princess, you are no better a liar than you are a ghost. I think you know exactly what I'm talking about."

"Mr. Delaney," she protested, drawing herself up in offense.

"I think we've gone beyond the Mr. and Miss, don't you, Gillian? Call me Jake." He sauntered over to her favorite chair and took a seat, stretching his long legs out in front of him before crossing them at the ankles. "A few minutes ago you said he stole something from Rowanclere and you went to England and got it back. That something was the Declaration of Independence."

"Mr. De . . . Jake . . . I don't think—"

"Here's the way I think it worked. At some point during the years your uncle lived in Texas, the document fell into his hands. He brought it with him when he returned to Scotland. It could have happened differently—this copy could be the one we believe was sent to the Texas Legation in London—but that part doesn't really matter. What does matter is that Bennet learned of its existence and went after it. Angus Brodie wouldn't give or sell or barter away the document, so Bennet tricked Robbie into giving it to him. He swindled a piece of history away from that darlin' little girl for the price of a bag of candy and a ham."

Gillian choked and covered it with a cough. How could he know that? He certainly didn't learn it from Robyn, because shame kept the child's lips sealed tight. That bit of news must have come from Bennet himself.

Jake continued. "Once y'all found out what happened, I imagine tempers blew. Not only did Bennet take advantage of a child, he took something your uncle valued. So you set out to right the wrong and stole the Declaration back from Bennet."

He had read the situation like a book, and Gillian did her best to hide any response. She couldn't confirm or deny anything, not until she talked to Uncle Angus.

He folded his arms and tilted his head to one side, making a show of studying her. "You snatched the Declaration right from beneath the baron's pointy nose, then hightailed it home. You must have suspected he'd try to get it back, so you were prepared for him. You stopped him."

While Jake talked, Scooter had dragged herself toward the chair and plopped down beside his feet. Jake leaned over, scooped her up, and set her in his lap. "Now, Bennet wasn't a man who liked being thwarted, hence the letters. You were right to be wary of the man and his ugly threats, Gillian. He was obsessed. He'd have been back for the Declaration eventually. So, what parts do I have wrong? Not much, I imagine."

Not anything. At a loss on how to answer, Gillian kept her gaze on Scooter, who whimpered with pleasure at Jake Delaney's attentions. *I know how you feel.*

"Gillian? How about it? It was the Declaration you stole from Bennet's home, right?"

She avoided answering by asking a question of her own. "Is that the true reason you searched our library? You were looking for this proclamation?"

"Declaration, as you well know. Yes. Like I said before, my family almost came to real grief at Bennet's hand due to the Declaration. Because of that, I thought it best to keep to myself the purpose behind my visit when I first arrived. Now I figure it's best to lay it all out for you. I believe I mentioned I am an attorney?"

Returning Scooter to the floor, he rose, reached into his pocket, and handed her a card that read *J. A. K. Delaney, Attorney at Law. San Antonio, Texas.*

Lovely.

"In this matter I represent the people of the State of Texas." His tone turned professional as he elaborated, "I have been sent by a group of concerned Texans who have organized a search for four handwritten copies of the Republic of Texas's Declaration of Independence. We traced one of the Declarations to England. My brother-in-law's inquiries then turned up Lord Bennet's name. That trail has now led right to you."

Then, with a wink, the solicitor disappeared and the rogue returned. "So hand it over and be done with the debt. This document truly belongs to the people of Texas. The only other copy we had burned a few years ago. A country deserves to own its own history."

"Tell that to the museums of the world," Gillian observed wryly. "I'm certain Greece would like the Elgin marbles back, too, but I don't see the British Museum handing them over."

"The British Museum doesn't owe me a debt and you do, princess."

"Dinna call me princess."

Wicked charm filled the smile he flashed. "You are a blindingly beautiful woman who lives in a fairy-tale castle. Princess fits."

His compliment warmed her and stroked her wounded sense of femininity. David never called her blindingly beautiful. Of course, David had never wanted her to give up an historical document, either.

No, he only wanted your virginity.

Gillian mentally slammed that door and cleared her throat. "I understand your concern, and I would be pleased to help you if it were in my power. However—"

"Not yours to give away, hmm? Must be your Uncle Angus's property, then. He's the one who'll make the call?" Jake pulled out a pocket watch and checked the time. "Now that we have an understanding, I reckon this can wait until later this morning. Mind if I bunk in one of those rooms downstairs near your sisters instead of up in the tower? I noticed it's warmer in that part of the castle, and after the day I've had, my bones are crying out for heat. We can both get some shut-eye, then I'll meet with your uncle at breakfast. If all goes right, I can be on my way home before noon."

"Wait. You have made assumptions and decisions based on your imagination. We have no understanding. What we have between us is—"

"Debt. You said it yourself, Gillian. You said it first. Don't try to fishtail when I want to collect."

"Fishtail?"

He moved his hand in a back and forth motion. "Back out of it. Change directions. Change your mind."

"I'm not changing anything. Nor am I admitting to anything or denying anything." Gillian closed her eyes and drew a deep breath in an attempt to calm her jittery nerves. Delaney wanted to sleep. Good. She would use the time to talk to Uncle Angus and explain the situation. Maybe together they could think of a way to pay the debt in a currency different from the one requested by Jake Delaney.

If that was what Uncle Angus wanted, she couldn't imagine it being otherwise.

The Declaration of Independence meant too much to Uncle Angus. He often said that in many ways, the document defined him as a man. He did not elaborate, other than saying it had something to do with what had happened on the San Jacinto battlefield where independence was won.

After Lord Bennet stole the Declaration, she'd been

surprised at the depth of Angus Brodie's sorrow. When the depression dragged on for months, she'd been motivated to go to great lengths to bring the document home. Now Jake Delaney wanted to take it away again. How would Uncle Angus react? Would the altruistic reasons Delaney presented make a difference to Uncle Angus?

Possibly. She wouldn't know until she asked.

"Well?" Jake folded his arms and scowled. "How long does it take for you to make up your mind? I'd just as soon not be standing here come dawn."

"I was trying to decide which bedchamber you would find most comfortable. I think the pink room on the second floor is the best choice. It's usually warmer than—"

"Pink?" He grimaced.

"Actually, lavender and pink. It's a perfect room for you, sir." His petulant expression made her grin. Nodding toward the dog, she said, "If you and Scooter will follow me, I'll show you to your room."

"Perfect room," he muttered. "Lavender and pink. What, did I kiss like a schoolgirl?"

They were halfway down the spiral staircase when Gillian first heard Robyn's shout. Immediately, she picked up her skirts and ran down the steps. Rounding the final turn, she spied her younger sister. Tears glistened in eyes rounded with worry.

"Oh, Gilly, come quick. Please, come quick."

"Angus?" Gillian asked, her throat tight with nervousness.

"No. It's Flora. It's the baby. Oh, Gillian, it's way too soon, but Flora says she's afraid she's having the baby."

*   *   *

Rowanclere was a castle in chaos.

Before disappearing into her sister's room, Gillian dispatched a stableboy to Laichmoray to summon Flora's husband and sent a maid to the nearest village to fetch the howdie, or midwife. Mrs. Ferguson, the cook and all-around caretaker, dashed up and down the stairs, checking on Flora's progress while seeing to preparations for the merry meht, a kind of post-birth celebration, from what Jake gathered.

Even young Robbie kept busy. Seated at a table in the sitting room across the hall from Flora's bedchamber, the girl made lists of items needed for the coming child. "We are not prepared to have a baby here at Rowanclere," she told Jake solemnly. "Birthing bairns is a serious event and matters must be a certain way to ensure the health and safety of Flora and the wee babe."

"I see," Jake said, even though he didn't. At home, babies were birthed with little more than clean sheets, soap, a pan of hot water, and a knife to cut the cord. Why would it be so much different over here? He could see the need for extra coals for the fire to keep the infant warm enough, but the girl had filled three whole pages with writing, and she didn't appear near finished yet.

Because he was curious by nature, Jake would have asked questions. Under the circumstances, he figured he'd better not. Calling attention to himself any more than necessary might prove dangerous. At the moment, while activity swarmed around him, Jake sat on a straight-backed, too-small, splintered-seat wooden chair within point-blank range of a Texas Paterson five-shot revolver held by a shaky Angus Brodie, Laird of Rowanclere.

Damned old man had gotten the drop on him.

Surprised was a mild term for what Jake felt when shortly after meeting his host, the Scot had pulled a gun. Hell, Brodie had to be eighty if he were a day, and he walked not just with one cane, but with a pair of 'em. If anyone from home saw Jake playing target in a chair like this, he'd never live it down.

Except for confirming Jake's identity after Gillian's hurried introduction, Angus Brodie did not address him at all during the first half-hour of the bairn watch. A time or two Jake wondered if the lord of the castle had forgotten him, but each time he so much as twitched, he found himself staring down the Paterson's barrel. Not that he couldn't have extricated himself from the situation if he'd wanted. The man had a sickly look about him. But Brodie kept demanding information from the women going in and out of Flora's room, and Jake wanted to hear their replies. He figured Brodie probably wouldn't shoot him without some sort of provocation, and he was a bit worried about Mrs. Dunbar, himself. So he'd settled down to wait.

Everyone breathed a sigh of relief when the howdie arrived with her daughter and another female assistant. Moments later, the midwife called for Robbie. The girl disappeared into the bedroom, then less than five minutes later, dashed out into the hall headed for the stairs. She returned a short time later carrying a huge knife.

"Careful, there, sweetheart!" Jake exclaimed, horrified at the sight of such a little girl carrying such a big weapon. As Robbie hurried into the bedchamber, he turned to Brodie. "Why the hell did they need a knife like that in the birthing room?"

Angus scowled in his direction, then explained in a voice that was a unique blend of Texan drawl and Scottish burr. "The butching-gullie. To ward off evil. Flora already has her Bible."

"Oh. Of course." Now that didn't make a lick of sense. Jake was still pondering the remark a few minutes later when Robbie reappeared, rolling her eyes theatrically.

"What's wrong?" asked her uncle, the last of the color fading from his already pallid face. "Flora?"

"Flora is fine." Before she could elaborate, a pain-racked cry sounded from inside the bedchamber.

"Never mind the noise, lass," the Scot said, his brow dipping in a frown. "Do not be judgmental. Birthing bairns is hard work."

"I know that," Robbie replied, her young girl's voice dripping with disgust. "If that were Flora squealing, I wouldn't say a word. But Flora is being very brave about it. Gilly's the one who is squealing."

"Gillian?" Jake and Angus asked simultaneously.

At that moment, the bedroom door opened and Gillian stumbled out, stooped over and holding her leg below the knee. "But Mrs. Cameron—" she protested.

"Bide a wee, Gillian. Your sister disnae need the distraction right now."

"I did not mean—"

"We ken," replied the midwife before she shut the door.

Gillian whimpered her way over to the settee and plunked herself down next to her uncle, massaging her leg as he asked, "What is it, lass?"

She winced. "I do not know. Every time Flora feels a pain, my leg cramps. I could not stop it, Uncle Angus. It does it all on its own. Mrs. Cameron thinks the fairies could be responsible. She says they may be trying to distract us from putting all the protection in place, giving them the chance to steal Flora's child."

"She has a point," Robbie said. "Fairies are wee wicked folk."

Angus Brodie sniffed with disdain, then used his free hand to pat Gillian's knee while he soothed, "Dinna fash yersel'. I'm certain your pain has nothing to do with the fairies. It is part of being a twin, I imagine. The pair of you are too close to go through this together without you being affected."

Gillian sighed and nodded. "I hope you are right."

"Perhaps you'd feel better if your mind were put to other matters." He motioned toward Jake with the Paterson. "Tell me about him, lass. I thought we sent him away."

"I did, too," she glumly replied. "He came back."

Robbie snapped her fingers. "I know how we can watch for fairies. Where is Scooter?"

Gillian replied, "Up in my bedchamber."

"Yours?" Brodie asked. "Why was his dog in your chamber?" He lowered the aim of his gun from Jake's heart to his loins.

Jake decided a diversion was in order. His gaze captured Gillian's. "Fairies? You mean ghosts aren't enough? Now I'm supposed to worry about fairies, too?"

"Not with Scooter around," Robbie insisted. "She'll sniff out those fairies and scare them away. I'll go get her now, all right?"

Without waiting for permission, she darted for the door, leaving a pregnant silence in her wake. As the moment dragged out, Jake rubbed his palms along the top of his thighs and asked, "What do y'all expect the weather to do today? Think we'll get any rain?"

Angus Brodie snorted. "That is how Texans start more than half their conversations. Tell me, lass. Do I want to talk to him at all, or shall I simply shoot him and be done with it?"

Damn the woman, she actually acted as if she had to consider the question. Jake hastened to say, "Tell him about the debt, Gillian."

"What debt?" Brodie asked, grabbing up one of his walking canes and rapping it on the floor.

Gillian scowled at Jake, then looked at her uncle. "According to Mr. Delaney, our worries concerning Lord Bennet are behind us. Mr. Delaney says his sister shot him. Lord Bennet is dead."

It took a moment for the news to seep through, then Brodie's bushy white eyebrows winged up. "Dead? The bastard is dead?"

Gillian and Jake both nodded. Brodie looked from one to the other, then angled his head toward Jake and asked his niece, "Can we believe him?"

Before she could open her mouth, Jake rolled the truth out like a rug. "I would never put your grandniece at risk."

He sat motionless, chin out and eyes glaring as Angus Brodie shot him a hard stare, measuring his worth. Abruptly, the Scot lowered his gun. "You will tell me the entire tale. Now."

Jake arched a brow, silently asking Gillian if she wished to tell it or have him do the honors. She wrinkled her nose, gave Flora's bedchamber door one more glance, then launched into the story.

While she talked, Jake took advantage of the unguarded moment to move to a more comfortable chair nearer the fireplace. There he stretched out his legs and settled in to listen, interrupting her twice to elaborate on a point, three times to correct a mistake. He didn't count the number of times Gillian paused to massage her leg muscles.

It didn't escape Jake's notice that she failed to mention that the Declaration of Independence was the object of his search. Jake decided she must be working up to that, saving the best for last, so to speak.

Once during the telling, they heard Flora cry out for her husband in a voice racked with pain. When a few minutes later they heard the laboring woman curse her man with invectives as blue as the lochs of Scotland, Gillian moaned and buried her face in her hands.

Jake felt the urge to reassure her, to touch her and kiss her cheek and tell her everything would be all right. He refrained, which appeared to be a good thing considering the unvoiced threat her granduncle shot his way when she shook off her worry and continued the story, picking up at the place where she awoke to find Jake in her bedroom.

At least she had the good sense not to mention he had tied her up.

During a pause in her narrative, Brodie eyed Jake speculatively and stroked his snowy beard. "Sneaking into the lass's room. I probably should kill you just for that. Gilly, tell me the truth. Did he dare to lay a finger on you?"

Jake held his own breath and eyed Brodie's revolver waiting for Gillian to reply. Hell, if he'd known he stood a chance of dying for his transgression, he wouldn't have stopped at a kiss.

Apparently, Gillian agreed he had not committed a death-deserving deed because she shook her head in response to her granduncle's question. "He didn't bother me, Uncle Angus. His impersonation of a ghost is even worse than mine. I think next week I—"

She broke off abruptly, gasped, then fell back against the sofa, her eyes closed as she turned her face up toward the ceiling. "Next week. Flora. I'm doomed."

Doomed? Jake silently repeated.

"The Earl of Harrington arrives next week." She hit her head against the cushion. "Oh, Uncle Angus. What will I do?"

Brodie clucked his tongue and shrugged. "Let's not concern ourselves with that today. The main thing to remember now is that you are safe from Bennet's evil threats."

"But what about you?" Indignation flashed in Gillian's eyes as she shoved to her feet. "Unless you've changed your mind about selling Rowanclere, next week is still vitally important. What about it, Uncle, have you changed your hard-headed ways? Will you move down from your Crow's Nest to a safer room?"

"I've kept my vow for fifty years," Brodie said, jutting out his bewhiskered chin. "I'll not break it now. Besides, changing rooms will not solve the problem. I'll see you and Robyn provided for before I die."

She folded her arms. "Stubborn Scot."

"You are one to talk."

The conversation had left Jake in the dust. Before he could pursue the matter, Mrs. Ferguson opened Flora's chamber door and dashed for the hallway. Gillian jumped to her feet. "What's wrong?"

"Nothing is wrong. Water. We need more water."

"Water." She glanced at Jake, blue eyes pleading. "Is that a good sign?"

"I think it is."

Of course, he didn't know it for a fact, but he figured it for a good guess. In Texas, water was always a good sign. Besides, the worry in her expression damned near broke his heart.

Gillian began to pace the sitting room, limping at fairly regular intervals as her leg continued to cramp. "I hope Alasdair is home and not off hunting or something. I hope he rides like the wind from Laichmoray and gets here in time. Flora needs him." She paused for a moment, then said, "He will be so angry. He wanted the bairn born at home."

"Let him be angry," her uncle said with a huff. "You needed your sister's help and she needed to give it."

"Because you are too stubborn to help yourself."

"Gillian Ross, dinna start that again." Angus Brodie waved a finger at his niece as he continued, "And you'll mind your tongue as will Alasdair Dunbar when he arrives. He will soon discover that it doesn't matter where a bairn is born. What matters is his health."

"Her health." Gillian grimaced and clutched at her leg. "I think Flora is having a girl. And you are right. All that does matter is that Flora and the baby are healthy."

"Of course I am right. Now, explain to me about this debt Delaney, here, claims we owe."

Gillian's lips moved but no sound came out. Jake decided she was praying, so he answered Angus Brodie's question for her. "Gillian told me about Lord Bennet's threats. She rightly admitted my sister did your family a huge favor by . . . eliminating the peril, shall we say . . . and that your family is in my family's debt. In turn, I explained the true purpose of my visit to Rowanclere, and informed her how y'all could clear this obligation."

"And that would be?"

Sitting up in his chair, Jake rested his hands on his knees, leaned forward, and watched Angus Brodie's face closely. "I want you to give me the Declaration of Independence."

Angus didn't twitch so much as a whisker. "You want what?"

"He has the idea that you have this item he is searching for," Gillian said. She then outlined the points he had made to her earlier. While she spoke, Brodie tapped his cane against the floor in an annoyingly sporadic cadence. His eyes, however, narrowed at regular intervals.

When Gillian finished, he said only, "Hmm . . . so that's the sorry way they teach boys to think in Texas these days. Such faulty reasoning. Sad state of affairs, if you ask me."

Before Jake could respond, Robbie returned with Scooter cradled in her arms. "I told her all about Flora having her bairn and how fairies like to steal newborns. Scooter is ready to protect my sister."

"Good." Brodie tossed her a pillow from the settee. "Make her a guard spot in the hallway outside Flora's door, then come snuggle with me, wee one. We will wait together."

The girl's return effectively halted any further conversation about the Declaration. Jake didn't mind. His own attention kept wandering to the room across the hall. He could only imagine how the rest of them were feeling. Besides, this would give the Scot some time to think about what he'd learned in the last few minutes.

Jake knew he'd taken a giant step forward in his hunt for the document. He was ninety-nine percent sure the document was somewhere here at Rowanclere. Their secrecy had told him he'd be wasting his time to search for it, however. If they wanted to keep it hidden, a man would need ten years to search all the nooks, crannies, and hidden passages in this castle.

Nope, they were going to have to hand it over, and after having met Angus Brodie, Jake felt confident he could make it happen. The Scotsman might be crotchety and stubborn, but those qualities couldn't hide his honorable core.

So Jake settled back in his chair, watching Robbie cuddle with her Uncle Angus and Gillian pace the room as they waited for nature to take its course. Eventually, Robbie fell asleep on her granduncle's lap. Gillian lapsed into contemplative quiet.

Twice during the next hour, she braved her sister's bedchamber. Each time she lasted less than five minutes before a leg cramp saw her banished to the sitting room once again.

Jake dozed as night gave way to dawn and dawn to daylight. He had slipped into a sound sleep when a disturbance in the hallway jarred him awake.

"Flora!" boomed a man's voice. "Flora, where are ye? Are ye well?"

Gillian stepped to the doorway of the sitting room. "Alasdair, thank God you've come."

"My wife?"

"In the green bedchamber across the hall. The howdie says she is faring well. The babe has yet to arrive."

He caught Gillian up in a bear hug, lifting her off her feet. He whirled her around and finally set her down in the middle of the sitting room.

He was a mountain of a man, with a voice that roared like the ocean in a storm. Concern mingled with relief in the brown eyes that pinned Gillian. "She is good?"

"Aye."

"Why are you nae with her? Ye are her twin. She needs ye with her."

Gillian sagged. "The howdie won't let me stay. I start feeling Flora's pains, and she thinks it weakens her labor, will make it last twice as long. Mrs. Cameron says Flora needs all the pain to safely deliver the bairn."

"But she's well."

"Aye. You can go in and see for yourself. Tell Flora you are here."

"Nae." He backed away from both Gillian and the door. "It is not my place. I will wait for the bairn and my Flora to come through this trial safely." He paused for a moment, scowled, and added, "Then I can kill her."

Jake couldn't help but grin. Gillian caught the look, glared at him, and he shrugged. "He sounds just like my brother-in-law, Cole. He's always threatening to kill my sister. Of course, Chrissy needs it more than Flora. She is always getting herself into trouble."

The big, burly Scot whirled on him. "Who are ye? What are ye doing attending my wife at this time?"

Jake sized him up. The man was shorter than Jake, but meatier. They'd be well-matched, but Jake figured he could probably take him. One scream from Flora's room and the man would be a sitting loon on a loch.

"I'm here to take Angus's Declaration of Independence home to Texas."

Alasdair Dunbar nodded hard. "Good. That thing has caused naught but trouble for the past year or more."

"Alasdair!" Gillian protested. "You have the biggest mouth in Scotland."

Jake grinned with smug satisfaction at having the truth out. Flora's husband waved the subject of the Declaration away and said, "Disnae matter now. Tell me what preparations have been made. Are all the doors in the castle unlocked?"

"Aye," Robbie piped up. "And she has a Bible and a knife in her bed."

"What about the iron? Did ye place a piece of cold iron with her to scare off the fairies?"

Gillian nodded. "I did that."

"And the cheese? Do ye have a cryin' kebbock for the merry meht?"

Gillian shared a worried look with Robbie before replying. "We have an uncut cheese, but I fear it will not be big enough."

Angus Brodie waved a dismissive hand. "We'll cut the pieces small."

"Nae." Dunbar raked his fingers through his hair as he stalked around the room. "I'll send a man back to Laichmoray. I should have brought it with me. And a fir-candle so they can be sained. Flora will need to be churched. The christening. My mother is in Edinburgh—I'll need to send word. So much to do, and nothing ready here, nothing ready yet." He stopped mid-stride and turned an anxious expression toward Gillian. "It's too early, Gilly. I am so afeared."

In the face of her brother-in-law's fright, Gillian appeared to bloom with strength. She stopped him mid-stalk with a hug.

Jake scowled at the way the Scotsman clung to his sister-in-law. Sure the fellow looked in need of comfort, and he obviously didn't know what he was doing, but that was no excuse for his hand to rest so low on her hip, damned near cupping her butt. Made Jake itch to knock Dunbar's hand away, dammit.

Gillian's voice was soothing as she stepped away from Alasdair and said, "Let me check on her progress for you, Alasdair Dunbar. Perhaps matters are happening faster now and . . . ow!" Gasping for breath, Gillian went stiff. She clutched her left leg, then her right. Moaning, then groaning.

Jake saw she was seconds from falling down. Shoving the helpless Alasdair aside, he swooped her up into his arms and headed for the first empty bed he knew of, the extra one in Flora's chamber.

Jake spared the chaos inside hardly a glance as he carried Gillian into the room. He ignored the flock of feminine voices raised in protest and dismissed Dunbar's shouted, "Ye canna go there. Get away. It isnae proper."

Gillian's moan blended with the pain-racked sound of her sister's groan. "To hell with proper," Jake said. "They're hurting."

"But the midwife said—"

"She's wrong. It'll help them both to be together."

He laid his burden gently upon the bed, then threw up the hem of her robe and nightgown, baring her legs to his gaze. The knots of muscle in her calves were clearly visible. Beginning with her right, he took her leg in his hands and started to massage. "Woman, your muscles are as hard as Texas red granite. Try to relax."

"I am trying," she snapped.

To his left, Jake could hear Flora struggling for breath. "Alasdair," she whimpered. "Is that you?"

"Aye, my wren. Look at ye. Ye tear my heart in two."

Gillian cried out and reached for her left leg. "Here's another one."

Flora mewled and panted. The midwife said, "That's it, dearie. Not much longer."

Jake kneaded Gillian's muscles until his fingers ached. Though he kept his concentration focused on the woman before him, he couldn't help but be aware of the chaos going on behind him. Dunbar kept scrambling in and out of the room. Robbie had joined the women and kept darting back to the doorway to holler out details of Flora's progress like "She's squeezing Alasdair's hand hard enough to break it" and "Her face scrunches up and turns red as a poppy when she pushes, Uncle Angus."

Jake did his best to turn off his ears when he heard the child say, "Oh, yuck. That is messy."

Gillian's leg cramps continued to come faster and faster until there was barely any break between them. Behind him, Jake heard the howdie say, "Look, a red-headed bairn. Let's get him born, Mama. Gie us a good push."

For another five minutes, Flora labored, Gillian cramped, Alasdair prayed, Robbie went silent, Angus yelled from the sitting room for updates, and even Scooter got in on the act by barking.

Then finally, blessedly, Gillian let out a sigh of relief and her muscles went lax. Alasdair said, "Flora? Oh, Flora," and the first thready cry of a babe strengthened into a full-blown wail.

Jake's gaze met Gillian's and his heart stuttered. Her eyes glistened with tears of joy, and in that moment she was without a doubt the most beautiful woman he had ever seen.

"Thank you," she said with a smile, her voice soft and sweet and barely heard over the infant's cries and the midwife's muttering about men being where they didn't belong.

"My pleasure," he replied, meaning it.

She offered him one more smile before focusing on the child. "A boy," she breathed. "Oh, Flora, you have a son."

The tears fell freely now and she scrambled to her feet. But halfway to her sister, Gillian cried out, clutched her leg, and stumbled. Jake caught her just before she hit the ground.

Flora Dunbar's second son was born five minutes later.

The females took the momentous occasion in stride. The father fainted dead away right at the foot of Flora's bed.

After preserving her sister's modesty with a sheet, Gillian asked Jake to remove her brother-in-law from the room. "We have much to do here, and he is in the way. Tell Uncle Angus I said to break out his best."

It took some muscle to move the dead-weight Scot, but eventually Jake dragged Dunbar to the stairs and tumbled him down to a lower floor, then heaved him into what Angus Brodie called his Whisky Room. The fumes wafting from a bottle of the malt finally roused him, and Dunbar began rattling on about sons and clans and history.

Brodie was the one who eased the conversation into toast-making. Jake's brain was buzzing a bit by the time they'd tossed back a dram to everyone in the castle from the new mother and her babies, to the stableboy and the barn cats.

That's why he was a little slow on the uptake when Angus Brodie lifted his glass and said, "To the successful haunting of Rowanclere. May Jake Delaney scare that Sassenach fool right out of his pants."

"Not out of his pants," observed Dunbar, a slight slur to his words. "My Flora will be abed a fortnight. I'll not have any bare-ass naked man around my wife."

Jake quit admiring the attractive amber shade of the whisky and said, "Now wait one minute. Why would I be scaring anybody? And make no mistake. I have absolutely no interest in men who aren't wearing their pants. I know it's tradition and style and such, but hell, I get cold just thinkin' about you Scotsmen and your kilts. Give me denim britches anytime, thank you very much."

"Well, you cannot be wearing denim when you're a ghaist," Angus declared.

Jake took another sip of the local malt. This Scotch kind of whisky took some getting used to compared to the Tennessee brand he was accustomed to drinking, but the taste grew on a man. That decided, he responded to the laird of Rowanclere. "I can be buried in my work pants if I want. As long as it's not my mother laying me out, that is. She'll insist on a suit. But my sister Chrissy, she's a good one. She'll bury me in comfort. All I have to do is let my wishes be known."

"I don't intend to bury you, Jake Delaney. We will set it up like Gillian did. You will make appearances." Brodie stroked his beard and studied Jake. "We will drag out the trunks. You're big enough."

Suddenly, Jake felt as sober as a Baptist preacher praying for souls at a San Antonio sporting house. "What the hell are you talking about?"

Brodie threw back his drink, then banged the empty glass on the table beside him. "I have reached my decision. Although I am thankful the bastard Lord Bennet is dead, your sister did not kill him on our Gilly's behalf. Therefore, my clan is not in your debt, Jake Delaney."

"Bennet is dead?" Dunbar asked.

"Wait a minute." Jake slammed down his own drink. "You aren't gonna weasel out of this. Your own niece said you owe us, and you do."

Dryly, Angus observed, "Despite what she likes to think, Gillian is not laird of Rowanclere. I own this castle and all its contents. I own the Declaration of Independence you are so determined to get."

"You are wrong. That document belongs to the people of Texas." Jake shoved to his feet and glared down at Brodie.

"Get your pride out of your ears, boy, and listen. I'm offering you a deal."

"What deal?"

The feminine voice floated from the doorway behind him. "My, Uncle Angus," Gillian said. "Are you not the canny Scot?"

Jake whirled around, bracing his hands on his hips.

"Have you been there long? Did you hear this nonsense he's spouting? The man is a thief!"

"No, he is not. He was given that which you seek. I heard what he said, and he is right. He has something you want and you can give us something we need."

Jake was tired and angry and a ways down the road to drunk. He didn't feel like playing around with words. "I know what I think you need, but what the hell do you think you need?"

"A ghaist. Rowanclere needs a boodie, Jake, and Uncle Angus is right. You'll be perfect."

She beamed a smile at him so bright and so beautiful, he felt it clear to his toes. Under the circumstances, that frustrated him even more. "Are you saying you want me to take over the role you've been playing so poorly the last few days?"

"That's right, Texas." Her smug smile made his eyes cross.

Angus said, "That's my deal. Flora cannot help Gilly, so you must. You help her convince Lord Harrington that Rowanclere is haunted, and I'll give you my copy of the Republic of Texas's Declaration of Independence."

"I'll be damned if I'll do that!"

"Better than dead if you don't," Gillian said, her eyes sparkling like jewels as she bit her lip and gazed pointedly at the gun once again in her granduncle's hand. "One way or the other, Texas, Rowanclere will have you for a ghaist."

seven

FLORA'S BAIRNS WERE five days old when Gillian descended the corner tower stairs, her arms overflowing with tartan. The trunks in the storage rooms had yielded a dozen or more setts from which to choose. After much internal debate, she had chosen a tartan in shades of the forest and the summer sky, not due to its history or marriage ties to Rowanclere, but because the particular shade of green reminded her of Jake Delaney's eyes.

Though she acknowledged that truth, it embarrassed her. So when she spied Robyn and asked if she'd seen the Texan yet this day, the tone of her voice was sharper than necessary.

Her younger sister took an exaggerated step backward. "What's the matter with you, Gilly? Did you not sleep well? Did the babies keep you awake, too? May I may change rooms until Flora and Alasdair return to Laichmoray after the christening? The howdie says it's a scandal that Flora won't leave them in the nursery with a maid, but I understand that Flora worries herself sick when they're not around. They are terribly tiny, even though Mrs. Ferguson says the bairns are too big to be two months early, and Flora must have been mistaken on her dates. What does she mean by that?"

"Ask Flora. I'm looking for Mr. Delaney. Have you seen him this morning?"

"Aye, he is in the muniment room. I think his idea to use the suits of armor in the haunting is a fine idea, don't you?"

Gillian rolled her eyes. "No, I do not. The man wants to play in them, that is all. He acts no older than you, Robbie."

It was true. Despite his vociferous protests, Jake Delaney had taken to the haunting like dye to wool. She had expected him to pout, but he didn't. Once he decided it was in his best interests to agree to Uncle Angus's proposal, he'd shown nothing but enthusiasm for the plan. He'd taken Gillian's ideas for haunting the castle and elaborated on them to the point of overkill.

The numerous presages of death he had ready to employ were prime examples. The Texan wouldn't settle for setting up a deid-rap, an unexplained knocking; he had to create a deid-spail, too. The man wasted a full dozen candles in the attempt to guide the melted wax overhanging the lip of the holder into the form of a shroud that could extend in the direction of one individual. But he'd eventually triumphed, and now they had a deid-spail to use along with a number of pictures waiting to fall, footsteps ready to be heard overhead, and clocks prepared to stop for no apparent mechanical reason. It was ridiculous.

And maybe, just maybe, Gillian was a little jealous the

Texan displayed such adeptness at something she'd struggled so to get right.

"I like Mr. Jake," Robbie told her with a shrug. "He tells good stories like Uncle Angus and he makes me laugh. He likes to laugh, too, and when he smiles, he's gey handsome. Do you not agree, Gilly?"

She attempted to ignore the question, much like she tried to ignore the man himself of late. She succeeded with both about equally well.

"Gilly, I said do you not think he is bonny?"

"Aye," she replied, sighing. There was no denying the Texan's appeal. The man was even handsome when he scowled. Noticing the fact had become quite a problem for her of late. Worse, he didn't even need to be around her for the trouble to occur. They could be at opposite ends of Rowanclere, and the moment she recalled the kiss or the tender way he'd cared for her while Flora birthed the bairns, she would be lost in a fog. Just yesterday her inattention resulted in a pan of burned scones, a broken Wedgwood vase, and a cut on her finger when the knife slipped as they were repairing a worn spot in the string holding together Young Fergus's bones. It was humiliating.

Especially since he'd not touched her or attempted to kiss her since the night Flora's sons were born.

Disgruntled now, Gillian shifted the burden in her arms. "The muniment room, you said?"

"Aye. But he was on his way to take Scooter outside."

Ah, that meant she now should search for him in a room warmed by a fire. The man had to warm himself if he so much stuck a big toe past the front door. Bidding her sister farewell, she looked for him first in the library, then the dining room, and the yellow sitting room. Finally, upon approaching the blue drawing room, she heard the dachshund's yip from behind the closed door.

Reaching for the doorknob, Gillian paused. She glanced down at the predominantly green tartan in her arms and silently admitted one of the red setts may have been the smarter choice. Convincing this man to dress his part as a seventeenth-century ghaist might well be a bloody battle. Scarlet did a better job at hiding blood-stains. Gillian took a deep, bracing breath and quietly opened the drawing room door.

Heat rolled over her in waves. As expected, in a room occupied by the thin-skinned Texan, a larger-than-necessary fire burned in the fireplace. Gillian shook her head. One would think a bitter winter storm battered Rowanclere's doors rather than a gentle summer breeze. This morning's weather was moderate, bordering on warm, even. She hadn't broken ice in her pitcher on her washstand for several weeks.

Jake Delaney sat on the floor in front of the hearth, his back to her as he wrestled with his dog over a bone. He wore his customary boots, denim pants, a long-sleeved blue chambray shirt, and a leather vest, and she couldn't help but think the clothing suited him. For a cowboy haunt, perhaps. Not a Scot.

Her hold on the feileadh mor tightened and she waited for him to notice her. Dreading the battle certain to come, she wasn't in a rush. Initially, it had taken Uncle Angus hours of negotiation to gain Delaney's agreement to haunt Rowanclere. Had the required mode of dress been mentioned, he might well have refused the deal.

Gillian could delay no longer. Lord Harrington was

due to arrive at Rowanclere tomorrow. While Jake had taken to playing a spirit with gusto, he had yet to attempt any of the haunts in costume. 'Twas time for a dress rehearsal.

Hearing him growl, she momentarily wondered if he had read her thoughts. When she realized he mimicked the mutt's rumble, a rueful chuckle escaped her.

Jake glanced over his shoulder. "Well, good morning, Gilly. What death defying tasks have you set for us weary ghouls today?"

Ignoring his question, she gave the bone a pointed look and made a query of her own. "Did you not get enough porridge this morning, Texas?"

He flashed a grin, then rolled Scooter over onto her back and scratched her belly. "When it's a choice between ham and haggis, I'll go for the bone every time."

Because Robbie's observation about the Texan's handsomeness plagued like a pebble in her shoe, Gillian glanced away from the man as he rolled to his feet. Since she wasn't looking at him, he caught her by surprise when he reached out and grabbed the black-hilted dagger from out of the bundle of cloth in her arms.

"Pardon me, princess, but something about seeing a killin' knife in a female's hands gives me the shivers."

She offered a false smile. "Such wit this morning, Mr. Delaney."

"Jake." He studied the knife, tested its balance, and nodded. "Nice little weapon. Is it for me?"

"Aye. It is a sgian-dhu, a small dagger." It was to be worn at the outside top of his stocking, although she thought she would wait to impart that particular detail.

"Thanks, but I don't need it. I have a Bowie knife I strap on when it's best to wear a knife. It's three times the size of this little thing. So, what's on the agenda for today? I hope in your planning you remembered to keep the afternoon free. I promised Angus a game of dominos if he's up to it."

"I remember. I do expect you will play. He claims to have felt better these last few days than he has felt in months. I think the babies have much to do with it. My fear is that he will suffer a setback once Alasdair takes his family home."

"Don't borrow trouble, princess."

He casually set the treasured dagger on the marble mantel, and Gillian tried not to be annoyed. He couldn't know it was an heirloom due respect, having been passed down from the maternal side of her father's family. He couldn't know an ancestor carried that very same weapon during the Battle of the Pass of Killiecrankie in 1689.

That aside, if this Bowie knife of his was substantially larger than a sgian-dhu, it wouldn't do as a substitute for her purposes.

Before she could argue the fact, he moved to relieve her of the entire burden she held in her arms. Setting the bundle atop a nearby table, he asked, "What is all this? New draperies?"

"No." Gillian cleared her throat. It wasn't an outlandish idea. Rowanclere had a number of rooms decorated in tartan from the window treatments to the furniture upholstery to the rugs on the floor. "It's the feileadh mor. Look, Jake. See how much cloth is here?"

She took hold of one end of the tartan and whipped it

out in front of her, unfurling the cloth till it lay in a long, straight band across the floor. "Nearly six yards. And notice its weight and weave. Here, feel it."

She held the fabric out for him to touch and when he hesitated, gave it a shake. "Nothing keeps a person as warm as good wool."

"All right." He slid his hand across the soft plaid, then shot her a cautious look. "So you're making a dress from this bolt of fabric?"

"Oh, no. It's not a dress. I know Americans tend to think of the feileadh mor as a skirt, but that is ignorance."

"Gillian," he began, a frown darkening his brow.

"It is a long and proud tradition, something that puts you upstart Texans to shame."

"Now wait one minute." Affront bristled in his voice. "What has you all puckered up? Did Mrs. Ferguson put lemons in her haggis this morning?"

Gillian's mouth was dry as an overcooked haddock. Nervousness sang in her veins, building up pressure and diluting her good sense so that when she finally managed to talk, she babbled forward into the fray with little regard for strategy. "I brought my own father's brooch and dirk. I have a bonnet, too, although I think we can do without that, and both stockings and truis, depending on your preference. Personally, I think you would be more comfortable with stockings. Oh," she snapped her fingers. "I left the sporran in the storage room. I shall need to go get it."

While she paused to draw a breath, the only sound to be heard in the blue drawing room was the muted tick of the mantel clock. Then the Texan replied with a short laugh.

"You won't believe the ridiculous thought I just had. This bundle of yours? For a minute there I thought you might be trying to get me to wear one of those Scottish dresses."

"It's not a dress or a skirt, it's a plaid. And you will wear it. That is the deal you made with Uncle Angus."

He folded his arms, lifted his chin, and looked down his nose, the very picture of an arrogant aristocrat. "No, it is not. The terms of our agreement are very clear. I am an attorney-at-law, remember? I wrote the contract. I agreed to haunt Rowanclere for no longer than a two-week period commencing with the Earl of Harrington's arrival and ending upon either the expiration of the time limit or the departure of your ghost-hunting guest, whichever comes first."

Her nervousness having eased some now that the first shot was fired, Gillian took a moment to shoot him a perplexing look. Who was the real Jake Delaney? This starched-shirt professional or the lazy-drawled rogue? Whichever, he was the most fascinating man.

But she and her granduncle Angus had bested him this time. Now it was up to Jake Delaney to honor his word. She squared her shoulders and smiled. "Pull out your contract and read it. Page two, paragraph three. Cowboy, you agreed to wear a kilt."

Jake stalked from the drawing room and marched to his bedchamber where he dug the signed contract from his saddlebags. "Page two, paragraph three," he muttered, paper rustling as he flipped to the second page.

His eyes skimmed to the third paragraph. It was the seventh sentence that stopped him cold. . . . *will play the part of Brian Brodie, deceased.*

Jake closed his eyes. Obviously, this Brian Brodie was no made-up name like he had thought. "Sonofabitch. Who is Brian Brodie?"

She had followed him up to his room, bringing the damned armful of tartan and toys with her. "Was. Brian Brodie was the fifth laird of Rowanclere. He died here in the castle in 1692, stabbed through the heart after accusing a companion of cheating at cards."

"A violent death? Then why isn't his real ghost haunting the castle? Why do you need a false one?"

Gillian shrugged. "Who is to know the way of the dead? Perhaps he is here and does not indulge in haunting."

"Just my luck. A selfish specter." Jake's gaze returned to the page. "I can't believe I left it wide open. I'm better than that. How did I miss it?"

"I believe you were smeekit at the time."

"Smeekit?"

"Drunk."

"That never mattered before," he snapped, his gaze returning to the words written in his own hand upon the page. "It was the cold. This damnable cold. It froze my brain to the point that even your whisky couldn't thaw it out."

"Stop whining, Texas."

"I'm not whining. I'm complaining." She was part of it, too. His thinking had been numbed by a sexual haze since almost the moment he stepped foot in Rowanclere. "I haven't done this poor a job at lawyering in years."

He couldn't believe he'd gotten himself into this mess. A skirt. A goddamned skirt. If anyone from home ever saw him he'd never live it down. "I want to renegotiate."

"No. Pull off your boots and your shirt. You can leave your trousers on for now."

"Pardon me?"

"I am about to demonstrate the proper way to don the feileadh mor, or belted plaid. It is a bit complicated, so you shall need practice dressing yourself. Rowanclere cannot have a ghaist who is not comfortable in his plaid."

All thought of his pending humiliation fled when Jake realized Gillian Ross was telling him to strip. His mind filled with images of a pair of naked bodies rolling on the bed before him.

Jake stood without moving, watching mutely, while the woman laid a brown leather belt across the bed, then spread the tartan lengthwise atop it. He stared from his bed to Gillian, then back to the bed again.

She was all business as she explained her actions. "Now watch how I fold the tartan neatly in transverse pleats. You will want to leave a foot or so unpleated as aprons on each end."

Jake need only lay his hand on her posterior and give her a tiny push and she would fall upon his bed, there for the taking. He cleared his throat. "I'm not doing this."

Impatience simmered in the look she sent over her shoulder. "Take off your boots and shirt and lie down, Texas. Align your knees with its lower edge."

"No, I said."

She stepped away from the bed and folded her arms. Her gaze swept over him in a scathing glance. "So law means nothing to you? And you, an advocate? Have you no honor? Your contract is not worth the price of paper and ink?"

He hadn't meant he wouldn't wear the skirt. He'd meant he wouldn't wear the woman. "Gillian——"

"I'm surprised, Delaney. Uncle Angus has often told us how Texans tend to exaggerate and redefine the truth to suit their moods. However, he also says that a Texan's word freely given was worthy of trust. He says a man's honor is held in great regard in Texas. It appears my uncle is wrong."

"He isn't wrong. That's not what I . . . oh, forget it." Jake sat on the bed and stuck out his foot, silently demanding her assistance at pulling his boots. "By the way, if I want to whine, it is well within my rights to do so. I may have to do this, but there is nothing in that contract that says I can't grouse about it while it's happening."

The relaxation in her shoulders and spine at his capitulation was subtle, but unmistakable. Jake realized then that despite her bravado, Miss Gillian Ross had harbored doubts about the outcome of the argument. Maybe with a little patience and a bit of thought, he could find a way around this nonsense.

She knelt and tugged at his left boot. The sight of her down on her knees before him was highly erotic, and Jake tried not to watch. He couldn't help himself. When the boot suddenly slid free and momentum carried her back onto her behind, she looked up at him and laughed, her blue eyes sparkling, warming him from the inside out.

Gillian Ross could be a damned fine substitute for a fire. She removed the right boot, set it beside the left at the foot of the bed, then rose gracefully to her feet. Automatically, Jake stood, too. Not six inches of space separated them.

The warmth in his blood burned hotter, his will power waned. Acting on instinct, he lifted his shirt over his head and tossed it aside. "You want me to lie down? How?"

She froze like a doe in a rifle sight. Time seemed to slow as her gaze traveled across his bare shoulders, then down his naked chest. Jake filled his lungs with jasmine-scented air that sent his senses reeling. Heat pooled in his loins.

His own stare focused on Gillian's mouth and he leaned toward her.

But she pulled back, whirled away, and reached for the bundle she'd carried upstairs. "We've no time to waste. Our guest arrives tomorrow and you need to learn this. Here," she tossed him a folded square of white linen. "I found this shirt in one of the trunks. I thought you might prefer to wear it as it will provide added warmth."

Jake inspected the garment, noting laces instead of seams at the sleeves and down the front. He slipped it over his head and flexed his shoulders. A tight fit, but bearable. At least it fell past his backside and helped to conceal his body's reaction to Gillian Ross's attentions.

"That's better," she murmured. "Next . . ."

The devil in him made him rumble, "I'm at your service, Gillian."

Her voice emerged in a thin, reedy squeak, ". . . the feileadh mor."

She wouldn't look him in the eye as she placed her hands on his arms just below the shoulders and positioned him beside the mattress. His skin burned beneath her touch and again, he scented jasmine on the air. It was all he could do to rein in his needs. It wouldn't do to rav-ish the woman, no matter how much his body urged him to do so.

Jake was a man in control of his own desires. He refused to be led around by his pecker. He'd sworn off that on his nineteenth birthday, the day he woke up in an Abilene whorehouse, three dissolute women in his bed, and a queasy sense of shame in his gut. He never wanted to experience that kind of self-disgust again.

Gillian Ross could make him feel it.

A spark smoldered between them that couldn't be denied. He sensed that even a little indulgence could feed the flame, make it flare and burn hot and out-of-control. In some cases, with some women, that would be a pleas-ant interlude. An enjoyable seduction.

With Gillian, everything would be different.

For as much as he liked to play with fire, he could not in good conscience dally with Gillian Ross. Despite her skill with feathers, Gillian was no sporting woman, and he would not treat her as such.

Yet, he could offer her nothing more. He would leave Rowanclere in a matter of days. Africa, China, the Polynesian Isles. He'd waited half his life to be free to go exploring, free of responsibility, free of the ties that bound him so firmly to family and San Antonio, Texas. Now, finally, his time had come. He wouldn't let a han-kering for a beautiful Scottish lass interfere with his plans.

The safest course was not to touch her at all.

Damn.

While Jake lectured himself, Gillian pushed him down upon the bed, trying to act matter-of-factly, betrayed by the tremble in her hands. When she leaned over him, Jake's erection battled with his brain to take charge of his thinking.

Maybe a little touching wouldn't be so bad. Maybe he could indulge a little. He could stop before it went too far. He was strong. He could handle this.

God, he wanted her to handle him.

As his gaze snagged on the generous swell of her bosom, another question occurred. Perhaps she wasn't as chaste as he assumed. Hell, she'd spied on him when he was naked. An innocent maiden would have run away screaming; Gillian made a most suggestive comment. Too, how did a beautiful young maiden come to learn how to dress a man in Highland garb unless she did a bit of the undressing that went along with it?

Wishful thinking, Delaney?

He didn't know. As much as he'd love to have her here and now, the thought of another man knowing her charms made his gut twist.

Meanwhile, Gillian forged ahead, obviously anxious to put this intimacy behind them. "This is the difficult part. You must fold the unpleated ends across your body, first right, then left, making sure you do not disrupt the pleated part while you're about it."

As she folded, her hands brushed his lower stomach, his hips, his thighs. Jake sucked in a deep breath as his cock swelled even more. Good thing he had his pants on.

"Next the belt." She hesitated, her hands hovering on either side of his waist for the space of a heartbeat before she fastened the leather strap around him. Softly, she said, "Stand up and we'll finish it."

He'd rather pull her down against him and finish it his way.

Jake wanted Gillian Ross. He wanted her with an intensity he'd never felt with another woman. It surprised him, shocked him. Disconcerted him.

He held out his hand for Gillian to help pull him to his feet. Her gaze flicked up, met his. He saw his own feelings of confusion and desire reflected in their depths.

She clasped his hand and tugged. Jake rolled smoothly to his feet, but was slow to release her. Her throat bobbed as she swallowed hard.

Gillian yanked herself free of him and took a big step back. "The sporran. We need it. I shall bring it." She darted from the room as quickly as Scooter after a bird.

Jake could breathe again.

Alone now, he tugged at the bottom of the skirt that hit him a good two inches above the knees. Funny how naked the garment made him feel even with his pants still on. But then, if he were wearing just the skirt and not these britches that got tighter every time Gillian touched him, wouldn't he be a helluva lot more comfortable? Maybe these Scots had the right idea after all.

"Hell, when in Rome," he muttered, his fingers reaching beneath the tartan.

Jake dropped his pants, then kicked them out of the way. Walking over to the mirror, he braced his hands on his hips and studied his reflection. Hmm. *Never realized my legs were so hairy.*

Turning sideways, he took two steps forward, then two back, watching the swing of the skirt. Hell, a good wind would bare him but good. Cool him down, too. Around Gillian, that would come in handy.

The female in question knocked briskly on the door

even as she walked into his room. "I have the sporran, Mr. De . . ."

Her voice trailed off as her gaze dropped to his bare legs.

"Laugh and I'll have to hurt you," Jake warned.

"Oh, my. I see nothing to laugh about. You wear the feileadh mor as if it were made for you."

With the approval in her tone, the tension returned. The air between them all but vibrated. "Gillian, I want—"

She pasted on a cheery smile that looked as fake as her voice sounded false. "Excellent. It's a bonny fold, too. I must say I did a fine job of it, considering I've never worn the belted plaid myself."

"I wondered about that. Just how did you learn to do this?"

Had he not been watching closely, he'd have missed the shadow that crossed her face.

"An old friend taught me."

Suspicious, Jake waited for further explanation, but it wasn't forthcoming. His eyes narrowed. That was a damned strange reaction.

Before he could pursue it, she gestured toward a gilt-edged mirror and spoke in an instructive tone. "Look in the glass. The hard part is done, and now you can adjust the plaid to suit your mood or the weather. Like this," she explained as she pulled the unpleated portion up over his shoulders, her touch brisk and businesslike. "You can wear it for a cloak. You'll like it this style because it is good for keeping warm."

She stood at his side, close enough for him to detect that jasmine scent again. Never mind the feather spiders, this was true torture. "Yes, I can tell."

If she heard the rueful note in his voice, she ignored it. "To wear it in the usual fashion, and in the manner in which our Brian Brodie should present himself, we shall drop the plaid from your shoulders so you are wearing the double skirt again."

"Skirt? Let's use a different term, shall we, Gillian?"

Damned if her lips didn't twitch into a grin. Damned if those beautiful blue eyes didn't sparkle.

Jake glanced away from the intriguing sight and gritted his teeth. He didn't want to laugh. He wanted to howl. He wanted to throw her onto the bed and teach her how a Texan undressed.

Instead, he tried to think of something else—anything else—and watched in the mirror as she took the outermost front part of the plaid, rolled it up a bit, then tucked it into his belt at the small of his back. Then, he found a distraction. "You've made me a tail," he protested.

"Quit whining or I'll find you horns to match. Now, we take the right portion in front and your tail in back and join them on the shoulder with the brooch," she said, describing the actions as she performed them. "When we tuck the rest of the front into the belt, it appears you are only wearing a sash across your chest."

Stepping back, she studied him, then nodded with satisfaction. "See how the left shoulder wrap allows freedom of your dominant arm for battle? Isn't that ingenious?"

"Uh huh," he said, his attention caught by the purse of her mouth.

"And Texas? That day you spent hiding at the watchtower? Had you been wearing the feileadh mor, all you'd need have done was remove the brooch like this . . ." she plucked the pin from his shoulders ". . . and you'd have had your pillow and blanket right there with you."

As she gathered up the cloth to demonstrate, her hands brushed his arousal. Gillian jerked back and the tension between them flared thicker and hotter.

Ever so slowly, Jake reached out a finger, touched the soft skin beneath her chin, and tilted her face up.

"You stir me, Gillian Ross," he told her, his voice low and rough with desire. "You warm me like a San Antonio summer, and you make me want to take . . . what I shouldn't."

"Jake . . . I . . ." She licked her lips.

And he was lost.

eight

HOW COULD THIS man complain of being cold so much? He was fire inside. Kissing Jake Delaney was like diving headfirst into a volcano.

His lips slashed across hers, urgent and insistent and hungry. His tongue probed and stroked and demanded her response. Gillian gave freely. Joyfully. With a wondrous sigh.

Jake Delaney wanted her. Quite badly, judging by his reaction. The knowledge eased the burden of self-doubt that had weighted her heart for months. Her femininity had needed the affirmation. Receiving it allowed her passion to soar.

Jittery with desire, Gillian poured herself into the kiss. She answered him nip for nip, stroke for stroke, and when he rumbled a low, greedy moan, she replied with a feral purr.

His hands glided up her sides, cupped her breasts. His nails scratched across her erect nipples and a bolt of pure lust, hot and dangerous, shot from the tips of his fingers to the core of her womanhood.

Unprepared for the intensity of the sensation, Gillian shied. She broke the kiss, stepped back from him, and wrapped her arms around herself, defensively, protectively. "I . . . I don't know . . . I didn't mean. . . ."

"Me either." Breathing hard, he looked away. Arms at his sides, his hands fisted, then flexed, then fisted again. "Kind of got away from us, didn't it?"

It was a far cry from a declaration of devotion most any woman would hope to hear after such an intimate exchange. Something of her feelings must have shown in her expression because he hastened to say, "Make no mistake. You pack a punch, princess. A powerful punch."

Uncertain how to respond to that, she settled for the truth. "So do you."

The grin he flashed was a brazen combination of arrogance, wickedness, and masculinity. He tipped an imaginary hat and Gillian had an absurd mental flash of Jake Delaney dressed in the feileadh mor, but wearing his cowboy boots rather than stockings, a gunbelt instead of a dirk, and a wide-brimmed straw hat as opposed to the traditional Highland bonnet.

That mental image burned away when he added a slow wink to the hat-tipping. A vivid memory replaced it—Jake Delaney standing naked in front of the fireplace his first night at Rowanclere.

Gillian felt the heat of a blush stain her cheeks.

"So very beautiful," Jake murmured. "Prettier than the scene outside the tower window. Why, if a man had that view to look at outside, and you in his bed inside, he'd have to wonder if he'd died and gone to heaven."

Her mouth was dry as Young Fergus's bones. "I cannot go to your bed, sir."

He arched a brow. "I don't intend to ask you."

She took it like a slap to the face, flinching backward as she said, "Oh."

Jake grimaced and waved a hand. "No, I didn't mean it that way. Believe me, Gillian Ross, I want you in my bed. I want that very, very much."

His deep, resonant tone rang with truth, soothing her hurt and stoking the still smoldering coals of her desire. "I don't understand. Why did you . . . ?"

He raked his fingers through his hair. "You questioned my honor earlier. Well, my own personal code has a paragraph or ten about how a man should treat a lady. I won't stay in Scotland, Gillian. I have plans . . . dreams . . . and for the first time in a very long time, I'll be free to pursue them as soon as I wrap up this business with the Declaration."

He spoke to her at length, then, about his travel plans. He painted pictures of tropical flowers and sugar-sand beaches. He spoke of deserts and pyramids and jungles. "I want to see a tiger in the wild. Don't know why exactly, but it's something I've always dreamed of seeing. With Chrissy settled and my mother happily established in London Society, I'll be able to board my southbound ship in good conscience. Do you understand now, Gillian? Do you see why this can go no further?"

"Aye, I believe I do."

He took her hand, brought it to his lips, and kissed it. "I will not take advantage of you, princess, no matter how much I'd like to do just that."

"Well." Gillian picked up the sporran and smoothed down the fur adorning the flap. "Not every man feels as you do, Texas. I think I like you."

"I know I like you." His laugh was rueful. "Too much."

She handed him the sporran and instructed him how to fasten the strap around him so that the bag hung in front. It would have been easier to do it herself, but she had learned the danger of that. When he had arranged it to her satisfaction, she asked, "So, where does that leave us?"

Jake sat on the bed and donned the stockings, then slipped the sgian-dhu in the right one at her direction. "This is one part of the costume I agree with."

"I thought you might."

Then he took a deep breath and added, "Since becoming lovers isn't in the cards, how about we give being friends a shot? I can always use another friend, Gillian."

Friends, not lovers. Yes, that was better. She tried to ignore the sinking in her stomach as she nodded and said, "All right, friends it is."

"Good. All right, then." His gaze stroked over her and he winced. "I think we'll be able to manage it, don't you?"

"Aye."

"As long as we don't touch. Touching is . . . dangerous."

"Aye. No touching." Carefully, she handed him a pair of leather shoes with buckles on the top. "I hope these are not too small. They were the largest I could find."

Jake attempted to squeeze into the footwear, but the fit was simply too tight. "Don't worry about it," he said as Gillian clicked her tongue in concern. "I'll wear my boots."

At that, she hung her head and sighed. "No. That will not do at all." After a moment's thought, she continued, "Agnes Armstrong might have some to fit. Her man

Ronald wore the feileadh mor in a theatrical production a few summers ago, and he and you are of a size. The arrangements have all been made for the churching and baptism in the morning, and all is ready for Lord Harrington's arrival tomorrow afternoon. A trip across the loch today will be most welcome."

"Across the loch?" Jake asked. "How? Will you sail? Who will take you?"

"I shall take myself, but I will row. It is a relatively short trip, and I am better with oars than sails."

"I'll go with you, then. Maybe we can steal an hour or two to fish. I have a couple of Castaway Bait Company fishing lures I've been wanting to try out in your Scottish lakes. Think you can rustle up a pair of poles to take along with us?"

She frowned. "You want to fish? With me?"

"It's a decent substitute. Besides, fishing is a good activity to share with a friend. What do you say, friend? Wanna go fishing?"

Friends. Simply friends. Gillian licked her lips. What would it hurt to spend a little time with a friend? Slowly, she nodded. "On the way back to Rowanclere. First we must find you shoes."

"It's a deal. When do you want to go? Right away?"

"I need to see Robyn settled into her lessons. Plan to meet me down by the water in, say, half an hour?"

"All right. It may take me that long to get out of this dress and back into my pants."

She rolled her eyes at his choice of words, then turned to leave. At the doorway, she paused. "You might want to stop and ask Mrs. Ferguson for scraps to use for bait in case you have little luck with your artificial lures."

"I reckon I could." Jake dragged a hand along his jawline. "Though I doubt I'll use anything else. I've a feeling the ice cold waters of Loch Rowanclere is just the place to drown my Throbbing Bob."

Jake wore two pairs of socks inside his boots and his wool coat as he rowed the small boat out onto the loch. They weren't fifty yards offshore before he stripped off the coat. A hundred yards out, he'd lost the extra pair of socks, too.

He tried to tell himself the exercise warded off the chill he had expected. He knew he was lying to himself. He knew responsibility for his unaccustomed warmth could be laid at his fishing buddy's deliciously bare feet.

He'd groaned aloud, then blamed it on the rowboat's hard seat when she took off her shoes and stockings. If she'd been trying to be seductive, he might have had an easier time resisting her appeal. But Gillian was all innocent delight in the "warm" summer afternoon and the attraction of a new-to-her pastime—fishing with artificial bait.

She was giving Jake's Musky Wriggler a workout.

"It's been months and months since I fished," she told him. "Uncle Angus used to take us out often, but his puir joints pain him too much now to get in and out of the boat. I have forgotten how much fun fishing can be."

"It's fun because I'm being a good sport about taking your catch off the hook for you."

"Hah. You would rather do it yourself because you are afraid I will lose your lure."

What he wished was that she would lose her allure. Instead, with every giggle or wriggle or flex of her toes, she reeled him in a little more. What an idiot he'd been to think he could look at her as only a friend.

The hours they'd spent together since leaving Rowanclere had made the situation worse instead of better. Sure they had laughed and talked as friends do, but learning about one another served to increase the air of intimacy between them rather than erecting a wall like he had hoped. When she dangled a toe over the side of the boat, testing the temperature of the water, he found himself fantasizing licking it dry.

Desperate, he searched for a distraction. He offered her an apple from the picnic lunch they'd brought with them, and took another for himself. Sinking his teeth into the sweet, crisp fruit, he chewed thoughtfully for a moment before asking, "So, why do you want to sell your home?"

"I don't want to sell it. I love Rowanclere."

Jake changed lures from the Castaway Bait Company's Texas Doodle Spring Hook to their Scalloped Spoon. "If you love it, why sell it?"

"Because it's Uncle Angus's decision, and he is too stubborn to know when to come in out of the cold. He thinks this is the right thing for me and Robyn."

It was a mistake to give her the juicy apple. Every time she licked her lips, Jake wanted to howl. He cleared his throat. "Why would it be good for you and the squirt? Y'all seem happy here."

"We are happy." Gillian lowered her half-eaten apple and scowled. "Actually, Uncle Angus is doing this more on my account than for Robyn. He fears if he doesn't sell the castle, I will someday find myself in a situation like David's. It's his way of preparing to gae doon the brae."

Jake deduced that "gae doon the brae" meant to die, but the rest of what she said remained a puzzle. Who the hell was David, what was his situation, and why did she have a bite in her voice when she said his name? "You've lost me."

Gillian set her apple aside, then flicked her wrist sharply and sent her fishing line sailing. "You've been up to my granduncle's room in the past few days, have you not?"

"Yes. He showed me the Declaration. What does this have to do with this David person?"

The sadness in her smile caught him by surprise. "It's all part of the tale. Now, when you visited Uncle Angus's chamber, did you not wonder why he sleeps in a drafty old room built on top of the castle wall?"

Jake didn't care about Angus Brodie's sleeping arrangements, but he tempered down his impatience. If telling her story in her own time would get rid of the melancholy air that had suddenly enveloped them like a fog, then he'd sit here all day. "Lots of things in this country of yours seem strange to me. Men in skirts, for instance."

She threw her apple at him. Jake grinned and added, "That Crow's Nest room is a curiosity. Tell me about it, princess."

She nodded regally. "My maternal great-grandfather had three children: John Brodie, my grandmother Margaret, and Angus Brodie, who is our Uncle Angus. Angus and John hated one another. The trouble started when they were little more than boys. It was over a girl."

"Isn't it always?"

She rolled her eyes at that bit of truth. "John Brodie's

first sweetheart was a fickle wench, and for some reason, she set her sights on Angus. Of course she made it look as if Angus had stolen her away from John, even though it was truly her fault."

"That hussy," Jake said, distracted by the way sunlight glistened in her golden hair.

"Aye. She turned brother against brother. John nursed his animosity toward Angus for years until he saw the chance to retaliate. After their father died and he inherited Rowanclere, John convinced Uncle Angus's one true love to marry him rather than Angus."

Jake's gaze drifted to the thick, curling lashes that framed eyes of brilliant blue. "An eye for an eye."

Gillian wrinkled her nose. "She was a weak woman, allowing John's money and title to sway her."

"Happens all the time."

"Uncle Angus was better off without her."

"Maybe so." Jake released the top two buttons on his shirt. He was getting hot. "Is that why he went to Texas?"

"It's part of the reason. He says he might have remained here just to cause them trouble, but John became stingy with the purse strings. He had control over Uncle Angus's trust, you see."

Jake didn't see, but he didn't interrupt. He wanted her to get to the David part and besides, when she was talking, she didn't wiggle her toes nearly as often as she did when she was quiet.

"They had a horrible fight—from what I am told, it is a wonder no one was killed. That's when Uncle Angus swore he would never spend another night beneath the roof of Rowanclere Castle. He soon left Scotland and eventually settled in Texas."

"Ah," said Jake. Now the story made a little more sense. "So when John Brodie died, your uncle inherited Rowanclere and—"

"He kept his vow. He built the Crow's Nest." She scowled at the Musky Wriggler on the end of her line. "It was fine at first, but once the rheums took hold of him, getting up and down all the stairs became pure misery. He's a stubborn old Scot and won't give in. As a result, he seldom comes downstairs anymore."

She set down her fishing pole accompanied by a sigh. "It's not a good way to live, Jake. It's always drafty, and in winter when bitter winds howl around the walls . . . well, ye can imagine the effect it can have on an elderly man's lungs. It's dangerous. If he stays here one more winter, I fear he'll either catch an ague or suffer a bad fall. Either could kill him."

Jake grabbed for her line and removed the lure, switching out the Wriggler with a spinner bait. "I see your point. Why doesn't he just build another structure on the ground and connect it to the main part of the castle with a hallway? That wouldn't break his vow."

"You are right, and he had agreed to do exactly that, then David's father died and everything changed." Gillian shifted in her seat, calling Jake's attention to her toes once again. "Uncle Angus realized the precariousness of my position and decided to put Rowanclere up for sale."

Requiring a little help in maintaining the friendship parameter, he reached out and grabbed the hem of her skirt, rearranging it to cover her feet. "I'm confused again."

"Our coffers are empty, Jake," she replied. "John

Brodie beggared the estate, mainly out of spite because Uncle Angus was to inherit. We've managed to get by, but once Uncle Angus passes on, death taxes will take what is left. He doesn't want me to be forced to marry for money."

"Hmm . . . that's something else that happens all the time. What about this brother I've heard mentioned? Why isn't he here helping out? Aren't you his responsibility?"

"I am responsible for myself, thank you."

Damn, but she was pretty when her eyes flashed like that. Jake held up his hands, palms out. "Sorry, didn't mean to pull your trigger. It's just that I have a little sister, too, and I know how I feel when she's in trouble."

"I'm not in trouble and besides, as far as we know, Nicholas knows nothing about what has happened here in the years that he has been gone. He doesn't know about our parents' accident, or that the Rosses were cruel to me and my sisters, and that Uncle Angus rescued us."

"Why is that? Are you not in touch?"

She shrugged. "He went exploring and we have not heard from him since the year Robyn was born. He sent Flora and me a gift for our birthday. Hair ribbons all the way from your state, Jake. From Dallas, Texas. Every month Uncle Angus sends out inquiries about his whereabouts, but nothing has come of them. In all honesty, I fear he is. . . ."

Dead, Jake silently finished.

Gillian closed her eyes, lifted her face toward the sun, and wistfully said, "It is one of my most heartfelt wishes that he return home someday."

Jake decided right then and there to send a letter to

Cole Morgan in Texas asking him to make some inquiries into the matter of one Nicholas Ross. "So, back to this situation you mentioned earlier. Who is this David person?"

Gillian yanked her fishing pole and the line came sailing from the water. The spinner missed hooking Jake's ear by less than two inches. "What the—?"

"Apardon." She laid her pole in the bottom of the rowboat. "I think we should go now. I am certain I have much to do."

Jake stowed his own pole, then grabbed the oars. *We're not going anywhere just yet, not after a reaction like that.* "Gillian, who is David?"

She frowned as if she'd tasted something bitter. "David Maclean."

Jake waited, then finally asked, "And David Maclean is . . . ?"

"We were to be married. He was my betrothed. But David broke his promise."

Her betrothed.

Her love.

He broke his promise and her heart.

Though she'd sworn never to cry over him again, today the memory of David Maclean brought the sting of tears to Gillian's eyes. She could feel the Texan's questioning stare upon her, then he asked a few too-personal questions. Gillian refused to address them. She refused to even look at him, in fact, keeping her gaze turned stoically toward the shore.

Jake finally dipped the oars into the water and rowed toward land. He asked her no more questions, and she was thankful for his silence. Her thoughts were a whirlpool of confusion and she needed quiet to sort them.

Why had she brought up David's name? Why had she talked of him now and with Jake Delaney, of all people?

You wanted him to know.

Gillian frowned and watched the white cap of a wave break upon the deep blue surface of the loch. She wanted him to know what? That she had been loved? That in times past another man had told her she was his sun and sky and moon and stars? That she had given him her heart?

And he had broken it.

Gillian sucked in a breath. No, she knew no urge to lay her pride at Jake's feet. Previous experience with David had taught her that road led only to humiliation.

Questions swirled around and around in her mind. David and Jake. Jake and David.

He wants nothing more than friendship. He told you. Believe him.

Don't let history repeat itself.

Back at Rowanclere, she thanked Jake for his time and assistance, then fled, leaving him to stow the boat. She avoided the Texan for the rest of the day. She could not, however, ignore him in her sleep.

Old ghaists and new emotions haunted Gillian's dreams that night, and she awoke early the next morning filled with a blue spirit. Seeking a remedy, she made her way to Flora's room and knocked softly on the door.

"Aye? Come in," said her sister.

Gillian found the new mother sitting up in bed nursing one of the boys. The second infant lay in his cradle, awake and sucking his thumb. "Where is Alasdair?"

Flora rolled her eyes. "The silly man was up before dawn, pacing the floor. He is fashing himself ill over the boys, but for now it is Reverend Gregor's problem, not mine."

Lips twitching, Gillian asked, "What has he done now?"

"He's afeared the reverend will forget the baptism. He rode into the village to make certain he doesn't go somewhere else this morning."

"But that's—"

"I know. He is anxious to see the babes named before something happens amiss."

"Your Alasdair has a difficult time leaving the old ways behind, doesn't he?"

"Aye." Flora smiled down at the son in her arms. "Although we are not much different. Are you not the person who first placed the silver coins in my sons' cradles?"

"And are you not the mama who made certain the first time the bairns left your room they were carried up the stairs for good luck, instead of downstairs and risk the bad?"

"Your Jake thought I was crazy."

"He is not my Jake." Gillian sniffed. "And why Alasdair trusted the Texan to carry one of his boys is beyond me. I thought he might faint when you placed the bairn in his arms."

The babe in the cradle squirmed and began to whimper. At Flora's nod, Gillian gathered up the child and sat in the rocking chair beside Flora's bed.

Peace stole over her like a new dawn as she rocked the bairn. For a time, the sisters did not speak, content to share the quiet. Minutes passed and the unsettlement that lingered from her dreams gradually faded. What was it about holding a wee one in your arms that made everything right with the world?"

"It is a lie, you know," she observed, breaking the silence.

"What is a lie?"

"The true purpose of rocking a bairn is not to soothe the child, but the adult. I shall miss this when you leave. I know it is best you return to Laichmoray today, but I shall miss you dreadfully."

"If you need us to stay. . . ."

"Nae. I heard that Alasdair's mother has returned from Edinburgh. I know she must be anxious to see the bairns."

Flora nodded. "Her note arrived last night. She said she will see our bairns today if she must walk to Rowanclere."

"We can't have that," Gillian said with a small laugh. "Not while Lord Harrington is here. Your mother-in-law is a dear, but she's a puir teller of tales and would surely give the game away." She nuzzled the baby in her arms, pressing little kisses against his downy cheek. Her sigh floated on the air like a bedraggled ribbon.

Gently, Flora asked, "I think it is more than our leaving here that has you upset. What is wrong, Gilly?"

"Nothing." Then, after a moment's pause, "Everything."

"You are nervous about the earl's visit?"

"Most definitely."

"When does the haunting begin?"

"Jake has a series of incidents planned for tonight."

Gillian sighed. "But you are right, it is more than simply the fact I will miss you dreadfully. It is more than just the haunting, Flora."

When she didn't continue, her twin prodded, "Yes?"

"I dreamed of David. And I kissed Jake Delaney."

Flora pursed her lips in thought as she switched the nursing infant from one breast to the other. "That is very interesting news, sister. And did the dreaming and kissing occur concurrently? Did you think about that man— and I will not say his name aloud because it might cause my milk to curdle—while you kissed the Texan?"

"Oh, no. My mind would not work at all while I was kissing Jake."

Flora's expression lit with interest. "No?"

"He made me as fuzzy as a lamb."

A smile blossomed. "My, my, my. So what is the problem? What does that-man-whose-name-I-will-not-say have to do with Jake Delaney?"

Gillian smiled down into Flora's squirming son's face, then lifted him to her shoulder. Rubbing circles on his tiny back, she said, "I am bothered by the nature of the dream, Flora. It was a warning."

"In what way?"

"I think . . ." Gillian's teeth tugged at her bottom lip. "I dreamed of the day I received word of David's marriage. I relived all that hurt and anger and grief once again. I think I dreamed of that day because Jake Delaney poses a similar risk."

"He does? Tell me."

Gillian didn't ken quite how to explain. "Jake Delaney makes me . . . yearn. Like David did, but different. More."

"More?"

"More."

Flora pursed her lips in thought. "I like Mr. Delaney. I think the two of you would suit. If you like him, too, which from the sounds of it you do, then what is amiss?"

"He took me fishing yesterday."

"And . . . ?"

"The man likes to talk while he rows a boat."

Flora watched and waited, and when Gillian didn't continue, spoke in an exasperated tone. "Please, sister. My bairns have more to say than you."

Gillian smiled ruefully, then attempted to make some sense of the thoughts rolling around in her mind. "As soon as Angus gives him the Declaration of Independence, he is leaving Rowanclere, leaving Scotland. He's going exploring, adventuring all over the world. In the meantime, he wants us to be friends."

"Oh." Flora's mouth dipped in a frown. "That is a bit of bad luck. And he wishes you to be friends and nothing more?"

"Nothing more. I thought it was a good idea myself when he proposed it. But tell me, sister, how does a woman go about being friends with a man who awakens all her feminine desires?"

"He frightens you."

"He terrifies me. He is attractive and witty and good-hearted. He is strong and masculine and just wicked enough to be intriguing."

"You are afraid you will fall in love with him."

Gillian shut her eyes. "Aye. Exactly. It is what I fear the most. That's all I need, to fall in love with yet another man who will leave me. God's truth, Flora, were it not for Lord Harrington's pending arrival, I would give Jake that document he wants so badly and send him on his way."

Her sister pondered the problem for a moment, then said, "Maybe he will fall in love with you, too. Maybe he won't leave."

Gillian gave a short, bitter laugh. "And did I not think David would return to me until the very day we received his wedding announcement? I can't go through that again. I *won't* go through it again." She pressed another kiss to the infant's forehead, inhaled his sweet scent, and was soothed.

Flora removed the other child from her breast and lifted him to her shoulder. Patting the babe's back, she gazed at her sister with concern. "Then don't. You are a strong woman, Gilly. You can resist him."

"Aye, that I can. I hope." Gillian sighed. "Oh, Flora. 'Twould be a much easier task if I did not like him so much and were he not such a bonny braw man."

The babe in Gillian's arms began to cry and the two women switched infants. Flora adopted the maternal tone she'd been practicing of late and lectured. "Aye, Mr. Delaney is a fine one, but he is certainly not the only fine man in Scotland. Perhaps you are making too much of this, Gilly. After all, he is the first man who has engaged your interest since That One cried off. Perhaps your reaction does not have as much to do with the Texan as it does with what is happening inside of you. Maybe you have finally healed. Maybe once this situation with Rowanclere is settled, you will find another man who attracts you in the same way as does Mr. Delaney."

As she considered her sister's words, a spark of hope

lit inside Gillian. Maybe Flora was right. Maybe this wasn't about Jake Delaney at all. Maybe it was all about David Maclean and the fact that she was finally over the man. Maybe she *was* ready to fall in love again.

With somebody other than Jake Delaney, that is.

Jake stood in the Great Hall watching with interest as the howdie carried both Dunbar babies into the room. The infants both wore white dresses twice as long as their little bodies. Jake was tempted to make a comment about training boys young to wear these Scottish skirts, but in good conscience he couldn't. His mother had proudly displayed Jake's own baptismal gown upon occasion, and it was even frillier than these boys' dresses.

In all honesty, Jake felt honored to have been invited to the baptism this morning. Everyone else in attendance could claim family ties of one sort or another to the Rosses or the Dunbars.

The reverend waited in the center of the hall beside a table draped in a snowy white cloth. Alasdair Dunbar and his beautiful wife stood next to the churchman, their eyes glowing with pride and emotion as they watched their sons. Jake couldn't help but note the differences in the kilt the Scotsman wore and the plaid Gillian had so enticingly wrapped around him yesterday. His was longer, thank God, and less fussy. And did these men truly need to wear knives in their stockings to a private christening?

Gillian stood beside her sister, misty-eyed and wearing an expression of such loving tenderness as she gazed at the babies that Jake had to look away. A sudden, uninvited picture flashed through his mind of that woman wearing that expression while watching another baby, his baby. Their baby.

Jake's knees went a little weak. Where the hell had that come from?

Maybe it was a leftover from the nightmares that had plagued him during the night.

He'd dreamed of missing his boat. Half the night he'd spent running, riding, and even swimming toward the ship that would carry him off on his adventures. Never once had he made it. Each time he'd been delayed by a wraith who wrapped chains around his legs. A wraith with long golden hair and bluebonnet eyes and a kiss as sweet as cane sugar, straight from the field.

Not too hard to analyze those nightmares. Gillian Ross posed a threat to his real-life dreams.

Only if you do something extraordinarily stupid. You're smarter than that.

That's what his best friend Cole used to think, too. Right before he bedded Jake's sister, Chrissy, and found himself posing that leg-shackling question.

With that unpleasant thought haunting his mind, Jake forced his attention back to the baptismal proceedings.

The howdie approached the table where a water-filled basin sat next to a Bible and the papers certifying the children's births. The midwife stopped in front of Flora and handed her the infant she'd carried in her right arm. Flora looked the child over closely, then, cradling the babe in her arms, faced her husband. Alasdair reached into his right jacket pocket and removed a slip of paper and a pin.

Jake spotted a tremor in the man's hands as he pinned

the paper to his son's gown. Jake wondered what the paper signified and became especially curious when the process was repeated with the second child, only this time Alasdair withdrew a paper from his left pocket.

The minister began the service with a prayer, giving thanks for a living mother and living bairns. He followed that up with a few passages from Scripture. Jake took the opportunity to make his way toward Gillian, telling himself he was moving closer to the children to spy what was written on the notes, not because the woman drew him like a frosty glass of lemonade on a hot summer day.

He caught a whiff of jasmine just as the minister began to ask Dunbar a series of questions. As the man answered "Aye" to each of them, Jake angled his head closer to Gillian, pretending that he was trying to get a good look at the babies. Mainly he wanted to lose himself in her scent.

"Present your child for baptism," said the minister.

Alasdair took one of the children from Flora's arms and held his head over the basin. The churchman dipped his hand into the water and sprinkled the child. While the baby puckered up to fuss, the minister frowned over the slip of paper pinned to the dress below the infant's feet. "Twa ells and a half o' plaiding? Wha ever heard o' such a name for a bairn?"

Gillian gasped. Alasdair choked and turned red as his tartan and Flora slapped her husband on the shoulder. "That is the merchant's account, you fool." She dug into his pocket, removed a second square of paper, checked it, then shoved it toward the minister.

"The child's name is Duncan," he stated, looking relieved as he spoke to the assembly. He then made the sign of the cross saying, "Duncan, I baptize thee in the name of the Father, and of the Son, and of the Holy Ghost, One God blessed forever. Amen."

Without pause, the minister repeated the procedure with Duncan's twin, sprinkling the water, then saying, "The child's name is Douglas."

This time the baby didn't cry, a situation promptly remedied when his father gave him a quick pinch. Jake just shook his head while the minister continued on with the blessing. Never in his life had he run across such a superstitious bunch of people. Just the ones involving infants were enough to make his head spin.

Gillian had run through some of them when Jake had the audacity to question what names the babies had been given the day they were born. You'd have thought he'd threatened their poor little heads the way Angus and Alasdair reacted. Those two had all but drawn their dirks as Gillian hastened to soothe waters. Later, she'd explained why. Apparently, one of the seemingly thousands of superstitions these Highlanders held dear to their hearts included a ban on saying a child's name aloud before his christening.

Jake would bet his favorite shirt that the pinch he just witnessed involved another one. He wondered what foolishness they believed might happen to the babe if he didn't cry when he was baptized.

However, both Duncan and Douglas Dunbar had successfully squealed while being sprinkled, and no one dared to speak their name before the minister said it. Judging by the collective sigh of relief from the small congregation, all must be well in the superstition department.

With the ceremony concluded, bread and cheese were

set before the guests, along with a glass of whisky. Each person present raised the drink in toast to the children. As the turn worked around to him, Jake tried to search his brain for pretty words with which to salute the infant's long life and good health. He kept losing his train of thought because Gillian distracted him. First with the sparkle in her eyes, then the light music of her laughter, and finally, when she lifted her glass and spoke with the burr of Scotland thicker in her voice than he'd previously heard. "Wissin the company's gueede health and grace and growan to m'nephews Duncan and Douglas." Then she leaned over, kissed her brother-in-law on his cheek, and added, "And givin' a special thanks to Reverend Gregor that the bairns dinna end up with the name of 'Twa ells' and 'half o' plaiding.' "

Jake thought a laughing, teasing Gillian Ross was one of the prettiest sights he'd ever seen. Absently, he wondered if the sun-kissed beaches of Tahiti could compare. At that moment, he wasn't particularly anxious to find out.

The realization stopped him. Shocked him. What the hell was the matter with him?

Before he could put his finger on it, his turn for saluting the Dunbar boys came round. Distracted, he offered the first salute that came to mind. "Here's hoping your lives are gooder'n grits."

The people in Rowanclere's Great Hall all smiled politely, though Jake could tell the Southern saying didn't quite make the translation to Scots. He didn't care. All his attention was once again focused on Gillian. She was playing with one of the babies, nuzzling his chin, her expression tender and brimming with love.

Gillian with a babe in her arms. So beautiful. So right.

Imagine how she'd look playing with her own child. His child. Their child.

Damn. He'd done it again. Hell, better he imagine her lying naked beneath him on a Bora Bora beach than this. Gillian Ross didn't need to dress in a filmy gown and carry a wooden head to haunt a man. The woman did it just by existing.

"I've gotta get out of here," he murmured.

Standing beside him, young Robbie heard him and asked, "What's the matter, Mr. Jake?"

"Uh, I need to check on Scooter. I left her shut up in my room and I imagine it's time she went out."

"I'll go with you." The girl slipped her hand in Jake's. "I haven't seen her all day and besides, I have an idea I want to talk to you about. You know the chair with wheels that Alasdair bought for Uncle Angus that he is too proud to use? Well, I've been thinking about it and I think we could make something like that for Scooter. What do you think?"

What he thought was that he was damned glad that his mother wasn't here to see his reaction to Gillian. "I'd find myself hog-tied before sunset," he grumbled.

"Hog tied?" Robbie repeated. "What does that have to do with Scooter?"

His mother would like Gillian. Of course, Elizabeth Delaney was so anxious to get him married that she'd like anything in skirts in whom Jake showed an interest.

At that point he realized Robyn was tugging on his arm. ". . . Jake . . . Mr. Jake . . . Please. Can we make one? It will give you something to do between the hoaxes you play on the ghost hunter. Gilly says you have to stay hidden, so you will be restless. I have been thinking about

Scooter. I don't think she needs to stay hidden away too since you are not using her in your haunts. She and I can still play together each day, can we not? We shall both be so sad not to take our walks in the woods. She does so love to bark at the squirrels."

"Sure, sweetheart. Whatever you want," Jake responded absently, his attention drawn to movement out on the drive. A carriage approached drawn by two of the finest matched bays he had ever seen. As the conveyance drew closer, he spied a crest on the door. He'd seen enough of these in London to know what it meant. "Gillian? Could you come here a minute, please?"

She met his gaze for the first time all day. "Yes?"

"Looks like it's time for me to adjourn to my grave. Looks like your guest has arrived a bit early."

She followed the path of his gaze, then said, "Guid fegs. Aye, it is the Earl of Harrington." She cleared her throat, and spoke loudly, "Excuse me, everyone. I'm afraid our merriment must draw to a close. Harrington is arriving now."

After a moment's calm, chaos reigned as servants fled to their place of duty. Alasdair all but pushed Reverend Gregor along his way back to his church, and Flora instructed the howdie to return the bairns to the nursery. Angus shuffled over to the window to peer outside. "Fine looking horseflesh, there."

Jake agreed. Behind him, he heard Flora wish her sister luck as her husband attempted to hurry her back to her bedchamber.

Gillian pulled on his sleeve. "Come away from the window, Jake. They might see you. You need to enter the passages now."

"In a minute," he replied. He figured the chances of

being seen were slim, and besides, he wanted to get a look at the man who would be his main target that evening.

He watched as the coach's door opened and a male figure descended to the ground. "Anybody got a spyglass on them?" he asked.

Damned if Angus didn't slap one against his shoulder. "It's my habit to carry it. Use it often up in the Crow's Nest."

Grinning, Jake extended the scope and held it up to his eye. The dapper earl was speaking to someone inside the coach. He held up his hand as though to offer assistance, and sure enough, a slipper and the hem of a bright yellow skirt came into view. "Looks like the earl brought—"

Jake broke off abruptly. *Oh God, I'm dead.*

"Mother?"

nine

GILLIAN SAW JAKE'S skin bleach white. His expression soured, reminding her of the look on Robbie's face right before she lost the contents of her stomach. Tugging hard on his arm, she said, "Best move away from the window, Jake. You do not wish to be seen."

And she didn't wish to have the draperies soiled.

Gillian's own stomach twisted nervously. The Earl of Harrington had arrived. The game was begun. "Hurry, Texas. I must go downstairs, and you need to disappear into the passages. Please!"

"What have I done to deserve this?" he replied, his feet all but glued to the floor. "Have I not been a loving, dutiful son?"

Trying to move this man was like pushing against an oak tree. He didn't budge.

"Have I not put my family's needs before my own for years?"

Gillian drew back her foot and kicked him hard in the shin. "Would you listen to me? This is not the time to indulge in rhetorical questions. Get ready to play a ghaist afore I make you one in truth!"

He scowled at her as he reached down to rub his leg. Pain must have cut through the fog. Good. "Why did you do that?"

"Just get in the passageway! I dinna have time for any more of this."

"Well, fine." Green eyes flashed. "Don't mind me. I'm only mired in a crisis here. You see that woman down there with your earl?"

"He's not my earl."

"Well, she's mine. My mother, to be precise."

Gillian glanced out the window. "You must be mistaken, Jake. That woman is much too young to be your mother."

"It's true she doesn't look her age," he said as he followed the path of her gaze. "It's all the scheming she does that keeps her young. You'll probably be just like her as you grow old. The two of you could be sisters-in-scheming. What is it about me that puts women like you in my life?"

She restrained herself from hitting him. "What is your mother doing at Rowanclere? Why is she with Harrington? This is too much a coincidence for my peace of mind."

"Oh, it's no coincidence. Not if it involves Elizabeth Delaney. You can count on that. The woman has only been in England since winter and she already has a spy network to put Scotland Yard to shame."

Gillian observed the scene out in the drive, noting how Mrs. Delaney laughed up at her escort. The resemblance to her son was plain to see. She was an extraordinarily beautiful woman. "If she's knowledgeable about the activities of Society, she may well have learned of Harrington's interest in Rowanclere. Perhaps she chose to accompany him in order to check up on your progress toward locating the Declaration."

"It doesn't matter," he muttered. "She's here. My mother has come to Rowanclere. Just butter my backside and call me a biscuit. My ass is baked."

Then, in the blink of an eye, Jake went from immobile tree planted in front of the window to a thunderous tidal wave sweeping through the Great Hall. He clasped her arm and pulled her with him toward the door. The passageways didn't extend to this, the oldest part of the keep, therefore the closest entrance was from a bedroom suite up one flight of stairs, something he was bound to know considering he had spent part of the previous week mapping the secret tunnels.

Gillian had to run to keep up with his long strides and concentrate to make sense of all the words he fired in her direction. "I don't want her to know I am here, not until I think it through. Warn the others, Robbie especially. Scooter best stay with me for now because she would give the game away. Meet me in your bedroom after you get them settled and we can compare notes. I'll watch the goings-on as best I can, but I'll need your insights, too. Oh, and tell your sister and brother-in-law I said good-bye, and that I wish them and their little ones a lifetime of happiness."

Inside the bedchamber, Jake tripped the latch that opened the passageway door. Then he paused and did the most amazing thing. He grinned at her, his eyes alight with mischief. "I love my mother dearly, but her med-

dling has worn me to the bone. Maybe it's time it back-
fires on her. What do you think? Are you with me?"

She was far from certain what he asked, but she found
that did not matter. This Jake Delaney was a rogue, a
pirate, and a highwayman all wrapped up in one. An
irresistible combination. "Aye, I am with you."

At that, he did what any good pirate would do. He
yanked her toward him, pressed a hard, quick, bone-
tingling kiss upon her lips, then disappeared inside the
castle's secret halls.

As Gillian greeted her guests, Jake spied upon the proceedings from a peephole in a portrait hung high on a
wall above the entry hall. He had to listen a minute or so
before his ears got used to the echo, but once it did he
was able to pick up the conversation just fine.

"Ah, Mrs. Dunbar," the earl was saying. "How pleasant
to see you again."

"Welcome to Rowanclere, my lord. I must confess I
am not Mrs. Dunbar, but her twin, Gillian Ross. My sister and her husband were recently blessed with twin
sons, so I shall be your hostess during your visit to
Rowanclere."

The Englishman's brows winged up. "Felicitations
upon the happy news, in that case, and may I say it is
uncanny how much the two of you resemble. Tell me,
my dear, are you married?"

"Nae, my lord. I am not."

Harrington beamed a smile at Gillian. "Excellent. I
shall be certain to introduce you to my son. For now,
allow me to present my companion, Mrs. Delaney."

Jake scowled as his mother and Gillian exchanged

pleasantries. *Introduce her to his son. Looks like Mother is running with her own kind.*

Gillian laughed at something his mother said, then added, "I am pleased to meet you both. I hope your stay here at Rowanclere will be a pleasant one."

"I am certain we'll have a lovely time." Jake's mother slipped her arm through the earl's and spoke in a teasing tone. "Miss Ross, I feel obligated to warn you it is well-known throughout London that Harrington is searching for a bride for his son."

"As if you're not about the same sneaky business, Elizabeth," observed the earl. Turning to Gillian, he added, "We are engaged in quite a competition to gain the best bride for our boys."

"It's true," Elizabeth confirmed. "It is my fondest wish to see my son happily wed. I confess he's grown quite weary of my efforts to assist him in finding a bride. Has he perchance mentioned that to you?"

Jake's stomach took a dip. The woman never gave up, and now she was going public, to boot. And what was all this touching between her and Harrington about? It was bad enough she'd traveled alone with the man. This sort of behavior bordered on . . . well . . . scandalous.

"Your son, Mrs. Delaney?" Gillian asked innocently. "Do I know him?"

"I believe he has been a guest of yours in recent weeks. Mr. Jake Delaney."

"Oh, the writer. Yes, he visited with us for a short time. I do not recall him saying much about his family."

Behind the wall, Jake gave her a thumbs up. His Gilly was quick.

"A short time?" his mother responded. "My son isn't still here?"

"No." Gillian glanced up toward the portrait. Jake had enough experience with women that the light in her eyes made him wince. He braced himself as she said, "He told us he'd learned all he needed to know about Rowanclere and was returning to his grandfather's home in England. Although, he did plan to visit Inverness, first. The kiltmaker there is the best in the land. Mr. Delaney fell in love with the Highland style of dress during his visit, and he intended to order a whole new wardrobe. First, though, he shall need to make up his mind about his choice of tartan. I've never seen a man dither so much over shades of green and which proved most flattering."

Jake's jaw dropped simultaneously with his mother's. *Why that ornery little scamp.*

"Jake in a kilt?" his mother asked, a bewildered note to her voice. "I cannot imagine. Maybe we are talking about two different Jake Delaneys. Did this Jake have a dog with him?"

Gillian nodded. "Scooter, the puir wee beastie." As the Texan's mother turned a baffled look toward the earl, Gillian continued, "Would you care to take a brief tour of the castle before I show you to your rooms?"

"Certainly!" Harrington replied, obviously enthused by the prospect.

Taking care to remain hidden, Jake trailed the party through the castle for the next half-hour until Gillian showed them to their rooms. Then he watched from a tower window as she gathered with Angus and Robyn to see the Dunbar family off to Laichmoray, waving goodbye with tears flowing down her face. Jake watched the coach depart and realized the castle would feel a little empty with the babies gone.

He also felt a strong urge to hitch a ride away from here.

His matchmaking mother had come to Rowanclere. "It's enough to scare the boo out of this ghost," he grumbled.

When the Dunbar coach faded from sight he made his way to Gillian's bedchamber to await her arrival. Feeling edgy, he paced the room, his thoughts retracing the events of the day. As a result, by the time she entered her room, he'd worked himself into a lather. He waited until she shut the door behind her, then braced his hands on his hips and bellowed. "Kilts? Most complimentary shade of green?"

"I believe I said most flattering shade."

He continued to glare at her, and she stared right back. "You forced me to lie, Jake. I dinna like to lie."

"This from the woman who tied on a feather pouch and pretended to be pregnant?"

She shrugged. "It's different lying to your mother."

A smile twitched at the corners of his mouth until finally, he abandoned the struggle and freed his grin.

"You are the cutest little thing. Mama will really like you. She will—" He broke off abruptly. He shut his eyes, grimaced, shuddered, and said, "Gillian, I want you to stay as far away from her as possible."

"What? I don't understand."

"Let me put it this way. No matter how nice and friendly and helpful she appears, my mother will not have your best interests at heart. The woman always has an ulterior motive for everything she does."

Gillian folded her arms. "That's not a nice way to talk about your mother."

"It's the truth, though. I can't let down my guard one little bit."

"Afraid she'll succeed in her matchmaking?"

Damn, cut right to the nut of it, didn't she? "It got rather nasty before I left London. My mother on the hunt is the stuff of nightmares, princess. You should have seen some of the gems she hauled home for supper."

"You think she'll act the same way here?"

"Sure. It got to where anyone in skirts would do, and considering the mode of dress for men here in Scotland, that tends to worry me a bit."

Gillian visibly bristled. "Since I'm the only marriageable woman at Rowanclere at the moment, ye need not fash yersel'. Dinna worry, Texas. Yer no in the least bit of danger from me. I widna have ye if ye were the last man in Scotland. Why, I'd rather be matched with a grumpy auld—"

It was too much for Jake. "Oh, haud yer wheest, Gillian."

"—bodach than someone like—" she broke off abruptly. "What did you say?"

"Haud yer wheest. Robyn taught it to me. It basically means shut up. Since you have me wearing a dress now, I figured I should learn a bit of the language."

"Oh my." She sank onto a chair, closed her eyes, and rested the back of her hand against her brow. "What monster have I created?"

Jake strangled back a chuckle. When he spied her peeking through her lashes, her own mouth twitching with a smile, he let the laughter loose. "Aw shoot, princess." He sank onto his knees before her and took both her hands in his. "Thank you for that. I didn't know how much I needed that laugh. Gillian, I apologize for how I said what I said. I certainly didn't mean to be insulting. My mother simply brings out the worst in me upon occasion."

"And this is one of those occasions."

"Most definitely. This desire of hers to see me wed gets my temper up, and when I'm in a temper, I don't think straight. I hope you'll forgive me, and that you'll still be my friend."

She sniffed. "I don't think it's temper, Jake. I think you're afraid of the woman. I think you're afraid she'll win."

"Damned straight I am. I wake up in a cold sweat sometimes from nightmares about it. She doesn't want me to go adventuring, you see, and she's wearing me down. I'm afraid that when it comes to my mama, I'm a cream puff."

"Cream puff? You?"

"It's humiliating, princess."

"I don't believe it, Texas. Not a cream puff." She paused and thumped a finger against pursed lips as she pondered for a moment. "You're more a marshmallow."

Damned if it didn't take all his strength not to take her in his arms right then and there. *Not a marshmallow, princess. When your eyes get to sparkling like that, I'm a red hot jalapeño pepper.*

She might have seen something of it in his eyes, because she cleared her throat nervously and said, "So, what happens next? Does your mother's presence require any changes to the haunting plan?"

Standing and stepping away from her, Jake blew out a breath and forced his mind back to the matter at hand. "I don't see why it would. Although, I'm having a hard time deciding which trick to use at the midday meal—your moving breadbasket or my swinging chandelier."

"I'd say the basket. It's a nice, simple start."

"You're probably right. Except, it might not be enough for a member of the College of Psychic Studies. I allowed my mother to distract me during the castle tour, I'm afraid. If I had paid Harrington closer attention, I might have picked up a clue as to what would work best for the first haunt."

"You have both wiles set to work, correct?" Jake nodded, and Gillian continued. "We have half an hour before luncheon is served. Watch him in his bedchamber for a bit. That might give you your clues."

"I think I'll do that. This first trick will set the mood for the entire week."

A few minutes later with Gillian at his side, Jake flicked back the peephole cover and peered inside Lord Harrington's bedchamber. Immediately, everything inside him froze. *Oh, my God!*

A strangled sound emerged from his throat as he jerked back and slammed the peephole shut.

"What's wrong, Jake?"

His hand trembled as he brought it up and raked it through his hair. "Dammit, Gillian, she's in his room. That sonofabitch Lord Harrington is kissing my mother!"

Gillian all but tackled him to keep him from bursting into Lord Harrington's suite. "Hush. They'll hear you ranting."

"Won't matter. Harrington will just think I'm a ghost, except he's too busy using his mouth to use his ears."

He grumbled continuously while she pushed, pulled, and dragged him through the passageway back to his bedchamber. There he stalked around the room like a caged tiger. He fussed. He fumed. He ranted. He raved.

He made a fist and punched the wall, declaring, "Some English Lothario has sunk his claws into my vulnerable, widowed mother!"

Gillian winced as she imagined the pain radiating up his arm. She felt a combination of amusement and dismay as he flexed his aching fingers and gave his hand a shake.

"Jake, I think you are overreacting."

"Overreacting? Excuse me. I just saw my mother swapping spit with a stranger in his bedroom. I think my reactions are right on the mark."

"Jake, be reasonable. She lost your father some time ago, correct? Do you want her to be alone and lonely the rest of her life? Is that the act of a loving son?"

He scowled at her, all but growled at her. "I love my mother very much. She knows it. Chrissy knows it. Everyone does. I've proved it time and again, have I not? I'm here, aren't I? In Scotland where a man can never get warm instead of in Bora Bora where women run bare-breasted on the beaches."

"Well!" Gillian snapped.

Jake waved his arm in a kind of silent, half-hearted apology. "You are right. My father is gone. My mother is too young and nice and yes, I'll admit, too pretty to be alone the rest of her life."

"So what is the problem?"

"I don't know, all right? It's just . . . I wish . . . no son should see . . . Damn." He threw out his arms. "I didn't have to come to Rowanclere after all. She could have sweet-talked the Declaration away from Angus. I could be sailing for Tahiti right this minute. But no, I'm stuck in Scotland learning to wear a dress!"

"Take care, Texas. Ye have crossed the line to insulting."

He blew out a sigh. "Look, I don't mean any of this against you, Gillian. I want you to know that if I have to be in Scotland, there's nowhere else I'd rather be than right here with you. And as far as my mother goes, I don't want her to be lonely. I don't mind her developing a . . . a . . . friendship . . . with someone now that my father is gone. Hell, if she's involved in her own romantic life, maybe she'll leave mine the hell alone!"

Gillian didn't know whether to hurt him or hug him. She settled for saying, "Your language is running toward the gutter, sir."

"Well it's that kind of night. I had a shock."

"That is one of the risks of spying on people."

Jake sank onto a settee and buried his head in his hands. "My mother is having a love affair. This is information no son should ever learn. It's almost as unsettling as the time I figured out my parents had sex twice."

"Twice?"

"Once for me and once for Chrissy. I think I was seven."

Gillian couldn't hold back the laugh. "Oh, Jake."

Chagrin and sheepishness twisted the grin he offered her.

"Ye sappie-headed fouter." She sat beside him and rested a hand upon his knee. "This was not the way to meet the new man in your mother's life, but perhaps once you've spoken to him you will find it easier to accept."

"And when do you think that will be?" Jake drawled. "Let me tell you something about my mama. If she is . . . friendly . . . with that man, she won't keep quiet about who is haunting Rowanclere. For all her scheming and conniving and womanly-wiling, she never once lied to my father. If she cares enough about that . . . earl . . . to kiss him in his bedroom, then she's not gonna keep quiet about me."

"Oh."

"Yes, oh. Princess, if you still want me for your ghost, my mother cannot know I'm here. You're gonna have to keep up the lie about my leaving, and I'm gonna have to stay hidden."

Gillian thought about that for a moment. "You don't mind? You'll wait to speak with her about her dealings with the Earl of Harrington?"

"Dealings? Well, I reckon that's one way of putting it." He paused for a moment, thinking about it. "I'll wait, Gillian. In fact, I'll be more than happy to wait because I have something else to occupy my time and interest."

"You do?"

"I do. Now that I think about it, I think I should make some changes to the haunting plan after all. My mother is quick. She's liable to catch on to my tricks pretty fast. I'd better make the best of every opportunity I get."

Gillian eyed him suspiciously. "And to think I was already nervous about tonight. Jake, what do you have in mind?"

His smile was total innocence. Gillian didn't believe it

for a minute. "I'm just gonna give Lord Harrington what he's been asking for. He wants a ghost? Fine. I'm gonna give him a helluva scare."

At dinner that night, the chandelier shook for no apparent reason. Lord Harrington was intrigued.

When Gillian and her guests adjourned to the drawing room to partake of an after-dinner dram, a picture suddenly fell off the wall. The Englishman sat up straight, stared at the broken picture frame, and beamed.

After an unusual tiredness gripped both Harrington and Mrs. Delaney and they decided to seek their rest, unexplained footsteps seemed to follow them down the hall. Harrington bemoaned the unusual fact that he couldn't keep his eyes open. He wanted desperately to explore the peculiar occurrences. Instead, he kissed Elizabeth Delaney sweetly on the cheek, then adjourned to his own room, struggled into his nightclothes, and barely made it to bed before collapsing into slumber.

Which was exactly what Jake had intended when he slipped the sleeping draught into the whisky.

So far, his recently revised plan was working perfectly. His mother was snoozing in her room out of the way, despite Gillian's objections.

Drugging her guests didn't sit well with the woman. She'd raked him over the drawing room coals about that when he added the sleeping draught to the whisky. *What kind of man drugs his own mam?* she'd demanded in a huff.

He hadn't answered at once. He'd been too distracted. Gillian Ross in a huff was a blamed beautiful sight.

Jake had admitted to feeling only a twinge of guilt over seeing his mother swallow the drug. He knew for a fact the stuff wouldn't hurt her because he'd tried it out himself when originally formulating his haunting plan. He'd slept like a baby the night he took the potion and awakened refreshed. A similar experience might do his mother a world of good.

Maybe she'd be rested enough to think straight and see how silly a romance with Lord Wanna-spook would be.

Besides, he refused to feel bad about doing the job she, herself, had sent him to Rowanclere to do. She was the one who stuck herself in the middle of things. Elizabeth Delaney owned up to being a meddling mother, and she'd be the first to admit it sometimes complicated her life. A good night's sleep wasn't too big a complication, not to Jake's way of thinking.

"Now, you," he said as he pulled the snoring lord into a seated position, then put a shoulder to his gut. Hoisting the man from his bed, Jake grunted at the weight. The fella was heavier than he looked. "With you," he repeated, "I don't feel a lick of guilt. You are getting exactly what you asked for, but with a nice Texas twist."

Bigger, in other words.

Jake couldn't wait.

He had chosen the muniment room for the site of the evening's entertainment. Through long, narrow slits of windows, moonlight pierced the old keep's thick walls like luminescent swords. Pockets of cold air clung to the corners, evading the ribbons of heat escaping from the fire Jake had burning in the pit of one wall. Firelight melded with moonlight to cast shadows throughout the room, some flickering, some simply looming.

The glint of light off metal blades of swords, knives, claymores, and battle-axes added an air of threat, or menace. So, too, did the moan of wind as it blew through the sheep's horn Jake had hung outside the muniment room for just such a purpose.

Puffing a bit with the effort of having carried the dead-weight man up and down several flights of stairs, Jake approached the large, thronelike lord's chair he'd prepared for Harrington. Bending over, he heaved the earl into the seat. Sort of. The Englishman's arms flopped over the armrests to dangle at the sides. His behind slid down until it hung half on, half off the seat.

Through it all, he continued to snore. "Loud enough to scare away the ghosts if we had any," Jake grumbled. Still, he was well pleased with the progression of matters so far. Now to make those final preparations, after which he would settle back and wait for the curtain's rise.

Which would happen, he hoped, before Gillian figured out that the spooking spot had changed, that he hadn't taken the earl down to the dungeon room, the setting of the original plan. The place where she awaited him even now.

Gillian was too soft, too tenderhearted in her own obdurate way. She'd try to interfere with the haunting Jake had in mind. But he wouldn't let that happen. He wanted it done this way, and by God, he was the bogle. "I get to be the boss."

He puttered around the room for a few minutes, rearranging weapons and stirring up the pot of old raw scraps and blood he'd hidden beneath Harrington's chair to add that special, battle-decayed odor to the scene. That done, he checked his watch and figured how much time had passed since Harrington ingested the medicine. Hmm . . . another half-hour or so ought to do it.

"Good," he murmured softly. That would give him just enough time to put on his makeup and get rewrapped in the damned dress. Dragging the earl around had played hell with the pleats in his plaid. Judging by the draft, Jake suspected he might be flashing a cheek, too. That would never do. How intimidating a ghost would he be with a flesh-and-blood butt hanging out?

Jake's lips twisted in a cocksure grin. "Now, flashing my sword would be a different matter entirely."

"How long from the moment of death would it take a Texan to transform into a boodie?" Gillian muttered, eyeing an old, rusted sword. If the timing were right, she might consider assisting Jake through the transformation.

Three o'clock in the morning, and he had her waiting for him in a dungeon room. A dungeon room a short distance away from the castle crypt. A crypt filled with Rowanclere dead going back centuries.

Not to mention spiders.

Gillian swallowed hard. She'd give him five more minutes, then she would leave.

She lasted three and a half. The scurrying noise off to her left sent her rushing upstairs.

Her heart pounded with both temper and fear as she escaped the dungeon and hurried to Lord Harrington's room. She wasn't particularly surprised to find it empty. And it wasn't because she expected to find him with Jake's mother.

Jake had him. She'd bet the Declaration on it.

As expected, when she peeked into Elizabeth Delaney's suite she found the lady alone in her bed, deeply asleep. A quick check of the other guest rooms along that section of the hall turned up nothing, and she realized she needed a more efficient way to trace Jake Delaney through Rowanclere's numerous rooms, nooks, and crannies. If the Texan got creative, finding him could take hours.

Gillian knew just the thing to assist her.

After a brief visit to her own bedroom where she removed the belt from her oldest robe, Gillian made her way to Robbie's room where Jake's crippled mutt lay sleeping in her sister's arms. Plucking Scooter from the bed, she tried to ignore the wet tongue that licked its way up her neck and onto her face. "Stop that, now," she murmured, turning her head away, trying to scowl, but smiling instead.

"Gilly? Is that you?" asked Robbie, her voice slurred with sleep as she twisted around in her sheets and sat up.

"Aye. I need to borrow Scooter for a short bit. I shall bring her back to you soon."

"All right."

She burrowed headfirst back beneath her covers and Gillian flipped the blanket up over her sister's bare feet before retreating from the room. Once out in the hallway, Gillian set Scooter on the floor, slipped the belt around her belly, and lifted her hindquarters off the floor, saying, "Find Jake, Scooter."

It didn't work quite like she had planned. Instead of taking her to Jake, the dachshund led her to the buttery and the bowl of meat scraps Mrs. Ferguson left near the dog's favorite spot beside the hearth. "Eat up quickly," she impatiently urged. In that much, at least, the dog obeyed her.

Once the food bowl was empty and the water bowl sampled, Gillian tried again. "Jake. Find Jake. Find that lying Texan."

Scooter sneezed twice, then started off. "Guid dog," she encouraged. "I was wrong to call you those bad names before. But we're getting along better now, right? Guid puppy. Find Jake."

She kept her gaze on the ground and the dachshund, lifting her up staircases, then setting her back down. Gillian kept up a whispered stream of praise the entire time, feeling quite proud of herself for thinking to use the mutt to find the Texan scoundrel. With her attention divided between the dog and what she planned to do to Jake once she found him, she didn't realize just where Scooter was leading her until they reached the bedchamber door.

"No," she groaned. All the mutt had done was use Gillian for transportation assistance to a late night snack and back to bed. Glaring down at the dog, she added, "I said find Jake, not go eat a steak!"

Scooter jerked from her hold and dragged herself quickly toward the bed. There she let out a whimper and Robbie lifted her head from her pillow. Leaning over the bed, she scooped the hound up into her arms, then tucked the traitor in beside her. "Thanks for taking her downstairs for me, Gilly. What did Mrs. Ferguson leave for her tonight?"

"Beef." Gillian, on the other hand, was left with a plateful of crow.

Briefly, she considered giving up for the night and finding her own bed. But the sense of urgency riding her blood wouldn't let her. Something was telling her she had best find Jake and Lord Harrington.

Quickly.

ten

LORD HARRINGTON SAT in the old laird's chair in the center of the room, his eyes round and wary, his face chalky.

Jake stood before a crackling, crimson fire dressed in the feileadh mor, complete with knife, sword, and shield. In his hands he held a broadsword, which he swung in a slow, steady effortless arch from right to left, over and over again.

He was having the time of his life.

Jake had submerged himself in specterhood. He'd bathed himself in bogledom and reveled in his wraithness. If he'd known playing a ghost would be so much fun, he wouldn't have spent all that time rigging up the tricks. This was working so good, he wouldn't need them at all.

"Let me tell you a story," Jake said to the cowering Englishman. He banged the blade of the claymore against a leg of the chair and added, "You can make up your own mind about how you want to act once I'm done."

The odor from the bucket of blood and sheep entrails

he'd set beneath the earl's chair floated up and smacked him like a fist. Maybe he'd gone a bit overboard with that. Hiding his reaction, he retreated to a more safely-scented position and spoke in the burr he'd been practicing with Angus. "Ye summoned me to study me, so ye must reap what ye have sown. Ye want to write about me own self in your Spiritualist Magazine, to invade me privacy, to disturb me unrest. So I will gie ye what ye want, Lord Harry. Do with it what ye will. I am Ciaran, younger brother to the first laird of Rowanclere. This castle has been my home for centuries. I was murdered in my sleep in my own bed along with my lover, a bonny, buxom lass from the village. She was a sweet piece, and how was I to know the knap to whom she was wed was more than mortal? She complained of his performance atween the sheets all the time."

Jake shook his head sadly. "Those fairies, they are a heckle to understand."

"Fairies?" the Englishman croaked.

"Aye. Cursed me afore he killed me, he did. And take note, Lord Harry. The curse extends to any and all men who step beneath Rowanclere's roof and dare to treat any woman with less than respect. Only gentlemen may sleep safely beneath this castle's roof. Succumb to a rogue's behavior with the lady with whom you travel and be prepared to die yourself."

"I haven't acted less than gentlemanly."

Jake released the claymore and it clattered against the stone. Softly, he demanded, "And you won't."

"Of course not. I would never insult my hostess, and my companion is a lady whom I love and intend to marry. I wouldn't dream of dishonoring my Elizabeth."

Jake froze. "What did you say?"

"I'd rather die than dishonor my lady love."

"No, the other part. You want to . . ." Jake cleared his throat. ". . . marry her?"

The earl nodded. "As soon as possible. We'd be married already, except she insists on my meeting her son and gaining his blessing first."

Jake slumped into a chair. "Why hasn't she agreed?"

"She must have her son's blessing first."

Damn. Jake dragged his hand along his jaw, ignoring the greasy slide of the paint against his palm. "How long have you known her?"

Harrington paused for a long moment, his eyes narrowed as he studied Jake. Jake could all but see the wheels turning in the Englishman's brain, and when the silent question entered the older man's eyes, Jake stared back boldly, challengingly. A moment of silent communication passed between them.

Harrington's voice was stronger when next he spoke. Stronger and almost, well, kind. "Years and years. We were children together. Our parents were best of friends. She recently returned to England from America and we've renewed our acquaintance during the past five months."

"Five months? And you didn't meet the son during all that time?"

"Elizabeth is nervous about the introductions. Apparently her son is extremely protective of her, having admirably stepped into his father's shoes following Mr. Delaney's death."

Hell. "And why was she so nervous? Is there a reason the son wouldn't approve of the match? Are you impoverished? Given to excessive drink? Do you have a bevy of mistresses established in houses all over London?"

His color restored, Harrington smiled. "None of those. I daresay my wealth rivals that of your grand . . . uh, of the Earl of Thornbury, my darling's father. I am only an occasional drinker and as far as mistresses go, I rid myself of any encumbrances when Elizabeth reentered my life."

Damn and hell.

The earl continued, "My love is nervous about a meeting between myself and her son because she worries he'll not take kindly to another man following his father's footsteps. She hopes he'll give me the opportunity to explain that I would never try to replace his father, that I understand Mr. Delaney will always hold a piece of Elizabeth's heart. We both pray he'll believe that I will cherish his mother, protect her with my life, and love her until the day I die."

Dammit to hell. "Does she love you?"

"She has told me she does and I believe Elizabeth Delaney is a woman of her word."

"That's true." Jake picked the claymore off the floor and began tapping the blade against the stone as he considered all he'd just learned. Why was this so unsettling? Wasn't marriage infinitely better for his mother than the clandestine love affair he'd previously imagined? And wouldn't marriage to a British earl make it all the easier for Jake to sail away on his adventures with a clear conscience? Then another thought occurred, and he looked up and fired a glare at Harrington. "Does this romance between the two of you have anything to do with her overly enthusiastic efforts to see her son wed?"

The earl shrugged, as best a man could do while bound to a chair, anyway. "She is in love. Her daughter is in love. She feels her son should find similar joy. And too, she dreads the thought of these travels he is so intent to take. She will miss him desperately, you know."

"I know." Jake sighed heavily. He continued to roll the matter over and over in his mind, his protectiveness toward his mother still strong, but under siege by the honesty in the Earl of Harrington's declarations. Finally, on the verge of surrender, he posed the only legitimate objection he managed to think of. "What about this ghost-hunting hobby of yours? That sort of thing can be dangerous."

Dryly, the earl replied, "So I have recently come to understand."

Jake shot him another glare.

Harrington said, "I have a true curiosity about the supernatural and I intend to continue to pursue my interests. Whether or not Elizabeth will come to share my fascination for the subject, I cannot say. I have said I will protect her with my life and I mean that. However, a man who dreams of sailing around the world should understand that a life worth living involves a risk or two, don't you agree?"

Jake couldn't bring himself to give in. Not completely. Not yet.

"I love your mother to distraction, Jake Delaney, and she loves me in return. Our fondest wish is to marry. Will you give us your blessing?"

Dammit to hell and back.

"Oh, I guess so. But mind my word, Harrington," Jake stood and pointed the claymore toward his soon-to-be stepfather's face. "If you ever hurt her, I'll kill you."

"On my word of honor, I will never hurt your mother."

Jake nodded, then realized he had another problem. "And while you're at it, I want you to swear you won't tell her about what went on here tonight."

Now the earl scowled. "I won't lie to Elizabeth."

"I'm not asking you to lie. I'm asking you not to say anything about my being here at Rowanclere, not until I've had a chance to explain it. I know my mother. She's not gonna be happy about . . ." He waved his arm around the muniment room. ". . . all this. You've got to promise to let me tell her in my own way in my own time."

"I don't like it, but all right. You have my word. I will not mention to Elizabeth that I have met her son."

"Good." Jake grinned, feeling a bit relieved. No one gave a tongue-lashing like his mother. He would be glad to avoid it in this instance.

He loosened Harrington's bonds, then helped him to his feet. "I don't know about you, but I can use a drink. Want to join me?"

Harrington clapped him on the back. "I'd be honored, Jake. I hear they make a damn fine whisky in this part of the world."

Gillian found the two men sharing a bottle in Angus's whisky room. They were laughing together—laughing!—as Jake the traitor said, ". . . she plopped down on her stomach to look for the gum and when she stood up, her 'baby' had dropped."

Feeling as cold as the icy waters of Loch Rowanclere in the middle of a hard winter, she stepped into the room. "Jake, may I have a word with you in private, please?"

He glanced up at her in surprise, then winced. "Gillian."

"So you do remember me? I thought you might have forgotten, considering you failed to meet me in the dungeon as promised."

She sailed into the room, temper sizzling in her blood. Through the haze of her anger, she spied the remnants of white paint upon his lying face and she noted his apparent comfort in the feileadh mor. "Lovely. Simply lovely. What a perfect way to cap off a perfectly wretched evening."

Lord Harrington eyed her, then Jake, and pushed to his feet. Tossing back the last sip of his drink, he set down the glass and said, "If you will excuse me, Miss Ross, I believe it is time I found my bed. Goodnight."

Gillian didn't bother to respond. She was too busy flinging visual arrows at Jake. When they were alone, she braced her hands on her hips and demanded, "Would you care to explain what happened tonight?"

Jake refilled his glass. "To be perfectly honest, no."

"You ruined it, didn't you? You gave the game away?"

"Uh, yes, I'm afraid I did."

"Deil swarbit on, Jake Delaney!" she cursed him. "I knew it when I saw the scene you set in the muniment room. That's where you took him, wasn't it? What did you do? Did you stomp around and swing a broadsword while threatening a man on account of his love interest? Never mind that the man is a scholar. Never mind he knows a billy-blin from a banshee and would know the moment you spoke that you were no apparition. You didn't give a care about convincing him Rowanclere truly is haunted, did you? You forgot all about Uncle

Angus and our need to sell Rowanclere to Lord Harrington."

Jake scratched at the paint that still clung to his face and winced. "Yes, you pretty much covered it."

Gillian literally growled at him.

He held up his hands, palms out, and said, "Look, Gillian. It'll be all right. I'll fix it."

"How?"

"I don't know. I'll come up with something." He raked an impatient hand through his hair. "Cut me some slack, here, woman. I haven't had time to think about anything except my mother's future. Harrington told me he wants to marry her."

"How lovely. Your mother is getting married." She advanced on him, feeling mean and angry and completely devastated. "In the meantime, my puir Uncle Angus will die because he's forced to endure another winter at Rowanclere! You've killed him, Jake Delaney."

"Wait just one minute. Angus is not gonna die, not because of what happened tonight, anyway. I told you I'd fix it and I will."

Suddenly, the emotion of the night caught up with Gillian. Weariness like she'd never known before overcame her and swept the starch from her spine. "I don't believe you. Why should I believe you? You're a man and when has a man in my life ever kept his promises?"

"Ah, Gilly."

She walked toward the hearth where a fire flickered and held her hands out to the soothing warmth. She was cold. She was cold and tired and sad to her soul. When Jake's arms slipped around her and he pulled her back against him, she didn't have the energy to fight him.

"You can believe me, princess. I don't make many promises, but when I do, I keep 'em."

To her dismay, she felt tears swell and slip from her eyes. Soon they were spilling like water over rocks in a burn.

"Oh, don't cry. Please don't cry. I really hate it when a woman cries." He reached up and wiped away a tear with the pad of his thumb. "Shush, now. It'll be all right."

Oh, how much she wanted to believe him.

He turned her around and held her close. He pressed a tender kiss against her forehead. "You know, princess? You got one thing right earlier. I am most definitely a man. A Texan man. And we Texan men have more than a measure of pride. I get the feeling that you're comparing me to that scoundrel who did you wrong. Now, that doesn't set well with me. I'll take the grief I've earned, but don't lump me in with another fellow."

At his gentle scolding, her tears fell even faster.

"Damn," she heard him murmur. "Stop, Gilly." He put a finger beneath her chin and tilted her face upward. "Please stop." He kissed away first one tear, and then two. Then he kept kissing her. Her eyes, her cheeks, the tip of her nose, and finally . . . finally . . . her lips.

His kiss was tender, sweet, and soothing. For the first few seconds. Then she whimpered softly and kissed him back and everything changed. Gillian needed. She needed comfort and care and respite from her worries. She needed escape. So she asked for it. "Love me, Jake."

He groaned and his kisses turned savage. Her head spun as she arched her neck to meet his mouth. Her breath came in gasps when his clever hands slipped inside her gown, cupped and kneaded her aching breasts. Wanting sang through her veins.

His thumbs flicked her nipples, the sensation a bolt of heat to her woman's core. Awakened, hollow and aching. Wanting desperately to be filled. Wanting to be taken.

Gillian recognized this need. Had known it before. Had indulged it before. As he ripped off the feileadh mor and made a blanket of soft wool before the hearth, as he tore away her gown, baring her skin to the warmth of the fire and the heat of his stare, as he lay her down and rose above her, trailed devastating kisses along her neck, across her chest, then suckled at her breast, Gillian put the name to the emotion whispering in her heart.

Love. She was falling in love with this adventuring man. Falling in love, yet again, with a man bound to leave her.

"Nae," she moaned, just as he released her breast and moved to give the other similar attention.

Jake paused, his breath raspy as he asked, "That 'nae' means no stopping, doesn't it?" He skimmed a hand down her stomach, leaving shudders of pleasure in its wake before teasing her womanhood with a slow, gentle stroke. "You want this, don't you, Gillian? You are wet for me."

She tried to think, to find words, but before she managed the feat, two of his fingers rubbed a slow, sensual circle around the bead of nerves at the apex of her sex. Ribbons of pleasure fluttered outward from the spot and instinctively, unable to help herself, Gillian arched her hips, allowing him freer access.

"Ah, you are so damned beautiful, Gillian Ross. I want you madly." He captured her mouth, stealing her breath and robbing her of reason as he slipped a finger into her slick sheath. His tongue plunged and plundered, stroking in rhythm with the magic he made with his hand between her legs. Gillian's tension spiraled higher. "That's it, honey," he urged, his voice a low, coaxing rumble as he dragged his lips down to nibble at the base of her ear. "Climb that mountain. I want to watch you. I want to see the flush on your skin and hear the sound you make when you fall. I want to smell the scent of your satisfaction. Then I'll taste your honey and we'll do it all over again."

"Nae," she whimpered, trying desperately to summon the strength to send him away.

"Oh, don't worry. I'll take my turn. When it comes to lovin', I like to take my time."

It was the word *lovin'* that finally brought her crashing back to earth. Jake Delaney was *lovin'* while she was making love. She went stiff in his arms. "Not again."

"Princess?"

"I'm sorry. I canna do this." She pushed him away, scooped up her gown, and rolled to her feet. Her breathing was hard and her hands trembled. Her voice shook as she told him, "This isn't friendship. We agreed to simply be friends, remember? You said you have a code of honor. What about that? Was it a lie, too?"

"No, it wasn't a lie. I wasn't lying. I don't lie, dammit." Standing, he faced her. Temper snapped in his eyes. "Be fair. You said 'Love me, Jake.' Now that's a powerful temptation for a man. You're a powerful temptation. I'm not perfect. Sometimes circumstances get out of my control and I make mistakes. But I don't lie, Gillian. I'll never lie to you."

She felt a catch in her heart and the sting of tears all over again. "I'm sorry. I was wrong. I let it get out of hand. I did not mean to tease you. I wish I . . ." Unable to put her thoughts into words, she failed to finish the sentence.

He bent and grabbed the plaid from the floor. With short, jerky motions, he wrapped the woolen tartan around his waist like a towel. "You wish what, Gillian? That it was somebody else rolling on the floor with you? Somebody like . . ." he sneered the word . . . "David? He was more than just your betrothed, wasn't he?"

So, he'd figured it out. Her own actions here tonight had given her away. Emotion thickened her tongue as she said, "Ye are wrong about what I wish for, Jake Delaney. But as for the rest of it, ye have it right. David Maclean was indeed my lover."

Jake took a long time falling asleep. What a night. And what a day before that. So much had happened it made his head spin. The christening seemed like a month ago rather than yesterday morning.

Tossing and turning in his bed, he thought of his mother and the haunting and Lord Harrington's revelations. Mostly though, he thought of Gillian.

He'd never known a woman both so strong and so vulnerable at the same time. Damn that David Maclean.

She must have been crushed when ol' David threw her over. Jake seriously doubted the woman would have given her virginity without giving her heart first. That right there proved the magnitude of Maclean's sin. Not only had he taken her innocence—which was bad enough—he'd also taken her heart. Then he'd broken it.

Hell, maybe he'd just kill the fella if he ever got the chance.

Probably wouldn't be too difficult. The man must be an idiot. Who but a fool owned the love of a woman like Gillian Ross, then threw it away?

Other thoughts darted through his mind. Thoughts he was better off not thinking about. Like, how long the two had been lovers. How good the bastard was between the sheets. What it was like to be Gillian Ross's first.

Roll that wagon on back, Delaney. That's not a good place for you to go.

How could dear ol' David have given her up? Shoot, it would be damned hard for Jake to leave her when the time arrived, and they were only friends. Not lovers. Well, more than friends. Almost lovers, if there was such a thing.

God, he wanted to be her lover. His body still ached with that particular need.

But it was one need he could not assuage. That would make him no better than love-her-and-leave-her David.

Not if you took her with you when you go.

Jake damned near rolled out of bed when that thought rumbled through his brain. Where the hell had that come from? He had no business thinking along those lines. That's the kind of stuff that got a man in trouble as fast as small town gossip.

No, if he had to be thinking at all, he would think about how he could salvage the sale of Rowanclere with Harrington. That's what mattered now. He'd given his word. Somehow, someway, he'd make sure that happened. Gillian was gonna learn that some men do keep their promises.

On that note, as dawn began to break on the eastern horizon, Jake drifted off to sleep.

He woke up too few hours later with a pain in his shoulder. Pain from being punched. He rolled away, groaning in a raspy croak. "What the hell?"

"Get up."

He pried open his eyes and winced. A furious Gillian stood over his bed, her right hand doubled in a fist as she switched from jabbing his shoulder to slugging his gut. "Hey there, wait just a minute." Sitting up, he grabbed for her hand. Still woozy from sleep, he missed.

"I will not wait a moment longer. Neither will you. You did it. Just as I feared you would." His breath whooshed out as she hit him square in the center of his stomach, just below the ribs. "You ruined everything."

"What are you talking about, woman?" he wheezed.

Her eyes shot fire. "Lord Harrington left Rowanclere this morning. He called off the sale. He said you yourself told him the castle wasn't haunted."

Jake's stomach took a slow, sick roll. "Wait a minute. He couldn't have left yet. What about my mother? She didn't leave with him, did she? She wouldn't, not without seeing me first."

"Apparently, she did not ken you were still here. For some reason, Lord Harrington chose not to tell her you haunted him last night. She thinks you've returned to England by way of Inverness, and once Uncle Angus handed over the Declaration of Independence, she was anxious to follow you."

Jake blinked hard. "Angus did what?"

"I overslept, but Robyn told me everything. Apparently, Uncle Angus came downstairs for breakfast this morning and had a nice visit with your mother. They talked at length about Texas, and she told him all about the Historical Preservation Society's search for the lost Declarations. I walked into the dining room as he handed over the document with a flourish. She promised to place a plaque in his honor on the case where the Declaration is put on display."

"He just gave it to her? What about our deal?"

"Angus knew the deal was done. Despite his ordeal last night, Lord Harrington rose early this morn. He met Angus on the way downstairs and they shared a visit, too. That's when he told Uncle Angus that he knew we had staged the haunts and that he was no longer interested in purchasing Rowanclere."

Jake shook his head. He couldn't believe this. "So they loaded up and left without anyone bothering to come tell me? No one bothered to tell my mother I was upstairs in bed and not on the road to Hartsworth?"

"You swore us all to secrecy yesterday when they arrived, remember? The people of Rowanclere keep their word, unlike others among us."

Jake muttered a curse and dragged his hand through his hair. What now? "I wanted to talk to Harrington this morning. Thought I'd come up with a way to convince him to buy the castle despite its lack of otherworldly occupants."

Gillian didn't even bother to ask what argument he'd constructed. *Stubborn woman.*

She reached into her pocket and removed an envelope. Handing it to Jake, she said, "Lord Harrington left you this."

Quickly, he scanned the contents of the note. Harrington had taken Elizabeth Delaney back to her father's estate in Derby. He expected Jake to follow. Otherwise, he'd tell Elizabeth the truth about the haunting.

Damn. Throwing off the covers, Jake reached for the pants he'd left draped over the back of a nearby chair. "I've got to go. Right away. Maybe I can catch them on the road. Gillian, I hate to rush off like this, but—"

"You are leaving," she said softly. Her teeth tugged at her lower lip.

"I've got to go to England."

"I see. And then where, Tahiti?"

Jake snorted in frustration. He didn't need this now. "Gillian, I'm coming back. Our dealings are not finished. I told you I'd find you a buyer for Rowanclere and I mean to do it. I told you I'd fix things."

"It appears you slept away your opportunity. Lord Harrington was quite definite in his refusal to purchase Rowanclere."

"I have a good argument to change his mind. That's why I need to follow them. Part of why, anyway. But I'm coming back. I'll be back, Gillian. I promise."

She stared at him for a long moment. "I want to believe you, Jake Delaney. But it's difficult because I've lived this scene before."

"What do you mean?"

"David told me a similar story when he left on a business trip to America. He's never returned to Rowanclere. His American wife wouldn't understand, you see."

Jake snorted and grabbed his saddlebags from inside the armoire. As he stuffed a few necessities inside, he said, "I'm trying not to let that make me mad, but I'm having to work at it. I'm not Weasel Maclean, princess.

You have my word I'll return just as soon as I can, and you can take it as gospel."

He paused long enough to give her a quick searing kiss, then headed out the door. At the top of the staircase, he paused, then retraced his steps to her. He dropped his saddlebags at his feet and took her in his arms. "Give me another one for the road, princess. Kissing you is the best way I know to keep warm."

eleven

Derbyshire, England

JAKE CLIMBED HARTSWORTH'S front steps with his hat in his hand and his heart lodged somewhere in the vicinity of his neck. He was late. He'd suffered one mishap after another along the road south and he'd missed Lord Harrington by a day and a half.

Now that he was finally here, he seriously debated turning tail and running. It was time to come clean with his mother.

All in all, he'd rather chew spurs.

Before he'd lifted his hand to sound the knocker, the door flew open and a bundle of energy streaked out and flew into his arms screeching, "Jake! You're finally here. Mother thought you were to be here days ago."

"Chrissy! You're supposed to be in Texas."

"We were. But we had to come. We couldn't wait. We've already told Mama and Grandfather." She drew back, beamed up at him, and lovingly placed her hand upon her stomach. "Jake, Cole and I are expecting a baby."

Damn. She was pregnant. His baby sister was having a

baby. She was having sexual relations with his best friend. Oh, hell. He really, truly, didn't want to think about that. It was as bad as thinking about his mother and Harrington. Never mind Chrissy and Morgan were married.

"Jake!" She folded her arms and glared at him. "Aren't you going to congratulate us?"

"I am, Bug, I am." He allowed his gaze to take a perusal from her head to her toes. He hadn't seen his sister since she and Cole departed on their wedding trip more than seven months ago. If anything, the girl had grown more beautiful. Her red hair shone and sparkled in the sunlight, her green eyes glowed like a cat's in the firelight. She looked a little softer and a little rounder and totally, desperately happy. Jake couldn't help but smile. "I'm gonna congratulate you just as soon as I beat up Cole for messing with my baby sister."

She gave an exaggerated roll of her eyes, then hugged him hard once more. "Come inside. Mother is out taking a drive around the park, but Grandfather is in the saloon. I was on my way downstairs to meet him when I saw you ride up. I'm dying to hear all about your visit to Scotland. Mother has this wild story about you and a kilt."

"It's a feileadh mor," he murmured, distracted.

She shot him a sidelong look. "Now this is one story I have to hear. That and how it is that you left that Scottish castle empty-handed while Mother left it with the Declaration of Independence in her baggage."

"It's a long story."

"Then you do know she has it? The news isn't a surprise?"

"Look, I'll explain everything, but I think I'd better talk to Mother about it, first."

His sister angled her head to one side and studied him. He saw in her eyes the moment she made up her mind. "I think I should warn you. Mother has a special guest with her. Jake, she has a beau. His name is Lord Harrington and he is very nice. I think she likes him a lot. I know she is anxious for you to meet him. Isn't it wonderful?"

"Wonderful, yes." Harrington obviously had kept his mouth shut. At least something had gone right.

Inside, waiting to face his mother and the music, Jake shared a lemonade and small talk with his grandfather and his sister, then wandered out back to look for Cole, who had gone for a walk in the statue garden. Jake found him seated on a bench, chucking pebbles at Zeus. "I thought you might be here. You are a creature of habit, Morgan."

"Well, well, well. If it's not Bonny Prince Jake, home from the Highlands at last. I hear you've taken to wearing dresses since the last time I saw you."

"Haud yer wheest, Morgan. That way I won't knock out your teeth when I hit you again for trifling with my sister."

"Haud my what?" Cole arched a brow as he rubbed his jaw. "Look, Delaney, I never once trifled with Christina. For me, it was always dead serious."

"I hear you got it right, anyway."

A quick smile slashed across Cole's face. "She told you?"

"She told me." Jake shook his friend's hand and clapped him on the back. "Congratulations. This is great news. Truly great. And by the way, just in case you're worried, I've recently learned all the ins and outs on how to prevent fairies from stealing a newborn baby."

"That's good to know. The fairy activity in Texas is on the rise." After a moment's pause, he warned, "Christina is already whining about you coming home with us and putting off your trip until after the baby is born. She's dead set against your running off to Australia, you know."

"I'm not running off. I'm going exploring. There's a difference."

"I know that and you know that. Tell it to Chrissy and Elizabeth."

The mention of his mother put a pall on Jake's spirits and he scowled and threw a whole handful of pebbles at Zeus. Cole clicked his tongue. "Looks like I touched a nerve. What's the matter? You look like you just lost your favorite dog."

"I sorta did."

"You have a dog?"

"Yes. I left her with a friend."

"Ah-hah. Female, I presume."

"Nine years old."

"Oh."

"Well, I guess you can't take a dog on your travels, can you? Now that Elizabeth has the Declaration, you're free to go. No more responsibilities and obligations weighing you down. Christina is my problem now, and it looks like your mother has found someone to keep her company."

"Mother wants to marry him, Cole. Has she told you that?"

The strange look on his brother-in-law's face told Jake the news came as no surprise. "Chrissy blabbed, huh? Your mother wanted to tell you herself."

"No, Chrissy didn't tell me."

"So how do you know about Harrington?"

Jake chucked a large pebble at the statue, hitting it square on the nose. "Let me put it this way. Do you know anyone who's in the market to buy a Highland castle?"

Cole eyed him thoughtfully for a long moment, then sadly shook his head. "Hell, I've seen that same look on your sister's face more times than I can count. What have you done, Delaney?"

Because Cole was more like a true blood brother than just a brother-in-law, Jake told him most of the story. When he was finished, Cole whistled soundlessly. "You spied on Elizabeth? She's gonna be mad enough to eat bees."

"I'm not going to tell her that part, and I didn't mean to spy on her. She was in his bedroom. Kissing him!"

Cole winced. "Don't. I don't need to know about that. I don't need the vision in my mind. What are you going to do?"

"I have to talk to my mother." He took a seat on the bench beside Cole and grabbed another handful of pebbles. "She's going to be furious with you. I doubt she'll be too happy with Harrington, either. I can't believe he didn't tell her you were there."

"He gave his word and he kept it. You can't fault a man for that," Jake replied glumly. After a few more minutes ticked by in silence, he asked, "You think she'll help me talk Harrington into buying a ghostless Rowanclere?"

"Honestly? You don't have a snowball's chance in San Antonio in August." Cole shook his head. "Don't ask me why, but he's really interested in this ghost stuff. He wants a haunted castle."

"I know, but I have an idea about that. Lots of castles and houses and inns in the Highlands claim to have ghosts, and Rowanclere offers a nice, central location for visiting many of them. If he bought Rowanclere, he could study dozens of places within a day's ride of the castle. He could keep himself busy for years. Lord Lothario doesn't need to actually live in a haunted house." Jake paused for a moment, scowled, and added, "Especially if he's living with my mother."

"Lord Lothario?" Cole dryly asked.

"Don't give me grief. I learned the term from you, after all. Remember? When you spoke of one of Chrissy's beaus?"

"Don't talk about that, either." Cole threw a rock that hit Zeus directly on his male glory. Both Cole and Jake winced. "When are you gonna talk to your mama?"

Jake sighed. "Just as soon as she comes back from her drive and I can work up my courage."

Cole rose and brushed dust from his hands onto his pants. "In that case, I think I'll take my bride and pay a visit to the fishing pavilion. It's just about our favorite spot here at Hartsworth, and it's nice and isolated."

"Thanks for your support."

"Anytime, son. Anytime." Cole slapped him on the back. "Good luck, Jake. You're gonna need it."

His words proved prophetic. An hour later Jake found himself wishing he'd brought his lucky rabbit's foot with him from Texas. It looked as if he might need some outside help to survive this exchange. He'd never before seen his mother this angry, not even when dealing with some of Chrissy's antics.

"I cannot believe this!" Elizabeth Delaney exclaimed.

"I cannot believe you would pull such a wicked, mean-spirited trick in order to deceive a fine man like Lord Harrington. Why, Jake? Why act in such a dishonest manner?"

"I was out-lawyered, I'm afraid." He told her about the "debt" Gillian and Angus felt they owed the Delaney family for Chrissy having rid the world of Lord Bennet last winter. "Besides," he finished, "no one can say with total certainty that Rowanclere isn't haunted. Could be that its ghosts are just shy compared to those in other abodes around the Highlands. That's part of the reason why I'm hoping you will convince Lord Harrington to purchase Rowanclere from Angus Brodie after all."

Flabbergasted, she sank into a chair. "What?"

Jake explained about Gillian and Robyn, and how they would be all but destitute upon their granduncle's death. He told her what a good person Gillian was and how hard she worked at caring for the little girl who, by the way, reminded him so much of Chrissy. He explained how desperately she wished to bring ease to her granduncle's final years. He also added in a bit about how guilty she'd felt for the necessity of pretending Rowanclere had ghosts, even though he skirted the truth on that one.

As he talked, his mother gradually relaxed. She sat back in her seat, folded her arms, tilted her head, and listened. When her eyes narrowed in speculation, Jake felt the first glimmer of unease. What was she thinking?

He figured he was better off not knowing.

When Jake wound down, having delivered all the arguments he could think of for encouraging his mother's help, she watched him silently, pensively for a few moments before observing, "You don't need Harrington to help, Jake. You have the power to solve this imbroglio yourself."

He laughed uneasily. "I don't see how. I may not be hurting for money, but I don't have near enough to buy a castle like Rowanclere."

"Think, Jake. I know you've dismissed me when I brought it to your attention months ago, but after hearing this story today, I don't think you can in good conscience ignore the fact you have a fortune at your disposal."

Jake didn't know what she was talking about. Well, at least, he didn't think he knew. He knew he didn't want to think about it too much. "Mother, I'll talk to Lord Harrington if you prefer. I thought it only right to explain what happened before I went any further with it. I thought—"

"Your trust fund, Jake," she interrupted. "You know your grandfather established a trust fund for both you and Chrissy earlier this year. You know it comes to you upon your marriage."

A shudder crawled up Jake's spine. "But that's—"

"More than enough funds to buy that pretty Scottish castle. It was beautiful. Right out of a fairy tale."

"I don't want—"

"You owe the girl, of course. I must say I did like Gillian. She's a pretty thing, too, don't you think? Yes, it's only right, Jake."

"But Harrington—"

"Wants a haunted castle, not Rowanclere. He won't bail you out of this trouble. You will have to take care of that yourself."

"Oh, no." His knees weak, Jake sat on a nearby settee and plopped his head back against the cushion. "No . . . no . . . no."

His mother reached over and patted his knee. "You do have a responsibility to Gillian and her family. You did ruin her plan. It's a matter of honor, son, and I know your honor is one thing you rightfully hold quite dear. Isn't it handy, though, that this problem can be solved so simply?"

"Simple, Mother?"

She shrugged. "You can be the new laird of Rowanclere Castle. Isn't that exciting?"

"Mother, you don't know what you are asking."

"I'm not asking anything. You are the one who must do that. Come, now, Jake. Don't be so glum. This problem you created for yourself is easily fixed. All you must do is marry Gillian Ross."

A heavy gray mist rolled in off the loch as Gillian arranged a cheerful bouquet of flowers in a vase to take up to Uncle Angus. It was the second arrangement she'd made that day, the first having been lost when Robyn chased Scooter down a hallway and careened into Gillian, knocking the vase from her hands.

She gave her sister a gentle scolding about running in the house, saving her most harsh remarks for personal grumblings about Jake Delaney. "How dare he go off and leave us to care for that pesky pet," she muttered to herself. "Never mind that Robyn begged him to leave the dog behind. That is beside the point. He kept the animal as long as it suited him, then dumped her on another without a backward glance. How like a man."

Unless he'd told the truth about coming back to Rowanclere. Unless he did intend to return for the dog.

Gillian would like to believe his promises, but she didn't. She had been burned by a man's promises before. A part of her realized her doubts in Jake might be unfounded. Perhaps he had told the truth when he'd promised to return with sales papers for Rowanclere ready to be signed. However, the cynic in her thought that about as likely as Loch Rowanclere going dry overnight.

As she climbed the stairs to the Crow's Nest carrying a breakfast tray for Uncle Angus, she wondered where Jake Delaney was at that particular moment in time. Two weeks had passed since his leave-taking. Was he already aboard a ship headed south?

"Oh, stop thinking about him," she scolded herself. Her lack of control over her own thoughts infuriated her. "You do not care where he has gone. Tahiti or Tipperary or Tibet—it does not matter. It likely won't be Rowanclere. You'll probably never see the man again."

Yet, if that was what she believed, then why did she keep finding excuses to climb the towers and watch the road? Unhappy with the direction of her thoughts, Gillian entered Angus's chamber wearing a scowl.

Her granduncle slowly opened his eyes, gazed at her, then shut them once more. "The death bogle has come for me."

"Are you not the funny one," she replied dryly.

" 'Tis a fearsome look you are wearing, lass." He struggled to sit up in bed, but when she went to assist him, he pushed her away. "You have the same expression as our Robbie once she realizes she's eaten the last biscuit in the tin. What has put the thistle in your skirt?"

"Naught is wrong. I am just wishing for a little sunshine, that is all."

Ignoring his disbelieving snort, she asked, "Where would you like your tea? In bed or at the table?"

"The table."

She placed the vase of flowers atop a bookshelf, then transferred his breakfast to the table beside the fire. Seeing his wince as he attempted to rise, she hurried to assist him from his bed. "You've a steenge in your joints this day, I see."

"Aye. It's a bad thing when a man canna climb from his own bed himself. I'll feel better once I've moved about a bit. I want to come downstairs today. Robbie tells me she's taught the bawtie a new trick."

"How to break vases," Gillian grumbled.

Once he was seated, Angus gestured toward the stack of papers atop his bedside table. "When you leave, please take these downstairs and see them posted. I have written notices for newspapers in London and America. If we do not hear from young Delaney within the week, I am placing advertisements about the sale of Rowanclere."

Dismay filled her. "Advertisements? But, Uncle Angus, we decided against that. We decided to be discriminating about potential buyers in deference to Mrs. Ferguson and the villagers."

"Yes, and we tried. We did. But we also made a mistake by not pursuing a potential buyer in addition to Harrington. We have no backup plan."

"Uncle Angus, maybe it is time to rethink your decision to sell Rowanclere. The situation has changed."

"How?"

"Bennet is dead. I need no longer fear his threats."

"True." He sipped his tea. "But that was not my only purpose in selling the castle, was it? You know that some-day the real death bogle will come for me. What happens then, Gillian? How will you pay the death taxes, hmm? The coffers are all but empty."

"I don't wish to think about it."

"An adult attitude, that." He shook his head. "I'll tell you what will happen, lass. The Crown will take the cas-tle and leave you with little more than the clothes on your back. I refuse to allow that to happen. I'll not go to meet my Maker having failed to provide for my girls."

She shook her head hard. "Stop right there, Uncle Angus. You provided the most important thing of all. You gave us your love, and that is more valuable than any cas-tle in all of Britain."

"I appreciate the fact you believe that, Gilly, but don't allow your heart to stand in the way of your head. We have discussed this a thousand times. While love is what makes a man—or woman—truly wealthy, one cannot ignore the importance of cold hard cash. Money gives you freedom, Gillian. It will buy you time to find the love you desire, the love you deserve. It offers the free-dom of choice."

The word "freedom" brought Jake's image to mind and she quickly shoved it aside. "But I would be happy in a small cottage somewhere. All I require is to be close enough to visit Flora often."

"But what of Robbie? Her happiness is important to you, too, is it not? What if in a few years she wishes to have a London Season? You will want her to make a good marriage. Such opportunity requires an outlay of coin. How will you provide it, Gillian, if I don't?"

Only one sure way popped to mind. Marriage. "A way exists."

Uncle Angus pinned her with a knowing gaze. "I wish more for you than a marriage like young Maclean's," he said. "Circumstances forced David to make a choice he'll pay for all his life."

"Pay? I doubt he sees it that way. Flora and I met his wife in the village one day. Annabelle Maclean is very beautiful."

"Oh, she may be bonny, but she is not you, Gillian. David wanted you."

Not enough, she thought.

"Think about it, lass. If you were in his position, if you were forced to choose between following your heart or seeing Robyn well provided for, which would you choose?"

"Uncle Angus," she said with a long-suffering sigh. He was right, she knew it. Nothing truly had changed. "I will see that the advertisements are placed, but I will hope on the village's behalf that only potential good neighbors inquire."

"Naught wrong with that. Now, sit down and share a piece of bacon with me. Mrs. Ferguson has once again sent too much food."

Gillian sat and nibbled at the meat while Uncle Angus ate. He was almost through with his meal when the rain began. Before long, it was pouring down and to Gillian's great dismay, the roof spouted four different leaks, one directly above his bed. "Oh, no. Not again."

Angus silently observed each drip, then said, "Hope the weather clears before tonight. Sleeping in the damp is hard on my bones."

Anger flaring, Gillian waved an expansive hand

around the room. "This place is nothing more than a cold drafty bird's cage. I understand your desire for independence, Uncle, and I respect the vows you made in your youth. But it makes me furious to think of you causing yourself added pain by refusing to act intelligently and move downstairs where we could better care for you."

He pushed his chair away from the table and struggled to stand. "Now, hold on there. As much as I love you, this is my life, my decision. I have lived in the Crow's Nest since my return to Rowanclere and I will be here until I die. It is my choice, and I will not tolerate another shirrackin from you about it. Now, I'm done eating. If you'll excuse me, I've more correspondence that requires my attention."

The stormy sky suited her mood as she made her way downstairs. Caring for an elderly loved one was no easy task. She never was certain which role she was to take, that of parent or child. Right now Angus was full of nettle, but she had seen that change in the space of an hour. She could return later in the day and find him filled with fear over a twitch in his side or a pain in his chest, and he'd be turning to her for comfort and advice. She took her cues from him and presented the role he required. Some days, like today, acting the child was more difficult than others.

"Why won't he listen to me?" she muttered as she dropped the breakfast tray onto the worktable in the kitchen. "He should be downstairs in the blue salon with southern exposure. As his caretaker, I should insist on it."

As his niece, she could not.

Two days later, she faced the question once more

when Uncle Angus stumbled on a step and tumbled down the stairs.

The physician summoned to Rowanclere afterward declared Angus lucky to have suffered nothing more serious than soreness and a broken ankle. "Not that a broken ankle at his age is a minor injury. He'll be confined to bed for now. You'll want to order a wheeled chair for him."

"We already have one. He refuses to use it."

"He canna refuse it now. He'll not walk on his own for a long time to come."

Gillian had no choice but to order Uncle Angus moved to the blue salon with southern exposure. Needless to say, he didn't take the news well.

As Jake strolled into the blue salon, a luncheon tray came sailing toward him, crashing against the wall. "If you've hurt her again, you rapscallion, I'll have your head."

Jake glanced at the soup stain—potato, from the looks of it—and said, "What do you mean 'hurt her again.' I just walked in. Where is everyone?"

"Delaney, is that you?" Angus grabbed his glasses off the bedside table and put them on. "Finally. Thank God. You are just the man we need around here."

Jake didn't like the sound of that. "What's wrong? Why are you in bed down here? I thought this room was a salon."

"It was. It's my bedchamber now."

Looking closer, Jake realized the blue salon had been transformed into a fairly decent approximation of the Crow's Nest. Angus slept in the same bed, gazed at the same pictures, lit the same lamps. The same books lined the shelves, the same clock hung on the wall, and his carpet lay beneath the furnishings. The salon even smelled similar to the Crow's Nest due to numerous vases filled with roses placed about this chamber.

"I fell down the stairs, broke my ankle." Angus snorted with disgust. "Nobody here would help me get up to the Crow's Nest. Fifty years I kept my vow and now in the very twilight of my life, it is taken from me. As we said back in Texas, it really chaps my hide."

"That's why you threw your potato soup at me?"

"It's a fish soup, not potato. And I threw it at you because I thought you were David Maclean."

Jake went still. "David? The David who—?"

"Aye, Gillian's David."

Well, by God, he's not hers now.

Angus continued, "Maclean came sniffing around Rowanclere about half an hour ago. He's with Gillian right now. They're alone."

"Alone? Where's Robyn? Mrs. Ferguson?"

"They're off to the village to do some shopping. You must go after her, Jake. Make sure he's behaving himself."

"Where are they?"

"The library, I suspect. That's where they always did their sparkin' before."

Jake immediately turned to leave, but as he moved, a portrait on the wall caught his eye and changed his mind. This might be better handled the sneaky way. He'd go to the library through the passages. Maclean better hope Jake didn't discover any surprises once he got there.

* * *

Gillian cuddled Scooter close to her breast. Ever since their midnight snack the night of Harrington's haunting, the dog had trailed her like a tasty bone. Time and again, she'd fussed to Robyn about the development. At this moment, she was thrilled to have Scooter to hold.

She felt as if all the air had been sucked from her lungs. Though his home was but a half-hour's ride from Rowanclere, this was the first time she'd seen David in well over a year.

The last time she saw him they met at the standing stones and he'd brought her flowers. They'd made love beneath a brilliant blue sky and spoken aloud their dreams of the future.

Six weeks later, he married his American bride.

Scooter fixed somber brown eyes on David and gave a low, menacing growl. Scratching the dog behind the ears, Gillian moved to stand before the window. She pushed aside the drapery, and gazed outside. "Why have you come?"

"A number of reasons. Mainly, I can no longer stay away. I've wanted to see you every day for the past sixteen months, two weeks and a day."

She knew without counting that he referred to the last time they'd been together. Her hold on Scooter tightened, and when the dog yipped, she set her down.

I wonder if she'd nip at his ankles if I told her to?

"Ah, Gilly. Robbie and I met up on the moors. She told me of Angus's illness and all the troubles you have faced. I've come now because I am finally in the position to help you instead of hurt you."

Turning to face him, she slowly studied him. David was still a handsome man. Blond with angel blue eyes and aquiline features, he was tall and broad and fine enough to catch the fancy of any lass. Sincerity shimmered like sunset on Loch Rowanclere from his eyes. That and more. Sorrow, compassion, chagrin, and . . . love?

Gillian closed her eyes. Not love. No. The man was married.

"Let me help you, Gilly. Please. I know it will not absolve me from my sins, but at least this misery I claimed for myself will do good for someone. Someone I love."

On the wall behind David a painting—the second laird, she believed—suddenly crashed to the floor. Both she and David jumped. "Guid fegs, what was that?" he asked.

Scooter barked and dragged herself across the room to investigate. Seconds later, she gave a series of excited yips.

Gillian's lips twisted. The falling painting was one of the tricks they'd rigged for Lord Harrington. Its timing made her wonder if David's appearance had stirred up an old ghost after all. *Wouldn't that be just my luck, now when it's too late?*

Scooter's barks grew louder and more annoying. Gillian crossed the room and picked her up once more. She scratched the dog's belly and silently paced the room. Questions bubbled in her head; emotions warred in her heart. So much lay between this man and herself, she hardly knew where to start.

Yet, what good could belaboring old hurts possibly do? Better to deal with the here and now, because in truth nothing else truly mattered. "How? How can you help?"

David tore his gaze away from the walls and cleared his throat. "I sold my soul for money, Gillian. I married a fortune instead of the woman I loved, who I still love. As foolish as that was, the fact remains that now I do have funds."

Muuu ... waaaaa. Muuu ... waaa. David's eyes went wide as the moaning sound reverberated through the room. His gaze jerked around the room. "Gillian, did you hear that? What is happening here?"

The dog went wild in her arms and Gillian realized Robyn must have returned and taken up the role of ghost. Any other time, she'd have stopped to investigate, but right now she wanted to hear what David had to say. "I think Robyn is playing. Ignore it."

Woof woof woof woof.

"Oh, Robyn. Well. Yes." His throat bobbed as he swallowed hard. "Between what Robyn told me and the information I was able to gather in the village, I understand Angus is anxious to rid himself of Rowanclere. I can buy it, Gilly. I can buy it and you and Robbie can stay here in your home."

"You want to buy Rowanclere?" Scooter scratched the back of Gillian's arm during her scrambling around. Taking the hint, Gillian returned her to the floor.

"I want to help you," he replied. Scooter came at him. She paused just long enough to snap once at his ankles, then barreled on toward the far wall. There, she skidded to a halt and started whimpering.

Gillian watched the dog, but didn't truly see her, so busy was she trying to make sense of what he'd said. *David wanted to help her? David wanted to save her home?* Now her knees went a little weak, and a lump the size of an orange grew in her throat.

More than anything she wanted to snatch the treat he dangled before her, but common sense and prior experience with this man urged her to step cautiously. "Why?"

"Because I can. Because I should." He stood directly beneath the chandelier. When it began to shake, he scrambled to one side.

David's response to the hauntings made him look exceedingly childish to Gillian's eyes. He wasn't at all like Jake when she'd played the breadbasket trick on him. Jake had talked back to the ghost.

"Because I love you and I've never stopped loving you and I never will."

Oh, please. She barely stopped herself from rolling her eyes. "You married another woman."

Ruff, ruff, ruff, ruff.

He approached her, his hands outstretched. "Out of duty, not desire. It was a sorry plicht. I had no choice, Gillian. I faced the same thing then as you do now. The Macleans would have lost everything had I not married an heiress."

The rattle of chains from the inner wall had him scowling.

"Robyn needs to find something else to occupy her time," he grumbled. But back to the matter at hand. "Apardon, Gilly. I am sorry for hurting you. I am sorry age has finally caught up with Angus and that it has brought you to this pass. But I can help you. I *need* to help you. It has been a misery living so close but never laying eyes upon your beautiful face."

At that, Gillian wished she had some chains of her own to shake in his face. Or maybe she should bite at his ankles, herself. "Your *duty* was to me."

He shut his eyes and absorbed the blow. "With my brother's death, I became the eldest son. You would have me turn my back on five hundred years of family history?"

"Aye." She folded her arms.

"No, love, of course you would not," he said. "You understand what Culbin House means to the Macleans. You understand ties to the ancestral home."

Angry now, she snapped. "What I understand is when the time had come to cut those ties."

The rattle of chains grew louder and he glanced uneasily over his shoulder. Grrrr. . . . growled Scooter, looking his way.

With a flash of bravery, he reached for her and pulled her into his arms. Gillian tried to pull away, but his hold on her tightened. Softly, he spoke against her ear. "Let go of your anger now, lass. Nae need for that. We can be together again. Will it nae be grand?"

Though she heard him, she didn't at first comprehend what he was saying. She was too busy staring into a pair of angry green eyes that glared out from the portrait on the opposite wall. A portrait whose subject had brown eyes, if she remembered right, which she did.

David pressed little kisses against her hair, and when she didn't respond, continued, "It will be just like the old days. I'll steal away and meet you, at the standing stones or even here, because Rowanclere will be ours. We will have a fairy-tale life here, Gilly. We will be so happy."

His lips trailed downward, finding that spot on her neck that had always made her shudder with pleasure. Now, she shuddered in a different way. *Together again. Steal away.*

He is married.

Shocked, she said, "Are you asking me to be your mistress?"

"Aye," he breathed.

She drew a breath to voice her outrage just as he took her mouth in a hot, searing kiss. Gillian struggled against him, wrenching her mouth away. "David, no!"

"Gillian, my life is horrible now. I've missed you. I need—ow! That dampt dog bit me!"

"Smart dog."

Gillian heard the slow, familiar drawl as she watched the barrel of a pistol come to rest against David's temple. "Turn loose of her, you ass. I like the rug in this room, and I'd hate to see it all bloody and soiled from the likes of you."

David's hands dropped to his sides as he stepped away from Gillian. "Who are you?"

Jake lowered the aim of his gun from Maclean's head to below his belt. "I'm your worst nightmare, son. You can call me the pecker poltergeist. It's my job to make certain all the peckers in the castle stay where they belong. Of course, I figure yours is so small that it's not much of a threat. However, it's best that you keep it off Rowanclere land. In other words, bring it over here again, and you'll be leaving without it."

He paused long enough to give Gillian a significant glance, then said, "I promise."

twelve

❦

"PECKER POLTERGEIST?" GILLIAN murmured.

Jake's finger itched to pull the trigger. He really wanted to shoot this sonofabitch.

Glancing at Gillian, he observed, "Why is it that every time I turn around, I find one of the females in my life kissing someone?"

She didn't reply. She was too busy gaping at him. She backed away from both men, her mouth working, but failing to utter a word. Jake might have laughed had he not been so all-fired angry. When Maclean dared to take her in his arms, Jake had seen so much red he almost mistook the library for the crimson drawing room.

He leveled a hard, narrow-eyed stare on Maclean. With his finger in the trigger guard, he gave his revolver a quick theatrical twirl before stowing the gun in the holster of the gunbelt strapped around his hips. "You need to skedaddle on home, Maclean. Back to your wife. You are not welcome at Rowanclere."

"And just who are you to say such a thing to me?"

"Who am I?" Jake reached into his pocket and withdrew a document creased into thirds. This wasn't the way he'd intended to go about this, and even now in the midst of it, he realized he was probably making a mistake. For one thing, the paper wasn't signed yet, since he'd walked into the middle of this David crisis and hadn't had the chance to get Angus Brodie's John Hancock on the page. But right now, Jake was riled, and sometimes a man had to do what a man had to do. He had to stake a claim, to mark his territory. *Better this than peeing on the rug.* Jake shook the paper until it unfolded. "This says it all, boy."

"What is that?" Gillian demanded.

"Back home we call it a deed of sale."

David Maclean went stiff as a bois d'arc fence post. "For Rowanclere!"

"And all its contents." Without glancing at Gillian to judge her reaction—he couldn't quite force himself to do that—Jake snagged the paper from the Scotsman's hand. "Of course I intend for Angus to run this past his own lawyer, but for the most part, the deal is done. So you see, Mr. Maclaundry, it's within my prerogative to throw you out of here, and that's precisely what I'm doing. Here's your hat, what's your hurry."

The scoundrel rocked back on his heels, swaying just as if Jake had cold-cocked him. Jake wanted to crow, but instead he jerked his thumb toward the door. "Don't let the door hit your butt on the way out."

"Gillian?" Maclean asked. Begged.

She nudged Jake's arm. "May I borrow your handkerchief?"

While handing it over, he finally braved a glance. She

looked . . . beautiful, of course. Weepy, but in a good sense. Still, she did have a bit of perk to her, a glow in her eyes.

Something deep inside of Jake—a part of him he'd failed to realize was strung tighter than a hoedown fiddle—relaxed. *She's glad. She's happy I'm buying her castle.*

Of course, she didn't know the rest of it yet.

Jake sauntered over to the window and gazed outside while Gillian finished wiping her eyes. "David, I think it is best you leave now. I appreciate your . . . offer, but you must know I never would have accepted it. Jake was right. You need to return home and see to your wife."

"Gillian, please. I'm not happy with her."

"You made your choice, David. Now you must live with it."

To Jake, she said, "I would like to discuss this situation with you, but first I must check on my granduncle. You will be here when I return, I trust?"

Jake tugged his gaze from the gray stone ruins of the old watchtower built atop a hill within signaling distance of Rowanclere. "Sure. I'll come right back once I show your . . . guest . . . to the door."

Into the silence left behind in the library in Gillian's wake, David Maclean said, "This is not over. She still cares for me. I know Gilly and I can tell. I'll not give her up without a fight."

"Son, it is so over that the carcass has been picked clean and fed to the dogs. And just in case you didn't understand it the first few times, let me say it again. You are not welcome at Rowanclere. Don't even think about trying to see Gillian again."

"Gillian will need somewhere to live. I'll provide her with a cottage." He shot Jake a scathing look. "You might be buying the castle, Delaney, but you are not buying the woman."

"Hell no, I'm not buying her." Jake slapped Maclean on the back and pointed him toward the door. "I'm marrying her."

While standing in the corridor outside the library, Gillian's foot started tapping. She couldn't seem to make it stop. Uncle Angus didn't know about Jake Delaney's proposition to purchase Rowanclere.

What is going on here?

Did she truly wish to know?

Guid fegs, she was nervous. She lifted her fidgeting foot and gave it a shake, hoping to rid herself of the twitch. She shut her eyes and drew deep, calming breaths, then touched her toes ten times. Finally, having gained a modicum of control, she entered the library.

The empty library. The Texan had disappeared.

Anger surged, burning away her nervousness. "He's had plenty of time to show David the door," she grumbled, stalking around the room. "He'd said he'd be here. Why was he—"

Gillian spotted the note lying on the library desk. Picking it up, she scanned the paper, then balled it up and threw it down in frustration. "The watchtower ruins. Why would he want to discuss this there? It is outside, for heaven's sake. Jake Delaney hates being outside in the Scottish weather."

The watchtower was a twenty-minute walk from Rowanclere. Gillian made it in fifteen. She was angry and anxious and foolish with a temper, so by the time she reached her destination, she was ready to rail at the man.

She scrambled up the pebbled path to find him standing with his hands shoved into his back pockets staring out over the flower-dotted countryside. "There you are. Ah, Texas, you make me angry enough to——"

He didn't give her the chance to finish her sentence. Before she quite knew what had happened, he whirled around, yanked her against him, and took her mouth in a hard, hungry kiss.

He tasted of mint and mayhem. His mouth assaulted hers, consumed hers, daring and demanding and devouring. His hands stroked up and down her spine, his touch both savage and possessive. No one had ever wanted her this badly.

Seduced by his urgency, his intensity, Gillian's body softened. Her bones melted as she gave herself up to the heat now thrumming through her blood. She sighed into his mouth.

He tore his lips from hers and stared into her soul. "Mine, Gillian. You're mine."

Then he nipped his way down her neck. "Only mine."

He cupped her breast, kneaded her, sending arrows of wanton desire shooting to her woman's core. Gillian could hardly think, so lost was she in Jake's delicious onslaught. But even as his lips followed the path of his hand, laving her nipple through the thin sapphire silk of her dress, the echo of his words gave rise to a niggling sliver of caution in her mind.

Only mine.

But she wasn't his. She wasn't Jake's, just like she had not been David's. Not legally, nor in the eyes of God. Look where that got her. "No!" She pushed against his chest. "No! Let me go!"

He hesitated briefly before loosening his hold. She wrenched herself away and retreated to the opposite, half-crumbled wall of the watchtower. "No, Jake. This is not why we came here."

His chest rose and fell with the labored force of his breathing. Emerald eyes burned as he stared at the wet spot his mouth had left on her bodice. Gillian's breath caught. Her breasts ached to be touched.

He dragged his palm along his granite jawline, then slowly licked his lips. "Ah, princess." His hands moved to the buttons on his shirt and he yanked the top one free, saying, "Yes, princess, I think it is."

He stepped forward. She retreated and felt cool stone at her back.

Determination rumbled through his voice. "I think this is precisely why we are here. I think this is why I'm in Scotland and not on a ship headed south."

"But——"

"I want you, Gillian Ross. It's a clawing in my gut and an aching in my bones and a hunger in my blood. I'll have you, here and now."

She was a candle, slowly melting. "You can't. We can't. It is not right."

"Sure it is." He shrugged out of his shirt and tossed it aside. "It's more than right. It's perfect."

You are perfect, Gillian thought, unable to resist the sight of his broad, muscular, naked chest.

He stalked toward her, predator to prey, stopping but a foot away. Heat radiated off him in waves that called to her and warmed her from the inside out. But still, Gillian resisted. "No, you're wrong. This is wrong."

"Only if you don't want me like I want you." He

traced her bottom lip with his index finger, and she shuddered. "You can't say that, can you, Gillian? You do want me. You're hot and hungry for me. Wet for me. Right?"

In that moment, she couldn't think of a single response.

Jake took it as a yes.

His arms snaked around her. He yanked her against him, taking her mouth in a kiss that was rough and ravenous. For a few moments, Gillian couldn't help but respond. She did feel the heat. She did feel the hunger.

But she also felt the danger.

She jerked herself away from him. Tried to catch her breath. "No. I won't do this. Not again."

"Again." Jake spat the word like a filthy curse, then wiped his mouth with the back of his hand, a mean, possessive light glowing in the gaze he fixed upon her. "Did he bring you up here for your trysts?"

"No, that's not what I meant."

"Tell me, then."

She tore her gaze from the feral light glowing in his eyes and turned to stare out over the countryside. How could she put her feelings into words when she failed to understand them herself? "We were promised, David and I."

He waited for a moment, then said, "And his word wasn't worth spit."

Surprisingly, Gillian felt a smile tug at her lips. "Aye, that does manage to convey the point."

His boots scuffed across a pile of pebbles as he stepped toward her. Gillian braced herself, not knowing what to expect.

But rather than touch, he used words as his weapon. "Listen up, then, because I'm fixing to tell you something about Texans in general and me in particular."

He gently cupped her face in his palm and turned her to meet the bold honesty in his gaze. "Real men keep their promises. I'm a real man, princess, and I give you my word I'll not betray you. You're mine, Gillian Ross. Consider yourself claimed from this moment onward. Legal stuff is just a formality, but one I swear will happen. Now," he reached out and grabbed her wrist. "Where were we?"

Real men keep their promises. Gillian tried to consider the words that rang through her mind, but the impatient hands tearing at her clothing distracted her. Soon she felt the soft caress of the summer breeze against the bare skin of her back, and she moaned with pleasure.

She fought to keep a slim hold on her senses. Promises. Legal stuff. What did he mean?

His fingers tugged desperately at buttons, laces, and hooks, and Gillian couldn't think; she could only feel.

A wild, reckless yearning thrummed in her blood as both her dress and her resistance yielded to his questing hands. She wanted him. Lord help her, how she wanted him. Gillian sobbed with the force of her need.

"I want to see you," he said, his voice fierce and urgent. "All of you."

He dragged her clothing from her body, piece by piece, feasting on her flesh as he did so. Soon she stood naked in his arms, her garments a froth of white and deep blue at her feet. He paused just long enough to gaze at her. "Damn, Gillian. You're a fantasy-in-the-flesh."

He dipped his head and licked her nipple—bare this

time—once, twice, before his mouth closed over her. He hummed a satisfied sound.

Gillian instinctively arched toward him, strained against him, and while he suckled, his hands slid over her, stroking and exploring and coaxing greedy shivers from her skin. Pleasure burned through her like whisky. It was torment. It was torture. It was heaven.

"I missed you," he said between the greedy, open-mouthed kisses he trailed across her chest before taking her other breast. Her knees buckled, and she started to slide.

Jake caught her, held her, backed her up against the stone wall, pressing their bodies together, his hard ridge against her softer mound. "You haunted me. My dreams. My fantasies. Make them come true, princess. Here." He slid his hand between their bodies and found her. "Now."

Gillian moaned as his touch sent a lightning bolt of desire through her. "I need—"

"Me." He slid one finger into her sheath and stroked the sensitive skin. "You need to be mine."

Just as Gillian needed him to be hers.

The truth of that basic desire rocked her. She needed to belong to him. She needed him to belong to her.

"Aye," she whispered, sinking her fingers into the thick silk of his hair. "And you need me, too."

He growled low in his throat, then took her lips. She returned the kiss greedily. She touched him hungrily. She craved. Oh, how she craved.

Fingers fumbling, she attempted to work the fastenings on his trousers. Jake groaned impatiently and took over the task. Seconds later he spilled hotly into her hand. She curled her fingers around him and slid up and down his length, exploring, teasing, tantalizing. When he sucked in a short, frantic breath, she smiled, delighted with the evidence of her feminine power.

"Witch," he murmured.

"Wraith," she corrected.

He laughed as he pulled away from her, swept her up into his arms, then carried her to a bed of clover. Gently, he laid her down, then rose above her, stroking her skin with a hot-blooded gaze as he spoke in a half-teasing, half-serious tone. "Sorceress."

He bent his head and licked his way down her body. He teased her. He tortured her. Gillian thrashed and moaned and whimpered. She writhed.

His eyes burned and he wore a wicked smile when he paused, poised above the soft curls between her thighs.

"You can't," she breathed.

Seconds dragged by. The world beyond them faded away. The light in his eyes blazed hotter.

"You won't," she panted, anticipation shuddering through her.

He did.

Gillian cried out, her hands fisting in the sweet green grass as his tongue swept over her, stroking, tasting. Then into her, stroking, tasting. Pressure built inside her, taking her up . . . up . . . up. Taut with tension. She hung suspended, trapped, at the very brink, and helpless whimpers of need rose from her throat.

"Gillian," he growled, his breath hot against her wet skin. He flicked her once more with his tongue, and then he sucked her.

Gillian flew apart, sobbing aloud as shock waves of

pleasure ripped through her, wave after wave after wonderful wave. He licked and probed and sucked, wringing her dry and it felt like it went on forever.

His hands skimmed her thighs, lifting, spreading her open. "Again, Gillian," he demanded, his hot, hard length probing her entrance. "Again."

She whimpered in response.

With one hard thrust, he took her, filled her. His mouth crushed down on hers, branding her, claiming her. His hips pumped and his mouth plundered as he took her up again.

Gloriously lost in the moment, Gillian met him stroke for stroke. Flesh slapped against flesh, primal now, driven by the need to mate. It was sweaty skin and urgent groans and greed for more—harder, deeper, faster. The second climax hit her without warning, a bolt of lightning from a cloudless sky. She clawed his bare back. Nipped at his neck. Cried out, "Jake, oh God. Jake!"

"Look at me," he demanded, plunging once. "Me." Twice. "Mine." Three times. "You're mine!"

"Yes!" she sobbed, quaking as she welcomed the hot, wet spurt of Jake Delaney's seed. "I'm yours."

"I'm hot." Jake rolled onto his back and smiled as a cool Highland breeze swept over his sweaty skin. Damn, but that felt good. He felt good. Wonderful, in fact.

He closed his eyes, and inhaled Gillian's heady scent as he filled his lungs with air. He exhaled in a rush, a loud, satisfied sigh. Life simply didn't get any better than this.

"Hot? Did you say hot?"

Jake pried open one eye at the disbelief in Gillian's tone. "I feel like a slice of bacon sizzling on the stove."

Then he reached out, grabbed her hand, and pulled it up to his lips for a kiss. "And you, princess, are one helluva frying pan."

She gasped, then grinned, and grabbed for her gown. "The romance in your soul leaves me breathless, sir."

"So that's what it was. And here I was thinking my kisses stole all your air."

"No, sir. Your kisses stole my good sense."

Lying buck naked atop a Scottish hillside, warm and sated and at peace for the first time in weeks, Jake stretched like a rattlesnake on a sunny rock and smiled. "I'll take that as a compliment."

"It wasn't meant as one," she groused.

Like any self-respecting snake-in-the-grass, he struck, lunging for her, dragging her beneath him. Once again, their joining was furious and filled with heat, and when she had wrung him dry for a second time, he felt more like an old hound dog run to ground than a viper. "No more," he told her, groaning as he slumped onto his side. "I'll be too worn out to stand up before the preacher. I'll be damned if I'll say my wedding vows on my knees."

Slowly, she sat up. She reached for her dress and wrapped herself in its concealing folds. Her voice trembled as she repeated, "Wedding vows?"

Caution blew in on the breeze and suddenly, Jake wasn't so hot. He reached for his pants. "Yes. Wedding vows. I sorta mentioned it earlier. I came back to Rowanclere to marry you."

She went as still as the old stone wall. Jake tensed a bit himself. Really, she didn't have to look so . . . stunned. Hadn't he all but said the words earlier?

"That's what you meant when you mentioned legalities?" she asked, her voice thin and thready.

"Yes."

"Oh."

He waited. *Oh? That's all she has to say? Oh?* Standing, he shoved his legs into his britches and yanked them on. She watched him, silent and serious, until he folded his arms and glared down at her. Then it turned out she had something else to say, after all, and that something else stumped him.

"Why?" Gillian asked.

"Why?"

"Yes, why?" She leaned forward, an intense light in her bluebonnet eyes, obviously anxious about his response. "Why do you want to marry me?"

The words "want" and "marriage" didn't fit together in any sentence that ran through Jake's mind, but he had enough sense not to mention that. Instead, he threaded his fingers through his hair, rubbing the back of his neck while he prevaricated. "Well, it's kinda complicated."

"Marriage often is."

"Well, this one's apt to be more complicated than most," he grumbled.

She waited expectantly, and a sense of impending doom drifted over Jake like a cloud. He wasn't a stupid man; he knew what she hoped for. She was a woman, and God help him, he knew women.

She wanted wine and roses and silvered moonlight upon a shadowed sea. She wanted pretty words. She wanted a pledge of undying love.

Well, hell. The very idea of it sent a frisson of fear skittering up his spine.

Love meant one thing to Jake. Responsibility. When it came to tying a man down, ropes and chains had nothing on love.

And Gillian's timing stunk. For the first time in as long as he could remember, he was free of love's responsibilities. A year earlier or a year from now, perhaps he could have taken a closer look. But now, today, he could promise her anything but that. Love, he couldn't give her. Couldn't she understand that?

She's a woman. What do you think, Delaney?

To hell with it. He'd lay it out like Sunday dinner and she could take it however she wished.

Jake drew a deep breath, then began. "Being friends didn't exactly work for us, did it?"

"No."

"The thing is, I still want to be friends with you, Gillian. I like you."

The color washed from her skin and the sparkle in her eyes died. "You like me."

Oh, hell, Delaney. Where's your silver tongue when you need it? "You're a real nice girl. I like having you in my life. The way I see it, this marriage can be good for both of us."

"I see."

Did she? He'd told the truth when he said it was complicated. Jake couldn't even explain it all to himself. Still, that was the bare bones reality of it. He hated that it turned her a bit green around the gills.

She turned away from him and donned her dress, and Jake couldn't help but mourn the loss of such a spectacular view. She caught him at it and the scorn in her gaze stung.

He tried again. "Look, Gillian, I'm trying to be honest here. I thought you'd appreciate that."

Now temper flared in her eyes. "Honesty? Is that what it is? I must say, Mr. Delaney, this Texan way of wooing is different from that to which I'm accustomed."

Guilt niggled at Jake and put him on the defensive. As a result, the words he spoke were less than well-considered. "Wooing? Who said anything about wooing? I'm not offering posies and poetry. I thought you knew that, Gillian."

Smoothing away the bits of grass and grime clinging to her skirt, she spoke in a voice that dripped sugar. "Perhaps it would be best if you spelled out exactly what it is you *are* offering."

Jake folded his arms. He hated it when women got all snippy like this. "I'm talking about the traditional British marriage—a convenient one. You marry me for what I can give you and I marry you for . . . well . . .

"Sex?"

"Yes! No! That's not what I mean." He dragged a hand through his hair. "Look, princess, it's a business arrangement of sorts. I can't get to my trust fund unless I get married. If I have my trust fund, I can buy your castle. That'll give you all the funds you need to do whatever you want to do. Shoot, you can handle the whole trust for me, too, if you want to."

"So you say you're offering me marriage so you can access your trust fund. You'll marry me for money? Like David?"

"Dammit, I'm nothing like David!"

She arched a challenging brow and frustration had him clenching his fists. "Look, I never did want the money. I'd forgotten my grandfather created the trust until my mother recalled it to mind. I don't need money to do what I want, which is to—"

"See the world," Gillian interrupted, her voice flat as the Texas plains.

Jake's back was up now, and his gut frothed like milk in a churn. "That's right. I've waited a long time for this. It's my turn. I'm not gonna apologize for it. I've been straight with you about it from the beginning."

"That's true." She shut her eyes, then, and swayed a little.

He'd hurt her. Dammit all, he didn't want to hurt her. "Look, Gillian. A thought occurs to me. Since we're good at being friends, and since it's always nice to have a friend to travel with, if you want to come with me . . . well . . . you're welcome."

He wished she'd look at him. He couldn't judge her reaction at all, so being a man, he kept talking, trying to dig himself from the hole. "This marriage is a good thing for both of us. It's convenient for both of us. You get to keep your home. Isn't that what you wanted most of all?"

He watched her eyes flame and her chin come up. *Oh, man. He should have shut up when he was ahead.* He recognized the look—living with his mother and sister all these years provided a certain education—and he braced himself for a full-fledged tongue-lashing. She surprised him, though, by saying, "You never said, Jake. What do you get? What would a marriage between us bring to you?"

"I get . . . well . . . I get you."

"For sex."

Now that ripped the old tartan rug right out from under him.

"It's more than that, Gilly." He wished she could see it. He wished he could figure it out himself. "I'm not trying to buy you, if that's what has your petticoat in a twist. What will this marriage do for me? For one thing, it makes me feel good to think I'm helping you. You and Robyn and that crotchety old man you have stashed in the blue salon. Also, my having a wife will put an end to my mother's matchmaking efforts. That is no small thing, let me tell you. And let's not forget you're in this tight spot because of me and the way I haunted Harrington. Marrying you will settle the debt I owe your family. I'd feel bad setting off on my journey with that hanging over my head." He paused for a moment, then added, "And in all honesty, Gillian, I'm kinda hoping you'll decide to travel with me. It's a long way to Bora Bora. I think it'd be nice to have a friend to pass time with."

She opened her mouth, then suddenly, she stopped. Her eyes narrowed and she studied him. Seconds dragged by like Scooter on a slow day.

When she folded her arms and tilted her head, he knew he had managed to talk himself right into trouble.

"Yes, you are right," she said with a smile. "I do prefer to have Rowanclere as my home. And now that I think about it, I recognize how your plan would be advantageous to me."

"You do?"

"I do. A marriage of convenience has much to offer. I will have my home, the protection of your name."

"Wealth," he interjected.

"Yes, that." She tapped her lips with an index finger and trepidation slithered up his spine. "Also, the point about your mother's matchmaking causes something else to occur to me. I imagine that on your travels— should I choose not to accompany you—you will find that your married state frees you from any similar pressures your paramours might attempt."

"My what?" he croaked.

"Your paramours. Come now, Jake, you surely do not intend to remain celibate during your adventures."

"Well . . . I . . . uh . . . I'll probably be gone for years."

"Aye, I assumed so. And of course, no man or woman should be expected to deny his physical needs for years. So," she smiled brightly. "You say we shall be married today?"

"Huh?" He felt like he'd been knocked in the head with a fence post.

"You arranged for a clergyman to arrive today?"

As Jake cleared his throat, he felt the urge to take a step backward, but his feet remained planted on the ground. "Yes. I brought the preacher with me to Rowanclere. He's waiting for us."

"Wonderful," she said as if she meant it. She retrieved her shoes from where he had thrown them in his hurry to have her. Balancing first on one foot, and then the other, she clicked her tongue. "If we are to marry today, I must hurry. We Scots have almost as many superstitions involving marriage as we do about birthing bairns. Will you come down the hill with me now, or do you wish to remain here for a bit?"

He needed time to think. He wasn't exactly certain what had just happened here. "Actually, I think I will stay here for a time," he said, shoving his hands into his back pockets. "Enjoy this pretty day."

Gillian sent a curious glance skyward where rain clouds had started to gather. "Aye. Until later, then." She turned to go, then a dozen steps downhill paused and turned around. "Oh, Jake? What time should I be ready? What time do you wish to have the ceremony?"

"Talk to the preacher. Whenever is convenient with y'all is fine with me."

Jake watched his bride-to-be descend the hill, and in his mind's eye, he saw a man waiting to escort her back to the castle. However, the man wasn't him, but that damned David Maclean.

Shaken, he turned away, stalking across the ruins to where his shirt lay balled up against a stone wall. Bending down, he scooped it up, but when he tried to slip it on, his arms got tangled in the sleeves. *Shackled. Paramours. Celibacy.*

David Maclean.

Gillian and David Maclean.

Rain splattered his back. Cold rain. Scottish rain.

Jake thought he might just get sick.

"Jake Delaney is an idiot," Gillian muttered as she dressed for her wedding. "A kae-witted mell-heid. Looking for a convenient wife, is he? Well, I'll give him convenient."

In fact, she intended to be very, very convenient.

Gillian had a plan. The seed of it had been planted in her brain when she'd watched him up at the watchtower. The man was a martyr on the altar of marriage, to hear him talk, but the message he had conveyed with his stance, his gestures, and aye, with his lovemaking, had told another story entirely.

Jake had feelings for her.

Gillian was willing to stake her future on it.

She didn't fool herself that he loved her, not the deep,

soul-binding, forever kind of love like Flora shared with Alasdair. Not the true love that would give her reason to follow him to the ends of the earth——literally, in this case. But he did care for her. His lackluster invitation to join him in his travels told her that much, as did the jealousy he displayed toward David. He cared for her and that was a start. With encouragement and a little time, love could grow, could it not?

Because, foolish or not, she loved the contrary man. She refused to give him up without a fight. He thought he wanted adventure? Well, she would give him adventure, all that he could handle, and neither of them would need to leave Scotland.

The adventure would begin with her gown.

It wasn't a traditional wedding dress, but then, this wasn't to be a traditional wedding. Part of Gillian, the dreamy, girlish side, bemoaned the fact. She would have liked to have had all the trappings of a Scottish wedding.

"This is what you get when you marry a Texan."

She found the perfect dress in the back of her armoire. The sky blue silk matched her eyes and revealed much of her bosom——too much of her bosom——which was why she'd never worn the dress. That, and the fact the dress was cut too snug. Gillian had made a mistake when she'd ordered it on the heels of a bout of illness. In this case, however, the gown would serve her purposes perfectly.

She was threading a ribbon through her hair a few minutes later when her door opened and Robyn darted inside. "Gilly? Are you ready? Everyone is waiting. Even Uncle Angus! He's all dressed up and sitting in his chair like a king on his throne. I think he looks better than he has for the longest time."

"That's wonderful," Gillian said, turning around.

Robyn's face brightened like a morning sun and she clutched the ever-present Scooter—adorned with a bright red bow for the day's festivities—close to her chest. "Oh, Gilly, you are so beautiful. You look like a princess!"

"I feel like a sausage squeezed into a casing."

Robyn didn't make her feel any better when she eyed Gillian's bosom in speculation. "I hope your brisket disnae pop out, though. Reverend Gregor's ears would turn red as his hair."

Gillian started to tug at the bodice, then stopped herself. She had donned her armor. Now it was time to engage the battle.

Minutes later, she walked into the green salon where her granduncle shared a glass of whisky with the minister, and her groom stood laughing with a woman Gillian failed to recognize from behind. Upon noticing her, the minister's eyes went inappropriately warm for a man of the cloth. Uncle Angus gave a misty-eyed smile. Jake broke off mid-chortle.

Gillian held herself regally beneath the heat of his stare. His gaze scorched a slow path from her head to her toes, then back up again, dawdling at her neckline both ways. His reaction was everything she'd hoped for when she chose her gown. The man might succeed in his intention to bed her, wed her, and leave her, but she wouldn't make it easy for him.

At some point during his perusal, the woman turned around. When Gillian managed to drag her attention away from Jake and see who had come to call, her stomach dropped to her ankles.

The American. David's wife. Gillian eyed the rug beneath her feet with the idea of crawling under it.

"Hello, Miss Ross." Annabelle Maclean's brown eyes sparkled and she flashed a brilliant smile. She was younger than Gillian and had a fresh-washed, friendly attitude that perfectly complimented her beauty. Today, however, she gushed. "It is such a pleasure to see you again. I understand I have happened upon a happy occasion. I was out riding, you see, and noticed the towers of Rowanclere in the distance. I decided the time had come to let bygones be bygones. Isn't it lucky I picked this particular time to renew our acquaintance?"

While Gillian fumbled for an appropriate response, the American entwined her arms with Gillian's husband-to-be. "Jake and I have proved what a small world we live in. Can you believe we have mutual friends in both Boston and New Orleans? Isn't that simply amazing?"

Gillian noted how Annabelle Maclean's breast nudged up against Jake's bicep and found herself wanting to rip her man away from the other woman. Instead, she forced a smile and said, "Yes, amazing."

Uncle Angus cleared his throat. "I don't mean to rush matters, but I'd like to see this settled this year. Are you ready, lass?"

No, she wasn't. Not now. She'd heard the stories about the elaborate society wedding Annabelle's family had hosted in Boston, and she did not wish to marry in such a shabby manner in front of David's wife. Gillian did have her pride, after all.

Then Jake stepped away from Annabelle Maclean and crossed the room toward her and Gillian realized she had nothing to fret about. All the champagne and edible delicacies could not overcome the superiority of her groom over Annabelle's. *And I should know. I've had them both.*

The embarrassing thought warmed her cheeks. The flush intensified when her groom took her hands, then dipped his head to brush a kiss across her lips. "You look beautiful, princess," he said softly.

"So do you," she replied. It was the truth. He wore a crisp white shirt beneath a coat of charcoal gray and matching trousers, and she was encouraged he had bothered to dress up for the occasion. Maybe this marriage meant more to him than he allowed.

More likely, the suit was his only clean apparel.

On that cheery note, with her former lover's wife standing as witness on one side, her younger sister and a crippled dachshund on the other, Gillian prepared to say her wedding vows.

It would have been nice, though, if her groom hadn't appeared on the verge of fainting dead away.

Wedding nights, Jake told himself, were not for the faint of heart. Particularly after a strenuous wedding afternoon on a hilltop.

Gillian had retreated upstairs almost an hour ago, and he figured he'd put off joining her as long as he should. After they'd said their vows and while Gillian reluctantly gave young Mrs. Maclean a tour of the castle, Jake's first act as a married man was to send a letter off to his grandfather informing the earl that he'd been altered at the altar, so to speak. Then he spent some time with Angus discussing the purchase of Rowanclere and the documentation required for the elderly man to officially bestow the proceeds of the sale upon his grandnieces. He found the familiar legal process soothing, and he had relaxed for the first time since the preacher opened his prayer book.

Then Gillian had to walk into the room. Barefoot. Everything had gone south from there. And, in the case of his blood to his britches, he meant it quite literally.

She'd stripped off her shoes because she'd stepped into a puddle of water, and she seduced him by wriggling her toes. From that moment on, he'd felt nervous as a virgin. He didn't understand it. He'd bedded women hundreds of times. Maybe even thousands. Hell, he'd bedded Gillian twice today. Why would he be nervous now?

Because, for the first time in his life, he would be making love to his wife.

Wife. Here came that sick feeling again. What was he going to do? A man couldn't concentrate on pleasing his woman when he worried about losing his lunch.

As he reached the top of the stairs, Jake realized he truly wanted to please Gillian Ross. Gillian Ross Delaney. His wife. He wanted to please her very, very much. He'd promised Angus he would remain at Rowanclere until such time that his trust fund was released and the funds safely transferred to Gillian, Flora, and Robyn. Until then, he wanted to make her happy, to be a good husband to her.

Maybe that way she would decide to make the trip with him.

As the hours passed, Jake had grown rather fond of the idea. The fact surprised him. Astounded him, actually. But he realized he'd told her the truth up at the watchtower. He did consider Gillian a friend and the notion of traveling the world with her set well with him.

Right now, though, they needed to get past this wedding night business. He faced the bedroom door as if a firing squad waited behind it, not Gillian. Swallowing hard, he reached for the doorknob and muttered, "I just hope she's gentle with me."

The moment he stepped into the room, he wondered if he'd get a chance to find out. Gillian wasn't waiting for him in bed. She wasn't in the bedchamber at all. Jake scowled and felt a spark of anger kindle. *Don't tell me she got tired of waiting on me. I wasn't that long.*

Then he noticed the yawning dark hole in the wall where the passageway door opened. Her wedding dress lay in a heap in front of it. The sight worried him at first. Could something have happened to her? Quickly, he crossed to the passageway door and stepped into the gloom. Off to the right, an arrow made of rose petals pointed the way. "Well, well, well. This is starting to look interesting."

He found a petticoat a dozen steps away. A stocking, a flight of stairs beyond that. By the time he'd collected a second stocking, two slippers, a bustle, another petticoat, a corset cover, and a corset, Jake was whistling, his trepidation disappeared in the enjoyment of her game.

When he found the wooden head, he laughed out loud. "My, oh my. Looks like I stand to get another peek at the Headless Lady of Rowanclere's breasts."

The trail exited from the passage at the bottom of a narrow, winding stone stair. There, he discovered another rose petal arrow. Jake began to climb.

It was one of the old towers, an uninhabited part of the castle. Jake had visited it during those early explorations of Rowanclere and from what he could remember, it had served as little more than a storehouse.

He couldn't wait to find out what was stored up here now.

Jake climbed all the way to the top where finally, another door stood open. He stepped inside and his mouth went dry as a West Texas summer.

Standing in front of a small arched window, she wore the delicate white ghost gown. She was naked underneath, her generous curves tantalizingly displayed. Heat slammed into Jake like a fist. "If you're a real ghost this time or a figment of my imagination, I think I'll just lay down and cry."

She offered a slow, Jezebel smile, then knelt in front of the fireplace and gestured for him to join her. He eyed the thick rug covering the hard stone floor and the more than a dozen pillows cozily beckoned. He saw a plate of cheeses and fruit. Wine. Woman. Oh, what a woman. The setting was a hedonist's dream.

Jake took half a dozen steps toward her, then stopped abruptly when a cloud of scent descended on him. Exotic scent, erotic scent. Gillian's scent. For just a second, he closed his eyes and enjoyed. "Mmm . . ."

"It is wonderful, is it not?" She held a small amber glass bottle in one and a cork in the other and she slowly poured a heavy liquid into a clay bowl. "Fragrant oil," she said. "I've warmed it. This is a drafty old room and I know how much you are bothered by the cold, so I thought I'd do whatever I could to help you to stay warm." She dipped her fingers into the bowl, then slowly, sensuously, rubbed the oil into her palm. "Take your shirt off, Jake, and let me warm you."

The last time he moved so fast, he'd been racing Cole Morgan for the last piece of his mother's pecan pie.

"Now lie on your stomach in front of the fire," she instructed.

"But then I can't see—"

"On your stomach, Texas." She reached out with an index finger coated in spicy-scented oil and trailed it down his chest from his collarbone to his navel.

Biting back a groan, he acquiesced. "Far be it from me to argue with an apparition."

He sank into the velvety texture of the rug, then reared back up again when he felt her straddle his hips. Her slight weight settled down on his buttocks and Jake tensed, his heart racing.

She laughed softly and the sound of it sent shivers streaking up his spine. "Relax, Jake. I won't hurt you, I promise."

Slick, warm hands settled on his shoulders, then worked their way down his back, kneading and massaging. She spoke of Scotland while she worked, the burr in her voice making music of unfamiliar Scots words like sykie and ripple-grass and bobbin-quaw. He breathed the scent of her, embraced the firm, yet gentle touch of her. He drifted into a warm sea of sensation where she was the siren, the Lorelei, luring him toward . . . something. Not danger. What could be dangerous about such exquisite pleasure?

At some point, her lips began tracing the path of her hands. His limbs went languid; his blood ran thick and lazy. His need was a steady, throbbing ache, but one he preferred prolonged, instead of rushed.

Then, she coaxed him to turn over and everything changed.

Jake watched her. She straddled him as if he were a

steed, her hair a veil of sun-kissed silk flowing loose and luscious past her waist. She closed her eyes, her gaze turned inward as her hands slicked their way across his chest. A beguiling smile lingered on her lips, and the sound emerging from her throat was a hungry, yet feminine, groan.

Then her fingers found the flat round disc of his nipples. She circled them with her thumbs, then her head dropped forward and she teased him with her tongue. Jake sucked in a quick, harsh breath.

His body no longer luxuriated in warmth. It burned. It shuddered. It ached.

He had to have her soon or die.

Then, witch that she was, she sat up once more. Crossing her arms, she grasped the hem of her gown and lifted it up and off. "Are you warm enough?"

"I'm warm," he choked out, reaching for her. "Plenty warm. I'm hot. I'm sizzling again." He shifted her, trying to switch their positions and take control of the moment. But Gillian wasn't having any of that. She resisted him, laughing, teasing, and tormenting him. Such sweet, delicious torment that he chose to let her have her way.

And have her way she did.

Gillian made love to Jake. A slow, drugging passion filled with mind-reeling kisses and lingering touches. She explored and indulged and aroused. She was sense-stealing sighs and slow, silky strokes that intoxicated Jake—made him dizzy and drunk with desire. His thoughts were sluggish, cold molasses slow. The rest of him was hot. Burning, blazing hot.

Finally, thank God, she took him. Inch by slow, aching

inch. With a passion that for all its spice was sweet and somehow innocent, Gillian took him on a journey of desire and delight. She showed him a world he hadn't known existed, and in doing so, made him wish the trip could last forever.

But like all things, it ended. As they lay together before the fireplace, catching their breaths, her head pillowed on his chest, his hand stroking gently up and down her side, Jake sensed something momentous had just occurred. It scared the bejabbers out of him.

"What was this?" he asked, as tension tried to work its way back into his languishing muscles.

"It's the Maiden's Tower," she replied, obviously thinking he'd asked of their location, not what had transpired between them. Gillian drew small whirls in the hair growing on his chest. "Legend has it that in 1536 on the eve of her marriage to a neighboring laird, the Maid of Rowanclere invited the Captain of the Guard to this tower room for a romantic rendezvous that would change the course of history of this entire region of Scotland."

"Got caught, did they?"

"By the bride-to-be's father. There was a battle, and the no-longer-a-maiden Maid managed to lock herself into this room. Along with her lover who immediately became her husband, marriage by declaration accomplishing the deed. The troops were divided between the laird and his man, so a standoff ensued. It took two weeks to negotiate a settlement between the laird, the new groom, and the rejected one. But the newlyweds enjoyed their time alone so much that every year thereafter on the anniversary of their wed-

ding, they retreated to this room for two uninter-
rupted weeks."

"Two weeks, huh?" Jake lifted his head off a blue velvet pillow and made a show of glancing around the
room. "I could handle that. Though you'll have to let me
rest some. Even a stud like me has a sinking spell now
and then."

She hit him with a red and green brocade pillow
trimmed in gold fringe.

The ensuing pillow fight set the mood for the next
two weeks. Gillian and Jake didn't spend the entire time
up in the Maiden's Tower. They spent their mornings
going about the business of the castle and of the family.
Afternoons, they played; exploring nearby ruins, fishing
in the loch, riding through the glen. Gillian showed him
nooks and crannies of the Highlands he'd never have
seen on his own, and Jake thoroughly enjoyed the education and the adventure of spending his time with Gillian.
And every night they retreated to the Maiden's Tower,
where they loved the night away.

As the days passed, Jake began to realize the wings on
his feet were enjoying their rest. He woke up in the
mornings looking forward to the day and went to sleep
each night with a smile on his face. He found himself
dreading the arrival of news from England that his trust
fund had been released.

Jake was happy. He was content. It confused the hell
out of him.

He tried to take each day as it came, to put off worry-
ing about anything until he could do something about it.
He succeeded at the task fairly well. Except that in the
very recesses of his mind he wondered why Gillian

wasn't more upset about his impending departure. Did she plan to travel with him? If not, what were her plans once he left? Did that bastard Maclean figure into the picture at all? What was Gillian's outlook on faithfulness to an absent husband?

The questions plagued him, but he did his best to ignore them. Then Gillian took him on a picnic.

thirteen

GILLIAN TOOK HIM to her favorite picnic spot where a stand of birks cuddled up next to a burn. It was a beautiful, sunshine-filled afternoon, though a bit cooler than in recent days. It amused her that her formerly thin-skinned Texan didn't seem to notice. It seemed that Jake Delaney had found a way other than southern sun to warm his blood. What was yet to be seen was whether or not the allure of an adventurous, ready-and-willing bride could overcome the lure of Tahitian beaches.

Gillian didn't want to trap him into staying; she simply planned to show him what he'd be giving up by leaving. She had great faith in the life and love she had to offer. Whether he realized it or not, Jake Delaney was a family man. His stories about his sister, his mother and late father proved it to her. Gillian honestly believed he could be happy here at Rowanclere.

And she didn't think she could be happy anywhere else.

"He'll be better off with me than in a South Sea siren's arms," she grumbled softly.

"What's that?" Jake rolled from his back onto his side.

"I thought you were sleeping."

"I was. Had to get my strength back. You wear me out, woman."

Gillian stretched languidly and flexed a bare foot. A sight, she had learned, her husband especially enjoyed. "Is that a complaint?"

"I don't know." He grabbed up her foot and nipped at her toes. "Wear me out some more and let me think about it."

When finally their passion was spent and they rose from the soft tartan blanket to gather their things, Gillian discovered a most unpleasant truth. At some point during their energetic love-making, all her clothing—shoes included—had been kicked into the burn where the water carried them away.

"Oh, no." As she stared in shock down into the bubbling burn, her husband broke into laughter. "Fine, carry on like a numpty, why don't you? See how funny you'll be feeling when you ride into Rowanclere wearing little more than a blanket."

"What blanket? My clothes aren't the ones that have gone missing." Yet, even as he said it he tossed her his shirt.

She attempted to convince him to let her wear his trousers, too, but Jake wouldn't hear of it. "I wear the pants in this family, Gillian Delaney, and don't you forget it."

She was giggling when the gunshot caught them completely by surprise. Chips of bark sprayed the air as it slammed into a tree off to the right of them, not too close, but certainly close enough. Before the sound of the shot died on the air, Jake threw her down behind a fallen log and surrounded her with his body. Shielding her. "Are you hit? Dammit, Gillian, say something!"

"I can't. I canna breathe. You are squashing me."

The pressure eased as he shifted the slightest bit. Gillian followed his lead as he waited, listening hard. Only forest sounds intruded. "Stay here. Don't move."

He was up and away before she could react, transformed into a gunfighter in the blink of an eye. Gillian was tempted to rise and follow him. Not because she feared being alone, but because she found this hard-edged, gunfighter side of Jake Delaney fascinating.

However, such action would be foolish at best. Odds were their assailant had been nothing more than a careless hunter. But what if she were wrong? What if a thief or murderer had taken refuge in these woods? Following Jake could make matters worse. So, she'd do as he demanded. This one time, anyway.

Time trickled by and her resolution became more difficult to keep. Where was he? What, if anything, had he found? Why hadn't he returned? What if he were hurt? She decided to give him to the count of five hundred, then she would try to find him.

"One, two, three," she whispered, peering through the trees. At four hundred twenty-eight, she heard his welcome drawl.

"A woman who does what she is told is a rare gift."

"Where have you been?" she asked as he grabbed her hand and helped her to her feet. "What happened? Did you find him? Who was it? Why did—"

"Quiet, woman! You are wearing out my ears. You know, it's flaws like a runaway mouth that keep you from being a perfect wife."

She wanted to hit him. When he didn't tell her what he'd found, she doubled up her fist and did just that, punching him in the stomach.

"Hey!"

"Jake Delaney, tell me—"

"I couldn't find anything. Or, to be more precise, I found too much. Despite the appearance of isolation, these woods are well traveled."

"Hunters," Gillian said.

"Yes." After a moment's pause, he added grimly, "Maybe something more."

"What did you find?"

He dragged a palm up and down the line of his jaw. She could tell by his expression that he debated telling her, so she pressed. "I did as you asked and didn't follow you despite how much I wanted to do exactly that."

He blew out a sigh. "I think someone watched us, Gillian. Someone spied on us while we . . . picnicked."

Someone watched them making love? Gillian shut her eyes and winced. She really wished she hadn't asked.

Jake brooded all the way back to Rowanclere. He fumed at the knowledge that they had been spied upon. He seethed at the idea that a bullet came anywhere near to Gillian. He chafed to get his wife delivered safely to the castle so he could return to the picnic spot for a more thorough investigation.

Initially, he'd made but a cursory search for the culprit, unwilling to leave Gillian alone a moment longer than was necessary. Now he wanted to scour the woods for clues to the shooter's identity. Jake had faith in his abilities. He'd tracked cattle rustlers through the Badlands of far West Texas and banditos beyond the Rio Grande. He could certainly trail a gun-toting voyeur from a patch of birch trees beside a Scottish stream.

His first priority, however, was making sure his wife was safe.

Which was why he was both relieved and alarmed when, while sneaking into Rowanclere a back way due to their state of undress, they stumbled upon a couple involved in a heated and decidedly carnal embrace up against the gray stone wall of the stable-block.

"Oh man," Jake groaned when he spied them. "I don't want to see this. I really, really don't want to see this."

"Go away," growled Cole Morgan, not bothering to lift his head from Jake's sister's neck.

"Jake!" Chrissy exclaimed, pushing at her husband's shoulders. Cole muttered some more as he withdrew his hand from beneath Chrissy's skirts and allowed her to edge around him and fly into her brother's arms. "Finally. We waited and waited and waited . . ."

"Quit whining. Looks like you found something to occupy your time."

"You're one to talk. Where's your shirt? Where's your bride?"

She glanced around, spied both objects of her inquiry, and then did the damnedest thing. Christina Delaney Morgan, Queen of the Chili Queens of San Antonio and acknowledged as the biggest flirt in Texas, blushed. Her cheeks went bright as the walls in Rowanclere's crimson drawing room.

Jake stood there gawking at her. He couldn't remember ever seeing such a sight. He would have pondered the anomaly another moment, but he happened to note the direction of Cole's stare—toward Gillian's legs, bare below the knees—and priorities took over. He tugged on the blanket she held wrapped around her waist, hiding as much of his wife as the tartan allowed.

He couldn't do a damned thing about the bare feet. *Well, at least this is family and not some peeking pervert.*

Cole flashed a wide grin and stuck out his hand. "Howdy, Mrs. Delaney. I'm Cole Morgan and this is my wife, Christina. She's—"

"Jake's sister," Gillian said with a hint of despair in her tone. Her complexion flushed as red as Chrissy's as she yanked the blanket up in that instinctive feminine response of covering the bosom—never mind about those alluring legs and feet—and primly added, "I am very pleased to meet you."

Chrissy brushed wrinkles from her skirt and didn't quite meet Gillian's eyes as she replied, "I am thrilled to meet you, also."

Cole burst out in a laugh. "Jake, my friend, our women are liars. They're both mortified, embarrassed clear down to the bone."

Jake gave his wife's blanket skirt another downward tug. "You're right. I reckon this isn't exactly the best of circumstances for meeting new in-laws." He paused, then added, "Kinda fits our family, though, doesn't it?"

Cole folded his arms and grinned. "We are manly men with fierce appetites."

Chrissy doubled up her fist and hit first her husband, then her brother, on the shoulder. Hard.

"Bug!" they exclaimed, simultaneously, leveling glares upon her that she fired right back.

Jake added, "What have I told you about hitting me? You're just like my wife. I'm not a punching bag and. . . ."

His sentence trailed off when Gillian began to laugh. "Mrs. Morgan, something tells me you and I shall get along famously."

Her voice was music that helped to relax a part of him that had been wound tight as a pea vine through a picket fence since the gunshot. "Look, I have a barrelful of questions for y'all and a thing to tell you in return, but I know I'd be more comfortable if Gilly and I make a quick trip upstairs first. How about we meet in the library in ten minutes. It's the room right off—"

"We know where it is, Jake. Robyn Ross gave us a tour of the castle shortly after we arrived."

"Where is my sister?" Gillian inquired.

Cole's grin slashed across his face. "She said something about chariot design."

Gillian winced and chewed at her bottom lip. "Knowing Robbie, that sounds dangerous. Maybe I should—"

"No, princess." Jake grabbed her hand and tugged her along with him as he headed for a seldom used side entrance to Rowanclere. "I know about this. It's something to do with Scooter. I've been helping her, and it's nothing hazardous. C'mon, let's get you upstairs and into some shoes."

She peppered him with questions while they dressed. Some he answered, some he had no answers for, only suspicions. Like the probability that his sister and her husband brought proof that the funds of his trust had been released, completing the sale of the castle. That would mean he had fulfilled the terms of his agreement with Angus Brodie. It would mean he was free to leave Rowanclere.

His stomach sank like a foot in a bog, but almost immediately, another thought occurred that somehow made him feel a bit better. He couldn't go anywhere. Not until he got to the bottom of the mystery about the gunshot and the watcher in the woods.

"That sonofabitch," he grumbled as he slipped his arms through the sleeves of a clean shirt. The dark mood that had lifted upon seeing the Morgans descended like a cloud once again. It followed him down the stairs and into the library where Chrissy and Cole waited.

Upon entering, he glanced around the room, fully figuring to see another familiar figure. "Mother didn't come with you?"

Chrissy shook her head. "She won't be arriving until shortly before the party."

"Party? What party?"

Chrissy and Cole shared a baffled look, then his sister said, "Uh, the party you invited us to. Invitations to a celebration in honor of your marriage arrived at Hartsworth along with your note. We left almost immediately."

Jake turned to Gillian. "Do you know about this?"

She shook her head. "It must be Uncle Angus's doing. A foy is a traditional way to celebrate a wedding. He's probably invited all the family and everyone in the glen." She addressed Chrissy. "When is the event to take place?"

"Ten days from now."

"Oh." Jake didn't necessarily mind, but he wished someone had informed him about it. "Like they say, the husband is always the last to know."

Chrissy rolled her eyes. "Come on, Jake. You know we would have paid you a visit, party or not. You sent a note saying you'd married. Surely you knew to expect us after that."

"Actually, I figured to see you ride in a few days ago."

Cole accepted the glass of whisky Jake offered. "I want you to know I delayed her as long as was humanly possible."

"You always were a decent friend, Morgan." He lifted his own glass in silent salute.

Their banter annoyed his sister so Chrissy, being Chrissy, fought back. "You have to admit, news of your marriage came as quite a shock. At least, to me it did. Mother didn't act too surprised. The last I heard you were on your way to Bora Bora. What happened, Jake? What happened to make you give up your silly dream of traveling the globe? How did you convince this lovely young woman to tie herself to the likes of you for the rest of her life?"

Jake darted a glance toward Gillian. She sat on the edge of her chair, staring hard at her hands lying laced in her lap. His mouth suddenly went dry; he felt like a rabbit looking down the barrel of a shotgun. Hell, only Chrissy would have found the one topic of discussion guaranteed to make this sorry day even sorrier.

Then his wife glanced up. Their gazes met and held. He saw the warmth glowing in their deep blue depths and in that warmth, he recognized the question. *Are you willing to stay with me?*

He asked his own in return. *Have you decided to come with me when I go?*

Since their marriage, the idea had grown on him and

now, the thought of traveling alone left him cold. How beautiful would he find Tahitian beaches if Gillian wasn't sitting on the sand?

But could he bear never seeing them at all?

Hell, he couldn't think about this now. He couldn't deal with this now. He grimaced and shoved his hand through his hair. And remained silent.

Gillian's expression underwent a subtle change. He wondered if anyone else saw the shadow that dimmed her sunshine smile as she looked at Chrissy and said, "Actually, you misread our marriage. Jake and I have an understanding. He will still be taking his trip."

He cut his gaze toward her. She lifted her chin. Well, hell. That didn't sound like she meant to come along.

Jake dragged his gaze from Gillian and focused on his sister, figuring it was time to change the subject. "All this socializing needs to wait, for now. I've got business in the woods. Need to look around. Somebody took a shot at my wife and me today."

"What? Why didn't you say something earlier?" Cole sat his whisky glass down hard and sighed. "Not more trouble. I was hoping we were done with that sort of thing."

Chrissy's expression turned fierce. "Why would someone shoot at you? What have you gotten yourself into now, Jake Delaney?"

"Me? Hey sister, I'm not the one who got herself sealed into a sarcophagus last winter, now am I?"

"That wasn't my fault and you know it."

"Please!" Gillian shoved to her feet. "The two of you whine louder than Flora's hungry bairns."

Brother and sister locked gazes. He grinned. "Isn't she cute?"

"I like her, Jake. Now tell me who would want to kill you."

A wheezing cough sounded from the doorway right before Angus Brodie said, "That's a tale I'd like to hear myself."

Gillian beamed at her granduncle. "Uncle Angus, it is wonderful to see you up. You must be feeling better."

"I am feeling well this day—at least I was. Tell me about this trouble."

Gillian nibbled at her bottom lip and wandered around the room during Jake's recitation of the events in the birk woods, afraid he'd say more than strictly necessary about their activities during the picnic. She had yet to recover from her embarrassment over her initial meeting with the Morgans. All she needed now was for Uncle Angus to hear the story.

Jake averted that disaster, however, by telling the tale in crisp, succinct sentences. She sensed his anxiousness to return to the woods to search, but he took care with her granduncle, answering all his questions before asking some of his own. Questions that took Gillian aback.

"What about this Maclean fella?" Jake asked. "Think he could have done it?"

"David?" repeated Angus.

"Not David," Gillian scoffed. She wiped a bit of dust from the glass and brass inkwell on the desk.

"Why not?" Jake sprawled upon a settee. "Jealousy does strange things to a man."

"Who is David?" asked Chrissy.

"I was once betrothed to David Maclean," Gillian replied. "He married someone else. Assuming that shot might have been a product of David's jealousy is sappie-headed."

Jake snorted. "You're the one being sappie-headed, whatever that is. Have you already forgotten what he wanted when he came to call? I don't doubt David Maclean is jealous as hell that you are mine and not his. In fact, I think Maclean took a potshot at me and missed. He watched us, Gillian. Spied on us."

"Spied on you?" Uncle Angus repeated. "What do you mean?"

She felt the heat climb up her neck. *Please, Jake, don't.*

"Some sonofabitch stood in the trees and watched me make love to my wife."

If embarrassment could melt the human body, Gillian would be a puddle on the library floor.

Angus thumped the tartan carpet with one of his canes. "Maclean would not act in such a dishonorable manner."

Jake sat up straight and leaned forward, resting his elbows on his knees. He stared Angus right in the eyes and declared, "The hell he wouldn't. He asked her to be his mistress!"

"Jake, watch your language," cautioned his sister.

Angus frowned and tugged at his beard. "He asked that of her?"

"Yes!"

Angus looked at Gillian. "Ah lass, the puir man loves you so much."

"Love?" Jake's eyes went wide and round as he shoved to his feet. "Excuse me, Gillian is my wife—" he thumped his chest "—not his. The man had his chance and he threw it away. He married someone else."

Angus gave another whack with his cane. "You don't ken, Delaney. He did his duty by his family, just like young men—and women—have done for ages. He is a good man." Angus paused, then threw down the verbal gauntlet. "Gillian would not have fallen in love with him were he not."

"That's right," Gillian agreed.

Jake made a fist and banged on a table. "David Maclean is married. And by God, Gillian is too. They both need to remember that." Green eyes blazed as he shot a look toward Cole and snapped, "I'm headin' back to the woods to take a closer look at the scene. Are you comin' with me?"

Cole Morgan followed Jake as he stormed out of the library, and moments later, the bang of Rowanclere's front door echoed through the hallways.

"Even with my puir hearing I heard that slam," Angus said, wincing. Then he cleared his throat and added, "Gilly, what is all this nonsense about David? Did he truly ask you to be his dunty?"

She sank onto the settee recently vacated by her husband. "Aye. The day Jake and I wed. Though I doubt Jake would admit it, I believe it is the reason he proposed marriage. He was angry at David."

"He was jealous. He is still jealous and that is why he suspects this David of being the culprit behind the shooting." Christina Morgan settled back into her seat with a pleased smile. "Green looks good on my brother. Matches his eyes. Mama will be so happy. You have hooked him but good, Gillian."

Gillian offered a sickly smile. Chrissy couldn't have been more wrong. "Our marriage is more an arrangement than a traditional union. Your brother made his wishes clear from the outset. He will depart for his travels as soon as some legal work is completed."

"And that's all right with you?"

She dusted the settee's wooden trim with her thumb. "I will admit I have harbored hopes of winning him, but I do not want him if he doesn't want to stay. I won't have a man filled with regrets."

"Regrets?" Chrissy wrinkled her nose. "No, not Jake. He's not the type. Oh, he may play out the line for a time, run with the bait, but I know my brother. He is well and truly hooked. I am thrilled about it too, Gillian. I think you and I will be the best of friends."

"You should talk to him," Angus announced. "Something is wrong here, I sense it."

"I will not." Gillian folded her arms and frowned. "I have my pride. If he stays, I want it to be his choice, not because of anything I said."

"Not Delaney," Angus said, waving a dismissive hand. "Maclean. Something is off about this entire business. I canna believe he would come to our home and invite you to become his mistress. That's not the David I know."

Gillian steepled her fingers in front of her mouth, tapping her lips as she considered Uncle Angus's suggestion. "I think that is an excellent idea."

"It's a terrible idea," Chrissy cried. "You cannot knock on a man's front door and accuse him of shooting at you."

"I will not be accusing David of anything," Gillian said, waving away Chrissy's protest. "You're right, Uncle Angus. Something about this situation smells like Scooter when she's wet. I'll talk to David today."

In the end, a trip to David's home wasn't necessary because the answers to all Gillian's questions came knocking at Rowanclere's door.

Annabelle Maclean had come to call, her face wet with tears.

Gillian showed Annabelle into the crimson salon and rang for tea. Though the other woman tried to launch into conversation immediately, Gillian put her off. From the looks of this, tea might not be enough. They might need to break into the barley-bree before their talk was over.

After Mrs. Ferguson brought a tray, and tea and biscuits were served, Gillian took a sip from her cup, then asked, "Now, Mrs. Maclean. What brings you to Rowanclere today?"

Her teacup rattled its saucer. Annabelle looked at Gillian with weepy brown eyes and said, "God forgive me. I'm the one who shot you."

Gillian choked on a bite of shortbread.

And Annabelle was off. "Of course, I didn't actually shoot you because I missed, and I only missed because I didn't truly mean to shoot. If I'd meant to shoot you, I'd have killed you. I'm a very good shot. My father is a wealthy man now but he started out poor and living in the slums of the city. He believes that females should know how to protect themselves, so he taught all his daughters how to shoot. I have two sisters, you see. I'm the oldest girl. I have four older brothers and they helped teach me, too."

She finally paused to take a breath and Gillian grabbed her chance. "Why in the world did you shoot at us?"

"At you. I shot at you. Because, I'm afraid I hate you, Mrs. Delaney. I know all about you. David told me you were lovers. He told me you are the only woman he will ever love. He told me he's asked you to be his mistress! I knew something was wrong the day of your wedding. That's why I paid you a visit. I thought once you married everything would be better, but it's not. It's only natural I should hate you, don't you think?"

"Uh . . ." Gillian took another sip of tea. How did one answer such a question? For that matter, why should she answer it? Why was she even listening to this American? The woman shot at her. Shot at her for something she not only didn't do, but had no desire to do.

She needn't have worried. Apparently, an answer was not required because Annabelle kept talking. "That's why I shot at you. I was taking a long walk because it's so very miserable to be home alone, even when the man you love is in the house. And what do I find? The very woman who has caused me so much grief cavorting in the woods with yet another man who is in love with her. By the way, I couldn't help but notice that Mr. Delaney is quite an admirable man. So well built. More so than David, don't you agree. My brothers would say he is hung like a horse."

Gillian spewed out her sip of tea.

"I might just tell David about that if I ever decide to speak to him again. He wouldn't like it. He wouldn't like it one bit. It might feel nice to hurt him. He's hurt me so . . . *sob* . . . so . . . *sob* . . . much—" She broke into tears heavy enough to fill a small loch.

Gillian didn't know what to do. Should she comfort the woman? Ignore her tears? Have her arrested? Lock her in the dungeon?

She chose to hand her a handkerchief. Annabelle sobbed into it.

The instinct to offer comfort caused Gillian to reach out and pat the woman's knee. Before she quite realized what was happening, David's wife had thrown herself into Gillian's arms.

"Now this is beyond strange," she murmured as her former lover's wife cried on her shoulder like a babe.

"Now, now, now," she said finally, after Annabelle had begun to hiccup. "It's all right. Everything will be all right."

With the handkerchief soaked, Gillian offered her a napkin from the tea tray. Annabelle blew her nose loudly. "I'm sorry I shot at you. I wasn't thinking. The two of you looked so happy and in love. I am . . . *sob* . . . *sob* . . . so mortally ashamed. Oh, Mrs. Delaney. I love my husband so much. David already hates me, but now he'll hate me even more. And I do so love him. I love him very much. For a while, there, I thought he loved me, too." *Boo hoo hoo hoo.*

Guid fegs, the woman could teach Flora's bairns how to cry. "Now Annabelle, we can keep this to ourselves. David need not know. No law says you must tell your husband everything, you ken, and this would only upset David."

"You won't tell him?"

"I will not." Nor would she tell Jake unless she was forced to do so.

"Oh, Mrs. Delaney!" Annabelle cried even harder. "David is right. You are nice. So much nicer than I."

As the young woman continued to sob, Gillian debated what to do next. She had no experience with women in such a state. She couldn't ever remember being this distraught, not even when she learned David had married this . . . girl. She was little more than a girl. "How old are you, Annabelle?"

"I . . . *sob* . . . just turned . . . *sob* . . . *sob* . . . eighteen. Will I go to jail for what I did? They'll call it attempted murder, even though I promise I didn't aim at you."

They'd been married over a year. *Why, the man robbed the cradle.* "Annabelle, I said I won't tell. You won't go to jail."

She looked up at Gillian, those round brown eyes filled with hope. *She really is a pretty thing. No wonder David chose her.*

In that moment, Gillian experienced a revelation. Annabelle clearly worshiped her husband. Knowing David, he undoubtedly preened under such regard. Though Gillian had loved him, she certainly never worshiped at his feet. That sort of attention would be bound to appeal to the man. *I bet he loves her, after all. I bet that visit he paid to Rowanclere had more to do with Annabelle than with me. David Maclean is in love with his wife.*

Surprisingly, it didn't bother Gillian a bit.

Anxious to prove her supposition true, she inquired, "So tell me about your marriage, Annabelle. You were happy for a time?"

"Yes, we were. I thought we were. At least, until last month."

"And what happened last month?"

She started sobbing again, even louder now, and Gillian lifted her gaze to the ceiling and shook her head, still dumbfounded at the notion that she would be offering marital advice to David's wife.

Annabelle gasped a breath and said, "Last month my . . . my . . . mother . . . came to visit."

Light dawned. A mother-in-law. One of the greatest challenges to any marriage. "Oh. I see. Is she still there?"

"Yes. She doesn't plan to leave for six more months. Mother can be rather difficult. She and David don't get along at all. I'm afraid . . . I think . . . he might . . . *sob* . . . leave. He's so angry all the time. Oh, Mrs. Delaney, he hasn't come to my bed in weeks!"

"That is a problem."

"It's a disaster, Mrs. Delaney. Please, you're obviously very happy in your own marriage. Do you have any advice for me? I should be more like you. If I were more like you, maybe I could make David love me. Please, Mrs. Delaney. What can I do?"

Gillian shook her head. "You don't need to be like me. He married you, not me. David fell in love with you. You need not change, it's your living arrangements that need some . . . well . . . rearranging."

Pursing her lips, Gillian considered the problem. When an idea flickered to life, she inquired, "What sort of woman is your mother, Annabelle? Is she superstitious at all? Fearful of anything?"

"Oh, yes. She's a terrible scairdy-cat. Papa says she has cold feet no matter how hot the weather."

"Excellent." Gillian grabbed a second napkin from the tea tray and handed it to Annabelle. "Dry up, lass. I'm going to help you."

Hope bloomed like heather in August in the girl's expression. "You are? Oh, that's wonderful, Mrs. Delaney. What are you going to do?"

"Call me Gillian, please. I'm going to help you get rid of your mother."

*　　　*　　　*

Walking beside the small stream near the picnic site, their gazes intent upon the ground, Jake and Cole searched for clues. Comfortable with the familiarity of such a task, they conversed while they went about their search. "Your missus has spunk," Cole observed. "She reminds me of Christina."

"In a way, I guess. She's ornery like Bug. You should have seen her play the Wraith of Rowanclere."

"The what?"

"Never mind." They had reached the spot where earlier Jake had found signs of a snoop. The two men hunkered down on either side of the footprint faintly visible in the soft dirt. Cole measured the depth of the indentation with his finger. "Look how shallow. Small, too. A full-grown man would have left a bigger print. Unless this Maclean fella is a tiny man, looks like your voyeur was a youngster, Jake. Probably a proud-and-primed boy from the village who was too busy recalling the look of your lady's, uh, charms, to pay attention to the gun in his hand."

"You're probably right. Otherwise, we'd have found something suspicious. I just wish I'd caught sight of whoever fired the gun. He could have hurt Gillian. He did hurt her by spying on us." After a moment's pause where he kicked at the dirt, he added, "Youngster needs his ass whipped."

"I can't argue with that." Cole stood and stretched. " 'Course, some might say a man who uses the great outdoors for a bedroom ought to expect less than total privacy."

"Considering how I stumbled across you this morning, you're one to talk."

Cole grinned. "So, do we let this go or do you want to keep looking for the shooter?"

"Nah, I'll let it go, for now anyway. If anything else happens, I'll reconsider."

"Fair enough." Cole nodded. "So, on to more interesting subjects. What's with this marriage of yours? Is it for real or not?"

Jake's gaze went to the pleasant picnic spot beside the stream, or burn, as Gillian called it. The memory of her needy, passionate cries that had filled the air not long ago reverberated through his mind. "Oh, it's real enough. Signed sealed and delivered. Or, at least it will be if, as I suspect, you brought word from my grandfather."

"You mean this?"

Cole reached into his pocket and withdrew an envelope. He handed it to Jake, who opened it, removed the folded paper, and quickly skimmed the page. The funds had been released, his draft honored. Rowanclere was his. "It's done."

"What's done, Jake?"

"Mother knows the whole story. Didn't she tell you any of it?"

Cole folded his arms and leaned against a tree. "Elizabeth didn't say much of anything—not that Christina gave her the chance. She was ready to head for Scotland the minute your grandfather read the letter announcing your marriage. To say your sister was anxious to meet your bride is like saying she flirts a little."

Jake snorted. "My sister is the biggest flirt in Texas."

"You gotta add Great Britain in there, too. Marriage hasn't changed that. Not enough to suit me, anyway. You're lucky your wife isn't like Christina in that regard."

"No, my wife doesn't flirt with other men." Silently, he added, *She beds 'em.*

Damned if that didn't stick in his craw.

"If Chrissy came up here expecting to find me getting all domestic, she's bound for disappointment." Jake returned the paper to the envelope and slapped it against his hand as he spoke. He elaborated on how he'd ruined Gillian's plans when he failed in his haunting of Harrington. He mentioned his guilt and the proposition he'd put to his mother and the proposal of a proposal she'd made in turn. "So, I married her. I bought it. The funds have now been transferred. Cole, my friend, you are looking at the new owner of Rowanclere Castle. And I don't know what the hell to do next. I don't know if my wife intends to travel with me. She dodges the question every time I bring it up. Guess I'll have to hang around until this party, anyway, and now with this bullet business, I wouldn't think of going until I have some answers there."

Cole was looking at him strangely.

"What?"

"Back this wagon on up a bit. Back to this ghost business. You haunted Harrington?"

"I told you about that when I was in England."

"But you didn't say . . . you dressed up like a dead Scotsman?"

"What else? We're in Scotland, not San Antonio."

"But you . . . you did it . . . in a skirt, Delaney? You actually put on a skirt? That wasn't all talk?"

"Gillian calls it a feileadh mor."

Cole's mouth gaped open. "Surely not."

"Watch it there, Morgan. Don't be calling me Shirley

just because I dressed like a Scotsman. I have to admit that once I got used to the draft, it was kinda comfortable."

Slowly, Cole shook his head. "No wonder you're confused about what to do about your castle. That skirt-wearing has probably put girl-thoughts in your head. That'll screw up your thinking but good."

"Tell me about it. I'm as mixed-up as a fly in a butter churn." He scooped a handful of stones off the ground, then pinged one off the side of a boulder a short distance away. So much had been packed into this day. Life had gone round and round like a lariat in a cowherd's hand and left him dizzy. "I can't wait to go, but I don't want to leave Rowanclere. I want her, Cole. I want Gillian."

"That's handy. Considering you're married to her and you own her home."

He threw a pebble hard. "But I don't want to want her."

Cole simply arched a brow and watched him, waiting.

Jake snarled at him. "You know how long I've waited to take off, Cole. I loved the freedom I had as a youth— hell, I'd still be a cowboy driving cattle north if I could. I was loath to give it all up, but I did because that's what was expected of me. Doing all that living up to the Delaney name and Delaney responsibilities was damned difficult, but I did it. I read law like my father wanted, because he wanted it. I gave my time to social clubs and political issues and one boring dinner party after another because I was J. B. Delaney's son. Yet, through all of it, I managed not to get caught. I stood firm against the not inconsiderable pressure placed upon me by my parents to marry a worthy young woman and settle in San Antone and raise the next generation of Delaney puppets."

"Delaney puppets?" Cole drawled, folding his arms.

"That's taking it a little far, don't you think? Christina has never been anybody's puppet."

"True. But Chrissy had an excuse. She's female."

"And I thank God for that every day," Cole solemnly replied.

Jake rolled his eyes. "I did what I was supposed to do, and I did it gladly. I'm proud of how I took care of Mother and Chrissy after my father died. It makes me feel good to know I was the kind of son he wanted me to be. But now I've fulfilled those commitments and I don't want any more. I want to see the Orient. I want to swim in an ocean that is bath-water warm. And I can do that now. Nothing is stopping me. Chrissy is married. Mother is . . . well . . . I don't want to go into that other than to say she no longer needs me around to support her. I am free. Finally, I am free."

"Hmm . . ." Cole rubbed the back of his neck. "Let me see if I have this straight. You are a free man. But you are married. And you have just bought a rather large house. And Gillian could already be carrying your child. That sounds like freedom to me."

Jake made an obscene hand gesture, and Cole's lips twisted into a grin. "Okay, maybe not freedom. How about something else? Love. That's it, Jake, my man. Sounds to me like you are in love."

"Love?" A noose slipped around his neck. "I don't want to be in love."

"Why not? I have to tell you, Jake, I really like being in love with your sister. And for more reasons than the obvious."

"Don't talk about sex. I don't want to think about you and Bug and sex."

"No, that's private. Spectacular, but private." Ignoring

Jake's groan, he pressed on. "Pare this down to the nut, Jake. Why did you marry Gillian?"

"Because I owed her, and marrying her was the way to pay her back."

"That's bullshit. Why did you marry her, Jake?"

The sharp edges of rocks bit into his hand as he made a fist. "Because I walked into Rowanclere and that damned Maclean sonofabitch was asking her to be his paramour."

Cole walked toward him, looked into his eyes. "Try again, idiot. Why did you marry Gillian Ross?"

"Because I wanted to. I needed to."

"Because you . . . ?"

"Love her, goddammit. I love her!" He wound back his arm and hurled the remaining pebbles. They crashed and pinged into the trees. "I love her and it has turned my world upside down. I don't want to love her. I don't want to live here. I'm cold here. I don't want to be stuck living here in perpetual winter raising children who've never seen a longhorn cow!"

"Actually, they have some longhorn cattle in Scotland. Shaggy things. Don't you remember? Bennet had some stuffed ones in his country house."

"Forget the damned cows. What about Gillian? Grandfather released the money. The sale is completed. So, unless I find out this nonsense here today was something more sinister than we think, I can leave. I can head out right after this party Angus is throwing. But what the hell am I going to do about Gillian?"

"Nothing." Gillian's voice was the second bullet that had streaked from those trees this day. She stepped into sight and stared straight at her husband. "Cole, could you excuse us, please?"

fourteen

❧

I LOVE HER, he had said. *I don't want to love her.*

They were not exactly the words a bride wishes to hear, but for Gillian, they were close enough.

"Uh, princess." Jake shoved his fingers through his hair. "Gillian, I didn't mean it the way it sounded. But no matter what, you shouldn't have been eavesdropping. Like my mama always told me, no eavesdropper ever hears good about himself. Didn't anyone ever teach you that?"

She arched a brow. Really, the man did his cause no good. Assuming she was angry about what she'd overheard, he obviously felt defensive, and in a natural, if misguided, masculine reaction, he went on the attack. "Dammit, woman. Don't act like a five-year-old about this. I swear, sometimes Robbie could give you lessons on maturity."

All right, now he'd gone too far. Biting the inside of her cheek to keep from smiling, feeling more alive than she could ever remember, Gillian jumped headfirst into the game—by letting loose a small sob and turning and running for the castle.

As expected, he took off after her. "Gillian! Wait, come back here."

She lifted her skirts and picked up speed, confident she could outrun him. She gave free rein to her smile as she ran, tamping it down only when she entered the castle and dashed past the obviously curious Morgans.

She headed for the Maiden's Tower and hurried up the winding staircase. She knew exactly what she wanted, and how she wanted to get it. Upon reaching what she'd begun to think of as the Honeymoon Room, she darted inside, then slammed and locked the door behind her.

Bang! Bang! Bang! Gillian hummed a song as she arranged pillows and blankets to suit her.

Bang! Bang! Bang! "Gillian! Open this door!"

Knowing that her time was limited—her husband was quite good with locks—she hurried to complete her preparations.

Gillian Ross Delaney stripped naked and waited for her husband to break into the room.

She didn't wait long. She heard a scraping sound at the lock, then the knob turned and the door was shoved open. "Dammit Gillian," he cursed as he barged into the room, "nothing is ever sol—"

Jake swallowed his words and quite possibly his tongue. Gillian lifted her arms toward him and spoke the words in her heart. "All I ever wanted was your love, Jake Delaney. I love you, too. If you still want my company on your adventures, I will go along."

"Yes. Oh God, yes." His gaze never leaving her, he

immediately began pulling off his clothes. "I thought you were angry."

"I know. You don't know me as well as I know you." When he looked like he thought to argue the point, she stepped up to help him with his clothes. When her hands brushed across his chest to slip his shirt off his shoulders, he sucked in a breath past gritted teeth. "I've been loved outdoors today already. I wanted you here, in this room, where I first realized how much I love you."

"Oh, princess." He bore her down upon the blankets and loved her with a fierce tenderness that both roused her to the heights of passion and wrung tears of joy from her soul. His warmth was her warmth. His heart, hers. She was complete, whole and happy and fulfilled for the first time in her life.

Still inside her, he rose above her and stared down into her eyes. Solemnly, he declared, "I do love you, Gillian Delaney. I love your heart and your energy and your spunk. I love your loyalty to those you love. I love the fire you bring to our bed." Then a quick flash of a grin. "And to our blankets."

He leaned down and kissed away the sweet tear that spilled from her eye. "I will make you happy, Gillian. You have my promise."

He kissed her lips, then, and kept on kissing her until his body hardened once again and her feminine core wept with need. She gloried in the intensity of his passion. Every touch, every taste, every sound a reaffirmation of the vow he made to her. When it was over, he cradled her against him. His hand brushed slow, soothing strokes across her heated skin and quietly, they spoke of the future they would share.

"I never thought I could convince you to come with me."

She smiled, though a bit sadly. "I thought I could open your eyes to all the adventure Scotland has to offer. I will be truthful with you, Jake. I dinna share your dreams of adventure, not the way you wish."

As his finger painted an imaginary swirl upon her stomach, she attempted to explain. "I have no ambition to see Egyptian pyramids or kangaroos in the Australian outback. My dream is different. I dream of tucking my bairns to sleep beneath the roof of my very own home. I dream of retiring to my bed each night with my husband who loves me to distraction."

His voice rumbled low and soft. "It doesn't seem to me that our goals are mutually exclusive. If we're willing to compromise a bit, I don't see why we can't both get what we want. I mean, you already have the husband who loves you to distraction and I'll be happy to work on getting you those babies any time you wish."

She smiled and stretched sinuously against him as his finger wandered upward to trace a path across her breasts. "That's what I realized. As long as I have you and your love, I dinna need the roof."

He rolled above her yet again, grinning wickedly. "I'll be your roof, princess. Anytime. Anyplace. Or your blanket. I'm versatile."

So saying, he set out to prove it. He accomplished his task admirably, then collapsed onto the floor beside her. "I think you've killed me."

Gillian wanted to reply, but couldn't catch her breath enough to speak. Minutes later, he said, "I hate to bring this up, princess, but I guess I'd better. What about Angus and Robbie? Are you all right about leaving them?"

She wondered if he purposely waited until she was completely exhausted to bring up the subject. "It winna be easy. But it is not like I will be leaving them to fend for themselves. Flora has long offered to see to their caretaking. They will be happy enough at Laichmoray."

"Good." He lifted his head and propped it on his elbow. "You wouldn't believe how often I've fantasized about you, me, and a Bora Bora beach. I can't wait, princess. Cole brought me the papers from my grandfather. The trust has been released, so I can complete the business about the castle with Angus. I'm not trying to rush you, but how soon do you think you can be ready to leave? As soon as this party is over?"

Gillian tried to ignore the sinking sensation in her stomach caused by his question. Glad to have something other than leaving her home and homeland to ponder, she sat up, pasted on a cheerful smile, and said, "Possibly. I've a task to complete, first. I've promised my help to someone, but I might be able to see it done by the foy. I will need to think of a plan."

"You and your plans. You scare me, Gilly. What is this task all about?" Jake followed her lead and reached for his pants. "Who are you wanting to help?"

Bracing herself for an explosion, she leaned over and pressed a kiss against his cheek. "Annabelle Maclean. She confessed to firing the shot that surprised us this morning. I've promised to help her win back David's love."

Jake Delaney's subsequent shout rocked Rowanclere's ancient walls.

*   *   *

It set the pattern for the days that followed.

To say Jake wasn't happy about Gillian's proposed meddling in the Macleans' marriage was like saying Scooter had trouble climbing up stairs. While he liked the general idea of a strong marriage between that damnable David and his wife, he despised the idea of his own bride being involved in the matter in any way, shape, form, or fashion. Though he'd never admit it to a soul, he felt a bit uneasy . . . well, more than uneasy. He felt threatened at the notion of Gillian having anything at all to do with Maclean.

It wasn't that he doubted her love or her integrity, because he didn't. Maclean, however, was another matter entirely. Jake didn't trust him any farther than he could throw him. Hell, any man who'd had a taste of the heaven to be found in Gillian's arms would be bound to come sniffing around for more. Especially when he wasn't getting his pistol oiled at home.

Such thoughts were part of the reason why, while the Lady of Rowanclere made plans for an assault on the wall separating David Maclean and his wife, the new laird of Rowanclere laid siege to his own castle, so to speak. Each day he fought a subtle battle with gifts and pretty words and acts of tenderness and kindness. Every night, he waged his war on the sometimes sweet, and sometimes stormy battlefield of their bed. And while the laird breached his lady-wife's defenses both physically and mentally, it was against his own fears and doubts that he waged war.

He worried that something would happen before they left. He worried that some catastrophic event might occur and prevent her from leaving.

The sooner they departed Rowanclere, the better. That particular certainty was the reason Jake agreed to participate in Gillian's latest bit of theater. It was the reason he was on his way to a strategy session in Rowanclere's library.

"Well, if it's not the Diabolical Duo," he said, spying his wife and sister with their heads together, giggling. "Where's your apprentice? I thought Quick Draw was supposed to be at this meeting."

Chrissy snorted. "If you're referring to Annabelle, then she'll be back in a few minutes. Robyn insisted on showing her the chariot y'all made for Scooter."

Jake nodded and poured himself a drink. Having already suffered two of these get-togethers, he knew he'd want a belt of good whisky sooner or later.

Judging by the first thing out of his bride's mouth after Annabelle joined them a few moments later, sooner was the applicable term. "Annabelle, I have considered your suggestion, and I believe you are right. I, rather than Chrissy, should be the one to pay particular attention to David at the foy."

Whisky burned a path down Jake's throat. "Wait just one minute. I thought the idea of this entire plan was to help repair damage to the Macleans' marriage, not cause more."

The three women shared a rueful look, then proceeded to ignore him.

Gillian took a seat at the library desk and removed a sheet of paper from a drawer. "Going over the checklist . . . Annabelle, you reviewed the guest list with Uncle Angus and confirmed he did not forget anyone?"

"I did."

"Chrissy, food preparations?"

"The supplies we ordered have arrived and Mrs. Ferguson is happily baking and broiling. She's not too keen about turning over her kitchen to me for an afternoon so I can mix up my chili, but we've reached a compromise. Everything should be ready on schedule."

"Excellent." Gillian made a check on the paper. "Jake, about the whisky and ale?"

He stretched out his legs, crossed them at the ankles, and folded his arms. "Angus told me what to order and I ordered it. It'll be here tomorrow. You know that, Gillian. I told you yesterday."

She frowned at him. "Don't pout, Texas."

As the discussion digressed into fashion and the ladies' own attire to the party, Jake sat sulking and sipping his drink. How the hell had he allowed himself to get involved in this? He should have called a halt to Gillian's plan the minute he heard about it. Cole had been right to call him nine kinds of fool for putting up with this nonsense. Of course, Morgan was one to talk. Wasn't he rowing Loch Rowanclere right this very minute, headed for the village to buy spices for Chrissy's chili?

"Well," said Gillian, dropping her pen onto the desk. "That should just about do it. Everyone knows their part. We'll plan to meet—" She broke off abruptly at the sound of Mrs. Ferguson's screech. "David Maclean, you get back here. Miss Annabelle is not here and you will not be bursting into my laird's library looking for mischief."

Everyone in the room realized they had been given a warning. Jake pointed at Annabelle, then to the desk. As she scrambled to hide herself, he joined Gillian and wrapped her in his arms. Giving Gillian a passionate kiss was a fitting distraction, he decided.

The door flew open. "Where is she? Where's my wife!"

Jake didn't have to pretend to be annoyed. "Maclean, what the devil are you doing here? I seem to recall warning you not to step foot on Rowanclere land at risk of losing your . . . pride."

The Scotsman's gaze flickered around the room. "So it's not you she's meeting. It's the other American. She said—"

Chrissy set down her cup and saucer with a clatter. In a weak female voice entirely unlike her, she gasped, then asked, "Sir, are you implying that your wife is with my husband?"

Gillian pulled herself out of Jake's arms, appearing delightfully mussed. Watching her, he wished he hadn't kissed her after all, because now she sparkled even more than normal as she gazed up at her former beau.

"Cole has gone to the village today," she said in a chastising tone. "He's picking up supplies for our foy. David, you speak out of turn. You winna find your wife at Rowanclere."

The man didn't like being scolded by Gillian, Jake saw. He also obviously believed what she said because he gave a curt nod, then departed.

No one moved until Jake said, "All right, Annabelle. I think it's safe for you to come out."

She crawled from beneath the desk and brushed off her skirts. "It's working. He's jealous, I can tell."

Jake watched the young woman study Gillian with

eyes alight with interest. What did she think when she watched the woman her husband still claimed to love? Glancing at his wife, Jake knew what *he* thought. The need to have her was a fever in his blood, a combination of his customary lust for her, the jealousy that surged through him at each sight of that damned Maclean, and the effect of the kiss they just shared.

Because his attention was focused on his wife, he didn't realize Annabelle had moved until she stood directly in front of him, her face lifted toward his. "I need to look all lovely and mussed like Gillian when I go home. You'd better kiss me like you did her."

Jake gawked at her pursed lips, then shot Gillian an entreating gaze. His wife sighed and shook her head. "Nice try, Annabelle, but I don't share. Go home and prepare for the foy."

Two days before the party, Gillian spent the morning with Robyn doing nothing more serious than playing. They held a mock sword battle in the muniment room, took Scooter on a long ramble across the glen, and chased Mrs. Ferguson from the kitchen long enough to make a batch of scones. They teased and laughed and giggled. It was such fun.

It was all Gillian could do not to burst into tears.

The preparations for the foy had helped her keep thoughts about her pending departure from Rowanclere at bay, but as the day grew closer, she had to face reality. As much as she loved Jake, the thought of leaving her family all but tore her in two.

She hadn't told them yet because she needed to talk with Flora first. While she knew her twin wouldn't hesitate to make a place for Angus and Robyn at Laichmoray, good manners required she wait for her sister to offer first.

Around lunchtime, melancholy settled over her and Gillian escaped to her bedchamber for some time alone. Walking to the window, she drew back the drapery. Outside, a small flock of blackbirds swooped and swept through the air before landing on a patch of green grass. From the periphery of her vision, she spied a couple walking hand in hand back toward the castle from a stroll along the shore of Loch Rowanclere. Gillian liked Chrissy and Cole very much. They planned to return to Texas when she and Jake departed for the South Seas. Watching them, Gillian wondered if Jake was at all disconcerted at the idea of being separated from his family by more than one ocean.

The blackbird flock took flight and as Gillian turned away from the window, movement out on the road caught her notice. A coach rattled its way up the road toward Rowanclere. Slowly, it drew close enough to identify, and in that instant, Gillian's melancholy disappeared. "Flora!"

Pausing only long enough to check on Angus, she raced for the entry hall and dashed outside just as the conveyance rolled to a halt in front of the castle. Seconds later, the sisters flew into one another's arms.

Flora burst into tears almost immediately. "Oh, Gilly, you got married and I wasn't here."

"I'm sorry. I wanted to wait for you, but—"

"I'm the one who is sorry. I'd have come the moment I received your letter about your nuptials, but first I caught the sniffles, and then each of the boys fell ill. We didn't want to bring sickness to Rowanclere.

"But, Gilly, I missed your wedding. What happened? Your note said little more than that the two of you had married. The last I knew, you sent Delaney away. When did he return? Why did you allow it? Why is Uncle Angus hosting a foy? You must tell me every little detail starting with why in the world you married that Texan."

"Why wouldn't she marry that *Texan?*" Jake's sister snapped as she swept through the castle's open door. "Jake is a fine catch. An exceptional catch."

With her sister and sister-in-law facing each other like a pair of hissing cats, Gillian quickly performed the introductions. The two women nodded stiffly.

Alasdair disembarked from the coach carrying a child in each arm. Gillian started to go to them, but Flora caught her hand and held her in place. Her twin was not to be put off. "Good catch or no, what I wish to hear is how your brother ended up on my sister's plate."

"A run of good luck, I should say." Chrissy lifted her chin, folded her arms, and scowled.

Gillian realized she had better intercede before a cat fight erupted. She took a deep breath and offered a condensed version of the facts surrounding her marriage. When she finished, Chrissy Morgan scoffed. "Gillian Delaney, how many times do I have to say this? If you think my brother married you to get his trust fund, you are a fool. Jake may have used this 'debt' idiocy as an excuse, but if he hadn't wanted to marry you, the Queen of England could not have made him do it."

She paused, thought for a moment, then added, "Shoot, not even our mother could have made him do it. Jake married you because he wanted to marry you. He loves you."

"I know that," Gillian quietly responded. "However, if he could have gained access to his trust fund without marrying, I doubt we'd be married today. He'd have bought my home, then run off to Rangoon."

"You may be right," Chrissy said with a shrug. "However, I still believe that deep inside himself, Jake wants to call off his travels. Remember, he is a man, that in itself is difficult to overcome. Men are slow to understand the workings of their own hearts, and we women must be patient with them. It's our duty as the more intelligent of the couple."

"Well." Alasdair Dunbar approached the women and observed, "I would like to stand up for the male brotherhood, but now is not a propitious time." He sent his wife a beseeching look. "The karriewhitchits both are in dire need of clean hippins."

Flora gave a long-suffering sigh. "More intelligent with stronger stomachs. How is it that a man who dresses deer without blinking an eye all but faints dead away when faced with his own sons' soiled nappies?"

While Flora took the babes inside to tend them, Gillian introduced Alasdair to Chrissy, then spent a few moments bringing him up to date on events at Rowanclere. "First of all, allow me to offer felicitations on your wedding, sweetie," he said, kissing Gillian's cheek. Then he cut a grin toward Chrissy and added, "Personally, I believe the fact Delaney managed to bind you to him shows exceptional intelligence and extraordinary taste in women. Now, where will I find the boy? I've brought a bottle of an excellent barley-bree for us to crack."

"I suggest you look for him in the muniment room.

He and Robyn are making a few adjustments to Scooter's chariot."

"Did you say chariot?"

"Aye, it is Robbie's idea. She believes Scooter has extraordinary powers of smell. She thinks that with more mobility, Scooter will help her locate treasure left behind by Norman invaders."

Alasdair shrugged. "Stranger things have happened. Who knows, the bouff might sniff out a ghaist or two."

"After all that we went through?" Gillian shook her head and groaned. "Aye, you are probably right, Alasdair. Such is the way my luck runs."

Jake woke up with a smile on his face. It didn't last long. Almost immediately he realized the significance of the day. At that point he wanted nothing more than to bury his head beneath the covers and hide.

Especially since a head buried in the covers of this particular bed was liable to stumble across something good to nibble upon.

Gillian lay beside him, dead to the world as usual. He'd never met a woman who slept as hard as his wife. But then, he'd never met a woman who loved as hard, either. This particular morning he'd like nothing better than to kiss her awake and pick up where they'd left off in the wee hours of the morning. But he knew he couldn't. Shouldn't, anyway.

Today was the day of Gillian's godforsaken party. Today was the day his mother was due to return to Rowanclere. Today was the day his wife planned to tell the rest of her family she intended to join him on his travels.

How much fun does one man deserve?

Last night, he'd joined his wife and the Dunbars for a private meeting in one of the upstairs sitting rooms. He'd promised Gillian he'd keep his mouth shut and allow her to tell the story in her own way. He'd kept his word, though he nearly bit his tongue in two while doing it.

Gillian had made it sound like leaving Rowanclere was all her idea. She'd told her sister that in listening to Jake talk about his dreams, they had become hers. Flora acted bewildered and disbelieving at first, then as Gillian continued to talk, a knowing look entered her twin's eyes.

"You must love him very much," Flora had said.

"I do," Gillian had answered.

That, it appeared, had put all Flora's doubts to rest.

Too bad it hadn't done the same with Jake. Even though Flora jumped at the chance of having Angus and Robyn live with her, he was nagged by second thoughts. Angus was a proud man. He wouldn't take well to giving up a major piece of his independence by going to live in another man's home. And then there was Robyn. Was a move to Laichmoray good for her? A girl her age needed lots of attention and the Dunbars had those new little babies. Jake knew they wouldn't neglect the girl on purpose, but what if they simply got too busy and didn't realize what they were doing? Such a thing could cause Robbie a good deal of hurt. She might have scars from it for years to come.

Jake rolled over and tried to banish the troublesome thoughts. Enough of this. He'd best get up and get moving. He had a lot to do today. Besides, lying here brooding wasn't going to solve anything.

Then Gillian shifted in her sleep and the sheet slipped to reveal one pert, naked breast.

"Twenty minutes," Jake told himself as he reached for her. The day's work could wait twenty more minutes, but that was all.

An hour and forty minutes later, he finally rolled out of bed. "Princess, we need to talk."

"Anything more strenuous is out of the question," she told him.

His mouth twisted into a grin. She was right about that. "Gillian, I love you."

Warmth filled the liquid blue eyes that looked up at him. "I love you, too."

"Something tells me it might be well served to remember that detail throughout the rest of today."

"Today?" She sat up abruptly. "The foy. Jake, the foy is today!"

Flinging back the sheets, she vaulted from the bed and hurried to dress. "I have so much to do. Why didn't you remind me? We should never have lazed around like this."

His gaze resting happily on the delicious sight of her bare behind, he repeated, "Why didn't I remind you? Princess, do you really need to ask?"

She fired off a glare that transformed into a smug little smile. "Chrissy said the note she received from your mother indicated she planned to arrive early. Is your mother a woman to whom 'early' is truly early, or just not as late as usual?"

Jake glanced at the clock. "If my mother said early, she's liable to be downstairs already."

"Hurry up, then!" She finished dressing, did something quick and simple with her hair, then departed the room on a run.

Jake sauntered downstairs half an hour later to find his wife, sister, and mother rearranging chairs and baskets of flowers in Rowanclere's Great Hall. This, after Chrissy had him and Cole doing the same damned thing for two hours yesterday. He crossed the room and kissed and greeted his mother, then turned to his sister. "Change your mind again, Bug? Thought we finally got the room arrangement right."

"It's fine for tonight's event, but not for this morning's."

This morning's event? Jake arched a curious brow at the women. His mother approached him, took both his hands in hers. "Receiving your letter about your marriage convinced me to change my own plans."

"You've left Harrington?"

"No. But I decided against a London wedding. I realized how much I regretted not being with you to witness your nuptials. I decided to avoid a similar disappointment in relation to my own."

Jake put it together right away. "You're marrying Harrington here?"

"Today. Will you give the bride away, my son?"

It was his chance to show what a good sport he was about his mother's decision. He could almost feel the air being sucked from the room as the women held their breaths. Well hell, what kind of man did they think he was, anyway? He'd given Harrington his blessing. Did his sister and his wife think he'd go back on his word?

He tossed them both a scowl, then lifted his mother's

hand, gazed tenderly into her eyes, and pressed a gentle, courtly kiss to the back of her hand. But in spite of his best intentions, when it came time to speak, he failed to keep the sullen note from his tone. "I guess so. If I have to. If you're sure this is what you want to do. But he'd better treat you right, Mother. I'll have his head for breakfast if he doesn't."

Elizabeth chuckled. "From you, my dear, that is a grand capitulation. I know how hard this is for you. Thank you."

Jake preened a bit. He couldn't help it. No man ever outgrew the boy who wanted to please his mama.

And an hour later, he clasped Gillian's hand and squeezed it tightly as he listened to the earl say his vows to his mother. When her turn came, Jake's stomach took a roll and he felt a bit woozy, too. Just when he thought he might need to interrupt the ceremony and find a place to lose his breakfast, Gillian offered him a surprising distraction.

She gestured toward the floor. Jake looked down and spied a bare foot peeking from beneath the hem of her forest green gown. When she wriggled her toes at him, his mouth went dry and at the same time, he wanted to laugh. *Ah, princess, you're just so damned cute.*

The woman was the perfect wife for him.

He handled the rest of the simple wedding ceremony like a champion and when the groom kissed the bride, Jake gave his own bride a delightfully thorough kiss. So thorough, in fact, that by the time they came up for air, the others had left them alone in the Great Hall. "We could lock the door," he suggested hopefully. "I am the new lord of the castle, after all, and this is my hall so I should get to use it how I want to."

"It's a lovely thought, Texas, but I'm afraid we don't have time."

"It won't take me long. I promise."

She laughed and pulled him toward the door. "It's a beautiful day outside, and I thought we would benefit from some time away from the hustle and bustle of the castle. I've scheduled an hour and a half, and I told Robyn and Uncle Angus we'd take them for a row out on the loch."

Well, hell. "That's when you'll tell them?"

She made a brave show at smiling, but it was sickly at best. "I don't want Robyn running off in the middle of the telling."

"Smart thinking, princess. But tell me, just in case, does the girl know how to swim?"

Gillian need not have worried about Robyn diving into the cold waters of the loch when she told them she was leaving with Jake. Her sister didn't jump from the boat. She didn't move so much as a muscle. She certainly didn't speak.

Angus gazed out across the loch, his expression difficult for her to read. A long minute ticked by while the only sound to be heard was the creak of wood and the gentle splash of oar into water. Finally, Angus reached over and squeezed her hand. "It will be a fine adventure for you, lass. We will miss you here, of course, but if I've learned anything during this long life of mine, it is that youth should be lived to the fullest."

Then he turned a solemn stare toward Jake. "You protect her with your life, son. Keep her safe and healthy and happy. She has given you the gift of her love, which is as fine a treasure as any man on earth could desire. Honor it and her."

"I will, Angus."

Her granduncle shifted his gaze back to Gillian, and the melancholy tenderness in his eyes almost brought her to tears. He cleared his throat. "A bit of advice, Delaney. When the time comes for her to give ye bairns, give her a home. I dinna care if it is a castle or a nice little home in an island village. Give Gillian a place to build her nest. It will be important to her."

Bairns. Gillian found herself stunned at the thought. Not at the idea of giving him children, but at the idea of giving him children while visiting the South Seas. In all the thinking she'd done since agreeing to accompany him, she'd never made that particular connection in her mind. The question popped out, "Do they have doctors in Bora Bora?"

"Don't fret, Gilly. I've promised to keep you safe, and that includes having our babies in a civilized location."

"Good." With that worry disposed of—for now, anyway—she focused on her most immediate concern. "Robyn? Talk to me, please, lass? Let me know what you are thinking?"

The girl dipped a finger into the waters of the loch and twirled it around. When her silence continued, Gillian tried again. "You're so young to have had so much change in your life already, and I know you're certain to be at least a little wary. But posy, just think. Flora's bairns will grow fast and they'll be crawling and getting into trouble in no time. Think how much fun you'll have playing with them each day."

Angus sat up straighter. "You're not sending my Robbie to live at Laichmoray."

"Actually, Flora has invited you both to live with her family."

"Oh, I didn't realize . . . of course, Rowanclere is your castle now, Delaney. I should have expected you would want the previous owner to vacate the premises."

"Now hold on," Jake protested. "It's nothing like that. Gillian, tell him."

"Uncle Angus, be fair. Robbie needs supervision. She needs schooling. She needs children her own age with whom to play. She'll find all of that at Laichmoray. And you, you'll enjoy acting grandfather to those boys as they grow. You know you will."

"Aye," he said softly, sadly.

Keeping her gaze upon the water, Robyn slowly reached out and clasped Uncle Angus's hand. It was an offer of comfort and a plea to be comforted. Seeing it made Gillian feel like a traitor. She slumped on her seat and turned her gaze toward the opposite shore from the one her sister watched.

Jake muttered a curse and poured his strength into rowing. As the boat picked up speed, he punctuated his strokes with sentences. "I thought better of the two of you. Think of all this woman has done for you over the years. All the love she has given you. Is this how you reciprocate? Is this how you show your love for her? Did you stop and think that maybe leaving is hard for her, too, and that your grudging acceptance of her news will only make it more difficult for her?"

At that, Robyn found her voice. Shooting venom toward Jake, she said, "Then you're the one who's being mean. You're the one making her go away. I wish you'd never come to Rowanclere."

He jerked as if she'd hit him and one of the oars slipped from his grasp. Robyn scrambled around on her seat, giving Jake and Gillian her back. Uncle Angus looked like he'd aged five years in the past fifteen minutes.

Gillian was heartsick. She'd known this wouldn't be easy, and she had been right. She swallowed the lump in her throat, then said, "Robyn, leaving here is my choice, and my choice alone. It's not Jake's fault. It's not even my fault. It is the way of life. You were sad when Flora left Rowanclere but you adjusted. It'll be the same way with me leaving. You'll enjoy living at Laichmoray. If I doubted that at all, I wouldn't go."

Uncle Angus tugged a handkerchief from his pocket and blew his nose. Gruffly, he said, "They're right, lass. You and me, we'll be right as rain. Think of all those swords and suits of armor Alasdair has on display. We can have a fine old time playing war. That we can. So chin up. Delaney is right."

He pulled Robyn into his arms, but looked at Gillian as he said, "If we love our Gilly—and we do, very much—we will wish her happiness and Godspeed on her journey. Now, let's head home and prepare for the foy, shall we?"

Jake docked the boat, then helped Angus into the coach for the short ride back to Rowanclere. Needing time to clear her head, Gillian decided to walk back. She took two steps toward the castle when Robyn threw herself into her sister's arms and held on tight. "I'm sorry, Gilly. It's just that I don't want you to leave me. Everyone always leaves me. Someday I'll be all alone and I won't have a home anymore."

"Nae, love, that is not at all true. You have family who loves you—me and Jake and Flora and Alasdair and Uncle Angus and even Nick, wherever he is. You will always have a home with one of us, you have my word on it."

Jake placed a hand on Gillian's shoulder. "You can believe her, squirt. She's a Delaney and Delaneys always keep their word."

fifteen

~

THE SKIRL OF pipes drifted through the Great Hall at Rowanclere that evening as close to seventy guests attended the foy. Against one wall, cloth-draped banquet tables were laden with meats and cheeses, fish and fowl, along with more unfamiliar items like cornbread and enchiladas and the groom's sister's famous Texas Red chili. Whisky flowed like water, and laughter and merriment were the order of the day.

Jake, Gillian, and Uncle Angus greeted their guests in the entry hall as they arrived, then Robyn and Scooter, resplendent in her flower-adorned chariot, led them to the party. Outwardly, Gillian portrayed the blushing bride excited about the evening to come. Inwardly, she fought a battle with low spirits. The scene with Angus and Robyn had affected her worse than she'd expected.

They, at least, appeared to be taking the news in stride. With the arrival of the first few guests, the tension that had hovered between them and herself had evaporated. Soon they were laughing and joking as usual, exactly as

Gillian had hoped when deciding the best time to tell her family about her plans.

A time or two she'd caught Jake staring at her, a worried look in his eyes. She gathered his concern for her around herself like a soft blanket on a cold winter's night and immediately felt better. She *was* doing the right thing by going with him. She knew that. She loved him. It was normal for her to feel a sorrow at the notion of leaving home and family, but once they were on their way, she felt certain she'd catch the excitement of the adventure. Wouldn't she?

Aye, I will.

Summoning determination, she dedicated herself to enjoying the foy.

Gillian was smiling at a story Robyn told about Scooter when she realized the Macleans had arrived. Immediately, her gaze flew to meet Jake's. His disgruntled expression told her he knew the game had now begun, and Gillian's smile widened. Her big, tough husband could be such a little boy at times.

As Angus greeted the Macleans, Gillian met Annabelle's nervous gaze and smiled her encouragement. Then she turned to David. "Welcome to Rowanclere."

"Good evening, Gillian. You look beautiful as always."

Jake stepped closer to his wife. "Hello, Maclean. Glad you could make it."

"You are?" David offered in a droll tone. "I admit to surprise. My recent visits led me to believe otherwise."

Jake's smile was not reflected in his eyes. "This is a party celebrating Gillian's and my thoroughly happy marriage. I figure that's something good for you to see."

With that he dismissed David, then greeted Annabelle

with a genuine welcome. Gillian observed closely as Annabelle introduced her mother to Jake. The clever man found just the right tone in greeting a fellow American and the older woman, Mrs. Lehrman, was properly charmed.

And so the plan progressed nicely.

Once the arrivals slowed down to a trickle, Gillian and her family joined the merrymakers in the Great Hall. A short time later, Angus called for the crowd's attention and officially welcomed Jake to the family. Jake then led Gillian onto the floor for a dance and for a little while, she forgot about the evening's scheme.

"That fool Maclean was right about one thing," Jake murmured into her ear as he pulled her close. "You are beautiful, princess. The most beautiful woman here tonight."

His voice sent a sensual shiver down her spine.

"Although," he continued, "I can't say I like your dress."

Gillian knew exactly why he didn't care for the gown, but she pretended to be affronted. "What is wrong with my dress?"

"There's not enough of it." His gaze dropped to her dipping bodice. "This whole scheme to shore up the Macleans's marriage might come to naught. If he gets too bold with his gaze, I might have to kill him and then the rest won't matter." He paused, considered it for a moment, and grumbled, "Maybe that's the best plan anyhow."

She laughed. "Oh, Texas, I truly do love you."

"Well, keep it in mind when you're doing your play-acting with Maclean. Speaking of which, looks like Cole just raised the curtain."

Gillian followed the path of his gaze and spied Cole Morgan leading Annabelle Maclean out onto the dance floor. "Yes, this is it, then. Kiss me once for luck?"

He kissed her twice. "A person never can have enough luck. Although I still think this whole effort is a stupid waste of time."

"Assisting the course of true love is never a waste of time."

A wicked light glimmered in his eyes. "In that case, why don't we find an empty room and take fifteen minutes to assist the course of our own true love."

Gillian rose up on her tiptoes and gave him a quick, hard kiss, then a wanton wink. "I dinna have fifteen minutes right now, but hold the thought, handsome."

"Ten minutes?"

"Later."

"Five. I can be quick."

She let her fingers trail suggestively across his chest. "Aye, but why should you? Slow is more fun. Patience, Texas. Now, we each have work to do. The sooner begun, the sooner finished."

"You're an evil woman, Gillian Delaney." So said, he waltzed her off the dance floor and left her standing a few feet away from her former lover.

Gillian kept her gaze trained on the dancing as she eavesdropped on David's conversation with Reverend Gregor. She smiled as she watched Robyn beg a turn around the floor from her husband, then make a game of stomping on his toes.

She knew the exact moment David noticed her. She braced herself, preparing to adopt her chosen role for the evening.

"May I have this dance, Gilly?"

"Yes, I'd like that."

They joined the other dancers in a waltz and took only two steps before he spoke. "You must know how surprised I was to receive the invitation to attend tonight's festivities. Your husband claims to have his reasons for inviting me, but what about you, Gilly? Dare I hope to read a hidden meaning behind my being included?"

You hardheaded man. How dare you dishonor Annabelle this way. A hidden meaning in the invitation? Count on it. Choosing her words carefully, she said, "You've always been observant, and this case is no exception. I needed to talk with you and this seemed the most expedient way. David, you must do something about your wife."

His grip on her hand tightened reflexively. "What do you mean?"

"After you interrupted our meeting the other day, my husband's sister grew quite distraught. Apparently, she believes her husband has developed an interest in your wife. Have you been aware that your wife goes riding with Mr. Morgan almost every afternoon?"

David looked past Gillian, a grim set to his mouth. "I am aware she disappears. But I have decided I don't care what Annabelle does. She matters not at all to me. I told you that. I don't love her, I love you."

She wanted to kick him in the shins and tell him to stop being so stupid, to recognize that he did, indeed, love his wife. Instead, she shook her head and sighed. "I don't understand what has gotten into Cole. Chrissy Morgan is a beautiful woman."

"So is Annabelle."

Ah hah. Quick defense there, David. I hope you noticed. Gillian shrugged. "Aye, that she is. Cole certainly seems mesmerized by her."

Encouraged by the set of her dance partner's jaw, she continued, "It takes more than mere beauty to captivate a man like Cole Morgan. What is Annabelle like, David? Help me help my sister-in-law. You may not care about holding your marriage together, but she cares about saving hers."

"Annabelle is——" He broke off abruptly, scowled, then cleared his throat. "I don't wish to talk about Annabelle, especially not when I am holding you in my arms."

Stubborn Scot. "Indulge me."

His gaze drifted downward, alighting on the expanse of bosom displayed by her dress. "Anytime, anyplace."

Oh, really. Mentally, Gillian rolled her eyes. "Tell me about your wife. Look at how she sparkles."

He followed the path of her gaze to where Annabelle was laughing and batting her lashes up toward Cole. *It's a wonder she hasn't started a windstorm in the Hall.*

David purposely turned his back toward Annabelle.

Gillian frowned, surprised and a little worried. She hadn't expected this level of resistance from him. Had something happened between him and Annabelle since his wife's last visit to Rowanclere? Were they on even less favorable terms than before? Judging from his reaction, she feared it might be so.

Lovely. As if this job wasn't difficult enough as it was. Looking over David's shoulder, she searched the room for her husband.

She hoped he was having better luck than she was.

*   *   *

It's a wonder Maclean hasn't killed her.

Courageously, Jake maintained a smile despite the ringing in his ears and the throbbing of his feet. Robbie was an amateur toe-stomper compared to this ol' gal. If he'd known the level of pain involved, he wouldn't have asked Mrs. Lehrman to dance.

As it was, he'd made that suggestion in an effort to shut her up long enough to lead the conversation around to the topic he needed to cover. He'd never met a person so adept at eating and complaining at the same time. Actually, he found it an amazing feat to witness. She never spoke with her mouth full—yet she never seemed to stop whining—and she went through a bowl of Chrissy's chili faster than a hungry cowhand.

As he executed a turn, she landed an extra heavy step on his right little toe and Jake felt his eyes cross in pain. That's it. He'd suffered enough for this cause. A cause he wasn't all that hot to support anyway. When this was all said and done, Gillian was gonna owe him big.

He couldn't wait to get her alone to tell her so, either.

He waltzed Mrs. Lehrman toward the edge of the dance floor, then interrupted her mid-whine. "I'm dry as dirt. How about I grab us a lemonade and show you around the castle a bit?"

Having learned his lesson, he headed for the drink table before she had the chance to reply. Moments later, he escorted her from the Great Hall. The nod from Angus assured him that Robbie, Chrissy, and Flora stood at the ready to do their appointed tasks.

Ever the gentleman, he bit his tongue to keep from commenting as Annabelle's mother rattled on incessantly about surly Scots and inhospitable lodgings and an overall dislike of everything. He led her slowly, but surely, toward the library. Once there, he decided a subtle approach wouldn't work with Henrietta Lehrman, so he broke into her soliloquy about the accommodations she'd suffered during the ship's passage from Boston and asked, "Do you believe in ghosts?"

She stuttered to a stop. "What?"

"Ghosts. Poltergeists, goblins, and ghouls. I never believed in them myself—not until I encountered my first one right here at Rowanclere."

She blinked. "A ghost? You saw a ghost here in your castle?"

"Actually, I've seen two of them. I'm told we have a couple more. They have different personalities, you see. Take Young Fergus, for instance. He's full of mischief, likes to make lots of noise and send stuff flying around."

Jake could tell he had her attention now, the big clue being the way her jaw gaped open but no sound came out. "Now, the Laird's Lady is different. She's more serious in her haunts. She likes to make a man . . . sweat."

Behind his back, he signaled with his hand. The lamps on the fireplace mantel flickered out. Mrs. Lehrman's eyes went wide. "Did you see that?"

"What?"

"The lamps. They went out."

"Maybe a draft blew them out."

"Both at once?"

Jake glanced over his shoulder toward the mantel. "That or Young Fergus. Although that's a tame trick for him."

The portrait crashed to the floor. Jake winced as his guest let out a shriek. *Too hard again, dammit. That's the third frame in a month.* "Now that's more like Young Fergus."

Henrietta Lehrman cowered in her chair. "Is he dangerous?"

"Oh, no." Jake sauntered over to the whisky decanter and poured a pair of stiff drinks. Handing her a glass, he said, "Rowanclere's ghosts are never dangerous . . . well, except for the Headless Warrior."

She tossed back a healthy swallow. "The H-h-headless Warrior?"

"Yes. He's our more unsavory spirit. Legend has it that he lived at Rowanclere in the fourteenth century. He fell in love with a MacGregor maiden and they married. They were happy for a time, but then her mother came here to live with them. She didn't approve of the warrior and she wasn't shy about letting him know. Finally, in a fit of anger one night and wanting to put a stop to her tongue, he drew his broadsword and lopped off Mrs. MacGregor's head. Though no one who knew her could blame him, clans being clans, this started a war. As fate would have it, he was beheaded in battle and has haunted this manse ever since."

Henrietta gasped. "Have you seen this Headless Warrior?"

Jake shook his head. "No. He only appears to women. Mothers-in-law who bring trouble to their daughters' husbands, in fact. What makes him so dangerous is that once he has chosen a woman as his prey, he not only haunts her while they're at Rowanclere, he haunts her until she either dies or leaves Scotland."

"Oh, my." Mrs. Lehrman giggled nervously. "If that is the case, I'm surprised anyone ever visits this castle of yours."

"You know, I said the same thing to my wife. She told

me I needn't worry, that the Warrior hasn't haunted anyone to death in almost fifty years. Still, I can't help but
worry. Seems to me if it's been that long, we're ripe for
trouble."

He sipped at his own whisky, allowing the echo of the
tale to hang in the air. All in all, he thought it had gone
quite well. He'd been a bit worried about this part of
Gillian's scheme, to be honest. What if Henrietta Lehrman didn't draw the parallels between the story and herself? What if she didn't identify with a mother-in-law a
son-in-law couldn't abide? From his point of view, it was
the weakest link—well, except for the part where Gillian
thought she would be able to convince Maclean he loved
his wife more than her. What man in his right mind
would prefer that feather-headed female over his Gillian?
Sure, Annabelle was pretty, and she was rather sweet, but
compared to Gillian? He held up his glass and gazed at
the amber liquid.

Hell, Annabelle Maclean was a sweet little white wine
compared to the finest Scots whisky, that smooth, sultry
kick to the senses that tasted like heaven and made a man
burn.

Mrs. Lehrman bolted back her drink, then set the glass
down hard on the table. "I think it's time we return to
the ballroom. You are an honoree, Mr. Delaney. You
should attend your own party."

As Jake followed her, he gestured again. Just as the
woman reached the door, it slammed shut. Jake looked at
her, his eyes wide. "I sure hope this isn't the Headless
Warrior playing all these tricks."

David Maclean's mother-in-law screamed loud and
long. Then she gasped and swayed, and Jake worried that

they'd gone too far. If she passed out and he had to carry her somewhere, he might strain his back. He had plans for his back, later on. Plans with his princess.

Hell, he could always just roll the windbag out of the way.

Robyn inadvertently saved the day. Eyes glittering with mischief, she stuck her head in the door and said, "Uh-oh. I didn't know anyone was in here. Sorry to slam the door on you."

"You!" Henrietta exclaimed. "That was you? What about the portrait, the lamps? Were those your doings also?"

Robbie shook her head, her expression the picture of childhood innocence. "I don't know anything about lamps or pictures."

She could go on stage, Jake thought.

"Oh, my." Henrietta fanned her face. "I must find my son-in-law and insist we leave. I do not approve of the idea of communing with spirits, and we certainly cannot sleep here as planned."

Jake dragged his hand along his jaw. "Well ma'am, I hate to see you leave the party early, and I don't like the idea of you traveling at night, but if you think that's what you need to do. . . ."

He led her back to the ballroom, then trailed her as she searched the room for her daughter. She found Maclean first, however. The damned fool Scotsman was still sniffing after Gillian. As mother-in-laws were wont to do, Henrietta Lehrman pecked at her daughter's husband until he agreed to leave, then continued to search the Great Hall for Annabelle.

The woman wasn't to be found.

Gillian managed just the right note of concern when she pointed out the fact that Cole seemed to be missing, too. Maclean's eyes narrowed dangerously.

Good, Jake thought. Everything appeared to be going as planned.

Gillian tried to pinpoint exactly when the plan began to unravel. Was it when David proved to be so granite-headed about admitting his feelings for Annabelle? She'd poked and prodded, but the man simply refused to admit he loved the girl. For that matter, he refused to admit he even liked his wife very much.

Still, he'd caught Gillian unaware by the tepidness of his response upon learning Annabelle had gone missing at the same time as Cole. A flash of temper in his eyes and a thinning of his lips had been the extent of his reaction. She'd expected a jealous furor. She'd anticipated some ranting and raving.

She never guessed he'd calmly inform his mother-in-law that they'd be leaving for home shortly, with Annabelle or without her, he didn't care which.

At that point, Gillian realized she'd made a major miscalculation.

"I don't understand it," she told Flora and Chrissy in the salon being utilized as a ladies' retiring room. "I know him. This isn't like David at all."

"It's the influence of Mrs. Lehrman," Flora said knowingly. "I've seen it at Laichmoray with Alasdair's aunt. Don't underestimate the destructive power of a single unpleasant female relative. Mrs. Lehrman is quite unpleasant."

Chrissy nodded. "I haven't always seen eye to eye with

my mama, but even in the worst of times, she never held a candle to that one. Poor Annabelle."

"Why poor me?" the young woman asked when the salon entrance to the secret passageway swung open and she stepped into the room. "What happened?"

Gillian rubbed her temples and said, "David intends to go home."

"What? But I'm missing."

"That doesn't seem to matter. He told your mother to gather her things, that you knew your way home. Annabelle, what happened? Why is he being so hard-headed? Did something happen between the two of you?"

She grimaced and dipped her chin. "Maybe. He said something especially mean to me, and I . . . well . . . I said something I probably shouldn't have said."

"What?"

"I told him mmpht mmpht mmpht mmpht." She kicked at the carpet with the toe of her slipper.

"Don't mumble, Annabelle. What did you say?"

"I just might possibly have made mention that in comparison to your Jake he comes up a little . . . short."

Flora and Chrissy looked puzzled. Gillian's chin gaped in shock. "You didn't."

She shrugged. "It's the truth."

"What's she talk—" Chrissy's eyes went wide. "No. Jake? You saw his . . . no, never mind. I don't want to know."

Gillian rubbed her temples. "No wonder he's furious. Annabelle, what possessed you to say such a foolish thing as that?"

"He compared me to you and it wasn't a favorable comparison. If I didn't like you so much, Gillian, I'd want to shoot you again. I'm very tired of hearing about how wonderful you are."

"Guid fegs," Flora breathed.

Gillian threw out her hands. "Well, we might as well give up. All our planning has gone for naught. He's leaving and—"

"You've got to stop him, Gillian." Annabelle clasped her hands to her chest and begged. "You must. I know I can fix the problems if I can get him alone in the dungeon like we've planned. I know I can. I've been practicing with the feathers, just like you told me to do!"

Chrissy and Flora exchanged interested glances, then turned their attention on Gillian.

"Please, Gillian. Stop him from leaving. Do anything, just give me a chance!"

"Oh, all right. I'll try. But I don't know what I'll say. This isn't what we had planned."

"You'll think of something," Flora encouraged. "You always do."

Gillian proved Flora right. She thought of something. Just not anything very smart. Her efforts to mend the Macleans' marriage appeared to be causing more harm than good. At least, that's what a furious and tearful Annabelle declared when she learned David had agreed to stay the night at Rowanclere, after all.

He'd agreed to stay because Gillian Delaney had promised to meet him for a romantic assignation in the dungeon bedchamber at three A.M.

"If he touches you, I'll kill him. In fact, if he looks at you, I'll kill him. Maybe all he'll have to do is say 'howdy' and it'll be off with his head."

"Haud yer wheest, Texas," Gillian said as she adjusted the pleats of the feileadh mor around her husband's hips.

In a temper, he ignored her. "I should have put a stop to this idea of yours the first time I heard about it. I knew it was stupid from the git-go. You're no matchmaker, Gillian Delaney. You're a matchbreaker."

"What a terrible thing to say!" She gave his plaid a sharp tug. "It was a simple plan that would have worked fine had Annabelle not been so cat-witted as to tell her husband his quhillylillie is smaller than yours."

Jake arched a brow. "Quhillylillie?"

"Your manhood."

"Oh." He proudly squared his shoulders and grinned. "Of course I'm bigger."

Gillian rolled her eyes, then slapped his behind. "Oh, hush and go haunt Henrietta."

"Aren't you coming? Aren't you gonna watch? This won't be any fun if you're not watching."

"I'll be there. I'll hide in the passageway and watch. I wouldn't miss this for anything. First I want to make a quick run down to the dungeon to check on the chamber room and Annabelle to see if she has any last questions."

"Think that's smart? Last time I saw her, she was angry enough to lock you in."

Gillian sighed. "I know. I hate to admit this, but you may be right. Meddling in the Macleans' marriage might not have been a good idea."

He hated seeing her blue. "Oh, don't listen to me. It'll all work out. I have a feeling that by sunup, Annabelle and her husband will be minus one meddling mother-in-law and well on their way toward reconciliation."

"You honestly think so?"

"Princess, I'm of a mind to be a damned convincing ghost, and as far as the reconciliation goes, well . . . if you taught that girl how to handle a feather half as good as you, then ol' David doesn't stand a chance."

Gillian carried a lantern as she hurried down to the dungeon. After the rough start to her plan, she wanted to be certain this next part went as smoothly as possible. She had grown to care about Annabelle and she'd always have a soft spot in her heart for David. She truly hoped that tonight's events would guide their marriage back on course. In fact, the success of the plan had become rather important to her. She couldn't put her finger on why, exactly, except that she thought it somehow involved the notion of leaving Scotland on a positive note.

"You're as crazy as Jake claims," she muttered to herself, making her way down the dungeon stairs.

David wasn't due for another hour, but she expected to find Annabelle already in place. From the first, the idea of a dalliance in the dungeon had been Annabelle's favorite part of the plan. They'd spent quite a bit of time choosing a gown for her to wear—or not wear, as the case may be. They'd collected rose petals to spread across the bed, stashed champagne and scented candles and a fresh batch of chocolate icing—Chrissy Morgan's contribution to the proceedings.

Gillian had half a mind to swipe that last supply for her own use tonight. After all, Annabelle wouldn't want to overwhelm the man. From Gillian's experience, the feather trick would certainly get the job done.

With such sensual delights on her mind, Gillian was

understandably shocked to walk into the dungeon chamber and discover supplies of another type entirely on display and ready for use.

David's wife sat in a bedside chair, polishing a torture device with a cloth. "Annabelle? What are you doing with that Cat's Paw?"

"Cleaning it. Really, Gillian, the housekeeping in your dungeon is appalling. I had to clean spider webs off the branks and oil the thumbscrews. The headcrusher is rusted in two and completely useless."

Gillian closed her eyes and massaged the bridge of her nose. "What happened to champagne and rose petals? What happened to chocolate icing?"

Annabelle paused and looked up. "I won't be needing them."

"Oh, Annabelle," Gillian said with a sigh.

The young wife threw down her polishing cloth and tossed the Cat's Paw onto the bed. "I'm done with him, Gillian. He's gone too far. I'm missing and in danger, and all he can think about is resuming his love affair with you. Well, I won't stand for it. He's going to pay for hurting me. I have the thumbscrews warmed up and ready for him, only it won't be his thumb that I'm putting the screw to."

"Now, calm down. I think I've figured out what's happening here. It's something he said tonight about how you liked to play games. I think he knows you're not missing. I think he's playing games just like you. That's part of what's wrong with your marriage, Annabelle. Too much game-playing and not enough truth."

"Well, the games are just beginning." Annabelle folded her arms, angled her head, and studied Gillian for a moment.

"What? What is it?"

"I've an idea. Perhaps I won't need to torture him after all?"

Oh, no. It was Gillian's experience that whenever Annabelle started thinking on her own, trouble threatened.

Standing, Annabelle walked over to one wall and lifted an iron manacle. "I'll use the shackles. It won't hurt him one bit. Come see how I fixed it, Gillian. I want to show you."

"No. You canna do this. I won't—"

"Oh, come on. I want you to see how smart I was. I fixed it so David won't even feel it." She held the manacle out. "See?"

Gillian indulged her, mainly because she was trying to come up with an argument to cool the young woman's temper. "How did you fix it?"

"I'll show you."

Before Gillian quite knew what had happened, Annabelle slapped the cuff around Gillian's wrist and snapped it shut. Gillian pulled on her arm, not believing what had happened. She expected the bolt to pull loose from the wall. It didn't.

"Annabelle!"

The young woman actually laughed. "I was right, wasn't I? It won't hurt David a bit because I'm using the irons on you instead."

She grabbed for Gillian's other arm and wrestled it toward the wall and the iron cuff. Gillian struggled, but Annabelle had an advantage in both height and weight. Soon both of Gillian's arms were chained to the dungeon wall. "What in heaven's name is going on here?"

"Give me your feet." Gillian started kicking when **Annabelle** went for her leg, but the blows failed to deter the younger woman. Moments later, Gillian found herself completely shackled to the wall. She was breathing heavy as a result of her struggles, but her tone nonetheless reflected bewilderment as she said, "Annabelle?"

David Maclean's wife looked at her, tears swimming in her big brown eyes. "I want him to choose me, Gillian. Not you. One time, I want him to choose me."

She started sobbing, then, her tears flowing like whisky at the foy. Gillian rolled her eyes and sighed. "There's a handkerchief in my pocket."

"Th-th-thank you."

Gillian waited for a few moments for the waterworks to subside, then asked, "Honey, I understand what you want of your husband, but explain this, please? How does chaining me to the wall present David with a choice?"

"I don't exactly know. It's just they were there and you were here and it seemed like the thing to do."

"It's uncomfortable, Annabelle. My arms are beginning to ache a bit. Please, fetch the key and let me loose."

"No. I'm sorry. I'm not going to do that. I'm going to find some way to restrain myself so that we're both in trouble. There's a rack in one of the other rooms. I wonder if I could somehow fasten myself to it. We'll both wait for him, Gillian, and then he must choose. He must choose between us, and he must choose me. I must know once and for all that he truly does want me and not you. Otherwise . . . well . . . I just might use the thumbscrew after all!" With that, Annabelle sailed out of the chamber room.

Gillian leaned back against the cold rock wall, she rattled her chains, then exhaled a tired sigh. "They were here. I was here. A simple plan. To borrow a phrase from Jake, 'Sometimes, Gillian, you don't have the sense God gave a goat.' "

sixteen

❧

JAKE WAITED IN the passageway outside Henrietta Lehrman's room for half an hour, but Gillian never arrived. It made him grumpy. He was doing this for her, after all. The least she could do was show up to watch. He'd been practicing his accent too. He'd wanted to impress her.

She was probably down in the dungeon holding Annabelle's hand. Ol' Maclean had his hands full with that one. The girl was pretty and fun to be around, but her mind traveled different paths than most folks'. Though he'd never say so to Gillian, the more time he spent with Annabelle, the more he wondered if helping the Macleans' marriage was more a vengeance instead of friendship.

He waited ten more minutes, then decided he'd waited long enough. The black face paint was beginning to itch and besides, he was worried a bit about Gillian.

Without an audience to play to, he wasn't much for dragging this haunting out. Still, he wanted to do a good

330 WOO GERALYN DAWSON

job and redeem himself for his poor showing at haunting Harrington. He marched over to the bed and moaned, "Woo . . . woo . . . woo."

When she opened her eyes, he grinned evilly and said, "I'm the Headless Warrior of Rowanclere and you are my chosen one."

Damned if she didn't pull a gun. "Get away! Get away! I'll shoot you!"

Idiot woman. "Why the hell would you do something dumb like that?" he said, grabbing the revolver away from her. "I'm a ghost. I'm already dead!"

"Oh. That's right. It's just that I'm frightened."

"You should be frightened. That's why I'm here. That's what ghosts do. We frighten people."

"M-m-mr. Delaney said you k-k-kill people."

"Aye, I scare them to death. I haunt viper-tongued harridans who cause trouble in their daughters' marriages. I'm a fine ghost, Henrietta Lehrman. You will look forward to dying by the time I'm through with you."

"Now that's an awful thing to say. Why I . . ."

Jake quit listening. In deference to her gender, he had intended to keep his haunting as tame as possible and still get the job done. Judging from the unending stream of complaints emerging from her mouth, he'd need to step up the threats or he'd be here all night.

Besides, he was worried about Gillian and he wanted this job done.

"Enough!" he yelled at the same time he secretly pulled a trio of strings at the ready. A vase flew off the mantel. A chair tipped over and one of the bed curtains came loose from its mooring and floated down on top of Henrietta Lehrman. "Consider this your only warning, madam. In order to save your life, you you must leave Rowanclere at first light, and Scotland within the fortnight. Otherwise, I'll haunt you daily until you give up the ghost, so to speak."

Cowering beneath the bed-hanging, she cried, "But I can't leave. My daughter is missing."

"No she's not. She's meeting her husband for a tupping even as we speak. Nothing's keeping you here, Henrietta. Can I count on your going or should I pack my bags to tag along?"

"I'm gone. First light, I'm headed for home. We don't have ghosts in Boston."

"No? But I hear y'all make a good baked bean."

In the musty passageway, he paused long enough to grab the towel from his pile of supplies and wipe the paint from his face before making his way downstairs. Ten minutes later, he entered the dungeon and immediately heard Gillian's voice and he breathed a heavy sigh of relief. Damn, but he'd been worried.

Now that he wasn't worried any longer, he remembered he was angry at her.

Pasting on a scowl, he followed the sound of her voice toward the infamous dungeon bedchamber. As he drew closer, he started listening to the words she sputtered. "The girl was not spanked enough as a child. That mother of hers needs more than a haunting, she needs a tongue lashing. And Annabelle, that girl needs a—"

"What?" he asked, sauntering into the room.

The second he saw her he stopped cold. His heart went tha-thump. "Gillian? What is going on here?"

"That pesk Annabelle chained me to the wall, that's what's going on. She's gone to sift through the torture devices."

"She thinks to torture you?"

"No, they're for herself. She's looking for one she can strap herself into that won't hurt too much."

Jake pursed his lips and nodded. "Of course. We wouldn't want a torture device to hurt."

Gillian scowled at him. "It's a test for David. After she chose not to use the breast-ripper on him, she decided to see who he would choose to rescue first—her or me."

"Breast-ripper?" he repeated, wincing at the thought.

"Just get me out of here, Jake. I think the keys for these chains are in the small wooden box just inside the door of the chamber next to this one."

Now that he knew the situation here, Jake took a minute to take stock. "Are you hurt, Gillian? In any pain?"

"No, not really."

"Good." My oh my, princess.

"My arms are going to sleep, though."

Every part of him was wide awake.

"Jake, get the key."

"The key. In a minute, honey." Jake was distracted. He was very distracted. He sucked in a breath past his teeth. "I guess it would be crass of me to admit that I'm having an erotic moment here."

"You need not admit anything. Your feileadh mor is tenting."

"I know. Believe me, I know." He was hard enough to drive a railroad spike.

"I thought you said this sort of thing wasn't a preference of yours."

"It's not. Hasn't been, anyway. But we keep finding ourselves in these . . . circumstances." His feet scuffed the floor as he walked toward her. He'd have pulled at his collar if he'd had one. "Damn, princess. This is making me hot. If you didn't have so many clothes on. . . ."

"Go get the key, Jake."

His blood hadn't boiled this hot since . . . well . . . this morning, anyway. "But—"

"Now."

"Oh, all right." He started to turn, but stopped mid-pivot. "Gillian, just one. . . ." Before she could voice the word to stop him, he knelt on one knee at her feet.

"Jake?"

"Just let me? Just a little?" Reverently, he removed her slipper, then slipping his hand beneath her skirt, untied her stocking. He caressed her soft skin as he tugged the stocking down, through the iron cuff around her ankle, and off.

"Oh God, princess." Bare toes and bondage. He thought he just might explode.

Her voice sounded thready as she repeated. "Get. The. Key."

"But—"

"Now, Jake. Annabelle could return any second. David is due soon."

"Oh, man." He grimaced and groaned. "What if I shut the door? It probably locks. I could be quick. Hell, wouldn't even have to take time to drop my pants since I'm wearing a skirt."

"Jake, you're begging."

"Yes. Oh, yes."

The witch wiggled her toes then, and laughed when he moaned with pain. "You are so pitiful. Listen, Texas, I'll promise to come back here with you another time if you'll go get the key and let me loose now. Right now."

"Oh, all right. This really is a torture chamber, isn't it."

He found the key following a brief search, then he made quick work of the manacles. He kissed her wrists, now chafed and red. "Why, you were hurting. You should have told me. I wouldn't have played around with you like that."

She wrapped her arms around his neck and pulled him toward her for a quick, hard kiss on the lips. "I like you playing around with me."

He shook his head. "Don't do this to me, Gillian. I'm hurting, too, and I don't think you want to be kissing it better right here and now, no matter how much I like the thought."

Chuckling, she released him and started for the door. "We'd better find Annabelle. No telling what trouble she's managed to get herself into."

They located her in a storeroom farther into the dungeons. She had moved a Chair of Spikes away from the wall and was attempting to push it out into the hall. Jake looked from the chair to his wife. "Princess, I'm beginning to wonder about your ancestors." Addressing Annabelle, he said, "Darlin', what do you think you're gonna do with that?"

"Sit in it," she said, wiping away her tears with the sleeve of her dress. "I'm going to move it next to Gillian and sit in it and see who he rescues first."

"Makes a person pucker just to think about it," Jake said, testing a spike with his finger. "Darlin', I understand your desire to test your husband's love—it's a female fault—but you have to realize that matters of the heart aren't always so black and white. I'm new to the in-love state myself, but I've known a lot of loving couples in my days, and one thing I've figured out is that love isn't proven in big, flashy rescues from a torture chair in a Scottish dungeon. It's those little rescues and rewards that accumulate day in, day out, year after year, that truly show what is in a person's heart."

"But I don't have years," she wailed. "I have tonight. Gillian said she's leaving and I must know before she goes. I can't wonder about this the rest of my life. If we somehow work out our problems but he's never been forced to choose, I'll always have that doubt. I need to know. I need to know if he loves me or Gillian."

"Oh, Annabelle, you don't need—"

He broke off at the sound of a man's voice calling, "Gillian? Are you down here?"

"It's David," Gillian said.

"Oh, no," Annabelle sobbed. "She's loose. I'm not stuck to the chair. We don't need rescuing. There's no test. Now I'll never know."

Jake raked his fingers through his hair. *Well, hell. The poor thing is purely pitiful.*

Gillian said, "Hush now, it's all right. We'll figure out another way."

The hell we will. I'm done with plans. We're takin' care of this right here, right now. He pushed Gillian into the storeroom whispering, "I'll take care of it. It's a dirty job, but someone's got to do it. The sacrifices a man makes for the women in his life. . . ."

So saying, he took Annabelle into his arms and commenced to kissing her just as David moved to within sight.

"Gillian?"

Jake broke the kiss, despite the resistance Annabelle gave him at doing so. *Little thing's got the suction of an octopus.* Acting as if he meant to shield her from Maclean's gaze, but in reality calling the other man's attention to her, he shoved Annabelle behind him. "I'll protect you, honey."

"Annabelle? Is that you?"

The boy is sharp as a marble.

Maclean rushed to meet them in the lantern-lit gloom. "Annabelle, my God! What are you doing down here?"

She stuck her head out from around Jake's shoulder. "I was kissing my lover, Jake."

Oh, shit.

Maclean's eyes flashed. "No. This is one of your dramas. One of your games. You are always say—" He broke off abruptly as if a thought had occurred to him. His gaze flicked down to Jake's skirt, then back up. He looked mad enough to chew nails. "You Texan bastard, you keep your filthy hands off my wife."

"Why should I? You're sure as hell anxious enough to get your paws on my wife. You're down here looking for her, aren't you? You had a rendezvous planned?"

"Yes. No." He waved his arm in dismissal. "I knew Gillian wouldn't be here. I know her better than that. She said what she did to keep me from going home which I took to mean that Annabelle put her up to it. I expected to find my wife in this dungeon, but I never expected to find her with the likes of you."

Annabelle stepped out from behind Jake, then threaded her arm through his and cuddled up against him. "It doesn't matter what you expected. You don't matter to me anymore. Jake and I are together now.

Gillian just married him for his money, you know. Just like you married me for mine. Now Jake owns Rowanclere, I'm moving in, and Gillian is moving away. If you want her, you're welcome to her."

"I don't believe you."

"It's true." She gave her head a toss. "Tonight's party was just for show, wasn't it, Jake?"

Jake nodded. He didn't have a problem with that. Tonight's shindig was certainly a show. "And Gillian is leaving Rowanclere. I expect her to be gone by the end of the week." His arm around Annabelle's waist, Jake gave her a squeeze and decided to bring this confrontation to a head. "So, Maclean, your wife tells me my johnson is a helluva lot bigger than yours."

The Scotsman was quick. A roar of rage echoed through the dungeon as he lunged toward Jake, his arms extended, hands aimed for the neck. Jake blocked him and they wrestled a bit. Then, finally, he threw the punch he'd dreamed of throwing since he first heard Maclean's name on Gillian's lips.

Knuckles cracked against chin. Jake knew Maclean had to see stars. Stopping to gloat was a mistake, as demonstrated by the whumph that blew from his mouth following a roundhouse to the gut.

After that, they got down to serious fighting. It was a regular dungeon brawl, rolling and pounding and punching. No biting or kicking, and Jake had to admire that in the Scotsman. He hadn't had this much fun since he left Texas—discounting sex with Gillian, of course.

Then Annabelle had to ruin it by dumping a bottle of champagne on them.

Jake rolled off Maclean and lay on his back, trying to

catch his breath. Having worked off some of the tension that had plagued him since ogling his chained-to-the-wall wife, he felt pretty damned good. *Too bad she didn't spill any champagne on Gillian. I could lick it up to celebrate.*

Then Annabelle started sobbing, popping the bubbles of Jake's good mood. "Get up, D-d-david Maclean. Get up and go to Gillian, to the woman you want. I never want to see you again."

Maclean scowled, wiggled one of his front teeth, and glared up at his wife. "Haud yer wheest, woman. You're not throwing me over."

"Yes I am."

"Nae, you're not. You are my wife and you are going to stay my wife."

"No, I'm not. We can't live together!"

"We can if I build a new castle for your mother."

She gasped and clasped her hands to her breast. "You would do that for me?"

Scowling fiercely, he nodded.

After checking his nose for breaks, Jake stood and readjusted his skirt. "No need to go to the trouble. Mrs. Lehrman is headed back to Boston at first light. Doesn't like our ghosts."

"It worked!" Annabelle wrapped her arms around Jake and hugged him hard.

Gillian must have figured enough was enough about then, because she emerged from the storeroom. David saw her and his eyes went wide. "Gillian, you were here all the time?"

"All of it. I heard everything." She glanced from Annabelle, to Jake, to David, then back to Annabelle again. "They told the truth, David. I am leaving Rowanclere. I want this finished once and for all. You need to choose which woman you want, now and forever. Who is it to be, sir. Annabelle or myself?"

The man looked like he'd swallowed a mouthful of green whisky. "Oh, Gilly—"

"Choose, David."

He looked from one woman to the other. Annabelle dried her tears, squared her shoulders, and lifted her chin. Jake was right proud of her.

Then the Scotsman met Gillian's gaze head on. "I love her. I love Annabelle."

Gillian beamed a tender smile as Annabelle threw herself at her husband. "Of course you do, David. You wouldn't have married her otherwise."

Extending a hand to her own mate, she said, "Come upstairs, Texas."

"Yes. Our business here is done."

"Aye, after I mention that if I ever see your lips on another woman's again, I won't be this understanding."

"I'll keep that in mind."

"See that you do."

Jake and Gillian made their way toward the staircase leading out of the dungeon. At the base, Jake paused. He held up a finger, signaling for her to wait. Detouring into the bedchamber, he retrieved what he wanted, then returned to his wife. "It's been a long night. Let's go to bed, shall we?"

Gillian eyed the handcuffs slung over his shoulder, smiled, and said, "Aye, my lord. Our bed. What a fine idea."

"We can save the wall for next time."

*   *   *

Following a few short hours of sleep, Jake and Gillian concluded their duties as host of the foy as those guests who had stayed the night at Rowanclere made their departures. First up and out was Henrietta Lehrman. So intent was she to leave that Jake was forced to return to the dungeon and bang on the bedchamber door. However, once he explained his reason for being there, the happy couple had all but run over him on their way upstairs.

It was only after the mother and daughter's tearful good-byes that Gillian noticed the evil contraption in David's hands. "David, one of the rules we have here at Rowanclere is that torture devices are not allowed out of the dungeon. Think of Robyn and her mischief."

"I'll take it right back down," he told her, his smile wreathing his face as he swung the branks slowly back and forth by its chain. "I brought it just as a precaution in case she resisted at the end."

Jake eyed the contraption in David's hand and said, "Let me see that."

He studied the metal cage designed to lock around a person's head with a spiked tongue-piece that fit inside the mouth. He gave a slow whistle. "What is this thing called?"

"Branks," Gillian answered.

"Or Scold's Bridle," David added. "It was principally used on scolding housewives."

"Really, now." Jake slanted a grin toward Gillian.

"Don't even think it," she snapped back.

The Macleans ate breakfast, then departed for home. By midmorning everyone but family had made their farewells. When Lord Harrington called for his carriage to be brought round, Gillian looked up with surprise from the important business of cooing at one of her nephews. "You are leaving?"

Jake's mother nodded. "Harrington has business in London. Cole and Chrissy will travel with us as far as Hartsworth. Cole will personally carry the Declaration of Independence home to Texas so we know it will arrive safe and sound."

Gillian put the baby to her shoulder and absently patted his back. They were all leaving. Jake would be saying good-bye to his loved ones for what was bound to be years. *Oh my. He is so tired.* This was a terrible time to face something so emotionally draining.

As it turned out, Jake took the leave-taking just fine. Gillian was the one who started crying and couldn't stop.

"There, there," said his mother, giving Gillian a hug. "No need to carry on so. It's not as if we'll never see each other again."

"But it will be so long."

"Time goes fast, believe me. I've much experience at this sort of thing. Miles don't separate loved ones; anger and hurt feelings are the culprit there. Believe me, in the twenty-plus years I was estranged from my father, it wasn't the physical distance that truly separated us, but the emotional distance. As long as you part on good terms, the time will fly by. Right, Chrissy?"

Jake's sister nodded and stepped up to give Gillian another hug. "She's right. You'll get used to these separations, honey. I promise. Time does pass quickly. We'll keep in touch with letters and before you know it, we'll be together again."

Gillian felt Jake's gaze upon her and she looked

through watery eyes to see his worried frown. Not wishing to add to his burden, she smiled. It was shaky, but she gave it a good effort. He pressed a kiss against her forehead, then handed her his handkerchief. Hers was already soaked.

She did a fine job of soaking his, too, as she watched him say good-bye to first Cole, then Chrissy, and finally his mother. She didn't eavesdrop on their short conversations. She didn't need to, the language of their bodies said it all.

They were sad to leave one another, but not devastated. Gillian didn't understand it. She knew they loved each other. She'd seen it over and over again. Why, if it were her, she'd be prostrate on the ground with grief.

In another few days, it will be you.

"Oh, my." Her knees suddenly felt like water. She thought she might have swayed, because Jake slipped his arm around her waist, supporting her as they waved good-bye to the departing coach.

They watched until it disappeared from sight, then he turned to her, lifted her chin with two fingers, and gazed solemnly into her eyes. "Princess, you gonna be okay?"

Gillian told herself she was tough and she was brave. "Aye, I'm fine. Tired, though. I need sleep."

He gathered her in his arms and held her for a long moment. She found the embrace comforting and in a way, almost healing, and when she went upstairs for a nap, she fell quickly asleep.

It was the last good sleep she had for days.

She is wasting away before my eyes.

Jake was supposedly overseeing the packing of

Angus's personal items for the move to Laichmoray, but in actuality, he was watching his wife be miserable. She'd been this way ever since the day his family left Rowanclere. She didn't eat, she didn't sleep. She seldom smiled and never laughed.

The woman was in mourning for a life she perceived as dying, and it was all Jake's fault. Oh, she never said anything, never complained, and even tried to hide what she was feeling. But Jake knew.

The idea of leaving her home and family was killing her. He'd always known she'd take it hard, but he never realized just how hard. His first realization of it had come while watching her say her farewells to his family. Her reaction had shaken him, and he'd tried to write it off as fatigue and letdown from the foy. But as the days slowly passed and he saw her bittersweet smiles and the hundreds of tiny good-byes she unwittingly betrayed, Jake began to realize the enormity of what he was asking her to do.

Gillian wasn't like him in this. She hadn't grown up in a world where family separations were frequent occurrences. In Gillian's experience, when people left, they left forever. Her parents, her brother Nick. Shoot, it was a wonder she survived Flora moving a day's ride away.

And now, he'd asked her to leave her loved ones for months and even years on end? To sail off into the sunset with him and leave the rest of her life behind? *You truly are a bastard, Delaney.*

The final straw came later that afternoon when Angus asked that a favorite dagger from the muniment room be included with the items being sent to Laichmoray. As Jake neared the room, the first sound he heard was

Scooter's whimpering, followed almost immediately by Robbie Ross's disconsolate weeping. Oh, God. Not more female tears.

He approached the doorway cautiously, filled with trepidation. Standing just out of sight, he eavesdropped on the conversation taking place between his choked-up wife and her broken-hearted sister.

"Please, Gilly," Robbie was saying, hiccupping a breath. "Please ask him."

"Oh, posy. I canna."

"Why, do you not want me to come with you?"

"Robbie, no. Of course I'd love to have you come with us. But it just isn't practical. I'm told shipboard is often not a place for ladies, so it certainly would not be proper for a child. And what about your schoolwork? What about Uncle Angus? I would feel so bad if we both went with Jake and left him behind."

"So let's take him with us, too! And Scooter. The whole family will go."

Sadness dampened Gillian's laugh. "And Flora and Alasdair and the bairns while we're aboot it, too."

"Aye!" Robbie sobbed as she said it. "Everyone. That way we'll not be apart. We shouldn't be apart, Gillian. It'll be too sad."

Oh, hell. The girl was right. It would be too sad. He couldn't do this to Gillian.

Jake sighed heavily and leaned back against the wall. He stood there for a full minute, thinking and considering, weighing his options. Except, there were no options, just a choice. His choice.

He closed his eyes, and silently bid his dream goodbye.

Then Jake squared his shoulders, pasted on a grin, and sauntered into the muniment room. "Oh, halt the caterwauling, squirt. I've got good news."

Robbie lifted her head from her sister's shoulder and two pairs of watery, bluebonnet eyes questioned him with a look. "No need to fret. Gillian and I aren't going anywhere. I've decided to cancel the trip and stay here at Rowanclere."

Gillian's heart leapt, and for one brief instant, joy filled her soul. Then she looked past the smile on her husband's face to his eyes now dimmed of their brightness. "Don't be silly, Jake. Of course we're going. The day after tomorrow, just as we planned."

"No. Uh uh. I've changed my mind. I want to stay here."

She knew what he was doing, of course. He thought to sacrifice his dream for her sake. Well, she wouldn't have it. "Robyn, please excuse us. I think it's time for Jake and me to have a talk."

"All right." Her sister walked toward the door, pausing beside Jake. "It's a fine decision, Jake. Dinna let her talk you out of it."

When they were alone, Gillian moved to the window and turned her gaze out to the sunshine-filled day. She needed the illusion of warmth. "I've imagined this journey of ours. I've pictured standing beside you at ship's rail watching the sunset. I fantasized about making love with you on a tropical beach. I'm looking forward to those moments."

"Your heart is torn in two, princess, and I can't stand watching it anymore. I can't stand knowing I'm the cause of your and your family's misery. No, I cannot in good conscience take you away from here. Not now. Maybe on down the road aways when you don't have so many ties. I've waited this long. A few more years won't hurt."

She shook her head. "In a few more years, with God's blessing, I hope we'll have a family of our own. I will not raise my children aboard ship or on a remote beach with no doctor within call. No, we must go now. Our plans are all made. It'll be fine, Jake, dinna worry."

Frustration shimmered in his voice. "Yes, it will be fine, because we're not going."

"Yes, we are."

"No, we're not.

"Yes, we are."

He shoved his hands into his pants pockets. "Stop it. Listen to us. This is ridiculous." He crossed over to the window, and placing his arms upon her shoulders, turned her to face him. "Princess, don't fight me on this. I can't bear to watch what this has been doing to you, to you and to Angus and to Robin and to Flora. My decision has been made. I had a choice and I chose you."

Her eyes flashed and she tore herself from his arms. "I am not Annabelle Maclean. I didn't ask you to choose, did I?"

"We're not going, and that's my final decision."

They fought about it for an entire month. Snapping and arguing and bickering each day, loving desperately each night. It was as if they sensed a coming change. Finally, a simple remark from Jake about the weather brought the battle to a head.

It was a simple comment about being cold, no different from any of the hundreds of complaints he'd voiced over the course of the summer. Gillian, feeling snappish in the wake of an argument with Angus, rounded on him and said, "What is wrong with you? One would think we live in Siberia by the way you talk."

"Well it's damn sure not Texas."

"Then why stay? Why stay where you are so miserable? I think you'd better go, Jake Delaney. Leave Rowanclere. Leave Scotland. You are liable not to last through a Highland winter."

They stood staring at one another, fuming, until to Jake's horror, tears swelled in Gillian's eyes, then overflowed. "It's no good, Jake. No good. You had it partially right a month ago. Leaving home is wrong for me. But staying, I'm afraid, is wrong for you. We're tearing each other apart. I think you should go. I think you should follow your dream, but I think you should do it without me."

Everything inside Jake went cold. "What are you saying?"

"It's what is right. You have wings on your feet, Texas. Mine are planted deep in the Highland moors."

An invisible noose was tightening around his neck, and he cleared his throat to get the words out. "My feet don't need to fly. I don't need the tropics to keep me warm. All I need is you, princess. You and your love."

Her smile was sad. "For now, when our love is new, that may be true. But what about when the yearning for adventure stirs within you once again? You know it will, Jake. What happens then? Will you come to resent me? Resent our home, our family?"

"I would never do that."

"Can you be so certain? Honestly certain? I'm not. That's why I've realized I canna go with you. I canna stand here and say without a moment's doubt that someday I would not come to resent you for taking me from my home and family. That is why you must go, and I must stay. It's the only way."

He wanted to argue with her, rather desperately, but the words to convince her of her error in judgment wouldn't come. Instead, frustration filled him. "No. I own this castle. You can't make me go."

Tears spilled down her cheeks. "Then I won't stay. I'll go to Laichmoray. I winna live with you any longer, Jake Delaney."

His heart cracked, then shattered. "Dammit, Gillian. Why are you doing this? Why are you throwing me out of your life?"

"No no no," she said, shaking her head. "I'm not throwing you out. I'm letting you go. And I'm trusting in our love."

She lifted his hands to her mouth and kissed them, first one, then the other. "I want you to go and live your adventure, Jake Delaney, but I'm asking for your promise to return to me when it is done. If you promise, I will believe it. I will wait for you, I will hold your love inside my heart and wait for you to come home to me. However long it takes. You have my word."

Jake held her gaze as if it were a lifeline. Love shone in their glittering depths, love deep and true.

And he believed.

His voice was gravelly when he spoke. "I will love you until the day I die, Gillian Ross Delaney. And I will come home to you, home to Rowanclere. You have my promise."

seventeen

THE FIRST PACKAGE arrived from Cairo. Gillian opened it to find a beautiful Persian rug.

Dear Princess,

Saw the pyramids. Kinda boring compared to barbicons and turrets. The rug is for Maiden's Tower. Lie on it and dream of me. Hate it here. Sand gets in everything I eat. Miss you. Love you. It's cold here.

Jake.

The next, from Madagascar. A diamond as big as her thumb.

Dear Princess,

Crossed the equator. Had to put on extra socks. Won the jewel in a card game. Hate it here. Bugs are worse than Scotland's midges and Texas's mosquitoes combined. Miss you. Love you. Still cold.

Jake.

The third gift arrived from Burma. A miniature tiger carved of ivory with amber eyes.

> Dear Princess,
>
> Look at this and think of me. Grrr. . . . Hate it here. Too much spice in the food—even Chrissy would agree. Miss you. Love you. Colder yet.
>
> Jake.

The fourth package arrived with an Australian postmark. Gillian frowned at the curved wooden stick and wondered just what it was.

> Dear Princess,
>
> Enclosed, please find a boomerang. Note that when you throw it, it always comes back. Hate it here. Scooter thinks crocodiles are something to play with. Miss you. Love you. My toes never thaw out.
>
> Jake.

Seashells filled the fifth box. "Tahiti," she murmured, blinking back tears.

> Dear Princess,
>
> Here I am. Beautiful beaches, crystalline sea, women who aren't too picky about clothes. Hate it here. I mean, I really hate it. Nothing about this place appeals. Not the beaches. Not the shark infested sea. Definitely not the women. Miss you. Love you. I'm beginning to think I may freeze to death before this nonsense is done.
>
> Jake.

As the months dragged by, Gillian waited for a sixth package to arrive. She began each day filled with anticipation. She ended each day mired in gloom. As time passed, the doubts grew. Why hadn't she heard from him? Had something happened to him? Was he hurt? Did he decide he liked those half-naked Tahitian women, after all?

When finally the sixth gift did arrive from Jake, it came in a most unexpected manner. She was sitting at a table in the kitchen discussing recipes with Mrs. Ferguson when the cook looked up and gasped. The dish she was holding crashed to the floor. Gillian twisted around.

"Hello, lass."

"Nicholas?"

He narrowed his eyes and studied her for a moment. "Gillian, right? Not Flora?"

"Nick!" Joy filled her heart as she flew into his arms.

He put off her questions until the family assembled a short time later in Uncle Angus's bedchamber. The introduction between Nick and Robyn brought a lump to Gillian's throat. Her big braw brother looked almost frightened of the lass.

Uncle Angus, expert now in manipulating his wheeled chair, rolled up to Gillian's brother, glared into his face, and demanded answers. Nicholas poured a whisky, tossed back a swallow, then said, "A man named Delaney hired a detective to find me. I understand this Delaney fellow now owns Rowanclere?"

"Jake Delaney is my husband, but never mind about him. Where were you, Nicholas? Why did you stay gone so long?"

His lips twisted into a crooked smile. "Actually, lass, when your husband's man found me, I was at a wedding in Fort Worth."

"A wedding?"

"It is a long, ugly story and I do not wish to darken this reunion day. Let's leave it for another time, shall we? Now, tell me of our sister. Young Robyn says Flora has bairns?"

With Nick home, the atmosphere around Rowanclere lightened to an extent. Still, Gillian waited for word from Jake. She soothed herself with the knowledge that posts from foreign ports were undependable. She worried herself with the fact she might never hear from him again. Boomerang or not.

Finally, more than a month following Nick's return to Rowanclere, a seventh box arrived. The packaging was plain, with no indications of origin. Her heart pounding, she opened it to find a framed canvas and a painting that literally took her breath away.

It was Rowanclere—but it wasn't. It was Rowanclere in warm, tropical shades of orange, yellow, and red. It was bright and brilliant and oh, so beautiful. "Oh, Jake," she murmured on a sigh. Then, she opened the enclosed note.

Dear Princess,

Adventure isn't external. Adventure is what lives inside a man.
I love it here. Everything about this place appeals to me. The people, the pets, even the ghosts. Especially the ghosts. I want to stay forever. Can you finally accept that? Can you finally believe me? Miss you. Love you. I'm warm again, princess. But I want to sizzle. I really, really want to sizzle. Hurry.

Jake.

The note fluttered from Gillian's hand. "He's not cold anymore? He's warm? He's . . . here! Oh, dear God, he's finally come home!"

She knew immediately where to look for him. She dashed from the drawing room and darted through the corridors of Rowanclere to the staircase leading up to Maiden's Tower. Picking up her skirts, she ran up the stairs and burst into the chamber room.

He wore the feileadh mor with no shirt beneath. He looked tanned and a bit tired. Nervous, perhaps. "Hello, princess."

"Jake!" Tears of happiness spilled from her eyes as she flew into his arms. "Oh, Jake. You're back. You're finally back."

"Finally is right." He sighed and buried his face in her hair. "Damn, Gillian. I have ached to hold you for so long."

She closed her eyes and absorbed this long anticipated moment. Jake had come home to her, just like he'd promised. Elation warmed her heart and joy filled her soul as she smiled up at him and asked, "How were your adventures?"

"Lonely. I see you got the carpet."

"Yes. And the diamond and tiger and shells and the boomerang. They were wonderful. And Nick, he's a gift, too. And the painting today. It took my breath away."

Jake nodded. "I have another present. Well, it's not really a present. Something I picked up on one of the islands."

"Is it catching?"

He scowled. "I was faithful to our vows, Mrs. Delaney. Now, do you want to see it or not?"

She shrugged. Looking at gifts wasn't at all what she wanted at the moment, but since it seemed to matter . . . "That would be nice."

"Well, I was sharing a bottle of whisky with an old Scots sailor in a bar in Australia, when somebody heard his burr and made a snickering comment about what Scotsmen wear beneath their kilts. One thing sort of led to another, and we ended up in a major debate about what Texans should wear beneath a feileadh mor. So here's what we decided." He yanked up the tartan to his waist.

Gillian blinked. "Um, that's impressive, Jake, as always. But you had that when you left home. I know. I remember quite clearly."

"Not that." He frowned at her, angled his hip toward her, then pointed at a spot of color on his buttock. "This."

She blinked again. "What is that?"

"It's my tattoo. It's a castle. It's Rowanclere—or what's supposed to be Rowanclere, anyway."

"You had Rowanclere tattooed on your behouchie? Why?"

"Well, some of the 'why' of it was lost in the whisky fog, but from what I recall, the conversation centered around a man's pride and how what he most valued hung between his legs, hence beneath the kilt. What I do remember distinctly is why I chose the picture that I did. Rowanclere and the flame."

"Flame?" She stared a little closer. Yes there was some sort of yellow blob hovering above a tower.

"I know it looks more like an upside down turkey wattle, but it's supposed to be a flame. I remember the

Brodie coat of arms and motto displayed on so many things here at Rowanclere, so I figured since the castle changed hands, it needed a new one. This is the Delaney coat of arms, Gillian. The motto is on the banner below the castle."

"Motto?"

"It's small, hard to read because it's long."

Actually, she could probably read it if she took her gaze off his "pride" long enough. But one did have one's priorities, after all, and he had been away a long time. "What does it say?"

"It's in Latin, but the translation is "I came, I saw, I loved, I stayed forever."

"And the flame?"

He allowed the feileadh mor to drop back into place as he put his hands on Gillian's waist and held her. Gazing deeply into her eyes, he spoke with simple sincerity as he said, "It's the symbol of my love for you, and my burning desire to live out my life at Rowanclere. You see, princess, this is the lesson I learned in my travels. No matter where I am—the Sahara Desert, crossing the equator at sea, or traipsing through the Burmese jungle—this world is a cold, cold place whenever I'm not with you. Let me stay and never send me away again. Be my warmth, Gillian. Be my home."

Love flowed between them, warm and sweet and free of any doubt. Smiling, Gillian pulled his lips down to hers. "Welcome to Rowanclere, Texas. Welcome home."

Later, after the first impatient rush of passion and a second more leisurely loving, Jake sat up and said, "Princess, about the gifts?"

Gillian stretched sensuously. "Mmm . . . hmm?"

"I did bring more home."

"More?"

"More." He wore a wicked grin, and his eyes sparkled with devilment. Gesturing toward a sea chest sitting against the wall, he winked at her and said, "Wait till you see the toys I picked up in Tangier."

Available from

GERALYN DAWSON

Simmer All Night

The Kissing Stars

The Bad Luck Wedding Cake

The Wedding Ransom

The Wedding Raffle

SONNET BOOKS

PUBLISHED BY
POCKET BOOKS   2352-01

**Visit the Simon & Schuster
romance Website:**

www.SimonSaysLove.com

**and sign up for our
romance e-mail updates!**

Keep up on the latest
new romance releases,
author appearances, news, chats,
special offers, and more!
We'll deliver the information
right to your inbox—if it's new,
you'll know about it.

POCKET BOOKS

2800.01